PRIMAL
NATURE

MONIQUE SINGLETON

BOOKS

By Monique Singleton

I would like to dedicate this book to Richard Butler.
He did a thorough read-through of my first draft finding countless typos and silly mistakes.
And thank you to all the rest of you who helped make this possible.
You know who you are.

Vinci Books

vinci-books.com

Published by Vinci Books Ltd in 2025

1

A CIP catalogue record for this book is available from the British Library.
Paperback ISBN: 9781036701505
The EU GPSR authorised representative is Logos Europe, 9 rue Nicolas
Poussion, 17000 La Rochelle, France contact@logoseurope.eu

What if we accept the impossible is only improbable?
Until someone proves that it exists.
The world is a big place.
Who's to say that what I dream,
what I write, isn't out there somewhere?

For everyone who believes in dreams.

Chapter One

I've lost count of how many times you've tried to kill me.

Hundreds, maybe even thousands. And not only in the course of the two global wars that so characterise the past two eras.

When will you get it through your thick heads that you cannot succeed? I'm here for as long as I want to be. You do not decide my fate. That prerogative is mine, and mine alone. I'm here to stay, I'm here for eternity.

But still, you try and every time you fail.

You're attempts can't kill me.

But man, it hurts.

Every time you shoot me, cut me, try to blow me up, it hurts, causing the pain and anger within me to build exponentially. It clouds my judgement, clouds my reserves and morals, with the expected result—I turn the tables and kill you.

I'm no stranger to pain. In the two-hundred and fifty-eight years I've lived up till now, pain has been the one constant factor.

That and death—yours, not mine.

I started off human, or at least I had no reason to think otherwise. I was born, grew older, got sick and better again —nothing unusual or even remotely interesting. All the human traits.

Until it stopped.

All of it.

I stopped growing old. I never got sick again. And life definitely got a lot more interesting.

Chapter Two

I'm cynical.

Eternity does that to you.

I've seen so much evil in humans it eclipses any good that might lie dormant.

As you will have guessed, I'm not a fan. But that's mutual. You don't like me. Not after you really get to know me.

It's not that you think I'm malicious, or inherently evil or anything superficial like that. Just different, and that terrifies you. That—and jealousy—colours any relationship between you and me.

Why? Well, it's too simple to exile all myth and folklore to the realms of fantasy. True, the majority of them are ninety-nine-percent fantasy. But somewhere, deep down, there is the origin. The reason for the myth; a small wafer of truth.

And that's the really scary part.

The enormous technological advancements that charac-

3

terise the last few hundred years lulled you into a sense of control. You think you can rationalise everything.

Well, you can't. There are still things in this world that defy reason; that your scientists or politicians can't explain. There are still things you can't control.

And that terrifies you.

I'm not human anymore.

That implies I once was. For the first forty years, my life was quite normal by your standards; nothing really strange or out of the ordinary.

I still don't have a definite reason why I am what I am. There was no poisonous spider, mythical animal bite, no radiation from a meteoroid as the catalyst or anything dramatic like that. Nothing that I can label "The Reason."

In my early forties my scars and wrinkles started to fade. I welcomed this and thought I was experiencing some kind of second youth due to better eating habits. Who wouldn't? At that age you begin to understand that nobody—not even you—has eternal youth and that you are starting to look remarkably like your parents did twenty-five years earlier. How's that for a nightmare? Wrinkles? Sagging figure? Cosmetic surgery comes to mind. Well anyway, I didn't need surgery. I became younger, or at the very least—didn't age.

Everyone around me of course did. My husband started off younger than me. I buried him looking like his grand-daughter.

People stalked me for an explanation. How did I do it?

Surprise quickly made way for resentment. I could at least share my secret. Let other people benefit from my "fountain of youth". I wanted to, but how could I, if I didn't know the answer myself?

I tried to find out.

One of the perks of longevity is you have ample time to learn. I studied biology, chemistry, anything that could help me understand what was going on. But the answers eluded me.

It's funny how friends and family turn into enemies when you have something they covet. Especially something as elementary as life. But be careful what you wish for. Immortality is not the eternal dream it's portrayed to be, more an eternal nightmare.

The resentment and jealousy finally drove me away from everything and everyone I knew. And that I was the subject of countless medical experiments and tests. Everyone wanted to know what stopped me from ageing. Everyone wanted a piece of me.

I was sick of it and left. Besides, everyone I really loved —every family member or friend—was already dead, even the ones born long after me. I'd said so many goodbyes, there was nothing left.

They still needed answers, so they brought me back.

There are just so many needles and tests a person can take before they snap. With me there was one too many. But instead of becoming abusive or just plain giving up, I changed. Changed in ways that defied science and belief. That was the real beginning of my exile. That was when they started to hunt me with a vengeance. It heralded my promotion from an anomaly to a major threat. In the end the whole weight of the government and military fuelled the hunt.

But even then, in those dark times, there were ways to disappear if you really wanted to.

I needed to.

Not just to evade them.

More than anything else, I had to find out and come to terms with what I was.

It would be nice to say I went to a sanctuary in Tibet, or somewhere exotic like that, where enlightened masters showed me my new path in life and my place in the universe.

But that's not how it went.

We'll pick up the story about that later. I want to finish what I see as the "management summary" first.

I've experienced things that would make you sick. Killed and healed. Loved and lost, as the clichés so eloquently say.

I've seen governments and nations come and go. Lived through both global wars in the twenty-first and twenty-second century. Come out the other side, sometimes even with a sense of direction and purpose.

In your human years, I would now be two-hundred and fifty-eight. Quite a life span. Me? I'm just beginning.

So, why am I writing this epistle? Why come out of hiding now? Well, by the time this manuscript becomes public in any way—if it ever does—I will be long gone. Back to my old ways of making myself invisible.

There have been many theories about what I am. Some extremely far-fetched, some have merit. None completely fit—save one. One reason. One explanation that sticks in my head. That just might offer the answers that I want, that I need. But I need to be sure. I need to put everything that happened to me in perspective. Review the timeline as it were. That will help me determine whether I really accept the theory as my basis. As my destiny. For that, I need to tell my story. I need to share what happened. I need to explain.

I've given up on acceptance. I have no illusion I will be one of you. Don't even want to be.

So, okay. Let's backtrack, go down memory lane. Go back to where it more or less really started.

Round about my ninety-third birthday, I was in quite a fix.

I had been the focus of medical interest and experiments for more than thirty years. Understandable—I looked the consummate thirty-four-year-old. I was in excellent health with a body to die for. Dr Karpatski, my old MD, was genuinely worried for me, he wanted to make sure I was all right. He could never have imagined the pain and torture his good intentions would cause. He and the initial scientists wanted the best: for me, and for others who could benefit from the "talents" I had.

That was the noble goal.

The other ones we will encounter further on. Be patient.

I was in and out of medical institutions, poked at, scanned, tested, and put through the mangle. I finally managed to disappear for a few years, started a new life and was subsequently kidnapped and transported to a secure facility somewhere in the Americas. There, the tests continued. That I was there against my will didn't seem to bother anyone. It was for the greater good, so I was designated a volunteer.

The first year the circumstances were reasonable. I had a "suite" of rooms and some form of privacy, however controlled. The doctors—and I use that term loosely—still wanted my cooperation.

But as time passed, the results remained slim. Somewhere down the line they decided that was my fault and subsequently tried to force me to cooperate. Problem was, I wasn't sabotaging the tests. I actually hoped they would find what they were looking for so that I could finally leave.

How's that for naivety?

I didn't know. I couldn't answer the questions. No matter how often I tried to make them understand, it didn't sink in. It was unacceptable, because that would mean they'd failed and that was not an option. There was too much at stake.

The initial group that "recruited" me still had illusions of saving mankind. Curing diseases like AIDS, Cancer and LKX-clones—quite enviable goals.

Changes in staff brought changes in incentive. Budgetary issues necessitated new partners; not so noble ones. Partners more interested in the monetary successes that could be achieved. Eternal Youth is of course the ultimate product.

The military came later on. After the cosmetic companies gave up. After the revolution started.

I see it all in my mind, clear as day. I relive what happened over and over again. And now I'll share it with you.

It's not pretty.

…You have been warned.

Chapter Three

The walls of the cell closed in on her again: sickly grey, damp and covered in mould. The small window at the top right of the far wall was dirty, filled with fly shit and grime so thick it barely let in the light. Not that the speck of clouded sky did much to relieve her dark mood anyway.

The room was spartan, fifteen-by-fifteen feet, grey walls, one solid metal door, a table, and a chair—not for her, naturally.

The ever-present stench of her stale dried blood and sweat hung in the air. In an attempt to get her to cooperate they left her on her tortured feet for more than forty-eight hours. They wanted to force her to answer the questions she had no answers to.

"Big nose," as she called the eldest doctor—the one who had been there from the start more than three or four years ago—was ranting and raving again. Spittle flew from his mouth and his face was bright red. One of these days she fully expected the veins pulsating in his prom-inent nose to explode. That, or he would have a heart attack. She was laying bets on which would hit him first. His nose was winning, the strained skin looking ready to erupt.

It was business as usual.

The doctor, a small thin man of about fifty-five with a big chip on his shoulder, did not impress her in the least. His demeanour was of someone who desperately needed recognition but wasn't getting any, despite all his intellect and effort.

'It's you; you're doing this,' he spat. 'You refuse to let us do our work. Do you have any idea of the trouble you're getting me and the staff here into?' Pacing the small interrogation room, she felt the agitation he exuded in the air around him. She didn't react. It wouldn't do any good, not that she could be bothered anyway.

The fatigue showed on her face and in the slight tremors in her legs and torso. All she wanted to do was lie down and forget everything for a few hours. Big nose had other ideas. He had a deadline.

'We need results.' His agitation coloured his face an even darker shade of red. 'You have no idea of what will happen to us, or to you for that matter, if we don't come up with something, anything.' His breath came in frantic bursts. Saliva landed on her face again. He stood so close she was forced to inhale his stale smelling breath and body-odour as he tormented her with his relentless questions. Looking up at him, her eyes showed the contempt.

'Whatever,' she replied.

He hit her. Slapped her across the face. She didn't flinch. The increased anger caused him to shake with pure rage and utter helplessness.

'You think we're tough?'

Could his nose get any brighter?

'Well, this is a picnic to what will happen when the military takes over, and they will.'

'They will break you,' he added smugly, contorting his face into what was supposed to be a grin. Moving around the table he lowered himself into the chair and smirked at her.

The past months had been bad. All the tests ended up useless. Time and again blood and tissue was extracted, and once it left her body it died quite spectacularly. The nucleus of the cells imploded, the DNA liquefied into a brown mush and there was nothing they could learn from the samples anymore. It frustrated the hell out of the scientists.

Initially they suspected malfunction of the equipment. Then they suspected each other of sabotage. Security checks were intensified. The scientists were interrogated, which formed a short reprieve for her. Finally, they ruled out sabotage or malfunction. That left her. But how was she doing it? Was it a conscious act? How could she control her body, her cells, like that? Even after they left her body.

She was tortured, physically and mentally.

Nothing seemed too depraved for them. They placed her in a cage not even fit for a small dog. She felt degraded, less than human, less even than a lab rat. They kept her there for five days. Not letting her out, not even for toilet breaks, she lay in her own excrement. Cramped beyond compare, with no way to avoid the stink, the filth and the inevitable bugs attracted to the waste, she felt humiliated... debased. When they finally let her out, all she could do was crawl out of the muck. Her seized-up muscles wouldn't work. She just lay there while they hosed her down, too cramped and depressed to even try to resist.

But still, they didn't get any answers.

Refusing to give up, they took samples again, and again,

and again. Anaesthetic was discarded. she healed anyway, so what did it matter. Any wounds and scars were gone within twelve hours. Biopsies were taken from all major organs, except the brain and heart because they didn't want to inadvertently kill her. If she didn't comply, they strapped her to the table. The only tests that showed results were the ones documenting her increasing strength and healing capabilities. The more they cut, the quicker she healed, and the more frustrated they became, yelling at her and subjecting her to further abuse.

The door opened. The youngest doctor Hardy—the nice one—entered the dim room, unintentionally hurting her eyes with the sharp light that followed him into the dim cubicle. He looked pale. Frightened.

'He's here, Doctor Collins,' he said. 'He's waiting for you in your office.' He fidgeted uncomfortably waiting for Big-Nose to reply. 'Doctor Collins?' Sheepishly.

'Yes, yes, I heard you.' Collins zoned back from wherever he had been. Standing up he looked at her with a mixture of disgust and pity. 'You brought this upon yourself,' he whispered.

She continued to stare at the small window as the two men left the room. She didn't sit. They were watching her. She knew any deviation to the current situation would bring repercussions—painful ones. She didn't need more pain, so she just stayed upright where she was and waited.

Chapter Four

Collins tried to regulate his breathing. It would not do to let the General know how much he resented losing control over the investigation. He would be the ultimate colleague, helpful to a fault. And when the General failed—which was inevitable—he would take control back. It was all a matter of patience and a straight face. There was no way in hell the military would take the credit for the project, not after all he'd invested in this undertaking.

Rounding the corner to his office, the doctor was instantly taken aback by the presence of the military force. He'd expected a small contingent of maybe two or three scientists and the General with maybe one or two additional soldiers. More than twenty people filled the hallway. The majority of them were soldiers in full battle gear. One even had a vicious looking dog straining at the leash. Heavily armed, they all turned to glare at him as he approached. The canine growled. Hanging on to the barest threads of his composure, Collins opened the door and entered his own outer office.

Sally, his assistant, immediately clamped a hand around his arm to stop him from moving on to the inner office.

'He's on the secure line and can't be disturbed,' she whispered.

Taking one more step towards the door, but reluctantly recognising the urgency in her voice, he stopped and turned. The arrogance of the man—locking him out of his own office.

He looked around the small anteroom and forced himself to calm down. He was in his own territory now.

There were much bigger windows here than in the cells, with a view of the park-like grounds around the institute. The walls were painted in a soft apricot to mimic the adobe style that was so popular in this area. In the cells the impression was of a clinical institution, far away from the inhabited world. Maybe even on an island somewhere. The truth was the institute was hidden in a beauty spa in a residential part of the suburbs; a hide-a-way for the rich. The grounds were reasonably secure. The laboratory was impenetrable, but in a non-imposing way. The paying residents were unaware of the tests performed in this part of the clinic; unbeknownst they were acting as the blissfully innocent front to it all.

That of course would all change now the military had arrived in such ridiculous numbers. What was the use of all this force? They weren't even attempting to disguise their arrival; hadn't they been briefed? There would be hell to pay.

Through the window Collins saw that the military vehicles and even more guards outside had already attracted a small group of nosy residents. The phone rang. Sally ran to her desk and pressed the button on the receiver next to her ear.

'Heaven Valley spa, Sally speaking,' she answered in a clear and composed voice. 'How can I help you?'

Even from where he stood Collins could hear the agitated voice on the other end of the line.

'Please calm down, Mr. Stark.' Susan managed to get a word in. 'The military are only here with regard to an investigation we are helping them with.'

She looked at Collins helplessly—an unspoken plea in her eyes. How could she explain the presence of such an excess of military force? As paying customers, the residents expected to be pampered and kept away from all the disquieting realities of the outside world and not to be confronted with violence or the ugly real world on their doorstep.

Collins shrugged and turned away from his assistant, leaving her to think up an acceptable story. His thoughts once again turned to the specimen; how would he be able to keep the General from finding out all there was to know about the creature? How would he keep on top of it all?

He wandered over to the door of his inner office and tried to hear what was being said on the other side. But the doors and walls were soundproofed. At his request, to offer absolute privacy when he had visitors or was entertaining. He heard nothing. Just as he turned to walk back to the water cooler, the door opened suddenly.

He was startled, and it showed.

The doorway was filled with the presence of the General.

'Ah Collins. Just the man I wanted to see.' His manner was pleasant, almost friendly. But Collins had heard stories about this man and was not about to let his defences down.

Walking past the General, he entered his own office. He hesitated for a moment. Where was he supposed to sit? The General solved the problem for him by closing the door and sitting in the leather seat behind the desk, forcing Collins to sit in the chair in front of his own desk. Both were equally aware that this was the first clash in the power struggle and that the General was now ahead by one point.

'Thank you so much for the use of your office,' he said sweetly. 'As of now these are the headquarters for the military side of the operation.'

An agitated Collins muttered, 'you're welcome.' Neither of them giving any credit to the statement. Collins felt surprised at the distance the desk and the elevated seat created making him actually feel small. Insignificant. The General observed him intently. This unsettled him even more and he felt compelled to speak.

'We weren't expecting you until next week,' he attempted feebly. 'Then we could have readied everything for you and your staff.' He refused to call them soldiers.

'No worries.' The General smiled at his discomfort. 'My men and I will feel at home here before the end of the day.'

His hard stare unnerved Collins. Silence was a mighty weapon when used correctly. Sure enough, the doctor's insecurity increased, and he flustered to take control.

'Why are all these soldiers with you?' he demanded in what he hoped was an authoritative tone. 'Our residents will need an explanation'.

The General dismissed the challenge with a wave of his hand. 'I'm sure that you will think of something, you can always blame the Revolutionaries.'

He shuffled the papers on the desk. Collins saw that many of them were test reports, MRI- and brain scans from the specimen.

'Bring me up to speed,' the General ordered. 'The results I have here are depressing, what is the status?'

The ground opened up beneath Collins. Depressing was

an understatement. In the more than four years she'd been here, no real advancement had been made.

'The specimen arrived here some four years ago; we commenced the tests...'

The General stopped him in full sentence.

'The abbreviated version please, doctor. I've read her file. What have you actually achieved in those years?' His tone was accusative.

Visibly rattled, Collins stammered. 'We've tested everything we could. We have a very competent staff, but she won't cooperate.' When cornered blame someone—or in this case—something else.

The General softened his approach. 'My dear doctor Collins, I have no doubt that you and your staff did all you could. But you must agree the results have been painfully absent, the Powers are getting nervous, they want results for their investments.'

His tactics worked; the doctor was lulled into compliance. The real enemies were the specimen and those in power. The man was so easily manipulated it was pathetic. What a schmuck.

'She thwarts all our tests.' The fatigue was back again. 'No matter what we try, we don't get any closer to the source of her healing abilities, or her longevity. She is now almost one hundred years old but looks barely thirty-five. Though we are certain the two things are related. We've found out the healing capabilities are intensifying.'

This caught the Generals attention.

Collins continued; glad he had something positive to say. 'When she came here the healing procedure took much longer than it does now. Any wounds we administer heal within twelve hours now, scars are gone within twenty-four hours.'

'Any wounds?' The General raised an eyebrow. 'Describe the extent of the injuries.'

'We tested her with inch deep scalpel cuts on her torso and her extremities; length up ten inches. We taped the healing process. I can show you the streams if you want?' When the General didn't react, he continued. 'We also observed that her strength is increasing dramatically. She is much too strong for a female, no matter what age.'

The General was quiet throughout the rest of the narrative. He was becoming more and more interested in the side effects of what the Doctor called "the major question". The doctor and the pharmaceutical companies were only interested in marketing eternal youth. They'd pumped millions into research in the last two centuries with no obvious results, and then to everyone's surprise, this creature crossed their path—an unexpected break.

What he saw was the full potential for her; unbeatable soldiers. An immortal army capable of healing itself. The opposition—any opposition—would be stamped out. Whoever controlled her talents controlled the world. He'd always scoffed at the thought of world domination. But the idea was getting comfortably more realistic the deeper he became involved in this project. The powers-that-be had no idea what treasure they held here. All he had to do was succeed where this annoying overbearing scientist had failed.

But he was walking a tightrope.

Though still formally in service to the government, he'd transferred his allegiance to the pharmaceutical companies. He moonlighted, as so many military personnel did these days. Due to the pathetic incompetence of the government, his extracurricular activities took up more of his time than his official duties. Sometimes the two goals coincided, and he served both his employers with one action. Fighting the rebels for instance. This was in the best interest of both of them. But in the end his main allegiance was to himself. To his own ideals and objectives in life.

The bitter war between rich and poor was a godsend for him.

He once again thanked his diligence and eye for a good money-making deal. Even the rich were now anxious about the shortage of energy. Their lifestyle was on the line, and they paid him to make a difference. It had been this way for the past decade. It was time to restore order, crush the incompetents and give the power back to the strong, the responsible politicians and most of all; to him.

This was the situation when Gareth Bremmer, CEO and founder of GB Inc, the largest pharmaceutical company in America, contacted the General.

'My major concern is for the continuance of the company,' Bremmer said in their first face-to-face interview. 'I look further to the future. Once this unpleasant situation has been resolved—and believe me it will be—we will need a new focus for the majorities.'

He was a silver-haired man with an almost military bearing. A strong man, the General recognised; a dangerous man, with more than one agenda.

'The decimation of the undesirables in this world will open up more opportunities and resources for the rest of us. The war and LKX will do that for us. As long as we make sure the power stays where it belongs; in the hands of the capable.'

He sat behind a magnificent oak desk bigger than the General had ever seen. The whole arrangement was designed to impress the visitor. To show how immensely important the owner of this office was and how reverent the visitor should be. The General understood the first but refused the last. Bremmer needed him, so the distance in stature was smaller than the CEO would like it to be.

He detested speaking to this obnoxious bully in a uniform. It was necessary, but he flatly refused to hide his distaste for the General, who in turn welcomed the sentiment. It was mutual.

'There will be a shortage of competent men in the new situation. That means we must make sure the good genes that are available will be able to propagate long enough to repopulate the world as we see it,' Bremmer continued his high-and-mighty speech. 'For this we must elongate the life span. We need the ultimate cure.' He stared the General in the eye. 'We are quite frankly in the process of developing a cure for death.' He paused for drama.

Reluctantly he added, 'the project has however encountered some problems and will miss its deadlines. Mutual acquaintances suggested I put you in change. I want you to take over and make sure it delivers on time.'

The General recognised the potential of the specimen at that precise moment. During the rest of the meeting, he listened intently, looking for Brenner's hidden agenda and slowly constructing his own. That ultimately brought him here—to the spa—to deal with such incompetents as Collins.

He let the scientist rattle on a bit longer until he'd heard all there was to know. The man was an idiot, as expected.

'This resulted in the brain scan you have in front of you.' Collins babbled on blissfully unaware of the General's thoughts. 'The initial analysis indicated the...'

'Where is the subject now?' The General rudely interrupted Collins who was immediately silenced, stung by the unbelievable lack of manners.

'She is in the interrogation room—a small cell in the basement,' the doctor stammered.

'In what state?'

'She was cut, has been up for more than fifty hours and is exhausted. We are trying to break her.'

The General looked up from the papers. 'Let her get some rest and heal, I will speak with her tomorrow or the day after.'

The meeting was over, the dismissal clear.

The General pressed the intercom button. 'Susan, will you ask Major Dimage to come in please?'

The General stood up and walked out from behind the desk. The door opened, and a military man entered. He saluted the General and stood to attention, ignoring the scientist.

'Ah Major, this is Dr Collins. He will be assisting you in your tests.'

'I'll be assisting?' Collins blustered standing up. 'This is my project. Surly he will be assisting me?'

'You have proven yourself incapable of leading this project Dr Collins, so the Major will take over. I am sure you have no problem with that, otherwise I suggest you explain to Mr. Bremmer why there is such a distinct absence of results.'

The gloves were off. The General moved the scientist towards the door. 'I demand results. Get them.' The "or else" was silent, but clearly implied.

The Major saluted once again, strode through the opening after the confused doctor and closed the door behind them.

Chapter Five

She stood in the dimly lit cell and tried to sleep on her feet without anyone noticing. The young doctor came into the room again and moved the chair around the table to her side.

'You can sit down,' he said softly. 'Have something to eat and then we'll bring you back to your room where you can sleep.' Silence followed. 'The military have arrived. The General wants to speak to you tomorrow.'

The door opened, and a white clad assistant entered the room with a tray of sandwiches and some water. The prisoner looked at the plate of food, not trusting the scientists. The assistant placed the tray on the table, turned around and walked out the door. She expected something to happen. This had to be another game they were playing with her. But the young doctor motioned her to sit and eat.

Slowly she lowered herself into the seat and let the smell of the food waft into her sensitive nose. She could not detect any strange smells, just the bread and cheese. With the dramatic improvement in her senses in the last few years, she could detect acidic elements quite easily. They tried to drug her before, so she was careful. But she was also weary and extremely hungry. She started out with small bites and then wolfed down the food. The water was hardly enough to quench her thirst.

'There will be more in your room,' the doctor offered. He knocked on the door and two assistants entered to escort her to her cell.

Chapter Six

I lay down on the cot in my cell and tried to figure out what they were playing at.

Why had they stopped now? In earlier sessions they'd kept me on my feet for more than sixty-five hours. Must have something to do with the military.

I tried to think about the new situation and how I would be able to steel myself for what was to come. But I was too tired and besides I really didn't have a clue.

I closed my eyes and slept.

All too soon, the lights came back on in the cell and the door opened. Once again, a tray of food was offered and placed on the small table to the right of the cot. No utensils, they stopped issuing those when I used them to try to escape.

I got up off the cot and moved to the back of the cell where there was a small lavatory and a sink. I still expected some kind of betrayal. But it didn't come, and all remained quiet. I returned to the tray, ate my breakfast and waited.

About thirty minutes later the door opened again and

one of the assistants motioned me to follow him. There were two soldiers standing outside the door, one took the point and the other followed our little procession. The assistant took me to the shower room, handed me soft white towels and left. One of the soldiers remained. I hadn't expected all of them to leave. Privacy was not something I'd enjoyed in the past years.

He sneered as I undressed and unabashedly scanned my body. I resolved to ignore him and enjoy the hot water as it cascaded down my back. The heat invigorated me and almost made me feel whole again. The food, sleep, and now the water, did wonders for me. My strength was coming back. I flexed the muscles in my arms and back, much to the amusement of the soldier.

After my shower I dressed in the new shifts the assistant left for me. No shoes, but I hadn't expected them. I'd been barefoot so long my feet sported calluses and I could walk without footwear on any surface. The assistant returned, and we made our way through the labyrinth to the interrogation cells. Home sweet home.

The door opened to the first room on the right. This was the most comfortable of the interrogation rooms. I spent a lot of time here during the first weeks of my stay. The room was high ceilinged, light, with big windows and colourful semi-transparent sunshades that let in the soft sunlight. The windows were too high to look through comfortably, but never-the-less welcome because of the abundance of natural light.

The military man behind the desk swivelled his chair when I entered the room and observed me with a smile on his thin lips.

He motioned me to sit down opposite him in the chair on the far side of the bolted down desk. I pulled the chair away, sat down and let the silence continue. Silence doesn't bother me. Obviously, it didn't bother the soldier either.

We continued to observe each other in silence.

He was a heavyset man of indiscriminate age. I guessed him to be somewhere in his early fifties. He had the bearing of a career soldier—born in the uniform. His eyes were his most striking feature. Bright blue, cold and piercing underneath his short greying sandy brown hair.

'We're both good at the game of silence I see,' he finally spoke. 'I am the General,' he continued, smiling. 'There has been a shift in the management, and I am now in command of the project, and naturally of you.'

He paused to let his words register. I remained silent. He stood and began to walk around the room, talking while he paced.

'Dr Collins has brought me up to speed with the test progress up till now. Progress is, as you know, very poor. He relates it to some negativity on your part. I think incompetence; his and his staff's, is more likely, wouldn't you agree?'

When no reaction came, he continued, 'things will be different from now on. You will be treated in a more civilised manner. You will help us do our job and together we will bring this whole sorry mess to a close within the deadline. I am not an unreasonable man, but I do not accept rebellion. You will assist our investigation. Then you will finally be able to leave and continue with your life.'

Yeah. Right. I didn't believe that last remark for a moment. He didn't expect me to. So, I guessed that the meeting was being taped. This was for someone else's benefit.

The hair on the back of my neck tingled and a feeling of dread spread further to every cell in my body with each word he spoke. The ease and conviction with which he declared my productive involvement chilled me to the bone. This was one determined man; not to be swayed or played with, as I'd done with Big-Nose. He would not be managed or tempered by social or humanitarian restraints. This was a man on a mission. With the clout to achieve it.

'Just so we understand each other. I will succeed where the good doctor failed, by any means necessary.'

The General was to my back. He stood behind the chair. I could almost feel him there.

He had a complicated scent. Pleasant to start with, but with something buried down deep. In hindsight, I realise that was the viciousness I was to encounter in later months.

He moved back to his chair and sat down.

'But enough of all this,' he said pleasantly. 'We will start the new sessions with my scientists soon. That will give you some time to gather your thoughts and decide how you can be of assistance.'

Chapter Seven

Returning to her cell she slept soundly most of the day and the whole night for the first time in God knows how long. Nobody came for her that afternoon or the next day, leaving her to recuperate.

Finally, mid-morning of the second day, two soldiers came and escorted her to the General's office.

He was all charm. He let her sit down in the chair opposite his desk and served her water or coffee, whatever her preference. Two obviously military personnel in white lab coats flanked either side of the General's chair. He introduced them as Dr Dimage, on his left and Dr Jacobsen— the woman—on the right. Big-Nose was seated in the corner, his face and predominantly his nose still in imminent danger of exploding.

'These two will assist me in the project,' he continued. 'I trust we will have a good working arrangement. I have read your file.' He rambled on for a while and quoted parts of the file that had accumulated in the past years. 'Dear me, they haven't really been nice to you, have they?' He glanced in the direction of Big-Nose. 'The file actually makes amusing bedtime reading.' His sadism showed around the edges. 'Not many results though.' Big-Nose was fuming, only barely controlling his anger.

'It's about time something was achieved here. Thank God we came on time. The good doctor will also assist if there is anything we need him for, not that I expect that to happen.' The soldiers joined in the chuckles.

Remaining quiet seemed the best and only thing to do. The General didn't expect an answer, he was too busy with his monologue and strafing Doctor Collins. He obviously enjoyed every moment.

'Enough already,' she heard softly from the corner.

'What was that, Collins? Did you say something?' The General stood up and walked over to the front of the desk, nearer to her and Collins. 'You have any comments on my summary?'

Collins mumbled a negative, 'no.'

The military man answered for him. 'I didn't think so.' Turning his attention to her, he sat on the edge of the vast desk, close—too close for comfort.

'Now as I said the other day, failure is not a word in my vocabulary. Things will be different from now on. We will start anew. You will help us where you can, and I expect that is more than you have done up till now. Make no illusion about me or my ambition. I have been entrusted with a job, and that job is you. I will not fail. You will not let me. We will come to an understanding.' His gaze was intense, the ensuing silence stifling.

Abruptly he stood, turned and went back to his seat behind the desk.

'Now, without further ado—I've always wanted to say that—let's get to the lab and redo some of the basic tests.'

On cue the two white-clad doctors left their stations and moved towards her. She stood and followed them out of the room.

Collins hesitated. He almost opened his mouth and voiced his anger. The General stopped him; his head bowed into the document he was reading. 'I wouldn't do that if I were you Collins. Now get along and join the others, like a good boy.' His laughter followed the doctor out of the room.

The day was spent with routine tests: blood and hair samples were taken, and her weight and height were measured. As every time before, the blood coagulated, and the hair and skin samples imploded, leaving only a gooey residue. They tried immersing the samples in formaldehyde or other preserving substances. Nothing worked.

The new team took it all in their stride, but then again —having read the file—they knew what to expect. They persevered, redoing the tests again and again until she once again felt bruised and irritated by the needles. The General dropped in on the tests in the afternoon. When Dr Dimage reported the lack of test results, he too was not fazed.

'Well, it seems that some things in the file were close to correct,' was the only comment he made. He smiled at her and left the room.

During the day, Collins remained silent, seated on a chair in yet another corner in the lab. The lack of success had a different influence on him—his self-confidence grew with every test that failed.

At the end of the afternoon, the military stopped their tests and allowed her to return back to her cell where dinner was waiting. She slept well throughout the night and in the morning, everything resumed.

The days became weeks. The military doctors were

relentless, but even they became frustrated. The absence of results took its toll on everybody, with the exception of Collins, who enjoyed every moment. The doctors and the General abandoned their "friendly" approach and hardened with every failed experiment.

History repeated itself.

She was blamed.

They were inventive; thinking up new tests, things that didn't have any obvious links with her healing capabilities. They tested her endurance, her stamina, her strength. All of which were way above average for even Olympic athletes, not to mention regular people who had almost no exercise; like her. Dutifully they reported back to the General, who himself was beginning to feel some extra pressure from the Powers-that-be. Bremmer was breathing down his neck.

Finally, the General sent for her again. She was escorted this time not to an office, but to the old cell where she was interrogated all those months earlier. His demeanour was still composed, but his steel blue eyes were colder than she remembered. She was unceremoniously pushed into the chair opposite him, her wrists clamped in restraints. They were taking no chances ever since the tests showed her exceptional strength. Nothing had happened up till now, but the violence and the pain levels in the tests were increasing exponentially, so it paid to be vigilant.

'Well now, my dear,' he began. 'It seems we are getting nowhere with you. And I thought we had an understanding. What exactly don't you comprehend about cooperation?' He didn't expect an answer.

'My doctors tell me you hardly ever speak, and even though you do not actively oppose the tests, you're not helping either. There are no results to speak of. No inkling about what the secret is of your longevity or why you heal so well. This is unacceptable.'

Still no reaction from her, so he continued.

'As I indicated before, there will be results. It's more a question of changing what we're actually testing. A new focus you might say.'

Shuffling the papers on his desk he located the one he was looking for. 'This' he waved the paper 'Is frankly your death sentence.' He paused for effect. 'The pharmaceutical company has given up. They no longer expect to get any results and want to distance themselves from you and from the investigation.'

He put the paper down and folded his hands in front of him. 'The Powers do not have a consensus about what to do with you. Some of them want you dead; they're afraid you'll pose a threat. Others are just downright disappointed at your lack of cooperation and the dismal results of all their investments. Some want to sell you to the highest bidder. Maybe some kind of freak show.' His cold blue eyes bore into hers. 'I, on the other hand think you may have some value, at least to the right cause. I have managed to find new investors who are interested in continuing the project, though with a different goal. The army wants us to investigate your healing abilities and why your strength seems to grow so exponentially. You already have more strength than any man I have ever known, and it still increases. These are handy traits for us. Some way we will be able to replicate what you have.'

The subsequent silence said it all—by any means.

'All this results in a different approach to the project.'

He stood up, picked up his baton and folded his hands on his back, walked around the table and moved to a spot behind her chair. She followed his progress with her hearing, refusing to turn her head.

'We are no longer interested in your well-being.' As if they ever had been. 'And I have instructed the good doctors to take a more disciplinary approach.'

His voice was close to her right ear, his body behind her back. 'There is no such thing as excessive force where you are concerned. There is merely another test to determine how much you can take.' His voice was menacing, and she shivered inside.

The General stood up straight, swung the baton and hit her squarely on the side of her head. The skin split and sprayed bright red blood over his desk and uniform. The force of the blow sent her seat tumbling to the floor. For good measure he kicked her in the back below the backrest of the chair, more or less in the vicinity of her kidney.

The pain was excruciating, but her body had already started to heal. The bleeding on the side of her head stopped and the edges of the wound closed. The pain took a lot longer to subside, especially in her kidney. She wanted to cry out, but stifled the sound and just lay there, willing the pain to go away.

The General walked back to the desk and sat down.

'Take this piece of shit out of here and resume the tests as indicated.' As an afterthought he added; 'and send someone to clean up this mess,' indicating the blood.

The scientists motioned the soldiers to right the chair and free her from the restraints. They made sure she could not attack anyone, re-cuffed her and shoved her out of the room.

They dragged her down the cold corridor and across the courtyard.

It was dark outside, but the fresh air was welcome. She looked up at the sky and saw the stars; the bright pole star to the right of her. The air was dry and warm, heat still radiated from the sandy ground under her naked feet. There was the slight scent of flowers, but mostly she smelled the odour of the people in the compound. The lingering scent of the meal that had been prepared in the kitchen to the right. The sweat that darkened the uniforms of the soldiers. Wherever they were, it was hot by day, that was clear.

Rushing her along, they once again entered the buildings and pushed her into the laboratory. Instead of clamping her down on one of the tables they pushed her into a small cage that stood on the floor in the middle of the room. She couldn't stand up in the cage or really sit comfortably; unable to stretch her legs either way. A bright light was positioned so it shone into the small space and the scientists left the room. The suffering and pain had definitely started again with a vengeance.

Chapter Eight

The days passed into weeks.

As promised, the "tests" were directed at how much pain she could endure.

They methodically cut and burned her, bludgeoned her and broke bones. The healing process was documented to the second as they repeated the same injury time and again to the letter, to determine whether the process had accelerated and to document any changes. They even cut off one of her fingertips to see if she could regenerate it. She did, though it took some weeks.

She was injected with all kinds of drugs, once again to see what the effect would be on her. Her body attacked the foreign substance the moment it entered her system. Hard drugs like Crack, Heroine and Red devil, caused her to hallucinate violently but briefly, and the more they subjected her to the chemicals, the better she was able to cope with them. In the end she would close her eyes, relax her breathing, and just wait until it passed.

In one session the scientists were baffled by the deep rips

that appeared in the two-centimetre-thick leather of the tables she was strapped to. They seemed to have been made by her fingernails, but upon investigation these turned out to be short and blunt. Repetition of the test with constant observation revealed nothing. No new rips appeared. It drove them crazy. Each test still resulted in more questions.

Truth serums like sodium pentothal were tried but had no effect whatsoever. They gave her tranquilisers used for large animals like rhinos and even elephants. Still the effects were minimal and wore off in record time. They learned more about how her talents manifested themselves but were no closer to why she had them in the first place.

As she lay on her sparse mattress in her cold cell, she willed her body to heal.

She was good at phasing out the pain. Even though the wounds healed quicker, and none of them had come anywhere near to actually killing her, they always hurt. Pain was something she got used to. Even in this magnitude.

She was even able to regulate the speed with which she healed and played with the scientist's minds when she sometimes intentionally screwed up the results. She learned to compartmentalise the hurt. Push it away into one of the darker recesses of her mind.

She left it there to fester.

Chapter Nine

Her moods became ever darker. Tension built up. She started to actively fight the soldiers when they came for her, relishing in the pain she inflicted on them and the knowledge they would not heal as easily as she did. The soldiers retaliated with tasers and cattle prods. They beat her into submission with batons, baseball bats and only just managed to subdue her with sheer numbers.

Collins sat in the chair opposite the General. He dreaded these meetings. After all these months he still hadn't been able to find anything he could use against the General. The man was a fortress. No one got in his mind or was privy to his thoughts. He was unreadable for the otherwise so talented doctor. The initial elation Collins experienced when the test failed, was long gone.

'I believe that you're carrying out additional experiments on the subject at night, without any of my scientists —without me,' the doctor accused the General. 'I think I should know about what's going on. I have a right to know.'

The General didn't react. He remained engrossed in the papers he was reading.

The silence once again got to Collins. He would never learn, and that was what the General was counting on. He enjoyed torturing the feeble excuse for a man.

'My people tell me one of your soldiers is in isolation in one of the cells. He also needed medical attention, is that right?' Collins hoped his question would come out as a demand. But instead, it sounded pathetic, like a feeble request. The General looked up from the papers he was reading. He deemed to answer.

'That's right.' Silence again. The General was once again engrossed in the reports.

'What's wrong with him? Did it have anything to do with the experiments?' Collins could not hide his curiosity if his life depended on it.

'She bit him,' the General said matter-of-factly, not even looking up from his report.

'Bit him?' The surprise in the doctor's voice couldn't have been more gratifying to the General.

'Why? How's that possible? How did she get so close? Wasn't she restrained? What kind of experiments are you performing anyway?' The doctor was stunned.

Slowly the General folded the papers into the document map, leaned back and observed the scientist. The man was about ready to explode. His face was bright red, and his nose was almost pulsating. He was exactly where the General wanted him.

'We have been conducting additional experiments for about a week now, because the ones you do have zero results. It is not necessary that you're present. They are of a different nature,' he said. 'The subject bit my man in the neck, just missing the jugular. Another thing that was weird

—the bite marks weren't consistent with the form of her teeth. We are keeping him in observation for the moment.' The General stood up and walked to the window. 'Who knows, maybe her condition is passed on with saliva, like the vampires or werewolves of old myths.'

'That's ludicrous,' Collins snorted, not even trying to hide his contempt. He was furious the military were conducting experiments without him. And this was too idiotic to contemplate, not to mention totally unscientific.

'How did she bite him, anyway? Wasn't she restrained?' he repeated his earlier question.

Amused the General turned from the view and regarded the scientist. 'Do you really want to know?' he asked, walking over to him.

'Don't be stupid, of course I do,' Collins answered angrily 'I have a right, it's my project.'

The General let that one pass, moving closer to Collins.

'She was restrained, hands and feet, but managed to bite him because he came too close to her head.'

'Why? What was he doing?'

The General leaned over, his face was extremely close to the scientist's; no more than ten inches. 'He was fucking her,' he said simply.

Collins paled. 'He was what?'

The General returned to his seat behind the desk and settled down comfortably. 'He was fucking her,' he repeated.

Now it was the scientist's turn to stand; outraged about what he'd just heard. 'Why?' he stammered. 'What do you expect to achieve with that? What kind of experiment is rape?'

'Oh, I wouldn't call it rape. For that she would have to be human, and we have more or less ruled that out, haven't we. So, consent is not an issue.' The General was enjoying this.

'Do you expect her to talk, to answer our questions because of this...this atrocity?' Collins could not believe what he heard.

'Talk?' the General answered. 'Are you really that stupid? Do you still expect her to give us the answers to all our questions? My God, you're pathetic.' He directed his contempt at the moron across the desk. 'She will never tell us.' He paused for effect. 'Because she doesn't know. Haven't you figured that out yet?'

The ground opened beneath Collins. He was sinking fast into the cavern. What did the General mean, she didn't know? She had to. Otherwise, how would they find out? How would he ever get the answers? All his hard work would have been for nothing. There would be no results, no glory at the end of these more than four years of hell. All his dreams of recognition in the scientific world, yes even the ultimate dream—the Nobel Prize—all were going up in smoke. 'It's not possible, she has to know,' he stammered.

'Has to know?' the General repeated needlessly. 'Well, she doesn't.'

It was finally quiet for a few minutes. Even the doctor had nothing to say. 'How long have you known?' he asked softly.

'Since about two days after we arrived.' The General was really enjoying this. The scientist was broken.

'Then there is no use in continuing the experiments,' Collins said flatly, totally deflated by the revelation. 'Why did you continue—let us continue?' Collins looked at the General with this last question. He finally realised the change of agenda.

'She has other uses for me, so I want to see how far we can go, what she can take before we break her.'

'But that's wrong,' Collins tried. 'Morally repulsive, unethical.'

The General laughed. 'You are accusing me of morality issues. My dear doctor. I don't seem to remember any complaints earlier when you still had your sights on glory and recognition.' Collins paled. 'Besides, it's moot. The subject is under my control. I will do whatever I want.' He stared directly at Collins. 'And you will continue to help me.' The threat was implicit, but just as present as if it had been screamed out loud. Collins flinched.

'What do you want with her?' Collins dreaded the answer.

'What do you think. If we can't replicate her talents, then she will at least become the ultimate soldier—my ace in the hole. Think about it. Even a moron like you must be able to grasp her value. A soldier who can heal her own wounds amounts to more or less invincibility. And her strength is fantastic.'

'Anyway,' he continued in a more reasonable voice 'Who knows, we may get lucky and get her pregnant, replicate her that way.'

'That's impossible,' Collins interrupted softly. 'She has no uterus, she cannot conceive.'

This got the General's attention. 'Why not? That wasn't in her file.'

'We didn't think it was important. Anyway, she contracted cancer of the uterus at a young age and had a hysterectomy. We think this was before her healing abilities kicked in.'

'Can't she regenerate it now?' This was a big disappointment for the General.

'No,' Collins resumed. 'It seems any damage done before she was about forty is irreversible.'

'Are the ovaries gone as well?'

'No, they're intact, not that it makes any difference. I know what you're thinking. Forget it, we tried that already. We removed some eggs from her ovaries, and they immediately imploded, like all her cells do once they leave her body. There's no way we can get her pregnant or use her cells for IVF. And if she doesn't know what made her this way, we have no chance to find answers.' The scientist had resigned himself to absolute failure.

'Well, that may be the case.' The General ended the meeting. 'But we'll continue to test her breaking point. I need to know that, and then break her so that she'll become our willing executioner. Then we can wreak havoc on the revolutionaries. Clean up that mess once and for all. Now leave.'

Collins was dismissed. The General's enjoyment tempered by the revelation that the subject was infertile.

Collins left the office—his office. The truth of what the General had stated, about her not knowing, rocked his world. In hindsight; he'd known. There was no way she would have been able to keep it from him after all that time. The doubts crossed his mind before. But he dismissed them, because the implied conclusions were just too overpowering, too debilitating. His work, his life, was useless. He felt empty, defeated.

Sitting in his office, the General pondered the confrontation with Collins. He regretted telling the stupid man so much, but the look on his face had made it all so worthwhile. Only now he would have to take care of the scientist sooner than he'd planned. That is, if the stupid fool jumped ship. Then again where would he go? The whole scientific community would shun him, he would be the laughingstock. But why run any risk if it could be solved by an unfortunate accident? After all, the man was fragile. Suicidal if the truth be told. He would have Jenkins take care of it.

The General pressed the intercom. 'Susan, get Major Jenkins in here, would you?' he asked pleasantly.

Chapter Ten

The Resistance stepped up their attacks on the pharmaceutical companies in an attempt to gain access to the cure for the introduced man-made pandemic. Biological warfare was turning out to be a very effective way to combat the insurrection. It decimated not only the enemy soldiers but also the families and sympathetic bystanders. It cut into the conviction of the Resistance like a hot knife through butter.

The attacks were often inadequately planned, sometimes the spur of the moment idea of a group of farmers or workers desperate for the cure for their families. Choosing not to wait for the more organised Resistance, they ran head-on into the military who guarded the facilities.

The Resistance was pulled into the fray in reaction to the hasty and amateurish attacks.

The military had a field day. They killed and captured the unprepared fighters in larger numbers than before. The jails overflowed, and the General was requested to interrogate some of the Partisans. Survival of the prisoners was not important. They would be executed anyway.

The General wanted to test the subject's empathy, so with Jenkins and the other military scientists, he devised tests where prisoners would be brought in and subjected to the same torture as the subject. That way they could measure how much more she could take than any normal human being, and at the same time see whether she reacted to others being hurt in her vicinity. They also wanted to test her reaction to them punishing others for her perceived lack of cooperation.

Chapter Eleven

It was getting more difficult to block out what the General was doing. He projected the pain and suffering he thought I should have onto other people. The fact I didn't know these people made no difference.

I was a spectator to the suffering, but I was also the cause. There was nothing I could do to stop it. It made me feel so small, so inconsequential, so helpless. I wanted to do something, anything. Make up the answers the scientist so desperately needed. But there were no questions that made sense. I screamed at them to stop. I threatened, cried, ignored them.

Nothing helped.

They carried on. Tortured and murdered men, women and even children; teenagers and some even younger.

The military scientists looked on and observed my reactions. They wrote everything down. Made it so clinical.

Initially, the civilians in the lab were shocked. Some adapted to the situation out of self-preservation. Others looked away, or even called in sick. Leaving the program was not an option. Nobody was permitted to tell the tale, the General made sure of that.

The military, including the General, were enjoying it. An added benefit of it all was that they were killing partisans, so it was more or less legal; they were just doing their jobs.

I cried for the victims in the darkness of my cell. Cried for the hopelessness of their, and my, predicament. Cried out of pain and rage.

Slowly the anger started to eat away at me. My nerves frayed, and I thought violent thoughts, wanted revenge for the injustice, to me and to others. The guilt ate at my soul. They died because of me. Hurt because of something that was expected of me, something I couldn't deliver.

Why?

That question burned in my mind all the time, kept me from sleep and drove me crazy. The only release was physical exercise. I exhausted my body to the extreme. In the coldness of my cell, that was my escape. I embraced the pain of exhaustion. I slept because of the extremes I drove myself to—hundreds even thousands—of push-ups and sit-ups in the pitch black of the night. Any exercise I could think of. My body welcomed the stress and my strength increased beyond anything even close to what had become normal even for me. The muscles toned to the maximum. In the deep of the night, I felt them to their deepest fibre.

The dark played tricks on my senses. It seemed as though my form blurred. My hands gripped the cold stone beneath me. I attributed the hallucinations to the dark and fatigue. But somewhere deep down a small voice told me otherwise. I could see so well in the dark, that it wasn't possible my eyesight misled me. Strange things were happening. I thought I was tripping, but the strange deep scratches in the stone floor and the wood of my bed disagreed. They were still there in the morning.

I held conversations with myself. In my head I thought, but sometimes out loud. Was I really going mad? Or just stir crazy?

During the torture sessions I ignored anything they did to me, didn't react to any form of pain or stimulation. I tried to cut myself off from the pain of the others, but with less success.

The days and weeks blurred into a regime.

Every day I cried inside, every night I got stronger.

Chapter Twelve

The door to her cell opened and the harsh light momentarily hurt her eyes.

Two soldiers stood in the doorway holding a bundle of rags. They unceremoniously threw their burden into the small cell. The man in the rags—as she deduced from his scent—tumbled on to the cold floor and mumbled in pain. The door closed once again and blocked out all but a small strip of light.

She waited for a few minutes, then stood up and made her way to the corner where the man lay. She could smell his pain. He was battered and bleeding.

'Lay still,' she said. 'Tell me what hurts most.' The man replied in a language she could not understand. 'Please. English,' she requested apologetically. The man tried to sit up, his back to the wall. She helped him.

'Everything hurts,' he whispered in near perfect English. 'I am so cold.'

She gathered the weathered blanket she'd received a few months ago and draped it over the man's shoulders. Even in the absence of light, she could see him well. She could see in almost pitch black, like a cat. The man seemed very old, but that could be the result of the bad treatment he had been subjected to. She estimated he was somewhere in his fifties. A small Latino man, slight of build, with a weathered face and body. His health was bad, especially because of the torture, but probably had never been too good to start with.

She sat down beside him.

'I'm okay,' he said, even though she knew the opposite was true. He was a tough one, this old man. 'My name is Julio.' He held out his hand, then pulled it away as he realised it was dark and she would not be able to see him. She left it at that, not wanting to complicate things.

Reaching to the plateau near the door, she retrieved the water and offered it to him, pushing it in his hand. Thankful, he sipped the cold liquid.

'Who are you?' he asked.

'Just another prisoner,' she replied.

'What is your name?'

'I don't have a name anymore. They call me subject 336.' Her voice was soft and without any anger. She had resigned herself to the impersonal way the scientist treated her a long time ago.

'Everyone has a name,' Julio insisted. 'If you have forgotten it, you must have been here a long time.' Softly he asked; 'how long?'

She rested her back against the cold wall and thought back. How long had it actually been? She was abducted in the summer of 2053, how long ago was that? About two or three years?

'What date is it now?'

'Sometime half October 2058,' he replied, 'I don't know the exact date.'

She was quiet for a while. More than five years. She'd been here in this hellhole for more than five years. The time had seemed endless, but then, five years was a long time. Much longer than she had thought.

'Five years,' she said softly. 'Five endless years.'

The days had blurred into weeks, then months. There was no way she could keep records of the days or know what the date was. In the cell she hardly noticed which season it was. Kept inside most of the time, her last real visit outside was months ago. The cell was in the basement of the building, and she was transported to and from the interrogations with a bag over her head.

How much had she missed? What was going on in the outside world? Was it any better than when she had come here? For that matter, where was "here"? She turned her attention to her fellow prisoner. 'Do you know where we are?'

'Probably in one of the facilities in the southern Mexican provinces, I think in Chiapas,' he answered. 'They blindfolded me, so I don't know for certain, but we know they have secret places all over the southern areas. The air is warm outside so that makes me assume we are somewhere near the desert.'

'Who is "we"?' she asked.

He hesitated. Maybe this was a trick to get him to betray his comrades. What if this woman was one of them and she was supposed to milk him dry about the Resistance? But his instincts contradicted this. Deep in his belly he felt she was a real prisoner; in the same predicament he was. Of course, it was possible they had bugged the room, so he would not tell any secrets. The military already knew who and what he was. They knew he was connected. They had celebrated enough when they caught him.

'We are the Resistance,' he continued. 'We fight the Americanos and try to liberate the southern nations. Last week America attacked the southern Latino countries, the next step in the expansion of the Americas. The northern countries were annexed years ago and formed the new states. The Americanos new offensive has a dual function: to gain control of the energy sources and to divert attention from internal to external enemies. The American government, like so many of its western peers, is losing control and this is a last desperate effort to salvage some of the influence they so desperately need. Their idea was to get the energy, offer it to the people and regain the loyalty the government so dramatically covets. The idea backfired. Our revolutionary groups are more connected than the government realised. A war against the Latino countries is a war against the brethren, against the poor people worldwide who inspire more loyalty from the common man than the bureaucrats could ever dream of.'

'All this is for the energy sources?' She felt as though she had been incarcerated for a lifetime. She'd missed so much.

'Whoever has the energy, has the power. The shortage almost shifted the balance of power for good. As you may know, more than twenty years ago the oil all but ran out. The western and oil countries had not invested enough in alternative energy sources and found themselves without options. Our countries—the poorer ones—were forced to look for alternatives long before then because of the exorbitant prices of the quickly diminishing oil products. We hardly noticed the absence of the oil. We still had our own sources. But the rich countries were in dire straits. They were forced to buy energy from us. The global balance was turned upside down. The "undeveloped" countries owned it, and the West wanted it. Nations in Africa and South

America found themselves catching up with the West at a breath-taking pace. The new rich of these countries, that is. The poor still didn't benefit. Worse yet, the contrast between rich and poor grew. Everywhere. In the West, the rich were the only ones able to buy the energy. In the rest of the world—in the energy countries—only the rich profited. Just when the Western countries were almost on their knees, help came to them from an unexpected phenomenon—LKX.' He sighed. The pain clear on is features.

'LKX killed indiscriminately, until the West found a cure a few years ago. Once again, they had the upper hand. They saw the dramatic loss in work forces due to the fatalities of LKX and distributed the cure to their own constituents. The energy countries got none. Resentment festered. And with it the revolutionary fire. We started working together over the country borders. We targeted the pharmaceutical depots, the cure for LKX our main goal. Casualties—mainly among our supporters—were high, so we switched our sights and started targeting ammunition depots and military encampments to arm ourselves.'

He paused for a moment. The memories were clearly difficult and painful.

'As to be expected, the military retaliated and targeted our supporters. They were hunted down, arrested and subsequently disappeared. Civilian casualties were countless.'

They continued to talk deep into the night.

It surprised her how much she'd missed simple conversation with another human being. The scientists treated her like a lab rat. An object without perceived feeling or intellect. Not a person. The only thing remotely resembling conversations were orders to get her to do something, and abuse when that didn't go as planned. No one just spoke to her. Well, the young scientist tried once or twice, but he was rebuked by Big-Nose. After the military took over, there was hardly any conversation at all, not to her, not to each other. All the tests were done with military precision.

Not that it helped.

The results were the same.

Chapter Thirteen

They talked about the Resistance in general terms and what was happening in the outside world.

She learned that the energy situation had deteriorated to such a level the countries were fighting each other for it. Disease and war were the order of the day. She asked about the Southern Provinces—where they probably were. What was it like outside?

He asked her about her life. Evading the whole story, she didn't elaborate. She indicated there was something strange about her that the scientists wanted, though didn't go into details, but that it had nothing to do with politics or anything like that. She was a personal prisoner, not a POW.

Julio was surprised about this strange woman he spoke to in the dark. Her voice was soft, but she emanated power and strength. There was something about her that spurred him on to keep talking. He actually enjoyed it.

His capture had been almost a week ago. He hadn't been able to really talk to anyone—at least anyone nice. The mission to raid the pharmaceutical company and liberate the cure for LKX for everyone had gone hopelessly wrong. The military were waiting for the Resistance. They knew. There was a traitor. In the heat of the fire fight, Manuel tried to run over to the soldiers, screaming at the top of his voice about the deal he had made with the Commandant. They cut him down, along with the rest of the group. As far as he knew, Julio was now probably the sole survivor. And the prize. The soldiers were ecstatic they'd captured him. They congratulated each other in between the kicks and blows they aimed at him. He was bundled in the truck and taken to the military enclosure. There they tortured him in an attempt to gain more information about the resistance, but he persevered and told them nothing.

An order came down the line and he was once again bundled in the truck with a bag over his head. A painful trip of more than a day brought him here, wherever this was. He thought he knew the general vicinity but could not be sure. The soldiers were jittery. The little conversation stilled as they neared the place, the tension in the air was palatable. Something was bad.

He didn't expect to leave here alive.

The next morning, they came for Julio. She was left in the cell on her own and missed his company already. The night had been very informative, and the contact with another human refreshing. In the course of the day, she noticed anxiety about her newfound roommate. That was probably the reason why the General had placed him with her to start with. Nothing here was without reason.

But there was no way she could help.

The destruction of the cell matter from her body was no

conscious action on her part. She was equally perplexed as to why all this was happening. The way her body was changing, and the strange healing abilities she seemed to have, were just as magical to her as to them. Deep in her heart she knew the military scientist and the General were aware of this. However, the torture didn't relent. If at all; it intensified. The questions were asked pro-forma—no one actually expected any answers. They were just an excuse. An excuse to be able to test the extremes they could go to. The General was trying to break her, but she had no idea why or what for. That it couldn't be anything good was obvious. Plain sadism and sociopathic pleasure on the part of the military were also elements in the continuance of the torture.

They brought Julio back late in the afternoon. He was covered in blood and had been beaten extensively. The light was left on, and a bowl of water and rags placed in the room. She asked him what had happened while she tended to his wounds.

'They torture me to find out where the Resistance is,' he answered meekly. 'But I don't know, the location is moved so often that I just don't know. Not that I would ever tell anyway. They can kill me—and they probably will—but no one else.' Julio rested and slept. She watched over him, waking him when their simple food came. He should eat. To gain more strength.

For three additional days they repeated the procedure. The guards dragged Julio out of the cell and on the third day they had to beat her to keep her from intervening.

She was worried, a few more days like this and it would cost Julio his life. But there was little she could do. They left her alone, in the cell, not subjecting her to any physical torture. Physical pain she could deal with, but this was killing her. The anxiety of what was happening to Julio proved to be more painful than anything they could have inflicted on her. Despite her resolutions, she'd became attached to this quiet man. Their conversations deep into the night gave her hope. She wanted to see all the things he told her about, all the things and people outside of the cell. In the years she had been here her mind had gone into survival mode where the option of ever getting out was pushed to some dark recess. It was plain survival; so she could not dwell on the idea, could not be consumed with the loss of her freedom.

During the past days and nights, her mind opened its restraints and she found herself dreaming of escape. Dreaming of a life outside of the walls.

Her moods darkened the more she missed her freedom.

She became frustrated and depressed. And aggressive. Every time the soldiers came in, she wanted to attack them, rip their limbs from their bodies. Her thoughts became more and more bloody, her body over-saturated with adrenaline. In the few hours that she slept, she dreamt ever more violent scenes. Strange creatures roamed her mind and killed everything in sight. Sometimes she would find herself a spectator, cajoling and urging them onwards, other times she would be one of the killers, enjoying the slaughter and devastation. Her dreams coloured bright red. In her waking hours—pacing her cell and anxious about Julio—her dreams passed over the line of consciousness and invaded her senses.

All this time, the tension built.

Her muscles hurt. They twitched, strained and grew even though she was not actively using them. She encountered a sense of detachment. Her mind and thoughts felt separate from her body. Separate, and ever more violent.

When the soldiers finally brought Julio back, they were forced to use the dog and tasers to stop her from attacking them. She managed to swat one of the soldiers hard against the wall before they retreated. The dog went mad, his nose assaulted by a strange wild scent that permeated the cell. The handler barely managed to restrain the canine. They fled the small room and left her to tend to her friend.

Julio collapsed on the floor the moment they let go of him. He couldn't stand on his own two feet. Her rage subsided a bit and she took the water and rags to clean his new wounds. Even though they were shallow and not directly life-threatening, the loss of blood was becoming an issue. She tried as best she could to stop the slow seep and wished she could project some of her healing abilities onto him.

The next day brought a change in the routine.

Most of the day was quiet. Late in the evening they came for both of them. The guards carried Julio and dragged her with a collection of Tasers, cattle prods, baseball bats—whatever they could think of to restrain her—and left the cell. Her sight coloured red again, she found herself half growling at the soldiers. Strange sounds emitted from her throat, her body strained, and felt as though she was going to burst. The same strange wild smell permeated the hallways, somehow this intensified her thirst for blood. The Military beat her almost senseless, and the combined soldiers and scientists only just managed to strap her to one of the two operating tables in the brightly lit examination room. Her wrists and ankles were encompassed in thick leather straps. The locks clearly reinforced. Still, she struggled. They stripped her naked for some unfathomable reason. Sensors were attached to her chest and head. Her table was rotated so that she was positioned vertically, as though standing up.

Julio was bound to the table opposite her with a lot less force. He'd resigned himself to the idea that this would be his last day on this earth. He couldn't take any more of this.

Her demeanour visibly rattled the scientists. They huddled near the stationary tables against the wall, not daring to come anywhere near her.

The door opened and the General entered the room.

The pressure in her head and body increased and blocked out any semblance of thought. The red haze descended over her, and she had trouble concentrating on anything other than the sound of her own heart pounding madly in her ears. She felt the blood running in her veins; it burned wherever it passed. All the nerves in her body screamed out in defiance. Never had she encountered such pain and agony. She felt herself losing control over her mind and body, as she became consumed by rage and raw primal violence.

Through the pain, she felt more that heard the General giving orders and the Major approach Julio's head with a scalpel in his hand. Julio's scream sent her over the edge, and everything turned bright red.

Chapter Fourteen

I stood in the centre of the laboratory and tried to catch my breath.

The smell of the blood and gore assailed my senses. I was covered in the stuff. Felt tainted, and unbelievably tired.

It was quiet.

Even the whimpering had stopped. I turned to face Julio on the table. He met my stare.

Fear shone in his brown eyes. He didn't know what to make of what had just happened. But then again, neither did I. I had no conscious knowledge of the past few minutes. They seemed like hours but were blurred at the same time.

All around me I saw dead bodies. The scientists and military had been massacred; pulled apart. Horrendous wounds covered the corpses.

Images played in my head. I just stood there.

'We should leave.' Julio brought me back to reality. He was right. There was no way this could go unheeded. The guards in the direct vicinity had all died after when they came into the room on the General's call. But there were more in the building and on the grounds. We needed to get moving and try to get as far from here as possible before they found out we were gone. No way would they leave this alone, that much was clear. I was counting on surprise and chaos. But that was just wishful thinking.

I moved to the table and freed Julio of his restraints. He focused all his energy, sat up and swung his legs over the edge of the metal plate. He dropped to the floor and almost collapsed. I managed to catch him, and he steadied himself. I looked around, searching for something to wear. I was still naked and covered in blood. That was bound to raise questions. No time to clean up, so I would have to cover myself as best I could. I grabbed a spare lab coat I saw hanging on a peg on the back of the door. I covered my head and hair with a cap that one of the scientists had been wearing. He wouldn't need it anymore.

I supported Julio as I moved him to the door.

We looked around the corner and slipped silently into the hallway. No one barred our way. It seemed as if the building was devoid of life. This would be temporary at most, and we hurried up the flight of stairs at the end of the hall, through another door and out into a courtyard. There was a door at the far end of the courtyard, and we silently made our way there, circumventing the middle of the open space.

No one challenged us.

It was dark. I estimated it to be late in the evening, almost midnight. The interrogation session, as the General so lovingly called them, had not lasted long. It was timed for the night when no one was around. It looked as though the rest of the building and grounds had long since gone into slumber.

We reached the door in the courtyard wall. I tested it. It was locked. But the lock was old and looked worn. With one wrench it splintered. I strained to hear whether the noise had alerted anyone. All remained quiet.

I pushed the door open, and we slid out into the night. Hugging the wall, we moved to the right. It was darker there.

Julio hung on to my shoulder and tried to walk. I bent down and picked him up. I would make better time if I carried him. He protested for a second, but his energy deserted him, and he surrendered. My astute hearing detected the first stirrings back at the buildings. It seemed that someone had finally found the courage to sound the alarm.

I increased my speed, leaving the relative safety of the wall. I moved through small streets while I kept to a general southerly direction. Why? I didn't consciously know. I didn't know where I was, or where I was going for that matter. Just away, away from all the terror of the past years and, most of all; away from what I had done in the laboratory. Because somehow, I knew I was responsible for the carnage. I ducked into an open gateway and stopped for a moment. Julio was silent. I listened to the sounds of the small town around us. In the distance I heard the commotion behind the walls we had fled. It seemed to be chaos. That would give us time.

'We need to keep moving south, get out of this town' Julio whispered. 'I know where we are, there is a small village hidden in the mountains about ten miles from here. There we have Sympatico's.'

The urgency in his voice spurred me on. I picked him up again and moved out of the gateway. There were no cars or other vehicles around to steal. There was no fuel, so there was no use anyway. We neared the edge of the town and moved out into the desert. A lone dog started barking, but I silenced him instinctively with a low growl.

We travelled all night.

Near dawn we found refuge in a dense patch of weeds. A small indentation in the ground offered some camouflage. I heard dogs in the distance. But I was not afraid they would follow or track us. The effect I had on canines did not invite close contact. I heard the chaos and defiance of the dogs. The angry shouting of the handlers was not audible enough to distinguish individual words. But the sentiment was clear. They were getting nowhere. It seems that what happened to me last night had some use after all.

Chapter Fifteen

We rested.

I tested the air for the scent of water. We left in such a hurry we were not able to take anything with us, so we had to find some moisture ourselves. The scent was most prevalent in the cacti that dotted the desert scenery. We waited till dark, then finally cut open one of the cacti with a sharp rock and moisturised our lips and mouth. There was barely enough to swallow, but it refreshed us. Julio insisted on walking. He lasted about three steps before he collapsed. I waited a few seconds, then picked him up and started out over the cooling sand.

We travelled almost all night, diving into a rift when a helicopter flew overhead. Its strobes pierced the night and turned it almost into day. By early morning we reached a small outcrop.

'Go to the right here,' Julio motioned 'There's a small cave up in that rock wall. It leads into a valley.'

Cautiously, I picked my way between the boulders and thorny bushes. My feet were calloused, but even they hurt on the sharp stones. We entered the cave. Julio struggled out of my arms and moved gingerly across the floor of the cavern.

Though it was dark, his eyes were accustomed to little light, and we picked our way to the back. The cave wall halted our progress. There we encountered two corridors that led off the back of the cave. 'This one,' Julio motioned.

I tensed—we were not alone. Julio continued. I grabbed hold of him and pushed him behind me, growling inside. There were three others in the corridor. Two in front of us and one to the left.

'Stop, don't do anything rash,' Julio cautioned me. He turned to face the two men who materialised out of the gloom. He called out in a language I didn't understand. I'd heard him speak it when he was delirious in the cell back at the spa. One of the men answered him gruffly, a question it seemed. I stood and waited as I tried to push down the rush of emotion that I felt. The skin on my back pricked and moved. In the dark my fingers disjointed. I felt the nails grow into claws.

Julio answered, and it was silent again. The turmoil inside of me was overwhelming. It was all I could do not to let the fury and pain engulf me. Julio put a hand on my arm. He felt the fur underneath his fingers and tightened his grip. It worked—his touch restrained me. Slowly, I started breathing again. I willed the chaos to subside.

The answer Julio gave was obviously the right one. A lamp was lit, and the first man peered into his face. A happy cry left his lips and all of a sudden, the cave was filled with enthusiastic banter. I remained where I was, willing my body to regain its normal form. The happy voices trailed away as the light moved my way.

'She is a friend.' Julio stood before the man who was

obviously the leader of the three. 'She saved me and brought me here—she freed me,' he said it in English for my convenience.

Reluctantly, the man turned the light from my face and headed out of the corridor the way he had come. I supported Julio once again and followed. Once the men realised Julio could not walk on his own, they hastened to carry him, rebuffing me as they pushed me aside.

At that moment, I wanted to vanish and leave Julio to their care. He must have read my mind.

'No please, continue with us, our journey has but begun,' he pleaded. The men stopped, turned to me and waited for my decision. I looked into Julio's pleading face and resolved to stay just a short time.

We resumed the trek through the corridors in the mountain. After about twenty minutes we left the compressing darkness of the caves and moved out into the early light of the morning. Before us, I saw a small sandy valley dotted with trees and bushes. The floor turned and changed direction in course with the meandering spring that dissected it. We walked for another two or three minutes until we rounded a corner and came across a small gathering of camouflaged tents.

There were few people there; most of them old or women and children. The typical refugees the world had become used to in the last decade.

No one spoke.

We were taken to a tent in the centre of the small community. There Julio and the men entered the open flap. I waited outside, not eager to venture into the unknown. My senses were working overtime, and I didn't know what to make of them. I smelled people, animals and the tangy scent of grease and gunpowder. Mercifully, there were no dogs here, although I did detect the residual scent of one that had been here the day before. I listened as the horses I identified nickered nervously. It was probably the blood that I was still covered with. Frankly I stank.

There was movement from in the tent and a woman of about forty appeared in the passageway.

She looked me over and said in perfect English; 'thank you for bringing Julio here. He vouches for you, and I trust his judgment.'

I nodded my answer.

'Don't make me regret it,' she added as an afterthought.

'You must be hungry, but first I think a bath.' She wrinkled her nose at my smell. If I could have without looking stupid, I would have done so myself. 'The stream is over there,' she gestured. 'Clothes will be provided—we will burn these.'

I moved in the direction of her hand and one of the guards followed me. I was used to constant observation, so it didn't bother me. At the edge of the stream, I stripped and entered the icy cold water, not paying attention to the surprised exclamations of the man. I gasped at the cold on my skin, but it felt wonderful. The water came up to my waist, so I sat down and submerged entirely.

I felt the grime and blood leave my skin.

If only the water would cleanse the inside as easily.

After almost ten minutes I left the water and dried myself off with the cloth provided for me. Next to it lay a pile of clothes. Old and patched in places, but clean: trousers, a shirt and some underwear. I discarded the shoes —my feet were tough—and I wanted to keep them that way. I was not staying and new shoes with the subsequent blisters would slow me down.

I was led back to the tent and this time I entered. Up till now I hadn't said a word.

'Thank you for the clothes.' I directed my thanks to the woman who was obviously the leader of this rag tag group.

'You're welcome.' She smiled.

Julio sat in a folding chair near the table. He looked a bit refreshed himself, although I don't think he had visited the spring itself. There was food on the table: bread and vegetables. The woman motioned me to sit in the remaining unoccupied chair. When I'd done so, she offered me food and water.

'Julio will not elaborate on the circumstances of your escape, or about your name for that matter. I wonder if you would like to enlighten me.'

'Not really,' I answered. She stared me directly in the eye, probing for information. Then she gave up and with a sigh, started eating herself.

'We must call you something. Julio calls you his protector, his Tonal. If you agree, we will call you that.'

I nodded. What's in a name? It was certainly better than "Subject 336". Julio smiled. He had been trying to think of a good name for me since we met.

'We are a small group here, mostly women and children,' the woman continued. 'The authorities do not know we are here, and it is important to keep it that way.' She spoke to both Julio and me. 'Therefore, it is not possible for you to stay here for long. We have heard of a commotion in a high-end spa to the north, and I suspect that you were the instigator.' She looked directly at me for that last comment. 'The blood you were covered in probably originates from there.' When I didn't react, she continued. 'The Policia and military are out in force. Looking for you two no doubt. I cannot jeopardise the people living here.' She stated it matter-of-factly.

Julio immediately answered. 'We understand completely, Mercedes, and will not be staying. If possible, we would like to resume our journey when night falls.'

'You are in no state to attempt any journey.' I directed my comment at Julio. He was extremely gaunt and fragile. His wounds had not healed since we left the Spa. 'You can't go anywhere.' Julio spluttered that he was able to move and that we could not stay here.

'You are both right,' Mercedes intervened. 'You do not have to leave immediately but you cannot stay much longer than a day or two. We will attend to your wounds Julio, and you will rest. Tomorrow we will decide what to do.'

She looked at me. 'Do you have any wounds?' she asked. It was a rhetorical question—she had obviously heard the answer from my companion at the spring. There was an accusatory edge to the question. How could I not be wounded, when Julio had obviously been tortured? The distrust was etched on her face.

'Please Mercedes,' Julio whispered. 'No more questions. She has no wounds that need to be tended to right now.'

No, I thought, none you could heal. Now that the direct danger was gone, and I was able to relax a bit, the true horror of what I had done was beginning to take over my mind. My appetite deserted me, and the surroundings suddenly seemed depressing and suffocating. I needed to get out into the fresh air.

I stood up, thanked Mercedes for the hospitality and left the tent. Immediately one of the guards, this time a youth of no more than fourteen, followed me.

'A tent has been prepared for you,' he offered in heavily accented English. 'Here to the right.' I thanked him but indicated that I would like to stay outside. I moved to the shade of a tree and sat down on the hard ground.

Later on, I moved into the tent and slept. Thankfully there were no dreams—just blissful darkness.

It was the early morning light when I woke. I had slept the whole day and night. I felt better, rested. But I was still apprehensive and confused.

I went looking for Julio and found him in the tent with Mercedes again. Four angry men had now joined them. Mercedes motioned me to a chair at the back of the tent. I sat down and waited. I didn't understand the heated discussion, but the sentiment was clear. They were very angry at our presence here. We were obviously endangering them and their families. One of the men gestured with his arms counting out loud and then pointing directly at me. Julio tried to intervene. They were respectful of him, but unfriendly towards me. I stayed where I was. I didn't move or react to the commotion around me. Mercedes finally stood up and silenced the gathering. The men complied and, with short goodbyes to Julio and vicious stares directed at me, they left the tent.

'As we expected, the authorities are looking for you.' Mercedes directed her words more to me than to Julio. 'It is worse than we expected. The military joined the hunt in large numbers. They scour the dessert for clues. My men managed to wipe out many of your tracks, but they are still advancing in this general direction.' She turned to Julio and added; 'I am sorry Patron, but you cannot stay any longer.' Julio nodded his compliance.

'We do not have any vehicles,' she continued. 'But we do have a few ponies. You can ride, Julio. One of the men will escort you out of the valley and stay with you until you are well away. Then he will take the pony and return here. I am sorry that we cannot give you the animal as a gift, but we need it too much ourselves. If the authorities find us, we will have to move the people in a hurry.'

'Please, do not concern yourself with our well-being,' Julio answered 'We will be all right. I thank you for the loan of the pony. I do not think I would be able to get too far yet.' He turned to me. 'And even you cannot carry me forever.'

That was settled, and we started making the preparations for our departure. Mercedes gave us some provisions. Most important were the water bags filled with fresh water from the spring. We both received large brimmed hats that would shade us from the midday sun and cover our features.

The young boy who guarded me the day before was assigned as our guide. He helped Julio mount the scrawny pony. It was agitated and skittish. I guessed it was my scent, so I kept behind the rest. Finally, the pony calmed down— or just resigned itself to the situation—and we said our goodbyes to Mercedes.

'Be well Julio,' she embraced the old man and turned to me. 'Take care of him, he is important to us.' It was not a request, but an order.

I nodded, and we left the clearing.

Chapter Sixteen

We followed the stream for the better part of an hour. Then turned into a rift that stood at right angles to the valley we came from. The scenery became progressively dryer and more barren.

We journeyed all night. Only stopping to relieve ourselves or to check the general direction we were moving in. The boy seemed to know the area very well and we made good progress. By early morning we reached another mountain range and sheltered from the sun under an outcrop of rock. Julio and the boy slept soundly while the pony grazed on the little shrubbery it could find. It was still wary of me. I napped but stayed more or less awake to the surroundings.

It was just as well. I almost nodded off when I heard the soft footfall behind me. I waited to see if I had imagined it, but no; there was a second step, and then the stupid fool pulled back the safety on his gun. The sound was so loud it almost hurt my ears. Turning instantly, I grabbed the soldier, pushed his gun up so the barrel pointed at the sky and couldn't harm any of us. The struggle was brief, but the soldier was big and managed to fight back long enough to fire his gun. The sound woke my companions. They jumped up just in time to see me snap the luckless soldier's neck.

He would not be alone. There were bound to be more soldiers in the vicinity and the sound of the shot would no doubt alert them to our whereabouts.

The boy caught the skittish pony, and I manhandled Julio on to its back. I ordered them to go and turned to stop any other soldiers from following them.

No more than three minutes after they left the scene, two more soldiers crashed through the underbrush to the outcrop. Both saw their fallen comrade and me. The shock of their dead friend was enough to give me the upper hand. With my speed and strength, they didn't have a chance. One was dead before he could move, his throat ripped out. The other whimpered and turned to flee. I was on him in a second, grabbed his head and wrenched to the left. The crack was sickening.

I stood and waited to see if anymore were coming while I caught my breath, not so much from exertion as from the nauseous revelation that I had killed again with so much ease.

Thirty seconds and no sounds later, I decided that this was it. I turned, pulled the bodies under the outcrop, and then left the place to catch up with Julio and the boy.

It was still bright daylight, and we needed a place to hide. The sun was scalding, and the military still used the occasional helicopter to scan the mountains. We kept to the side of the mountain and under the sparse shrubbery. We travelled for another hour until we found a small cave. The pony was coaxed into the cave where we all settled down to wait for the sun to set and to rest. When it finally dropped over the horizon, we set out again.

We travelled in this manner for two more days. Julio and the boy exchanged stories and observations on the way. The further we got from the valley the more relaxed the journey became. We were rudely brought back to the extent of the search when we barely managed to escape detection on the third day after nearly stumbling on a sleeping soldier as we turned a corner in yet another rift. The unfortunate man died before he woke up. We listened for any other soldiers, then took the man's gun and a few more items that would be handy for the trip.

We were more careful after that.

The extent of the manhunt surprised us. We only expected the soldiers to be in the vicinity of the lab, but no matter how far we travelled, we still encountered them.

At one point, while we rested and waited for the dark, I left Julio with the boy to hunt for small animals to eat. The pickings were sparse. Most of the animals would be in the security of shade until the killing sun had set. I decided hunting would be better at night, but I found water and filled my flask.

As I returned to my small party of companions, I heard Julio cry out. Once again; we were too complacent. There was a soldier in the small clearing, his gun pointed at Julio who lay on the ground. The soldier kicked him for no apparent reason. I think he'd surprised Julio and woken him. The boy was nowhere to be seen. To the side the pony pulled at its tether.

Just as I was about to storm into the clearing, the boy beat me to it. Concealed in a shrub he waited for the non-suspecting soldier to move closer to him. The soldier concentrated solely on Julio, kicking him all the time. The boy rose from his hiding place, grabbed the soldier from behind and drove his knife deep into the man's side, up into the heart. He was dead before he fell.

As glad as I was that the situation was resolved, my heart broke to see the ease with which such a young boy killed his enemies. This wasn't the first time, and it probably would not be the last. The finality of the revolution hit me there—there was no turning back for these people.

After I made sure Julio's wounds had not reopened with the battery he'd endured, I once again hid the body, and we left the area in daytime. Julio was hunched over the horse's saddle, but he managed. His new injuries were thankfully more superficial than I'd thought.

On the evening of the fourth day, the boy declared we were far enough from the village and that he would leave us. He gave us most of the supplies that were left, said goodbye, took the reins of Julio's mount and mounted his pony.

Chapter Seventeen

Julio and I continued south.

Julio was the navigator. I was the packhorse.

He'd recovered enough to be able to walk part of the way. However, we didn't make the progress of the previous days—the pony was dearly missed.

At the end of the night, in the early light of dawn, we found a deserted shack and decided to stay there for the day. We would continue to travel at night. It was deemed safer.

Unpacking the few provisions we had left, we sat down on the packed earth. After a small meal of stale bread and some kind of jerky, I set about searching the shack for anything usable.

We were obviously not the first to try—there was nothing. A long piece of rope was the only thing of value that I found. But maybe it would be handy. I carried Julio on my back for most of the night. My arms were tired from supporting him. If I could make some sort of support with the rope it would leave my arms free. I started to weave and knot a seat that I could sling over my shoulders and tie around my waist. Julio understood what I was doing and helped.

We remained silent for a long time.

'Tonal.' Julio put down his work. 'It is maybe time to talk about what happened,' he stated matter of fact, as if the subject was something as trivial as the weather.

I'd dreaded this moment. There was no one around, so that was no excuse to stop me. But I was reluctant to speak about what I saw as a massacre. It was foremost in my mind every night while we travelled. In the daytime I dreamt about it. I relived it again and again.

'It's eating you up inside,' Julio continued. 'You must talk.' After another silence he added; 'it will not go away.'

I stopped knotting the rope and looked at him. 'What is there to talk about?' I tried. 'It happened.'

'What happened?' Julio was not about to let me off that easily.

'I don't know.' I finally gave in. 'I've tried to make sense of it since we left the lab, but I can't.' Julio listened intently. 'I relive it time and time again—what I know about it—and still it's so alien. What happened to me there Julio?' I turned the question around.

'You were pushed beyond your limits. I have heard of people who become abnormally strong and fierce when provoked as they had you, but never have I heard of an actual change into another being.'

'What did you see... feel... hear?' I wanted to know— all blockades had dissolved.

Julio sat back against the wall of the shack.

'The butcher cut me in the scalp. I remember it hurt terribly and I screamed. Then I heard a strange noise from your table and looked that way. There was blood in my eyes, so I thought I was not seeing things clearly.' He paused to gain his composure. Or maybe because he had nightmares about it too. Perhaps the subject was as difficult for him to speak about as for me.

'You looked strange—warped. Your face contorted. Your nose and mouth extended; all I could focus on were the teeth. They grew and grew. Your body was lightly covered in what looked like yellow-brown fur. Your whole stance changed. You fell to all fours once you'd freed your arms and legs through your massive strength. Everything blurred and suddenly you stopped. It was quiet. Nobody moved. I couldn't even breathe. Then the General shouted for the men to do something. I don't know exactly what he said. I wasn't listening. I couldn't take my eyes off what you had become.' He shifted his body as though to move farther away from me, then realised what he had done and made a conscious effort to move back to where he was before.

He saw that I noticed, and it obviously pained him.

'I am sorry, Tonal. A reflex. It will not happen again,' he apologised. When I remained silent, he continued his story.

'There was the smell, the wild scent that I'd noticed from you before when you were stressed. Only now it was much stronger. It fuelled the terror as well. As if the sight of you was not enough. You know Tonal, that I come from the jungle. I was born in a time that the mighty jaguar was still the lord of the jungle. I have seen him. But what I saw in that room was beyond anything I have seen before. The size of the cat—you—was immense. You were almost as big as a horse.' He paused in awe.

'You roared. It chilled me to the bone. Paralysed me. That was the moment you attacked the General, you ripped out his throat and turned on the soldiers and scientists. You were everywhere. I've never seen such claws.' He stopped his narrative. It was obvious that recanting the tale took its toll on him. After a few minutes he continued.

'I closed my eyes then. I didn't dare to look. I prayed. Then it was silent. I opened my eyes and saw you standing in the middle of the bodies. You were still the gigantic cat. You heard a noise and moved to the desk. The young scientist was crouched under the table, wounded and terrified. You moved to him and dragged him out from under the table. Then you stopped, looked around and backed off. You seemed smaller. That was when you changed back to how you are now. The rest you know.'

The story taxed him.

I remained silent.

'Enough,' he said. 'We must rest, tomorrow we talk further, now we sleep.'

I nodded my agreement.

Chapter Eighteen

Julio lay down on the hard earth, closed his eyes and was soon overtaken by his fatigue. I, on the other hand, was not so lucky. What he had told me haunted me. It made sense to rest, but I had so many questions and no answers.

Finally, I sank into a restless sleep.

The dreams returned.

In the dreams things were even more exaggerated than it had been in real life.

The blood coloured everything red. My claws were enormous, too big and heavy for me to lift. The General, his throat ripped to threads, refused to die. He kept coming back no matter what I did. He repeated the same guttural incantation again and again.

'You can't kill me. I will return and make your life a living hell.'

Wasn't that what he had already done? What more could he do?

In my dream, I was the helpless one. Weighed down by my claws, my mouth unable to close because of near sabre teeth. All the scientists and the soldiers that I killed crowded around me and started shouting and screaming. I was helpless.

I woke with a start because Julio shook me. I stopped myself from attacking him. Still lost somewhere in the dream.

'You had a nightmare—a bad one,' he said and indicated my right arm. The hand had once again morphed into a paw with long claws. I had been clawing the wood of the shack wall. Shocked, I tried to get my hand back to its normal shape. I was filled with dread at the thought that I could have wounded or even killed Julio in my sleep.

He understood my anxiety. 'I am all right, you did not hurt me. You won't, otherwise you would have done that in the lab.' His voice was soft. 'My pain was the reason you escaped your bonds.'

'Yeah, and killed all those people,' I added in my mind.

'Now breathe slowly, try to let the energy go,' he almost whispered. I had to concentrate to hear him. Slowly I inhaled and tried to relax all the tense muscles. I closed my eyes and listened to his slow and sure speech.

'You can turn this around,' he continued. 'Like you did in the cave, when the Partisans came.' I felt the tension ebb. The joints and muscles in my hand pulled and strained. Slowly, everything went back to normal. Or as normal as it would ever get from now on.

'We must teach you to get this under your control,' Julio said. 'It must become something conscious, not part of your instinct. It will take time, but that we have.'

I marvelled at this quiet and wise man. He had seen what I was—what I was capable of—and still he wasn't afraid of me. My own disgust at what I had become was one of the main feelings I experienced at that moment. I could not reconcile myself with what I had done. Sure, they were no innocents. The doctors and the soldiers tortured me, and others to get at me, in every way thinkable. They were responsible for so much death and pain and anguish. They might have deserved to die, but not like that. Not to be massacred, pulled apart, faced with a monster without a hope in hell of getting out alive.

Julio read my thoughts or maybe just translated the anguish on my features.

'Don't rebuff yourself so much, they brought their deaths upon themselves. It was not of your choosing.'

Chapter Nineteen

They travelled by night. Hiding from probing eyes in the daytime.

The trip was reasonably relaxed as long as they avoided any areas where there were settlements, so they skirted major highways and civilisation.

They slept in the morning, then awoke halfway through the afternoon and practiced. Julio insisted that she work at the change as much as possible. Reluctant to go too far, she restricted the transformation to small parts of her body. She found that she could control the area of the change reasonably well by focused—and conscious—thought. Concentrating on her hand as she channelled the blood through that specific area, she was able to determine where the change would take place. The speed of the change was beyond her control. Sometimes it would be instant, sometimes it would take excruciating long minutes. The pain was intense.

The first few times it seemed impossible to continue, but in time she got used to it and was able to funnel the agony away as she had learned in the past years at the lab. Her first unconscious reaction was to concentrate her healing on the body part that she was changing. But that stopped the transformation process, and she was forced to bear the pain if she wanted to practice. Foremost in her mind was the fear that the change would come over her fully, that she would not be able to control it or herself, and that she would hurt Julio. So, she was restrained and only let the change go as far as she felt comfortable with. After her hands transformed to paws, she inevitably started to feel the pull of her facial muscles and the creaking of the bones as her jaws attempted to morph into the feline form. There she stopped.

With practice she came to enjoy the sensation and the enormity of the change.

It was fascinating.

When she concentrated on her hand, she would see the nails grow longer, curved, thicker, harder and much, much sharper. A fine haze of ochre coloured fur pierced though her skin. It started on the back of her hand and moved down over her fingers and up to the top of her arm.

It tickled. Turning her hand over she saw that the skin on the inside of her hand was toughening and darkening—the pads became visible. The fingers fused between the last knuckles and the hand. The outer digits lengthened and bended. Her hand enlarged into the paw of an enormous feline with claws more than twelve centimetres long, curved and vicious.

The feeling of power in her paw was addictive—she wanted to continue the change. Let it roll over her whole body. Let loose of the stupid human form. Reluctantly she stopped the process. Subdued the feeling of elation that so often accompanied the pain of the change.

She alternated between hands. Sometimes even changing her feet, but that process was much more painful. The bones between her heel and toes needed to extend more than ten times their current length, the effort and the pain was enormous, the toes bending, the nails elongating into claws. Her legs warped, but she always stopped the process when it neared her knees. Her face and head were out of bounds for the practice. She was too scared she would lose control. Her body screamed for the change, but she didn't dare. The frustration sometimes seemed unbearable, but the guilt from the massacre was still heavy on her conscience.

In addition to the change, they practiced languages. Julio taught her Spanish and his local native language. The last was used by the Resistance as their formal communication language. It passed the time while traveling and she found it a nice challenge. It kept her occupied, her mind distracted from the other worries.

Most afternoons, when they woke up and waited for the camouflage of night, Julio told her about the world outside of the lab. The world she'd missed for more than five years. There was so much to catch up on. Five years was a long time anyway, but the past years felt exponentially long because so much happened in the outside world she was isolated from. She enjoyed the long talks and quizzed Julio about points she didn't understand. Slowly she came to understand and sympathise with the Resistance.

Chapter Twenty

We were travelling again, this time to the southeast. We'd probably crossed the border between Mexico and Guatemala about two weeks ago. As usual, Julio determined the direction and the destination.

'My brother lives a few miles to the east,' he said, after we walked for most of the night. It was almost morning; the sky was no longer black but that strange dark blue that heralds the rising of the sun.

'We'll stay in this area today and in the evening and see if we can make contact. He may be able to help us, and at least let us know what the situation is in this region.'

I had my doubts about the idea. We should keep as low a profile as possible. Not make contact at all. For our safety and for that of his brothers' family. But Julio was getting excited about seeing one of his siblings again. He was desperate for news of his kin. I knew he was scared his wife and children had been taken prisoner or maybe even worse.

'It'll be good to see my brother and his family. He has two children, a daughter—a teenager now, and a son, who is a few years younger. He lives on an isolated farm near here. Maybe he will be able to help us with some kind of vehicle or something.' He babbled on happily. Julio had walked part of the day. The past two hours he was back in the sling on my back.

'Now we must find a place to spend the day,' he said and motioned to the right. I walked on another mile, and we came to a cluster of trees and bushes that offered some protection from the sun and was well camouflaged from any passers-bye. We settled into the centre of the bushes, careful to make sure no tracks led to our hiding place.

We wouldn't make a fire today. Just huddle in the clothes we wore and hope the bushes and trees sheltered us. The day would warm up, so that was no problem. It was more the moment; it was cold now we'd stopped moving. During the night, we'd tried to gather some roots and other edible plants. The darkness complicated things, but we at least had some cacti fruits and roots to gnaw on.

After we settled, I broached the subject of his family and our intended visit later that day. 'I don't think it is a good idea to visit your brother,' I indicated.

Julio looked up from the knots in the sling he was repairing. I refrained from looking directly at him. I didn't want to disappoint him, but this ate away at me. My instincts were all over the place.

'You have been thinking about this a long time,' he stated. In some strange way he instantly knew how I had been mulling over my remark all day. 'That's why you were so quiet.'

'Why do you think this?' he finally asked.

I raised my head and looked at him. The light was dim because of the leaves of the bushes. It danced over his features, enhanced the lines in his face.

'They know he's your family. They probably guessed by now that we're moving south, so they'll expect us to come here and may even be waiting for us.'

'You overestimate their tenacity,' he remarked. 'They will not follow us for so long, nor will they look this far.'

He seemed very certain. But I was also sure. Sometimes when we walked, I picked up scents. Scents I linked with the soldiers at the lab. They knew where we were headed. More or less. And Julio's kin were slap-bang in the middle of the route.

'Please Julio,' I tried again. 'We shouldn't go there. We'll endanger them and us needlessly.'

But he would not take "no" for an answer. He could be very stubborn, as I found out several times in our long time together. He would not be swayed.

'Where exactly is the farm?' I asked.

He motioned to his right. 'You see that hillside, there between the large trees?' I nodded. 'Well after that hill is a lower one. On the far slope of the second hill lies the farm,' he explained. 'So maybe an hour's walk.' That surprised me. It was also much too close for comfort. I would have preferred to camp further away from any inhabited area, even if there were sympathetic people there.

I decided to stop and not push the subject. We were relatively safe in the enclosed area we were in now. No one could see us without actually entering the bushes themselves. That would cause a lot of noise, so we would be alarmed.

I wasn't afraid of animals; they shied away from my scent. The practice we had done in the past weeks made me able to start and stop the change when I wanted. Oddly enough the first thing that happened when I started the transformation of one of my hands or even a foot, was that the nails grew into claws. No matter how I tried to make something else the first step, I always ended up having claws before anything else. It was confusing. I could determine which major part of my body was to transform, but the change in that part still followed its own template. I wondered why but could not find any other answer than that my body was protecting itself when transforming. The change itself took time, and it would not do to be helpless while it happened.

I was getting used to the idea that it was a part of me, but I was still no closer to understanding what it was, or what that made me. Julio was equally fascinated by what I could do. He was an educated man and knew—as I did— that this defied all rules of nature. Or science for that matter. As did the longevity and my healing powers. But nothing was as dramatic as seeing parts of a human body physically change before your very eyes.

I noticed I'd practiced a lot the past few days. While we were walking, and before I slept. It was easier now. I had the pain under control and didn't wince anymore when the bones popped and stretched. That was probably one of the most painful parts, up till now anyway.

My senses become even more astute. I had twenty-twenty eyesight—even at night. My sense of smell was incredible, and I could hear a mouse move in the under-growth. The heightened senses came in handy in our trav-els. I recognised danger before it was anywhere near and saved us from many a confrontation. It also gave me an edge when I hunted. Night vision made traveling in the dark possible. All in all, it seemed the changes in my life were not all bad.

We had been moving now for almost four weeks.

I practiced a while and then decided to get some sleep.

Julio was already in a deep slumber. Thankfully neither of us snored. We didn't want to give away our position. Not even by something as rudimentary as snoring. I lay down on the dry leaves under the bushes and closed my eyes. My senses remained on high alert even though I slid into a fitful sleep.

Once again, I found myself back in the lab.

There was chaos.

Chapter Twenty-One

Numerous voices were shouting at the same time, and it was difficult to make out the individual words. A shot was fired, and then two more.

I opened my eyes, and a fourth shot battered my ears. This was no longer in my dreams. I heard the rhythmic sound of hooves on the hard granite valley floor. I woke Julio and indicated that he stayed quiet.

A horse came past our hiding place about a hundred metres to the right. It came from the general direction of where Julio indicated the farm was. The rider was hunched over the saddle. It was a man, or rather a boy, sliding further and further down in the saddle.

I smelled the blood. He was wounded. I connected this to the shots I'd heard.

In the distance I heard more horses. They were mulling around. I estimated three.

The horse stopped, and the boy fell from the saddle.

'Alejandro!' Julio exclaimed. We left the safety of the bushes and went to the boy. I already sensed death on him.

'Julio,' I said, 'Get the horse, there are more people coming.' He wanted to refuse, go to the boy. 'Please Julio, don't argue. The horse won't come to me. Get it and take it over the ridge, hide there. The boy is dead, there's nothing we can do for him anymore.' I reached the body and sure enough; he was lifeless. I estimated him to be about eleven years old. He was shot in the back, between the shoulder blades.

Julio just stood there. Too shocked to move.

'Julio! Now. Move!' The urgency in my voice snapped him back to the here-and-now. He grabbed the horse's reins and coaxed it away.

He mounted, turned the animal and directed it towards the ridge. And none too soon. The pursuers had determined their direction and were coming our way. I ran back to our shelter, careful to go over the hard ground so as not to leave any tracks.

Just as I was flat on my stomach, three riders came into the clearing at a slow walk, scanning the track for any signs. There were two Latino and one Caucasian—soldiers, all brandishing rifles. The Caucasian was obviously in charge and extremely impatient. The Latino at the point saw the body and called out to the others.

'Capitan, there,' he pointed to the boy then looked around. 'The horse is gone; the boy must have fallen off.'

The soldiers approached the boy's crumpled form. Following an order from the Capitan, one soldier dismounted and turned the boy over to inspect the body.

'He is dead Capitan,' he stated the obvious. 'Should we look for the horse?' I desperately wanted them to leave as soon as possible, not extend their search any further. It would be disastrous if they found Julio with the horse. I started the change—only my hands—but it was enough.

The result was as I intended. The scent of an unknown predator invaded the already skittish horses' noses, and they became noticeably terrified. The officer had difficulty controlling his steed, the urge to flee from this unidentified but very present danger was so strong in the animal. The dismounted soldier's horse shied away from him, and it was all he could do to grab the reins and hang on. He calmed the horse a bit, but it was temporary at most.

'What's gotten into them?' the Capitan was perplexed.

'There are wolves here in these hills,' the second Latino soldier explained. 'Maybe they are near.'

The answer seemed to be sufficient for the Capitan, who basically only wanted to leave the scene so his horse would calm down.

'Do we leave him for the wolves?' the soldier asked the Capitan.

After a moment of thought he answered, 'we take him back with us. The Major will want proof he is dead. He can burn with the rest of them. Give him to me.'

Handing the reins to his horse to his companion, the soldier picked up the boy. He was unceremoniously flung over the Capitan's horse in front of the saddle. As the body was so small the horse barely noticed. The officer chose not to wait for his subordinates to mount, turned his steed and galloped back the way they had come. The private cursed in Spanish, mumbling something about the waste of killing the young girl at the house so quickly and the missed fun. He remounted his horse, joined his companion and followed the Capitan. I waited for a few more minutes and listened intently to the sound of the three horses gallop off into the distance.

The clearing was quiet again. I let out the pent-up energy and changed my hands back to their normal form. I hardly noticed the popping of the joints and the receding claws.

I grabbed the few possessions we had and crept out from under the bushes. I kept to the side of the ridge and moved in the direction Julio had taken. After ten minutes I found him. The horse shied when I came into view, but Julio kept it under control. He rode well, as was the case with lots of people here. The energy crisis had reintroduced the horse as a means of transport, so most people learned how to ride. Judging by his proficiency I guessed that he had been able to ride long before the gasoline ran out.

'Alejandro?' Julio asked in a whisper.

I shook my head.

'They took him back,' I said. This caused even more anguish on his already broken features.

'The others!' he exclaimed. 'We have to help them.' He was about to turn the horse and head to the farm. I took hold of the reins—much to the horse's discomfort—and stopped him.

'No,' I said quietly. 'We can't.' I looked up at him. 'There is nothing we can do.' He almost protested, but the truth was evident. His eyes clouded over, and he started to cry.

'The whole family?' It was more a statement than a question. I nodded. The conversation between the two Latino soldiers convinced me there would be no survivors. Julio dismounted, walked two steps from the horse and fell to his knees—weeping.

'You were right,' he finally said between sobs. 'We should never have come this way. It is my fault that they are dead. They died because of me.' I tied the horse's reins to a stout bush and moved over to Julio. I took him in my arms. He felt so fragile.

'No Julio,' I whispered. 'They are after me, so if there is any fault, it is mine, and mine alone. for what I did at the lab.' He didn't answer, just softly cried.

After a few minutes, he coughed and extracted himself from my embrace. He stood up on wobbly legs and walked back to the horse. He started to pack the few possessions on to the back of the saddle.

'We must leave.' He was back in control. 'They might come back this way looking for the horse.'

I got up and moved over to him. He mounted the horse and made room for me. I declined.

'No, you ride, I will run,' I said. 'The horse will not let me ride, and anyway we can make better time this way.'

Chapter Twenty-Two

We headed off to the east, circumventing the farm. It was near the end of the afternoon, about four or five o'clock. Just this once we would travel in daylight.

After two hours we changed direction and moved to the south again.

Julio was silent. He hadn't said a word since we left the terrible scene. We travelled most of the evening and night in this manner.

We stopped to let the horse rest and drink at a stream, and by early morning I estimated we had put about thirty miles between us and the farm.

A little further on we found a large cave at the bottom of a steep hillside and decided to stay there. There was some scattered grass and water nearby. I unsaddled and hobbled the horse to let it graze. It was used to me by now and had decided that I was no immediate threat, though it was still apprehensive. At least now I could approach it easier.

Julio found some jerky in the saddlebag and offered it to

me. I accepted the stringy food and sat opposite him in the mouth of the cave.

'Tell me about them,' I suggested. It would do him good to talk about his family. He needed to grieve.

Julio told me about his youth growing up in relative peace. That lasted until the America's ran out of energy and annexed the Latin countries. He talked for more than an hour.

'I grew up near the town of Rama in Columbia, near Mitu, to the southeast of Bogota,' he explained. 'We were a close-knit family, with all our aunts and uncles, cousins and the grandparents. The family was reasonably well off, we owned a big estate, with wineries and many cattle. We also bred horses; for racing at the local fests as well as to work on the farm.'

That explained his prowess at riding.

'The farm was more or less self-sufficient like the other properties in that region. We had large wind and sun energy collection facilities, good water and good soil as long as we took care of the waterways. The people were prosperous.'

'I was the eldest of three boys, destined to take over from my father so I was sent to university in Managua. I studied economics and geology. Things that would come in handy when I took over the business. It never got that far. The America's attacked our government, with soldiers and with disease. LKX disseminated the population. The Americans purposely infected the paysans. The rich were offered the antidote if they joined the American cause. My father deceived them. He pretended to support the Americanos, gained their trust, got the antidote and distributed it among the people.' He was quiet for a few minutes—the memories were still vivid for him.

'Naturally we all supported my father and the partisans,'

he continued. 'The Americanos found out—there was a mole in the partisans—and my father was taken prisoner along with my mother and an uncle. In a mock trial in Rama, they were convicted of treason and sentenced to death. They shot them in the town square. It was like an old spaghetti western.'

He paused to take a deep breath. 'The rest of us escaped and witnessed their deaths on a stream. It was broadcasted throughout the whole of the Latin countries, as a deterrent. For us it had the opposite effect, we continued to fight the Americanos and joined the Revolutionaries. My brother Inno and I still fight them. Alejandras was tired of the violence and left the revolution with his family to go back to farming. He even moved to Guatemala in an attempt to distance himself from his earlier life. He thought the wrath of the Americanos would be quenched by now. But obviously it wasn't.'

Once again, the silence descended upon us.

'My family lives in constant danger. We move around a lot, never stay in one place long enough to be found. I hope we can get word to them, so that we can find them once we are back in Columbia.'

'How did they capture you?' I asked him.

'There were five of us, we planned to rob the depot in El Estor, here in Guatemala, looking for medicines. But once again, we were betrayed. They were waiting. Three of our group were killed in the shooting. They left Miranda and me alive though she was severely wounded, probably fatally. They knew who I was and sent me to the General. Miranda, I don't know what happened to her, but I can imagine.' He paused. 'She was a beautiful woman. They will have had their way with her before they killed her.' There was nothing more to say. We made ourselves as comfortable as possible and bedded down on the long dry grass we'd collected.

We slept.

I woke once to hear Julio crying softly.

In the twilight we retrieved the horse, saddled her again and headed off—Julio rode, I walked and sometimes ran alongside.

The scenery changed during the night as we entered the rainforest. We travelled through valleys that were more and more densely wooded. It became increasingly difficult to move in the dark. Fallen branches and trees barred our way and had to be cleared or circumvented.

Around midnight it was so dark that it would have been too dangerous to continue. We stopped and set up our meagre camp. The horse was once again hobbled, and we lay down to rest. There was no moon, only the stars lit up the night sky. My eyes took in their light, and it was easy for me to see what was around. I heard a lot of animals moving in the dark as well. The woods were home to a variety of mammals and other creatures. Maybe we would get lucky and catch something. I left the campsite and set up some primitive traps along a wildlife trail I recognised by scent. Small animals went this way.

I returned to the traps in the first light of the morning. One was empty, the other contained a small rabbit. I dispatched the animal and brought it back to our camp. We didn't dare to cook it, in case it would alert anyone to our whereabouts with the smoke from a fire, so we both ate some of the flesh raw and saved the rest for later. Julio had problems forcing the raw meat down. I—on the other hand —had no such scruples.

I felt at home in the forest. Some long forgotten or unknown instincts started to kick in.

We decided that while we were in the forests, we would travel early morning until about noon and then again at the end of the day until it got too dark.

Journeying this way for three days, we finally came to a small lake. We were all tired. The horse flatly refused to take another step, so we decided to stay here for a while. There were no scents of other humans, neither recent nor old. It was devoid of human life.

With our last breath, we set up camp in the hollow of a very big tree at the edge of the forest. The horse didn't need to be hobbled anymore; she chose to stay with us. She was used to my scent by now, and even stayed in the area when I practiced the change. She kept an eye on me, but that was to be expected. Grateful for the rest she stuck her nose in the grass and proceeded to graze.

Chapter Twenty-Three

It was another clear day, the fourth of our stay in the clearing. We'd recovered our strength and planned to start traveling again the next day. I hunted and caught some small Agouti and a Capybara. Some of the meat Julio dried in the sun for the days to come. Fishing had also been good and as an extra we gathered fruits and nuts in the forest. We were well fed, rested and felt good.

I swam naked in the small lake created by the stream and a natural dam a little further on from our camp. It relaxed me. The water was cool and refreshing. I got into the habit of swimming at least twice a day. After the long journey—when water was at a premium—it felt great to be clean again.

Julio was in the lean-to, busy weaving some reeds into baskets he wanted to attach to the saddle. That way we could take more provisions with us which would make us less dependent on foraging and prevented unnecessary delay. We needed the rest, but it cost us four days. One way or the other we had to get back on the road and make up for some of the lost time.

The clearing was tranquil. The smell of the brightly coloured flowers, trees and the tall grass was overwhelming and there was a small breeze from the direction of the tiny waterfall. The birds were plentiful and noisy. I heard the horse grazing. She'd wandered further from the lean-to. The relative quiet and safety lulled all of us all into carelessness.

An unknown scream and the terrified nicker of the horse abruptly broke the peace. She tried to run towards the lean-to and to us, but a large puma jumped out of the tree line and in one mighty leap was on her back with its teeth locked deep into her neck. The horse bucked and tried to free itself, but the cat was tenacious.

I swam to the edge of the lake as fast as I could, calling all the time. Julio left the lean-to and frantically tried to scare the cat away. The horse was on the ground. Its legs flailed with the puma at its throat. Julio grabbed some stones and desperately started to throw them at the carnivore. One hit the ochre coat and the cat growled menacingly. It let go of the horse and hissed at Julio. Without any thought for his own safety, Julio interpreted this as a good sign and renewed his attempts to chase it away with more stones aimed at its head and body. The puma was enraged and turned its full attention to Julio. It advanced on him menacingly. Finally, Julio understood that he was dangerously in over his head and slowly walked backwards, all the while he kept his terrified eyes on the advancing danger.

In the meantime, I'd left the water and ran towards the rapidly escalating drama.

The Puma growled.

I shouted, or at least that was what I wanted to do.

The sound came out of my throat as a deep and powerful roar.

Chapter Twenty-Four

In mid-stride she fell to all fours and continued to advance on the puma. She changed. Fully this time, no holds barred.

The puma was astounded. It stopped its advance and turned towards this gigantic animal that ran unsteadily, but full tilt, at it. It hesitated, unsure of what it was seeing and that gave the newcomer the edge. The enormous feline ran full force into the puma and drew blood with the claws on her massive front paws. More agile, the smaller animal managed to minimise the damage, turned sharply to the side and out of reach. In mid-turn it clawed at the sudden and unexpected threat and opened a row of slashes on its adversary's left shoulder. The big cat reacted unsurely, the blood bright red on her tawny coat. Her body felt alien and wouldn't function as she wanted it to. This offered the puma the chance to flee the scene, and that was exactly what it did.

The cat fight was over before it really begun. The gigantic feline took a few unsteady leaps after its smaller cousin, but soon stopped when the attacker disappeared into the dense forest.

The clearing was silent. Nothing moved. She turned and walked back to the bloody scene. The horse was still alive, but barely. The damage the puma had done was irreversible. The horse's throat was almost ripped out. Blood poured from the damaged neck and seeped into the ground below. Tonal sat down to change back into human form when Julio stopped her.

'No,' he said softly. 'Please, stay as you are. Don't change back. Be the cat for a while. Get used to your new body and what it can do.'

She looked at him and seemed to ponder his words.

'And please help the horse. It's suffering.' She understood what he wanted. The poor animal was in a great amount of pain. Her feeble attempts to move her legs and head were pathetic. The cat strode over to the downed horse. It took the horse's neck into its great jaws and with one quick jerk, broke the vertebra. The horse died instantly. With surprising softness, the cat laid the horse's head back down on the grass.

The light from the clearing and afternoon sun shone on her tawny coat. The gashes from the puma were already beginning to close. The edges of the wounds moving together and knitting as though they had never been rendered, the blood was the only reminder of the fight.

Julio looked at the gigantic cat in wonder. At the lab, he'd closed his eyes for most of the time she was in this form and wasn't able to appreciate what she'd become. She was more than one and a half metres high at the shoulder and had to be almost four metres from the nose to the tip of her tail. That made her larger than any lion or tiger he'd ever seen or heard of. Her coat was a tawny brown-ochre, with a hint of shadow stripes over her back. Her belly and under her muzzle were almost white. The head was enormous. The fangs, still red with the horse's blood, showed slightly under her closed mouth. But her eyes were the same deep ochre as when she was in human form. Julio swept his eyes over the enormous body, the paws—almost ten inches in width—the heavily muscled body and softly swishing tail.

'You are beyond words,' he said out loud. She merely observed him, which made him slightly uneasy, but he reminded himself that it was her—Tonal. That she was his friend, his saviour.

'Stay like this for a while, run a bit, use your legs and get used to the feeling. Learn how to be you.'

He saw her hesitate.

'Don't worry,' he added. 'You won't hurt me.'

To put value to his words; he approached her. Trembling slightly, he reached out to touch her. She followed his hand with her gaze and when she didn't move, he placed it squarely on her enormous shoulder. The feeling was exciting and terrifying at the same time. Her pelt was soft and warm, pleasant to the touch. Beneath the fur he felt the muscles and the enormous power they represented.

He didn't know whether to stroke her or not. She wasn't exactly a house cat. He compromised and just left his hand where it was. She seemed to appreciate the gesture, and relaxed. A little later she lay down on the grass. He sat down next to her. Enjoying the silence for a few minutes.

'You must practice more, now that you see that you still have full control over yourself, it is safe to experiment with what you can do. You don't have to be frightened anymore.' He knew this had been her biggest fear; that she would turn on him if she changed fully. That she would not be able to control the feline and nature and instinct would take over. That she would ultimately kill him.

She felt fantastic.

The power, the strength she felt was beyond anything she'd ever experienced. She didn't want to change back. This felt too good. She stood up and gingerly moved forward. Julio sat back and watched her discover her new body. She became more confident with each step. Soon she was turning in mid-air and changing direction.

The cat sprinted out into the clearing, stumbled over her paws and rolled over in the grass. If she could have laughed out loud, she wouldn't have stopped. It felt so good. She leapt up and bounded away again—like a small kitten, playing and finding unimaginable pleasure in everything around her. She jumped, ran and leapt at twigs and insects. Sharpening her gigantic claws on a tree near the edge of the forest, she left furrows five inches deep in its bark. Birds and other animals screamed a warning to each other, unsure what to make of this strange predator, and of its even stranger actions. The pure joy was contagious and soon Julio found himself laughing. She stopped at the sound, looked at him, turned and bounded back to where he was, barely stopping in time. Julio jumped to the side as she came to a shuddering stop exactly where he had just been. She rolled over on the grass and sat there. He approached her and joined her on the soft ground. He took her giant head in his hands and looked her in the eyes.

'Enjoy Tonal, this is also part of the miracle.' She licked his face with her rough tongue, lowered her head on to her paws and sighed. Julio shifted sideways and sat back against her flank, together they watched the clearing settle down again. They stayed that way for more than an hour, both reluctant to break the magic of the moment. Finally, she stood up and moved into the forest. Julio watched her move, a majestic feline in the afternoon sun.

She stayed away for more than an hour. When she returned, she walked up to Julio and greeted him. She was hungry. The change cost an enormous amount of energy. Even the partial changes she had done in the past weeks all but drained her energy. The elation of the cat fuelled her for a while, but now the hunger took over her urges.

Julio had cut some strips off the horse haunches while she was away. He had to be practical, and it was a shame to waste the meat. He'd placed the strips on the hot coals of the small underground oven he'd built.

He indicated the carcass of the horse. 'Go eat,' he said. 'You need it.' She strode over to the animal, lay down near its haunches and proceeded to gorge herself. After she finished, she once again disappeared into the forest.

Tonal stayed away all night. Julio was anxious until he noticed the birds were protesting again. Sure enough, there she was at the edge of the clearing walking into the early morning light. She padded over to the lake, waded into the water and swam for a while, cleaning the dried blood and dust from her fur.

When she emerged from the water, she'd regained her human form.

Tonal walked over to the lean to, dressed and sat down next to Julio. For a while they stayed silent, basking the moment and each other's company. The night in his own had made Julio aware of how much he valued her company. It emphasised how alone and fragile he was in the enormous forest, and how he missed her companionship. He was glad to see her again. In whichever form she chose.

'I am glad you are back, Tonal,' he voiced his feelings. 'How was it?'

'It was unbelievable, Julio.' She lay back on the damp grass, gazing at the treetops bordering the edge of the clearing. 'My senses are even better then. I can see, feel, smell everything. I became part of the jungle.' Her enthusiasm was touching. He had never seen her so happy.

'I stumbled a lot at first, I was so big, and heavy too.' She laughed. 'I fell through a rotten branch. It couldn't hold my weight. I can't begin to explain how it felt. I'm reeling.'

'You look tired,' Julio answered. 'Rest now, and we will discuss our options when you wake.'

Chapter Twenty-Five

The situation had changed drastically. The loss of the horse was a major setback and meant the plans had to be revised. Julio glanced back at Tonal and saw she was already asleep. He decided to follow her example. He hadn't slept much during the night; too anxious about how she was doing and whether she would come back. The thought had crossed his mind that she may be so exulted by her new form that she would choose to stay in the forest—would discard her human form for the feline world. But here she was again. So now the trip would continue.

That evening they discussed the possible scenarios and decided to leave the clearing the next morning. They would continue on their way to Julio's family and the partisans they were staying with. Their search would start in the general area where Julio thought his family would probably be. The trip would take them further south through Guatemala, Honduras, and Costa Rica.

All the southern provinces were under American rule.

But the further they got from the States, the bigger the

influence of the partisans became, and subsequently the smaller the American's. The American military didn't have the money or resources to patrol all their new territories and were losing their grip. The military previously stationed in the middle Latin countries had been sent to assist the invasion of the southern American countries like Brazil, Venezuela and Chile. The Americans were hopelessly spread out, their supply lines thin and fragile. On top of that, the resistance they encountered in the Latin countries and provinces was much greater than expected and quickly exhausted the limited facilities they had. Naively, they had counted on a quick and unexpected attack with easy subjugation.

The remainder of Julio and Tonal's trip would probably be less dangerous than it had been so far. There were more sympathetic people, less military, which meant they would not have to hide all the time, but it was by no means safe. The Americas still had money and continued to corrupt people. The nobles were America-voiced, dreading the possibility that the revolutionaries might gain control, and they had spies in all layers of the communities. Julio expected they were still looking for him—for them both probably. It was difficult to determine which of them was the most wanted. The sparse news they heard was not encouraging. The military were out in full force, luckily, they were still concentrating on the area from the spa down to where they massacred Julio' family.

Slowly they made their way further south, through Costa Rica, Panama and finally into Columbia. Occasionally they encountered people Julio knew. Every time he introduced her as a sympaitica who'd helped him escape from the Americano's. Never did they embellish on the story. The reaction was always the same. They stayed wary of her but in reverence to this small man who played such a large part in the resistance, they tolerated her presence. Though she was inevitably excluded from important discussions.

In the beginning Tonal allowed this to happen and waited outside wherever Julio went to have his private discussions. After one unfortunate incident where one of the people turned out to be a mole and tried to recapture Julio for the military, Julio insisted she attend every meeting. She sat in the corner, pretended ignorance of the language and absorbed the proceedings.

The resistance generally deferred to Julio on important issues, but sometimes they encountered eager, often young, people who were uncomfortable with the slow pace of the resistance and the meagre successes. Usually, knowledge and experience prevailed.

Inevitably news of their journey reached both sides. The military streamlined their search efforts further south, and the resistance gave Julio and Tonal aid where necessary.

Finally, in one of the meetings with trusted resistance people, Julio learned the vicinity of the resistance compound where his family was. As a precaution, the compound moved constantly, that, the secrecy, and the impenetrable jungle formed the initial security of the location.

Word travelled fast, and the resistance journeyed out to meet them.

In a clearing almost twenty miles from the compound there was a tearful reunion.

Chapter Twenty-Six

She felt their presence. They were doing their best to be invisible, but the scents and the noise were like a detailed picture in her mind. There were five of them. All men, well, one was a boy. They were spread out around the clearing she and Julio approached.

'Julio,' she whispered. 'There are men here. We should be watchful.'

Instantly he stopped at the sound of her voice and stayed on the fringe of the clearing. Listening intently, they waited for what would happen. Julio took a few steps forward and exposed himself in the clearing while she stayed in the shadows of the trees. Nothing happened for about ten minutes, then a heavily built man stepped out of the trees twenty metres to the right of Julio. Tonal circled around behind the men ringing the clearing and was ready to intervene if necessary. She felt the tension in the men, especially in the boy. He could hardly be restrained. His scent was similar to that of Julio, and she deduced that they were probably related.

Chapter Twenty-Seven

The big man walked over to Julio, who stood beaming.

'Jesus,' he called out to his old friend. 'It is so good to see you.' The men embraced. This was the sign for the others to emerge from the jungle. The boy ran to his father, throwing his arms around the man he'd thought he would never see again. Tears filled Julio's eyes as he hugged his son.

'You have a companion?' Jesus asked looking back behind where Julio stood. 'A woman if I am correctly informed.'

Julio nodded. 'Tonal, please come out, these are friends.'

She emerged behind the men and startled them. They had been unaware of her circumventing manoeuvre and were expecting her to emerge from the jungle behind Julio. Her presence behind them made them nervous and the guns were levelled at her.

'It is okay,' Julio informed Jesus. 'She is my saviour.' With a chuckle he added 'and as you can see; she protects me well.' His humour was lost on the others who felt threatened by her.

Slowly she moved around the group until she stood behind Julio again.

Julio's son was staring at her; fascinated by this beautiful woman who had brought his father back to him.

'This is Tonal,' Julio introduced her. 'This young man is my son, Alex.' He fondly indicated his son, then continued the introductions as he turned to the large man to his left. 'This is Jesus, the leader of our motley group.'

The remainder of the group moved closer and one by one they greeted Julio. He named them as they shook his hand or hugged him close. She remained distant, not wanting to intrude on the familiar terrain for the others. She was an outsider and painfully aware of this in the constraints of the small clearing.

Jesus approached her. 'Tonal, a strange name, full of mythical connotations, but if you are a friend of Julio's I welcome you.'

He wasn't entirely convincing.

She shook his offered hand and murmured, 'likewise.'

Appreciating the humour Jesus smiled. 'Come, let's go home. It's still a long walk.' He turned back and led the group out of the clearing onto a trail in the dense jungle. Julio was totally taken up by the rambling of his son Alex. Constant chatter—interspersed with secretive glances at the woman who followed them—characterised the walk for the boy.

After a three-hour trek through the hot and humid jungle, they arrived at a small ravine. This proved to be the location of the compound. The gorge was fifteen metres wide at its narrowest and widened out to several hundred metres. The overhang of one of the cliff walls provided a natural defence against any enemies and effectively hid the compound from sight. Most of the buildings and tents were situated in the shadow of the rock and the trees that littered the ravine floor. Another major benefit of the overhang was that the direct sun was screened. She smelled water in the form of a stream nearby and some animals as well as the people.

Tonal saw a small collection of vehicles and carts under camouflaged tarps; most old and damaged, bullet holes testament to the battles they had endured. In a paddock to the left there were a few nervous ponies. One or two dogs shied away from their group, unobserved by all except Jesus. She met his eyes. This was a clever man. He refrained from any comment. There would be time enough later.

Several people came out of the tents and buildings to greet Julio, and naturally to gape at her. Julio stood taller than she had ever seen him—almost swaggering. He was enjoying his homecoming no end.

The door of one of the wooden buildings was flung open with a loud bang and a large woman of about thirty-five with jet-black hair ran out of the opening screaming Julio's name. He quickened his step and caught the woman in his arms.

'It's true, you're back,' she stammered between sobs. 'I thought you were dead.'

'Maria, how could I have died, I promised you I would come back to you, and I always keep my promises.' Julio tenderly stroked her hair and held her close. She pulled back from angry and slapped his chest.

'I told you not to go, let the others do this, you have done enough... I nearly lost you.' Folding back into his arms, her anger momentarily spent, she renewed her sobs. A few minutes later, she disentangled herself and desperately tried to regain her composure. She looked at the others and spotted Tonal. 'Who is this?'

'This, my dear Maria, is the woman responsible for bringing me back to you; Tonal.'

Maria walked the short distance to Tonal and immediately engulfed her in a massive bear hug. 'Thank you, you have no idea how much this stupid old man means to me.'

Laughing Tonal answered, 'oh, I think I got that message.'

Hooking her arm in Tonal's, Maria led her into the building. 'He is such a stubborn man, always insisting that he should accompany the others on the dangerous missions, leaving me here to sit and wait.' Her familiarity was contagious and Tonal started to feel less the outsider and more a welcomed guest.

'You must be hungry, sit yourself down here at the table and I will get you BOTH something to eat.' She directed her comment as much at Tonal as at her husband who followed the two women into the building.

Julio clearly enjoyed the banter and loving abuse.

Chapter Twenty-Eight

The room was small but cosy. The wooden walls decorated with colourful Mayan blankets. Six sturdy chairs bordered the wooden table in the centre of the room, a child's high-chair stood up against the wall. To the right was a makeshift stove and sink. This was the hub of the house. Tonal smelled freshly baked bread, a meat stew, fruit and coffee. Her stomach rumbled; the last meal they had eaten was just a faint memory.

Alex managed to seat himself directly opposite Tonal. When she noticed and smiled at him, he went bright red and turned his face away.

'I will leave you alone with your family, but tomorrow we need to talk Julio, Tonal.' Jesus walked to Maria, gave her a peck on the cheek and left the building.

A small girl of about two years old shyly moved into the room and hid behind her mother's legs, thumb in her mouth and clutching the ever-present worn teddy bear. Julio's eyes watered as he walked to her and bent down, his arms open.

'Dulce… My beautiful Dulce.' The child kept one eye on the stranger sitting at their table, let go of her mother's leg and moved into Julio's arms. He picked her up, sat down on a chair and held her close, blinking back the tears. She hung on to her father, but the curiosity of the toddler got the better of her and she glanced at the stranger.

'This is my friend Tonal. She is a new member of this family.' She glanced up at her father's face and continued to fiercely suck her thumb, then once again turned her attention to the stranger.

The meal was brought to the table, the smells so intoxicating and warm. They feasted on the home baked bread, cheese and venison from the jungle. Fruit, vegetables and fresh clear water rounded off the feast.

The love and warmth of the family soon calmed Tonal's nerves and before the end of the meal, the small girl Dulce seated herself on her lap and babbled away in her toddler language. Totally incomprehensible, but very amusing. The little girl had decided that Tonal was her new best friend and before too long, she was curled up on Tonal's lap, fast asleep with her thumb in her mouth. Maria carefully picked up the tiny form and put her to bed.

Alex stayed, caught somewhere between child- and adulthood he felt he should remain. On her return Maria addressed Tonal. 'You must be tired, both of you. A good night's sleep and then tomorrow you can tell us all about your adventures.'

'Mom…' Alex—with the curiosity and absence of patience of so many of his peers—wanted to hear everything now.

'Tomorrow.' End of discussion, his mother was infinitely more convincing.

'I will show you your room.' Tonal followed Maria to a

door off the hallway. It opened to a tiny room. A bed with clean sheets and a pillow was up against the wall, next to the window. The candle on the small table next to the bed glowed in the twilight. It had been so long since she'd slept in a real bed, the idea alone was enough to put a smile to her lips.

'Thank you.'

'You have no idea how welcome you are.' With a smile, Maria left her alone in the room, not quite closing the door. Tonal welcomed the sounds of the family. Outside the light was beginning to wane and the compound was coming to rest. The familiar sounds of the jungle crept in and filled her sensitive ears.

Next morning, she woke early and listened to the noise of the compound as they woke up. She'd slept well, the bed comfortable and the compound secure and safe. Maria was the first up and already busy in the kitchen preparing breakfast. Tonal dressed and walked to the warm room.

'Did you sleep well?' Maria inquired, not at all surprised by her soft approach.

'Yes, thank you, very well, can I help you with anything.'

'No, no, you sit and rest, I have it all under control.' She busied herself with several pots and pans on the wood burning stove, Tonal believed her, she was so accomplished and had the routine down to an art.

A soft tug on her trouser leg made her turn her head to Dulce who, once again accompanied by her teddy bear and with her thumb in her mouth, wanted to be picked up. Complying with the little girls wishes, she picked her up, upon which Dulce leaned into her chest and cuddled up and promptly fell asleep again.

'You have a new best-friend, Tonal.' Julio stood in the doorway. He looked more rested and at peace than she had ever seen him. 'Usually, Dulce is quite restrained with strangers. But with you she knows. She is already a good judge of character.'

Halfway through the breakfast Dulce woke up and Julio placed her in her own highchair, freeing Tonal to eat. Alex joined the family and was still obviously infatuated by her.

Chapter Twenty-Nine

After the meal they were shooed out of the house by Maria who "needed her space to clean up". They walked through the compound and neared the building that turned out to be the command post. The sentry let them in, and they moved to the table where Jesus was seated. He raised his head and greeted them.

'Please sit.'

He pointed to the empty chairs next to and opposite him. Motioning to the sentry at the door, he called for the others of the council to join them. Slowly they trickled into the room from different sides and took their places at the table. Water, mugs and coffee were placed on the surface and passed around.

Jesus introduced the members of the council to her. There were seven people in total, two women and five men. Angel Rivera, a small wiry man of about thirty-five, and Diego Diaz, more than ten years older and physically his opposite—she'd met the day before. They'd accompanied Jesus and Alex to the clearing. The women: Isabel Mendez and Adriana Gomez, were in their late twenties. Young to be in a council, but with hard eyes and weathered features that made them old beyond their years. The elderly Jose Lopez, his nephew Juan Torres and the shy Miguel Soto completed the group. The men were without exception hard men, all had experienced too much, and it showed.

Then it was time to introduce Tonal to the council

'This woman is the reason I am sitting here. She saved me in the laboratory where they held me prisoner and she brought me home. She is Tonal. I trust her with my life and that of my family,' Jose said.

'Please tell us your story,' Jesus kicked off the meeting.

Tonal experienced some problems understanding all that was said during Julio's answer. In the long journey south, he taught her the language, but here the pace of the conversation was too high for her to be able to grasp everything. Julio noticed and slowed down his story. He pronounced his words clearly and without the accent that some of the council members used. Jesus continued in the same fashion. He rarely missed anything, Tonal thought. This was a special person, someone not to underestimate.

Julio continued the emotional tale of his capture. The betrayal by one of their own lay heavily on the group. Moving on, he talked about the Spa and the torture at the hands of the General. He spoke about the stranger in whose cell he was unceremoniously dumped and who took care of his wounds, the journey south and finally the reunion. The council as one refrained from any comment or interruption and allowed Julio to end his tale before they voiced their questions.

'How did you escape?' Adriana asked. This was the one hole in the tale, the one discrepancy. Julio had described the spa, the military and the laboratory. He left out the actual escape, jumping to the journey. Hoping against hope that they would not expect more detail.

'The military kept wild animals in the same laboratory,' Julio continued. He avoided eye contact with Tonal, who kept her head down, wondering how he would explain. 'During one of the tests they tried to put us in a cage with the lions around us and something went wrong. The animals escaped and killed the scientists and the soldiers, but miraculously left us alone, I think they were spent. Tonal managed to loosen her bonds after the lions left the lab and freed me. She helped me out of the compound, and we escaped to the south.'

Validation of the tale came from an unexpected side. 'There was a rumour on the internet, that scientists and soldiers had been slaughtered by wild beasts in the spa in Chiapas,' Isabel opted. 'About twelve people were killed. There was one survivor according to the sources. But they said nothing about any escaped prisoners.'

'Well, they wouldn't, would they?' Julio was relieved he'd pulled off the lie. 'The Americanos will never admit anyone escaped from their prisons.'

All this time Jesus observed Tonal. She raised her head and looked him in the eye. He was not buying the frankly unbelievable story, however much it was collaborated by Internet. There was more to this tale, and he would find out, one way or the other. He glanced at Julio but refrained from comment. Details would come later, when the council had retired.

The council voiced their sympathy at the deaths of Julio's kin. He lowered his eyes; a tear ran down his cheek and he took his seat again. His tale had been extensively detailed and tired him both emotionally and physically.

Jesus took centre stage. 'Thank you, my friend, for your

difficult narrative. It is clear you endured too much. He turned to Tonal. 'It is also clear we have much to thank you for. Julio is very important to this council and to our struggle, and I thank you that you brought him back to us. I welcome you to our compound and our family.' He paused. 'It is obvious that Julio trusts you totally and values your input and opinion, we will extend this trust and invite you to join our council. First as a spectator, until we find your special talent that will aid our goal.'

'Thank you,' she replied. 'It means a lot to me.'

'But...'

She smiled, 'But I will not stay long.'

'Of course you will' Julio protested, standing up from his chair. 'This is your home now.'

'Please Julio, we will talk about this later,' she replied.

Jesus stopped Julio's protests with a wave of his hand. 'For as long as you wish, you are welcome.'

'Thank you.'

'The council meeting is closed.' Jesus resolutely stopped any other protests and closed the discussions. 'You must both be tired from your ordeal. Take some time to recuperate and we will all talk again later.'

Chapter Thirty

Slowly the group dispersed to their daily tasks.

Tonal stayed in her seat. Jesus would have to be made party to her special talents. It was only right, and besides he was not one to give up probing for a more believable explanation. He was amused that she understood why he sent the rest of the council away. Julio looked at Tonal, then glanced at Jesus and he sat back down in his seat.

'So,' Jesus said. 'Now you tell me what really happened.'

With a sigh Julio answered, 'you won't believe it, my friend.'

'Try me.'

Tonal took up the story with a question to Jesus. 'Do you believe in the supernatural, Jesus? In strange things that are impossible, strange animals?'

'I am open-minded.'

'You may have to be more than that.'

That caused a raised eyebrow.

'In the laboratory they were trying to find out why I have some, shall we call them "special talents".' Jesus raised

127

an eyebrow again but remained silent. 'Some years ago, I found out that I was different than other people. I do not age—at least not noticeably—and can heal very quickly.' Taking a bread knife from the table she made a two cm cut in her lower right arm. Within seconds the two sides of the wound knitted together, after a minute only a slight scar line was visible. There had been virtually no bleeding.

'Now that is a handy talent.' Jesus handled it well.

'It turned out it wasn't the only talent that I have… or the most dramatic.'

She took a long breath and continued. 'Tension had been building up inside of me for quite some time at the laboratory. My strength increased beyond anything I—or anybody for that matter—could imagine. The scientists and soldiers tested my healing capabilities and strength every day. They cut and burned me to see how quickly I healed. Slowly it drove me mad, or so it felt. I started to have strange and violent dreams. In the dark I felt strange forces at work in my muscles. I didn't dare to look.'

'She can see in pitch black,' Julio volunteered.

'They brought Julio one night and every morning they dragged him out of the cell and tortured him. In the evening, he was returned to the cell, and I did my best to take care of his wounds. The constant torture they rained down on Julio compounded my anger, that and the helplessness I felt when they came to drag him away each morning. Slowly the rage built up inside of me and I was literally seeing red.' Putting her hands on the table she looked at Jesus. His face was passive, his eyes the only betrayal of his intense interest.

'One evening, they took both of us. I fought them, but it didn't help. They clamped us on to individual laboratory tables and righted mine so that I could see what happened to Julio. The tension was excruciating and when they started to cut Julio, I snapped.'

'You killed the scientists and the soldiers?' It was more a statement than a question.

'Yes.'

'How?'

A demonstration would say more than a thousand words, so she placed her right hand on the table and started the change. Jesus' mouth dropped open and his eyes spread as wide as they could go. He glanced at Julio, almost to make sure that he was not dreaming. Julio nodded, and Jesus turned his head back to the spectacle.

On the table he saw a fully formed feline paw, gigantic in size and girth, connected to Tonal's human arm. The paw sported enormous claws. To emphasise the power, she unsheathed them and softly dug them in the table, leaving long scratches.

'Madre de Dios.' Jesus found his voice. 'This goes all the way?'

'Yes, the change can be complete.'

Slowly he extended his fingers to the enormous paw, to touch the miracle that was in front of him. It was so difficult to get his mind around, he had to physically feel what his eyes said was real. It defied anything he thought possible. He thought he was hallucinating, but when he touched the fur, it felt warm and soft, the muscles underneath apparent. The claws were cold, hard and unbelievably sharp.

'And you can do this at will?'

'Whenever I want.' Tonal changed the paw back to her human hand.

'What is the end result, what do you turn into?'

'Some kind of feline. Not exactly a lion, but close.'

They remained silent as Jesus digested what he had seen. 'I understand your reluctance to tell the council.'

'I was afraid of panic and superstition,' Julio explained.

'And rightly so. This would go in like a bomb. No, we will keep to the explanation you gave for the time being, until further notice.' Turning back to Tonal he asked 'this tension that you experienced before the incident, does it come and go? Even now?'

'I didn't dare to change fully after the massacre at the lab, so it took quite a long time before I did it again. There was no real build-up of tension, like in the lab. But then again, there was no torture. The tension seems to rise when I get stressed, or exceptionally angry.'

'Or protective,' Julio added. 'I was attacked by a cougar and that triggered her next full change. But I know what you are thinking—she was no threat to me at any time in her cat form. Not even in the lab. I trust her fully.'

'That I already know, and I am pleased Julio, but I had to ask.'

'No problem,' Tonal answered.

'By the look of the paw, you must be enormous when fully changed?'

'She is almost the size of a horse, absolutely magnificent. The largest cat you have ever seen in your life.' Julio's enthusiasm was contagious.

'I'm sure she is. This is a very special miracle. I would like to see the end result someday. But now it is time for you to rest. I also need to process all I have seen and heard. It is hard to believe. But I saw the change and I felt the fur. Only my brain—my rationality—screams at me that it is impossible.'

His mind mulled over what he had seen and how this could benefit the cause as he settled down to a good think.

Tonal and Julio stood, left the room and walked back to their own dwelling.

'Well,' Julio said. happily, 'that went well.'

Tonal stopped and looked at him, and then she burst out laughing. 'I never knew you could be such a convincing liar like that.'

'Jesus didn't believe me.'

'Jesus is an exceptional person.' She wondered what the future would bring now he was party to her special talents. She had no doubt Jesus would find a way to use them for the cause. He was an opportunist, and this was just too good to ignore.

For the time being she would just wait and see. Her intention was to leave the compound soon, not to stay as Julio wanted. She needed to have some time for herself. Get her own mind around what she could do; what she had become. Test the limits and get to terms with all the changes that had happened in the past months.

Despite Julio's unwavering trust in her, she was not so sure she could control the change as well as she wanted. She often had nightmares about the laboratory and woke up in a sweat with fur covering parts of her body. She refrained from mentioning this to Julio, but it gnawed at her confidence and left her anxious about the safety of those around her.

Chapter Thirty-One

The days passed, and I did my best to get used to life in the compound.

It was quite busy. The settlement housed more than one-hundred men, women and children. There was always something happening. The council met every two days and discussed what should be done to further the cause. Some of the council members were only temporary residents of the compound and left after the meetings to go back to their homes in the villages or towns nearby. Others lived there permanently.

I was not party to all the meetings and only occasionally joined the group when specifically invited. I didn't feel at all sure of my status here and didn't want to create any lasting ties.

My nights were filled with nightmares and my days with cautious meanderings. I struggled to act normal, or what I thought would pass for that.

I felt stifled, but there was nowhere else to go.

The horror of what I had done in the laboratory and

on-route to the compound haunted me day and night. Before the lab I'd thought of myself as a peaceful person. Not capable of violence. And now? I couldn't get my head around the fact I 'd murdered not one, but countless people. How many were there? In the lab, there had been twelve. On the move down here another five or six. I felt dazed as I counted the dead. It seemed so surreal. How could this be me?

Okay, it was self-defence. Or so I tried to convince myself.

Julio would not hear of my guilt. He was adamant it had been necessary and that they brought it on themselves.

But every one of them was a human—with a family, a mother.

They robbed me of many years, tortured me physically and mentally.

But I surpassed that. I robbed them of life.

It killed me to think about it.

Chapter Thirty-Two

I tried to help Maria where possible and enjoyed the company of the woman and her children. Both Dulce and Alex vied for my attention. The small girl usually won when she crawled up on my lap and fell asleep. Alex almost interrogated me as he tried to find out as much as possible about me. He was completely infatuated. It was cute, but somewhat embarrassing. His face coloured bright red if I caught him looking at me, which invariably brought a smile to my lips.

Occasionally I accompanied someone into the jungle, looking for fruit or wood for the fires. I thoroughly enjoyed the walks, finally away from the compound and surrounded by the rich plant and animal variety. The smells and noises soothed my senses, and I could finally relax, revelling in all that was around me.

I tried to go out as much as possible, but Jesus was reluctant to let me go out alone; unsure of my jungle skills and sensing my resolve to leave permanently had not abated. He did not want me to go, not until he had answers and maybe until I'd aided the cause. Since the first council meeting, we had not spoken of my changing capabilities. I felt that he had many questions but was waiting for the right time to ask them.

I left it at that.

I doubted whether I would be able to answer them anyway.

Chapter Thirty-Three

They had been at the compound now for three weeks.

She was more or less used to the hustle and bustle of all the people and animals. The dogs stopped barking at her, even though they stayed wary. She had not changed at all in the time she was here, and Jesus had decided not to tell anyone else of her abilities just yet.

Julio regained his strength and actively participated in the strategy and war room meetings. He was obviously one of the movement's leaders, and his opinion was highly sought after. They didn't see much of each other, even though she stayed in a separate room in the building Julio's family shared with some close friends.

She preferred to be alone, but that was getting more and more difficult. Alex still had a crush on her. He managed to find excuses to be near her as often as possible. Even though she really didn't need the company, she found herself spending more time with Alex than with Julio.

Finally, she managed to leave the compound for a short time. She accompanied the partisans on two trips into the jungle to follow up on rumours that the military were in the area. Both times they returned empty handed without encountering the soldiers. The partisans were wary of her at the beginning but came to accept her presence and her heightened senses were a big benefit on the forays.

Julio was adamant. She belonged here, this was her home, and he would hear no arguments. Not even from her.

The partisans had spies and informants in the towns and villages in the area, and they regularly received information and streams of suspicious or alarming events. It was one of these streams that caused Jesus to call her into the war room.

'There are four strangers in San Maestro.' He opened the meeting. 'They are not military, although they look, and act like them. Probably mercenaries.'

A hush went over the congregated partisans. In these times where the military was for sale to the highest bidder, the mercenaries were even higher on the sadism scale. They did what was too atrocious for the corrupt soldiers. They had no ethics, no sense of guilt or compassion and answered to no one, all of them sadistic psychopaths. Their main drive was violence. Not money. Most had been kicked out of the military for excessive savagery. To be excessive— even for the sadistic military—was quite a challenge.

'We have a stream of them. They are dangerous men. They already killed two farmers we know of because they didn't get the information they wanted, or maybe just for fun. The farmers were tortured, the bodies left unrecognisable. Even the military in San Mateo avoid them like the plague.' He turned to Tonal. 'Watch the stream and tell me if you recognise any of them.'

'Why should she know any of them?' Julio asked surprised.

'Because it is her that they are looking for,' Jesus answered.

The silence was complete—all eyes on Tonal. She walked up to the table and looked at the computer screen. The stream was taken from a window higher than the street the four men were standing in—through a transparent material, probably a curtain. They stood in a circle around a fifth man who lay on the sandy ground with his arms over his head as he tried to ward off the blows from the mercenary's boots. They kicked him in an almost relaxed and uninterested manner—business as usual.

The scene unfolded in the middle of the street. She saw people on both sideways as they hurried away from the drama with their head down. She even saw soldiers watching the beating. No one intervened. Most attempted to leave in the opposite direction as quickly as possible. The victim was covered in blood and screamed at every vicious kick.

The camera zoomed in on the mercenaries. One was bald and Caucasian. His body—what was visible—was heavily tattooed. Another was a small and stringy dark-skinned man—probably Jamaican—with an intricate pattern of scars on the right side of his face. They looked to be deliberately inflicted. The third man was a blond Caucasian, though she could not see him well because he was turned away from the camera. The fourth man was enormous—almost as wide as he was tall—with a long ponytail of jet-black hair. She judged him to probably be Samoan.

She didn't recognise any of them but continued to watch the stream.

The men stopped beating the victim. Obviously bored. The Samoan spat at the whimpering and bloody mess huddled in the street. They laughed and started to leave. At that moment, the blond turned his head. His piercing blue eyes looked directly into the camera.

Her blood turned cold. She felt the hairs on her back ripple and start to grow, her fingers wanted to warp.

'Those eyes, he…' Julio said softly, he was pale.

'Has the General's eyes,' she finished the sentence. She could not take her gaze from the monitor.

'Who is the General, and who is this man?' Jesus demanded, looking from her to Julio.

'The General was one of the people at the spa,' Julio explained. 'He was in charge, responsible for our torture and the death of our companions.'

'And why is this man looking for her?' Jesus pointed to the screen. She looked up from the screen.

'Because I killed the General,' her answer was soft, but in the silence, it could have been as loud as a shout. 'This I expect, is his son.'

Jesus took control. 'You have made yourself a dangerous enemy.' He walked to the screen and froze the image. 'Because you are here, he is also our enemy. We must find out what we can about these men so that we can decide what to do about them.' He turned to Alex, Julio's son. 'Find out what you can about this General and his family.' Julio protested but was silenced when Jesus added; 'use the Internet.' Alex approached the computer and sat down behind the screen. Within seconds he was browsing the web, where he used the information supplied by his father.

Tonal retreated to the back of the war room. She left the building when nobody acknowledged her presence anymore. Jesus followed her. 'Don't leave the compound.' he ordered. 'I won't have you endangering us any more than necessary. You are here as Julio's guest. Our sanctuary for you is because of him.'

She had no illusions about why she was tolerated or where their loyalty lay, so this was no revelation. She chose not to answer.

'Don't take me wrong,' he added, his tone less accusatory. 'We are indebted to you that you returned him to us. But we can't risk our survival because you have angered the wrong people.'

It would serve no purpose to point out that saving Julio necessitated the killing or at least angering of the General and subsequently his clan.

She nodded, turned around and walked back to her quarters.

Later that day Alex reported on what he found on the Internet.

'The General is quite a high visibility person. Not just as a military man.' He consulted his notes. 'He started off as the son of a drunken sergeant and kind of fell into the military life naturally. I expect to escape from the old man. His Mother died under suspicious circumstances. Father was arrested, but never convicted, he finally died about ten years later. A domestic accident. Or at least according to the report.' He took a breath. 'The future General made rapid promotion in the ranks, mostly because of his valour and recklessness. He led his troops into the biggest forays. Lots of casualties, but just as many medals.'

The tale continued. The General's career blossomed. He rose in the ranks and made a name for himself as a ruthless leader who got the job done. Finally, he reached his pinnacle. His lowly heritage slowed and ultimately stopped his climb to power. He didn't fit in with the multiple-generation military families. Even though he managed to marry into one of the debutant new-money families, he never made it all the way to the real power. This aggravated him no end, and his name was connected to a number of "accidents" that seemed to plague the powers-that-be.

In the meantime, he started his dynasty. Four legitimate sons and three daughters, along with more than ten illegitimate children he semi-acknowledged when he brought them into the "family fold". Not as equals, but in the inner circle none the less. The competition between his spawn was second only to their loyalty to the General. His wife tolerated the multiple mistresses and their bastards. Not that she had any choice. She was hospitalised frequently with her own in-house accidents.

His daughters—with the exception of one who followed her brothers—married into wealthy and powerful families. His sons all followed their father into the army and often excelled in their loyalty and valour and on close inspection, also with their viciousness and outright sadism.

The man in the stream was the General's son Scott, he was the second child. He had one of the blackest souls in the family and was forcibly retired from the military after an especially bloody mission deep in the unruly part of the capitol. Unofficially—in sealed records—he was named as the cause of seventy-six civilian deaths that could not be attributed to terrorism. One of the victims was the estranged daughter of the Governor, who tried to make a difference by helping the poor. Here even the old man couldn't intervene. Scott was dishonourably discharged from the military and became a blemish on his father's record. Leaving the regular military, Scott unsuccessfully tried his hand at different careers, but finally re-found his calling in a semi-military environment—the mercenaries. He was linked to a multitude of skirmishes and wars in many different countries. Occasionally, he freelanced for his father's forays into Resistance territory.

From a revolutionary point of view, getting rid of the General was a good thing. But the fallout that was to be expected from the General's clan due of the loss of their patriarch, concerned the council.

For the time being, Jesus resolved to do nothing about the mercenaries. Tonal would have to stay under wraps and they would count on the invisibility of the compound and secrecy.

Life continued as usual.

Chapter Thirty-Four

I wanted to leave. I needed to.

The compound stifled me.

Since the sighting of the mercenaries last week, I was restricted to the small area—not allowed to leave the collection of buildings.

The tension built up inside me again.

I tried to convince Julio it would be better if I left. Better for them and better for me.

He wouldn't hear of it, every time adamant I was safest here, with the rest of them. But it wasn't my safety I was worried about.

He dismissed my fears for the safety of the small community if the mercenaries were to find me here. 'They will not find us or you,' Julio declared. He refused to accept any other option.

What about the danger I posed? To Julio, his family and everyone in the compound.

I didn't dare to sleep at night but couldn't keep myself awake. The fatigue overwhelmed me. The moment I let myself drift off to sleep, my mind immediately filled with nightmares of the lab.

Every single night I relived that scene, the massacre.

Only the scientists and soldiers didn't die. They bled, their bodies ripped open, and they should be dead, but they weren't. They crowded around me and screamed their accusations. Screamed that I was a monster, and they were innocents. Shouted that I would keep on killing, keep on murdering, that I would not be able to stop myself.

I felt they were right.

The last few nights the recurring nightmare became increasingly more terrifying. In my dream I retaliated, slashed and bit everyone around me. Some of the victims were new; people I encountered daily here in the compound. People that were alive in real life. Only in the dreams they were ripped apart.

I saw Julio, bleeding as he stumbled away from me, feebly begging me to stop.

I saw his wife Maria, with her throat clawed out.

Jesus with the back of his head caved in from my fangs.

This was all my work.

I advanced on Julio—my claws slippery with blood.

Alex ran over and tried to stop me, I turned on him and slashed at his young face but wounded his arm instead, because he threw it up in front of his face, in an attempt to protect himself as he fell back.

I jumped on him, my fangs near his pulsing throat.

Chapter Thirty-Five

She woke up at that precise moment.

Her muzzle two inches from Alex's neck. She smelled the blood and looked into his surprised and frightened visage. Immediately she jumped back, stumbling over the bed she'd just left.

Alex's arm bled profusely. He'd cried out when she attacked him, and she heard the rest of the building's inhabitants rush to the bedroom. The door flew further open, and a number of people—Julio and Maria among them— crowded into the small space. Maria instantly kneeled on the floor next to Alex.

Julio took in the scene; his son on the floor bleeding from slashes on his arm, his friend in full human form, almost in a foetal position huddled in the corner—rocking back and forth. He sent the remaining family members and friends from the room.

'Leave now,' his voice was commanding and everyone but Alex, Maria and himself left the scene. Julio checked to see his son was all right. The wounds were bleeding but did not seem life threatening. Maria had already torn a strip off her nightgown to staunch the blood.

Julio turned to the pathetic being huddled in the corner. He advanced slowly.

'Tonal,' he said quietly. 'Look at me.'

She continued to rock back and forth as she keened softly and didn't react to his voice. He persevered; his hand outstretched to her.

'Please Tonal, don't do this to yourself. Alex is all right, he's not badly hurt, he will be okay. You just scratched him, no more.'

His hand hovered above her form, slowly it descended and touched her shoulder. She was wet with sweat but quivering. She didn't react immediately. He kept his hand there.

Slowly she raised her head. 'Julio,' she whispered 'I am so sorry; I didn't mean to...' her voice trailed off.

He nodded. 'I know Tonal, you would never intentionally hurt him.'

'But I did,' her voice was breaking. 'I nearly killed him. I would have if he hadn't called out and woken me.' She was crying.

'But you didn't kill him.' Julio moved closer to her. He turned his head to his family. Willing Alex to say something. His son understood.

'I'm okay,' he said, sounding more convincing than he felt. 'It's nothing. It was my fault. I heard you scream and came to see what was wrong. I shouldn't have touched you.'

He was surprised at his own reaction to what had very nearly been his demise. He wasn't frightened or angry. Just surprised, amazed and sympathetic to this strange person he called his friend and whose image filled all his waking moments.

She regained part of her composure. 'Julio.' A pause. 'I

have to leave… Now,' she pleaded. 'Please don't try to stop me. I must go, get away from everyone.'

'Tonal, you need people now, to help you,' he countered.

She pulled away from him, angry that he should try to keep her—even after this.

'I attacked your son Julio, what do I need to do to get you to let me go? Kill someone?'

She stood up off the floor and sat on the bed. 'I have to go,' she repeated, her voice once again soft and barely audible. 'It's building up inside me. The rage, the tension. Like in the lab. I need to let it out, and I can't do that here. I dream every night. Dreams full of blood and murder. I see myself killing the scientists again, the General.'

The statement was difficult for her, and she looked at him.

'And then you, I see myself as I kill you and your family, everyone here in the compound. I wake up with claws, blood in my mouth from where I bite myself.' She opened her clenched hands, the fingers once again ending in the enormous claws. They receded back into her flesh, but the effort it took was obvious.

'And now this,' she whispered. 'Now I hurt Alex. Next time I will kill someone, what then Julio? How will you be able to live with that? How will I?'

No one spoke.

Julio sat down next to her on the bed. 'Where will you go?' he finally asked.

'Into the jungle, far from here, far from any settlement,' she answered resolutely. 'Someplace where I can do no harm.'

'I know such a place.' It was Alex who spoke. 'There is a valley about fifty miles from here, in the jungle, I read about it on the Internet. But it is a dangerous place, no one wants to live there. There are rumours that it is haunted.'

She almost laughed. 'Sounds perfect.' Now it will also have a monster.

'I will bring you there,' Alex continued. With help from Maria he stood up, cradling his wounded arm.

Tonal looked at him, touched by his offer and his trust, even after what she had done.

'No,' she answered 'Thank you, Alex, but I must go alone. Tell me where it is, and I will find it, or somewhere else where I can stay.'

'Come Alex.' Maria supported her son and directed him towards the door. 'Your arm needs care, probably stitches.' There was no anger or reproach in her statement. He let himself be steered out of the room and left Julio and Tonal alone.

'How long will you be gone?' Julio broke the silence.

She looked at him, fascinated that this man could still bear to be near her. She almost killed his only son, and still he trusted her.

'I don't know, as long as necessary.'

She found herself pleading to Julio again 'I need to get this under control. If I don't, I'll never trust myself near anyone again.'

'What will you do?'

She sighed. 'I have no idea,' she confessed. 'See what happens. But I must go, that much I do know.'

Julio stood up and started collecting the few possessions she had. 'You will need the GPS,' he bustled. 'To be able to find us again.' She walked over to him and softly put her hand on his arm.

'I won't be taking anything with me.'

He understood what she was telling him. 'You will change?' it was not really a question.

'I will make better time that way,' she explained. 'And I feel I need to, to relieve the energy.'

He nodded.

They moved into the small kitchen of the wooden building. Maria was tending to Alex's wounds as she stitched the three gashes—her medical knowledge gained from practice, not from a formal education. The revolutionary's life had given her more than adequate experience in nursing.

Alex explained where the valley was, his attempts to convince her that he should accompany her once again fell on deaf ears. She listened intently and memorised the directions.

Once again, she apologised to Alex and Maria. They reassured her it was ok.

She said her goodbyes.

Julio walked with her to the edge of the compound. The moon was high in the sky, there would be another five hours of night at least. They embraced. Julio wanted to say something, but he found his throat constricted with emotion. Tears slid down his weathered cheeks. It felt as though he were losing one of his children.

'Be well Tonal,' he managed.

She nodded, turned and left. Her eyes were moist, and she felt like a knife had been jammed in her chest. The only thing she could do was move away as quickly as possible. Pushing her way into the underbrush, she was soon swallowed up by the dense jungle.

Julio stayed there and watched the space where she'd disappeared. He hoped against hope, that she would change her mind and come back. He knew she wouldn't. Knew it was the best decision.

He decided to inform Jesus in the morning.

Chapter Thirty-Six

After I travelled the dense jungle for almost an hour, I came to the first focal point Alex mentioned—a small waterfall.

I took off my clothes, buried them in the undergrowth and in the pale moonlight I allowed the change to come over me.

Immediately the tension fell away.

The familiar pain of the change was welcome. It made me feel alive.

I revelled in the change, threw my head back and roared at the moon.

With that, I bounded off into the jungle, headed for the haunted valley.

The trip south was a relief for me, the sounds and smells of the jungle refreshing and sweet. For the sheer joy of it I ran and jumped over fallen trees littering the jungle floor, I chased birds and small animals that scattered before me. The birds cried out in anger as they warned all other jungle inhabitants a predator was underway.

I didn't mind. I enjoyed the ruckus I created. I wasn't

hunting, so stealth was not necessary. But when I did hunt, nothing was safe from my claws and fangs. I was the top predator in the jungle and relished the thought.

Late one afternoon I reached a small cliff that jutted out of the jungle floor. The face rose up about fifteen metres at its highest point and tapered down to the jungle floor three-hundred metres to the right. The left side ended in a steep drop to the edge of a small river. A tiny clearing bordered the cliff, surrounded by the high trees and vegetation of the tropical jungle. It was a quiet place. Peaceful. With the water close by and the cliff to protect my back, I decided this would be the place where I would stay—at least for a while.

About six metres up the cliff I saw a cave. It was reasonably accessible, even if it would be a stretch for a human. In feline form I could get up there in two leaps. To the left, the cave connected to a ledge that would offer a great vantage point to view the clearing and part of the jungle beyond till the vegetation got too dense even for me to be able to see anything.

I jumped up to the ledge and tested the air of the cave for scents—in case any other predator called this place home. Then I investigated the dark opening in the cliff wall. The cave was empty, and I didn't find any signs of recent inhabitants. It turned out to be a collection of caves that went into the cliff for about twenty metres. The first cave—the entrance—was the smallest and led off to a larger cave to the right. All in all, there were four caves that were usable to live in, including the entrance space. I retraced my steps back to the ledge, lay down and enjoyed the sunset.

Night descends quickly this close to the equator and soon it was dark. The sounds of the night dwellers tickled my sensitive hearing.

My stomach informed me that it was time to eat which meant time to hunt. I leapt down from the ledge and softly padded off into the jungle.

In the morning, I returned to the cave with a small deer. She quelled my immediate hunger, and I rested on the ledge. My direct future was unclear, but to start with I would just wing it.

One day at a time.

Get used to my feline form. Practice my skills and just experience what it was like to live in this beautiful jungle.

Chapter Thirty-Seven

She watched them from a distance, hidden by the dense foliage.

They were not bothered about noise and didn't even attempt to be quiet. Laughing and shouting to each other, they were enjoying themselves.

The girl was passed from one to the other, screaming. They tore her clothes and groped her. The Samoan held her close, pinned her arms and tried to kiss her lips. She spat at him which caused him to laugh even more. He turned her around, pushed her to his companion and slapped her buttocks.

The only one not actively involved in the game was the General's son. He watched from a short distance, enjoying the girl's fear. He had inherited more than just his father's eyes—also his sadistic character.

Scott focussed and looked past the scene to the man who lay on the floor. They had beaten him almost to a pulp. Scott strode over to him and cocked his pistol. The sound caused the girl to cease her fight with the tattooed mercenary who held her and plead with the General's son to let her husband live. She cried she would do anything, but please, please don't hurt him anymore. The piercing blue eyes watched her anguish as he slowly put the muzzle of the gun to the man's head and—laughing—pulled the trigger.

The girl screamed.

Anger boiled in Tonal's veins. The wounded man had been too far-gone to save, she'd smelled death on him, but to kill him just to distress the girl was more than brutal.

The gun once again holstered, Scott joined his companions as they stripped the girl naked, tearing off the last remnants of her clothes. The Jamaican mercenary had already unbuckled his jeans when Tonal stepped into the clearing.

'Wouldn't you prefer a real woman.' Her voice was seductive, her presence totally unexpected.

The sight of a beautiful naked woman emerging from the trees was enough to stun all four of the men. They gazed at her first with surprise, then with unbridled lust.

Scott was the first to recover. 'That's her,' he called out.

The urgency was lost on his men. They dropped the girl and turned to this perfect spectre. As one they advanced on her while Scott frantically searched through his backpack. He finally found what he was looking for—another pistol.

In the meantime, the three mercenaries surrounded the naked woman and pulled off their shirts and pants in reaction to her seducing and inviting gaze.

When they were all within a yard of her, she exploded, killing the Samoan first with the claws of her right hand. She'd identified him as the most dangerous in close contact. The bald man struggled with his shirt to free his arms that were pinned in the sleeves. He was the second to die. The Jamaican turned and fled to where Scott stood. In the panic, he ran into the shot that was meant for Tonal and fell over the General's son. Scott pushed his companion away, but she was almost upon him now in almost full feline form. He managed to take another shot. It entered her chest, on the left side. It didn't stop her. She continued her pounce and swiped the gun out of his hand.

'That's impossible,' he said surprised, no other emotion in his voice 'Those are silver bullets, they should kill you.'

'Don't believe everything you hear.' The words were barely audible through her elongating fangs and snout. The change completed. The last things he saw were the enormous fangs that advanced on his face as she took his head in her mouth. Her canines bore deep in his skull, cracked the bone and sank into his brain, killing him instantly.

She retreated from the body, changed back, looked for the girl, and found her huddled over the body of her husband, crying softly.

Tonal searched through the mercenaries' backpacks and found spare cotton shirts and jeans. She took two of each and went to the girl.

'Here,' she said. 'Put these on.' Tonal offered her one set.

They both dressed. The clothes were much too big, but with belts and rope they managed to make them reasonably comfortable.

'I'll take you back to your home,' she told the girl, astounded at the resilience of the young woman. Her husband dead, her attackers slaughtered by this strange nightmarish creature that was now helping her.

'I won't leave him,' she indicated her husband stubbornly. 'He must be buried properly.'

Tonal nodded. 'I will carry him, let the jungle have the others.'

She picked the man up and slung him over her shoulder in the fire-man's hold. Together they retraced the girl's foot-prints back to where the mercenaries abducted the couple. They arrived at a small village within two hours. The girl ran into the arms of an older man who advanced on them as soon as they were spotted. The elder was armed with a spear like utensil. He lowered it when he saw that the two women were not joined by any of the mercenaries.

The girl sobbed uncontrollably as her emotions finally took over. The old man gently passed her to an equally ancient woman and indicated to others they relieve the unknown woman of her burden—their dead friend.

'Take care of her.' Tonal said indicating the girl. 'She has been through a lot, seen a lot—strange things.'

The man nodded. 'Word had come to us that you were here, Tonal' he said. 'You are welcome in this village. We are forever in your debt.'

She shook her head and turned back to the jungle that had become her home.

They knew her name.

Chapter Thirty-Eight

I heard that they were looking for me. The matriarch of the village sent her youngest son to warn me. There were two people asking for me: a man and a woman. These were good people. partisans—Julio's children.

I watched from the edge of the cliff that overlooked the village. Alex, and a woman I didn't recognise, were welcomed enthusiastically by the village elders. I'd suspected the village kept Julio up to date on how I was doing and where I was. The ease with which the people accepted the two travellers was testament to that.

I turned and left the cliff, secure in the knowledge they would set out for the vicinity of my camp the next morning. Tonight, they would enjoy the village's hospitality and be drilled about any news of the outside world. The village was not often graced with visitors from outside the jungle. That was one of the reasons I liked it here, there was nobody to be wary of, and the villagers respected my privacy. Since I saved the young girl from the mercenaries almost twenty years ago, they looked out for me in subtle ways, nothing too overt. Small indications, like the blanket that had been left in the clearing before the colder season set in.

The girl, Marianna, recovered well from her ordeal, finally remarried, became the matriarch of the small community and followed in the footsteps of the old couple who had long since died. The community stayed small over the years and protected their independence courageously.

Sure enough, in the early hours of the following afternoon I heard the two visitors crashing into the clearing that had become the communication site with the villagers. They were accompanied by one of the elders. People always think they move quietly, but the truth is that usually even a deaf animal can hear them from a mile off. Alex and his companion were no exception, though the noise was intentional on the part of their guide. They crashed through the dense undergrowth—the villager using the noise to notify me. There were paths in the jungle that were clear and where little noise was made when traversing. They were not using one of those now.

In spite of myself, I was curious. What brought Alex here after all this time?

I could guess though.

Chapter Thirty-Nine

The two visitors stopped in the centre of the clearing and looked around. It was a beautiful place, full of light and flowers, the ground covered in lush grass.

'How do we find her from here?' Alex asked.

The man looked at him and replied, 'you don't. She will find you if she wants to. Just stay here. If she does not appear today, then take that track back to the village.' He turned to leave.

'And then try again tomorrow?' the woman asked.

'No. If she doesn't appear today, she does not want to see you. Then you go home.' He left them in the sunlight.

Alex and his sister settled down on the grass, ready to wait out the afternoon while the villager retraced his steps back to the settlement.

She let the siblings wait for an hour as she observed them through the trees. The woman was impatient. Tonal guessed she was about twenty-five or twenty-six years old. That would make her an infant when she had been in the compound. She remembered the small child that had hung on to Maria's skirts. What was her name? … …Dulce. Yes, that's right. This must be her.

Dulce had grown into a good-looking young woman. Alex was as she expected. He had matured into a broad-shouldered man, with dark wavy hair hanging to his shoulders. He was patient—secure in his conviction she would appear. He surveyed the clearing and the trees beyond and wondered where she would emerge.

'She's not coming,' Dulce declared and stood up to leave.

'Be patient, Sis,' Alex chuckled. 'She will come.'

'And how will you know it is her?' Dulce was determined to have the last word. 'You haven't seen her for more than twenty years, and she's been in the jungle for so long she will have turned into a wild woman.'

Tonal smiled and walked into the clearing.

'Oh, I recognise her,' Alex answered. 'And she is exactly as I expected.' He looked past his sister's shoulder to the figure who approached. She was exactly the same as when he saw her last—all those years ago. That fact alone was stunning. His heart felt the familiar tug as he smiled at her. His crush had survived the test of time.

Dulce spun around. Startled by how close this woman was and how she had been able to approach so soundlessly. She stared at the vision.

Dulce fully expected to see a wild, half-mad woman of late middle age. Everyone told her the strange visitor was about thirty - thirty-five when she was at the compound. But now she didn't seem a day older than the same thirtyish she had been then. Dulce herself had been too young to have any real memory of the woman who shared their dwelling in those months so long ago. Her agelessness confused Dulce. That, and the fact that no one in the family would tell her what was so special about the hermit. Okay, she saved her father Julio, brought him back to them, but there was more, only no one would tell her. Seeing her here in person didn't help much. It only brought up more questions.

'Hallo Tonal.' Alex breathed again and noticed he had held his breath until she was near. He was reluctant to make any move that could shatter the vision.

She smiled at him, turning his legs to jelly.

'Alex,' she answered, her voice soft and sensual to his ears. She turned her head to Dulce. 'And you must be Dulce,' she stated, startling the young woman who could only nod, no sound came out of her lips.

Alex laughed, Dulce tonged-tied, now that was something new. He stood up, slowly walked over and hugged this woman he had not seen for so long, but who had dominated his dreams for so many years. It felt so good to see her again, the years fell back, and he was once again the love-struck teenager.

'It's good to see you Alex,' she said. 'You have matured well.'

He smiled. 'And you look exactly the same as when I saw you last, only your hair is longer.' He touched the brown locks that fell to her waist. In the compound she had kept her hair short. 'It suits you.' Talk was light and meaningless. But it felt good. They sat down.

'You have been gone for a long time.' Alex became serious. 'Much has happened in the years you have lived in the jungle. I hoped that you would have tired of living alone and come back.' She didn't acknowledge the subtle reproach. 'Anyway, we are here now, and I will fill you in on the most important things.'

She smiled internally. Alex hadn't changed much. He

was still the enthusiastic boy that talked her ears off—sometimes for hours on end—back in the compound. He had been full of dreams, righteousness and determination to make a difference in the world. Totally confident his view on every subject was the correct one.

'My father died two months ago,' he said. Alex and Dulce bowed their heads slightly.

'I'm sorry, he was a good man.' She'd expected this to be the reason they'd sought to find her, but the news touched a tender spot anyway. Julio was a very important part of her past, and it had been comforting to think she could see him again if she wanted to. But so was the way of the world. Everything died. Well, almost everything.

'He was murdered,' Alex continued. 'It was too soon, not his time. He had problems with his health from the time you brought him back to us. The torture had long-term effects, so it seemed; he was fragile. But still, he was the driving force behind the revolution. The government knew this, and they continued to try to kill him. Two months ago, they succeeded.' The resulting silence gave Alex a moment to gather his emotions. 'We are grateful to you for bringing him home. He was very important to us, and to the revolution. Now we continue his legacy.'

Alex talked on for most of the afternoon, about Julio, about the family, and most of all about the revolution.

'We are at war,' he said. 'Officially now. The conflict between the rich and the poor has escalated throughout the whole world. The powers frantically try to keep their supremacy. Presidents and kings became tyrants. All over the world the two camps are fighting each other. The rich with weapons, the poor with guerrilla tactics and sheer numbers. There is extensive cooperation between the revolutionary parties in all the American and Latin countries.

And even further than that—with those across the seas. The wealthy distrust each other as much as they hate and fear us. They are not united and are subsequently being attacked on all fronts. But still, they have the weapons, and it is our people who are dying in large numbers. Last year the war escalated to a full global struggle. The whole world is now the battle arena.' He paused for a minute. Dulce continued the story.

'The Americas are falling apart. The northern states concentrate on the internal struggle and have pulled almost all their troops out of the Latin states. Slowly, more and more territories come under partisan control.' She was no less driven than her brother.

'When you came to the jungle,' Alex picked up the narrative again. 'The Americas had started a campaign to gain control over the southern Latin countries for their natural resources. They managed to conquer Brazil, Peru and Ecuador, but some of the other countries: Chile and Argentina, proved more than they could handle. Because their focus was on the southern countries, they lost their grip on the Middle American states, like Nicaragua and Puerto Rico.' He paused for breath. 'Their direct lines to the southern countries were constantly under fire from the partisans. Supply trains were hijacked, and we gathered more guns and ammunition—at their cost. They tried to bomb us out of the jungle but couldn't find us. We moved the compound many times. Finally, we lived in the caves in the mountains. But we persevered. And now we finally make some headway. There are even some rich people on our side. Others see their faith in the government and military is misplaced and try to make amends with us. We are wary of course. These are not true allies, only supporters of coincidence. They see who's winning and take a new side.

Anyway, we use their money and influence and bit-by-bit we conquer more terrain. Politically we also rally more people to our cause.'

Tonal listened intently and waited for Alex to inform her of the real reason they had trekked the hundred miles to her valley.

'There are countries that have already been liberated. They support the revolutionaries in those that are still at war. We receive much support from the Scandinavian countries. And from Alaska and Italy.' Alex was so into his story he didn't notice how the light of the day was waning. It was late in the afternoon and time to retire to a place where they would spend the night.

Tonal interrupted his narrative; 'Alex, we must leave the clearing now before it is too dark to travel. My camp is not far—near the caves. You must eat, and you will need a place to sleep.'

He sighed and nodded when he noticed for the first time the sun had started to set behind the trees. This close to the equator, night came suddenly with twilight going to instant darkness within minutes.

They stood, gathered their packs and followed Tonal out of the clearing. The walk took almost half an hour, and it was pitch black by the time they reached the cliff wall. There they saw the small cave and a lean-too. Tonal lit some lanterns in the lean-too, picked them up and placed them strategically around the clearing and on the track to the cave where she placed the packs.

'You will be staying in the cave' she explained. 'There are less animals here, less chance you will be bitten or stung.' Dulce shuddered at the thought of which creatures could sting and bite her this deep in the jungle. She had heard the rumours of monsters in this part of the dense forest. Although she was well educated, she could not escape the superstitions of generations of her kin, what if... ...

'Stay here, explore the cave, be careful with the climb.' Tonal stood by the lean-too. 'I will get something to eat.' She left them alone.

Alex and Dulce explored the small camp and the caves.

With the years, the climb to the caves had become less steep, worn away by wind, rain and Tonal's paws, but still it amounted to quite an effort for the siblings. The main cave was clean and cool, almost twenty metres to the back, and set to the right of the entrance cave. They found some old backpacks, a variety of ancient clothes—all very practical and most made for men—some with rips Alex seemed to recognise. There were also containers, many woven from leaves and filled with other products of the jungle.

They found cured animal hides—mostly capybaras—but occasionally a larger animal like a tapir or deer. The cave and the lean-too were devoid of any furniture, decoration or other items other than the lanterns they'd seen earlier.

After about thirty minutes Tonal returned with a dead capybara. She immediately began to skin and dress the animal while Alex started a fire with wood from the pile behind the lean-too. By the time she had prepared the carcass, the fire was hot enough to cook it. They pierced the body with a long thick stick and placed it in the two X-shaped holders on either side of the stone framed fire area. Dulce found fruit in the storage in the cave and brought this to the fire. They all sat down and waited in silence for the meat to cook.

'Have you lived here all the time?' Dulce finally spoke to the strange woman. 'I mean, it's been more than twenty years.' The woman made her nervous. She couldn't say why, but there was something very strange about her, and not only the fact that she lived in the jungle on her own and seemed to have eternal youth.

When Tonal turned to answer her, Dulce probed her eyes, trying to see what it was—to get a clue as to what her parents and Alex had spoken about all these years. Every time Dulce walked in on the conversations about this woman, they changed the subject. When her father Julio was on his deathbed—mortally wounded by the assassin— he called both her and Alex into the bedroom. He made them promise they would find her and speak to her. Try to convince Tonal that she should come home.

'Most of the time,' the mystical woman answered. There was a smile in her eyes, she was still quite taken by Dulce; so curious and vibrant. 'I found this cave complex straight away but decided to go further after I found there was a village close by. I wanted peace and quiet. I stayed in an old hut about two miles south for a few months, but there was a reason it had been abandoned—red fire ants. They arrived one day and went through all my stores in less than ten minutes. After that, I decided the cave would be a better place to stay permanently. It was empty and dry. So, I came back.'

'Where did you get the supplies and stuff from. The village?' There were so many questions.

She smiled. 'I had some visitors occasionally. They left their things here and I recycled them.' She caught Alex's eye, and he smiled back knowingly.

'The mercenaries?' he asked. She nodded.

'The mercenaries and others. It seems the General had a large extended family. Other than that, it has been nice and quiet. I enjoy the peace.' The last comment was a challenge to Alex. She was happy here, or at least content, and didn't plan on moving soon.

The food was ready, and they ate. The herbs she had scattered over the coals had scented the meat. The animal was quite young, and its flesh was tender. They complemented the protein with the fruit and coal baked sweet potato-like roots Dulce found in the cave.

Stars lit up the dark sky. The sounds of the jungle were of nocturnal creatures. Bats circled the edges of the cave and the lean-too, preying on the insects that were drawn by the light of the fire.

The three people were quiet. Conversation had drawn to a halt during the meal.

'You have seen where you can sleep.' Their host pointed to the cave—Alex nodded. He wanted to talk more, but she cut him short. 'Tomorrow we will talk, and you can tell me why you are really here.' The last comment was accompanied with a sly smile. The look on Alex's face amused her. He had forgotten how obvious his body language was, and how good she was at reading it.

Brother and sister retired to the cave. Tonal vanished. Dulce's curiosity was killing her. From the comfortable layer of dry grass she lay on, she quizzed her brother. 'Where has she gone to?'

It was pitch black in the cave, and she couldn't see the amused look on Alex's face. But she certainly could hear the laughter in his voice. 'Dulce, Dulce, you are so nosy. She has gone into the jungle and will be back again tomorrow.'

Ignoring the banter Dulce continued, 'but isn't it dangerous? There are predators out there, she could be attacked by something. Hurt maybe. There are jaguars here.'

Alex laughed out loud. 'Don't worry,' he managed to

say. 'Nothing will happen. She is the biggest predator in this jungle.' He knew his answer would confuse his sister even more, and he so loved riling her. 'Go to sleep, sis. Tomorrow we must speak to her.' He turned over in his sleeping bag and closed his eyes.

Dulce grumbled a bit more, but lacking any reaction from her big brother, she gave in and settled down to sleep.

Chapter Forty

The first light flowed into the opening of the cave. Alex had been awake for a while, watching the jungle rouse. Dulce opened her eyes and saw him sitting at the edge of the ledge, just outside the cave. The woman was sitting next to him. They were talking softly. Crawling out of the sleeping bag Dulce crept towards the cave opening where she strained to hear the conversation.

'Good morning, Dulce.' Tonal startled her. How could she have heard her—she hadn't made a sound. Alex hadn't heard her, he turned around smiling.

'Hi sis, slept well?'

'Yeah,' she conceded. 'Not bad.' She sat down between the two, determined to be included in the conversation, but nature called. She frantically needed to relieve herself.

'In the jungle,' the woman said to her. Fuming, she nodded and made her way to the jungle edge.

Alex called after her; 'watch out for poisonous plants,' he laughed. 'And snakes.'

Dulce returned four minutes later. Alex was cleaning the

cooled meat off the carcass of the capybara. Tonal had gathered fresh fruit. Dulce was surprised that she was hungry again and breakfast was welcome. They ate in silence and washed the food down with water from the stream nearby. It was cold, but clear and fresh.

'So, Alex,' Tonal broke the silence. 'Why are you here?' She was direct, almost rude.

'We want you to come back with us,' Alex was just as blunt. 'We need your help.' She waited patiently for him to explain. 'The Revolution is going well. We have the support of ninety-five percent of the people. But the remaining five percent are the ones with the money—the ones in power. We need to break that power. We have tried to talk to them, come to an understanding, to no avail.'

'They literally sent us the negotiator's head in a bag,' Dulce added.

Alex continued. 'There is no room anymore to talk or to reason with these people. But they still have the money and the soldiers. They have the power. They raid the villages, murder all, even women and children and leave them staked for the animals as warnings to anyone who supports us. They wage a war of terror. Young women and girls are kidnapped and taken to the walled compounds. There, we hear their screams as they are passed from soldier to soldier. A few days later what is left of them is dumped back in the villages. No one is safe. Their tactics are slowly working. People are too scared to help us much as they used to. Some even join the landowners in an attempt to protect their families. Young children are pressed into military service. They are brainwashed and sent back to kill their families.' He paused.

The images were too frightening to contemplate. Alex had seen the devastation wreaked by a twelve-year-old from the village near their compound after he massacred his family. He'd hacked his parents and young sisters to pieces with a machete. They were forced to kill the boy when he attacked the villagers who rushed to the screams of their neighbours.

'The landowners are federated. They work together, and their goal is to break the resistance. We need to get them out of the picture to be able to start the final attack on the government. But that's difficult. The villa's they live in are heavily armed compounds. Almost castles. Mercenaries and their own armies protect them. We can't get to them.'

'Our main target is General Ortiz. He isn't really a General.' Dulce and Alex alternated the narrative. 'That is what he calls himself. He's a pure sadist. He takes his tactics from history as he calls it. He stakes people and leaves them to die agonising deaths. The road to his mansion is framed with more than fifty bodies—dead and dying—the sound of their agony can be heard miles away. The smell of decaying flesh is sickening.'

'He is unreachable for us. But much of his power lies in his allies. We plan to take them out one by one and then—when he is most vulnerable—we will kill him.'

'How will you get to them?' she asked. Already knowing the answer.

'That is where we need you,' Alex answered. 'You and your special talents.'

No one spoke.

'It's not my fight,' she finally said. 'I live here; far away from everything. That's a choice I made long ago.'

Disappointment clouded Dulce's face. She was about to say something, but Alex restrained her with his hand on her arm.

'I know you value your peace. But the war is coming

down here as well. There will be no peace for you or anyone else if we let them continue their reign of terror. They will stop at nothing. Twenty-two miles from here they raided a village,' he continued.

'I saw the smoke,' she answered.

'It is only a question of time before they get here. You can fight them then, or you can help us save as many people as we can, and then get back to your life if this is what you want.' He looked her straight in the eye. 'You kid yourself if you keep thinking you are alone in the world. That you don't care for anyone else. If that were the case you wouldn't have saved Julio, or Marianna for that matter. She told us about the things you do to help them when danger presents itself. How you killed the rogue jaguar and the mercenaries that threatened them.'

'They came for me, killing them was in my own interest.'

Unable to keep from voicing her opinion, Dulce entered the conversation. 'How can you be so selfish?' she exclaimed —unbelief clear in her voice. 'There are people's lives at stake here, not just your precious peace and quiet. Try to think of what my father lived for. Didn't you learn anything from him? Didn't he mean anything to you? Does his murder leave you cold?'

Her eyes pierced into Dulce's as Tonal shot back. 'You have no idea what my "peaceful" life is like and what it costs me. Your father was my mentor. He helped me resign myself to what I am, to what I can be. He helped me find my peace, and I will protect it without restraint.'

'Then come back with us and protect it once and for all. Help us return this country to what it once was—a peaceful and good place for everyone to live in. Without the pain or the torture and death. Come back to avenge Julio,' Alex tried. 'Please, at least think about it. You don't have to decide now. You can find the way to our compound if you want, I'm sure.' Pushing would not help here. 'Please remember Julio, remember what he lived for, how he helped. How, and why he died.'

Silence settled on the threesome once again. Dulce was livid. They had travelled all this way for nothing. Alex constantly rattled on about this special woman. And now they were here she refused to help in any way. She was about to say something when Alex stood up.

'Please Tonal, think about it. Please, come to us. We need you.'

He picked up his pack and slung it over his shoulder. 'Thank you for your hospitality, and for the memories. It was good to see you again.' Turning, he addressed his sister. 'Come on Dulce, it's time to go back.'

She didn't try to stop them. Just watched as they left the small clearing, Alex turned to wave to her. She acknowledged his wave. He smiled, confidant he would see her again.

Chapter Forty-One

I took my clothes off and did what I always do when frustrated or angry—I changed.

The big cat bounded off into the jungle, in search of release from the tensions the discussion and my refusal brought.

Night came and went before I returned to the clearing.

I changed back, gathered some of my few possessions and took the trail Alex and Dulce walked the previous day. Despite my initial intentions, Julio's memory forced me to review my decision. I would see what I could do to help.

The memories of Julio opened my heart again to the man who was so instrumental in my acceptance of what I had become. His patience and complete trust in me and the inherent good he somehow saw inside me, was what brought me back from the brink of insanity. He set the foundation for the life I had now. When I hadn't seen any way out, any way to live with myself, he showed me how. Somehow, he helped me accept that whatever it was, it was irreversible, and it wasn't my fault. He helped me believe in myself again.

My nightmares always ended with Julio offering his hand to me, helping me out of the abyss. He had been my anchor.

If truth be told I always knew it wasn't eternal—this paradise. It was just a question of time before the conflict reached even these outposts. The attack on the village brought it all close to my door.

And now it was here.

I could of course just move further south, deeper into the Amazon.

But even there, the question was when they would come, not if. Alex's words strengthened my resolve not to be pushed away. The villagers, the country, had been good to me, it was time to return the favour.

Tracking the two siblings was easy; their tracks were clear and visible in the forest. Alex and Dulce stayed the night with the villagers, so they hadn't really made good time. They told me they were traveling on foot and that the journey in had taken two days. The compound would therefore probably be more to the south of where I had last seen it more than twenty years ago. I didn't have to rest as much as the siblings and caught up with them after their second night's sleep. I stayed under cover of the jungle as I followed them on the last day of their trek. We passed a clearing that resembled where I changed so many years ago. They veered off to the left and followed the bed of a river. The side of the valley rose steeply on the right and was bordered by dense jungle on the left.

I noticed sentries hidden in the trees. I circumvented them and stayed behind the two revolutionaries without too much effort.

Primal Nature

After about two hours they reached the compound and walked up to the waiting council.

Chapter Forty-Two

Tonal observed the reunion from the cover of the jungle.

She'd climbed a tree and had a reasonable view of the clearing where the compound was situated. There were no permanent buildings, only tents of all sizes. She estimated there would be about fifty to sixty inhabitants in the compound. There were no vehicles anywhere in sight, transportation was probably on foot or horseback. A dog barked at the far end of the compound. It may have caught her scent, but the revolutionaries didn't take much notice. They quieted the dog and welcomed Alex and Dulce back. Tonal recognised Jesus: still the same big and burly man, though his hair had turned an even grey. Now he sported a beard and walked a little stooped, but he was still unmistakably the man in charge—he must be in his sixties at least by now. She vaguely recognised some other faces but couldn't really put names to them. It had been a long time.

The group was obviously disappointed Alex and Dulce had returned empty-handed and after some back patting and shrugging they retired to one of the tents.

Tonal decided to stay in the tree for a while and observe the compound. Occasionally the dog barked but was silenced by its owners, there was no apparent danger, and the inhabitants were too sure of their sentries to imagine anyone could have breached the defences and entered the compound. They were too complacent. Well, her appearance would probably stir things up.

The sun started to set when she finally left the tree and strode into the compound.

Sure enough; panic broke out.

A woman screamed, men came running from all sides, brandishing weapons. She calmly continued her walk, her small pack slung over her shoulder, her bare feet treading the soft sand, and a slight smile on her lips. The council came running out of the tent they had been all afternoon. Alex was one of the first. When he saw her, his face lit up.

'You came after all.'

'No promises, but we can talk and see.'

'No promises,' he agreed.

'Hello Jesus, you are well?' Tonal turned to the older man. The surprise finally showed on his weathered face. He recovered quickly as was his practice.

'Yes, thank you Tonal, and you have not changed a bit.' He smiled at her. 'Still like the dramatic entrances, I see.' On a more serious tone he turned to the guards. 'It's okay, she's a friend.' Then more accusatory; 'we will talk later about how she could breach our defences without any of you noticing.'

Mumbling amongst themselves, the guards returned to their posts. It was a mystery to them how she was able to pass by them undetected. Now they would have to answer to Jesus.

'In all fairness, Jesus,' Alex came to their defence. 'She moves without sound—she could go anywhere undetected.'

'Be that as it may, they must remain vigil, complacency costs lives.' He turned and re-entered the tent holding the flap open for the rest. 'Come, we have much to discuss.'

They all took their seats around the table in the tent and the council meeting resumed, now with a different setting.

'It's good to see you Tonal,' Jesus started the proceedings. 'You fooled Alex here; he wasn't sure you would come. I take it he informed you of the current situation.'

Alex and Tonal both nodded. 'As you see, there are new faces in the council, to be expected after twenty-three years.' Jesus introduced the two people she didn't know. 'Elena Alvarez.' Pointing to the petite woman to his right. 'And our high-tech wizard Joaquin Cruz.' A young man with flaxen hair and skittish dark eyes behind thick glasses nodded somewhat embarrassed at the compliment. 'The council of course knows about you; Alex and Dulce were asked to recruit you in the name of the whole council. We have followed your life from a distance while you lived in the jungle. It has been quite uneventful most if the time. Julio wanted to know how you were and just in case the necessity arose to ask you for assistance.' He paused. 'And now here you are. Thank you for coming.'

She nodded, and he continued.

'The war has progressed to the point that the revolutionary movement needs to start a big offensive. The combined leaders have decided this will commence between now and a month. The different cells have been allotted specific tasks. Ours is to sabotage the supply lines to the military in the southern countries and to terminate certain key figures.' He stood up and moved easily to the board in front of the table.

'These are the main supply arteries we will disrupt.' He pinned photos to the board and pointed out the intended targets.

Tonal saw train lines, make-shift runways for small planes, and bridges that spanned important waterways. The state of the roads was atrocious to say the least. Still the inaccessibility of the jungle and the wildness of the river necessitated their use. Large convoys of trucks were heavily guarded, as were the crucial bridges. More photos and streams of the targets on a laptop showed the presence of the military stationed to guard the strategic objects. Large barracks framed the roads leading to the bridges. High wire fences shut off any other clandestine routes.

A timeline was created for the most important targets. The natural order of the attacks and the availability of ammunition and people determined the sequence, keeping in mind the military presence. The debate on the best way to attack the various targets and what the outcome would be was heated. Tempers flared when Jesus cautioned not to be too impatient. Finally, to calm them down and eliminate the discussion, Jesus decided that the detailed plans would be made later in another meeting. Reluctantly, the rest of the council agreed. Faces were still hot and flushed when cold drinks were brought in and placed on the table. They took a short break; many stretched their legs outside of the tent.

Tonal stayed seated and quietly hoped she'd made the right decision to come here after all. There would be fierce fighting. How she could play a part in this was something that would have to be discussed later. Sabotaging the supply lines and disrupting the military was more the forte of the revolutionaries. Okay, her healing abilities would be handy because she could take more risks than anyone else. But that would not be what they had recruited her for. That left the personal targets.

Jesus asked everyone to take his or her seat again, and the meeting resumed.

'Joaquin will fill us in on the personal targets.' He nodded to the young man and sat down.

Joaquin looked much too young to be caught up in the revolutionary struggle. Barely more than twenty or there-abouts, but with a much younger babyface. He moved to the front of the table with a stack of photos under his arm and a laptop in his right hand. He attached the laptop to the generator cable and placed it on the table in front of him. Without a word he proceeded to pin the photos to the board.

All in all, there were six portraits on display when he turned to face the council. Five stern looking men and one woman looked down on the council from the board. None of the faces were familiar to Tonal. But that was to be expected after twenty-three years of absence. The news that reached her was verbal. No faces accompanied the stories.

'These are our targets' Joaquin explained. 'Most of them will be familiar to you, but to make sure we all have the same basic information I will introduce them anyway.' This was more for her than anyone else, but Tonal was grateful for the explanation. He pointed to the first photo and continued.

'This is Arsenio Flores.'

In the photo Tonal saw a round-faced man with an exceptionally thin moustache that appeared to be almost drawn just above his upper lip. His eyes were deep set and cold, his mouth slightly crooked.

'He's a drug baron in the northern province. His main

crop is coca—the basis for cocaine—farmed by the people who are no more than serfs on his massive holding. He terrorises the villages in the vicinity. Flores is one of the main advocates of President Esposito. The drug business plays a major part in the financing of Esposito's regime. He is a close friend of the Presidential family and stays at the palace often.' Joaquin continued after passing some photo's around.

When the photos reached her Tonal saw a variety of scenes, in all of them the same man was prominently present. One photo showed him with an elderly woman with sad eyes, another with two strapping young men.

'Flores lives with his wife and two sons. His elder daughter Domminga married Reyes and left the family home. But we will talk about her later.' Turning back to the board, he intently observed the photo of his subject. 'If we take out Flores it will be a major blow to Esposito's finances. Most of the money is used to pay the mercenaries that secure the Presidential palace and train the soldiers. We hope that they will leave the President's employment when they are no longer paid.'

Moving to the next two photos he pointed out the woman Domminga and a muscular man with dyed blond hair and tattoos showing from the lapels of his shirt.

The hair on Tonal's back tingled while she observed the prints. The violence emanated from the faces. The beautiful but vicious contours of the woman and the hard, square features of her husband. This was a partnership made in hell.

'This is Domminga Reyes, formally Flores. She is Arsenio's daughter and a real chip off the old block. She and her husband are Flores's right hands. They extended their combined reach to the south and west of Flores' territory. Rolando Reyes is a psycho, only surpassed by his fair wife. There are tales of kidnapping and murder. The couple seem to enjoy raping and torturing young teenagers—both male and female. The bodies are thrown in the river afterwards. The assassination of these three targets must be perfectly timed. They must die at precisely the same time, otherwise the fall-out will be extensive to the people who live in the neighbourhood.'

The next photo on the board was of the country's president Raimundo Esposito. The photo showed a friendly looking man with a big smile. This was obviously a promotional photo from one of his campaigns. If you looked closer you saw the intensity in his eyes and his smile seemed crooked, or at the least very cosmetic. His friendliness was skin-deep, if even that. He looked to be in his late fifties or early sixties, his hair a very distinguished grey. A man comfortable in his pose.

'El Presidente. He will be the last on our list. Esposito is heavily protected and hardly ever comes out of his palace. We must undermine his confidence and his influence by taking care of the others first. With the demise of his lieutenants and the absence of finances he will lose the cooperation of the mercenaries quickly and become more vulnerable.' Joaquin paused to drink a little water.

He moved on; 'this is Sebastian Herrera.' Joaquin pointed to the next photo. The print was of a long-faced man with a dark complexion. His visage was heavily pockmarked and made him look older than his years, the scars were more prolific near his right eye. 'He is a minister in Esposito's government and takes care of all the communication with the Americanos. He is the official liaison. If we take him out, we will disrupt the line of support from America.'

He paused for a moment then turned to the final photo. A handsome man—forty-something—with a dark complexion and black hair. His smile was superficial—painted on—his gaze intensive and frightening. He was impeccably dressed and could have been mistaken for a movie star. Throwing more photos on the table Joaquin continued his narrative, his voice laden with pent up revulsion and anger. 'And this is our final target, Alejandras Ortiz. He is going to be the most difficult to reach.'

The silence was complete. Tonal had heard of this monster, the stories penetrated even deep down in the jungle. He was legendary—the stuff of nightmares. Elena closed her eyes at the mention of the name—there was a lot of hurt there, the tension was palatable.

'He is also the most important of all. His power is second only to El Presidente's, maybe even more in certain regions. This man is a monster. He regularly massacres whole villages, just to make a point. He employs the scum of the earth to do his dirty work, even though he actively participates in the murders himself. The man is a sadist. But he is also very intelligent and extremely careful. His home is a fortress, surrounded by difficult terrain, supposedly protected by wild animals as well as the mercenaries. He will be a challenge. We must plan his demise well. To fail is not an option. His retribution will be unbelievable. I welcome ideas if anyone has any.'

The council was silent. The atmosphere in the tent had gone cold. Everyone was obviously touched by the photos that were passed around. Dulce gasped and quickly pushed them into Tonal's hands. Her face was pale, and she tried her best not to gag.

Tonal lowered her eyes to the prints that upset Dulce so much and observed the scenes they portrayed. Chills moved up and down her spine. The snapshots were exceptionally bloody and vicious. Men and women staked on wooden poles set up-right along a road. The agony was clearly visible in their faces and showed they had been alive when this was done. In another photo three mercenaries posed next to a pile of corpses, laughing and holding up the decapitated head of a young girl. A third image was of the intended target Ortiz as he held a machine gun in one hand and a bloody machete in the other, his foot on the hacked remains of what had once been a human and his camouflage shirt bright red with arterial blood. Thankfully the remaining photos were scenes of a mansion and the grounds around it.

'We do not need an answer or plan today but keep it in mind.' Joaquin sat down in his seat again.

Jesus resumed the discussion. 'Now we should start with the general plans for the bridges and roads.' He referred to one of the council members who led the reconnaissance parties. The council immediately started to plan the actions they would take.

The meeting lasted all evening, only interrupted by the entrance of food and drinks. By eleven o'clock at night they had detailed plans for two missions, and the basics for three more. During the meeting no more attention was given to the assassinations. This would be done at a later date.

Alex and Dulce led Tonal to a tent further on in the compound. She would share it with Dulce.

'Thank you Tonal.' Alex held her close. 'Thank you for coming.'

'You're welcome, Alex. You were right, there was no

chance I would be able to ignore what is happening. I don't know how much help I can be, but we'll see, won't we.'

'Oh, I think your special talents will come in very handy.' Alex smiled.

'Will someone please tell me what these special talents are?' Dulce exclaimed totally frustrated.

'Soon Sis, very soon.'

Chapter Forty-Three

Alex caught up with Tonal in the afternoon of the following day. They had not been able to speak with each other in private yet and he had a bundle of questions to ask.

'It's good to see you again Tonal. I have often wondered how you were and what you were doing.' They were seated in the shade of a large tree, far enough from others not to be overheard. Dulce was accompanying some other women into the small town nearby where the revolutionaries bought the few supplies they needed. For the most, the compound was self-sufficient. But some small items still needed to be purchased elsewhere.

'What happened after you left us?'

She settled down with her back to the tree and told her story.

'I travelled down to the valley you described. It took me about two days. I was in no hurry. It just felt great to finally let the whole change come over me. I was enjoying it immensely.' Alex had never seen the whole change, but his father described it to him and his mother after Tonal left so suddenly.

'The valley was very comfortable. I found the stream and there was more than enough wildlife to sustain me. I stayed there for about six or seven months, I think. Then I decided to go further south and found a really nice place near a deserted village. As I said, I lived in one of the houses and found out why it had been deserted when the fire ants came.' She chuckled. 'Even I don't appreciate red fire ants. They sting.'

'So, like I told you in the jungle, I went back to the caves in the haunted valley. I tried to stay as far from people as possible, because I didn't really trust myself not to hurt them. I even tried to scare them away for a while. But they're tough, these people. They don't scare easily.'

'Julio informed the elders of the village.' Alex explained. 'He assured them that you would not hurt them and that you actually needed people nearby whatever you may think.'

'Well that explains a lot,' Tonal replied 'Now I know why they didn't seem surprised when they were faced with the cat.' She smiled. She had expected something like this. Leave that kind of thing to Julio. 'I finally started interacting with the villagers after the mercenaries entered the area, more than a year after I first came to the caves.'

'Were these the same ones we saw in the stream? The General's son and the others?'

'Yes, the same four men.'

'Do I have to ask what happened to them?'

'Not really. I killed them. They'd kidnapped a couple from the village and forced them to guide the group to where I lived. They killed the man and were about to rape the woman, so I intervened. Later I brought the woman back to the village. You met her there; Marianna—the matriarch of the village. After that, the villagers would sometimes leave supplies for me in the clearing where I found you. Occasionally Marianna would be there and would wait until I showed myself. We would talk, and she would bring me up to speed on the news they had of the outside world. She helped me through some difficult times when I really started to lose my way. Marianna is not scared of the cat. She is much like Julio in that respect. I suppose she's seen me at my worst—when I killed the mercenaries— so all else was less imposing.' She had fond memories of the tenacious woman. Now that was a woman who really didn't take "NO" for an answer. Tonal laughed at the memory.

'I stayed in the area and got more and more familiar with my "special talents". There were ups and downs. Times that I thought I would drown in the blood and killing urges. I sequestered myself in the caves for weeks on end. I hardly ate, didn't do anything but feel sorry for myself, I guess. A red haze descended on everything I did or thought. Once again Marianna hauled me out if it. She left me food at the mouth of the cave and stayed there for a whole day and night until I finally showed myself. I was wild then, but still she stayed put. She talked to me, like a mother talks to a child. She reassured me that I would not hurt her, that I could control this. Slowly, very slowly her words started to sink in. When I came out of the cave I was partially changed, I must have looked frightening. But she persevered. She stayed with me for three days. Slowly I reverted back to human form and finally spoke to her. We talked for a long time. After that she left and told me to come to the village within the next few days.'

Alex saw that the story still had an emotional impact on Tonal.

'I didn't dare to go to the village. But Marianna's belief and blind trust pushed me there anyway. I didn't want to disappoint her. So finally, I dressed, picked up the little self-esteem I had left, and walked into the village.'

'Marianne was waiting for me at the entrance to the village, her young child on her arm. She welcomed me, introduced me to a lot of people and basically organised a party to celebrate my visit. It was so unexpected. So foreign to what I had thought would happen. Initially it frightened me, but I was soon caught up in the enthusiasm and genuine friendship these people radiated. I only stayed at the village until the next day. Then I left. Baby steps. But Marianna steadfastly included me in festivities and looked me up. My visits to them became more and more frequent and lasted longer. We have basically looked out for each other since.'

'Were there other visitors in those long years?'

'Jesus came to visit once, after I had been there for about three years. He stayed for a few hours. Other than that, most of the visitors were the General's family, or others that were linked to him. I believe I must have killed about four or five direct members of his clan in these years. Them, and a multitude of mercenaries that accompanied them. They don't seem to be able to get it in their thick skulls that they cannot kill me, however much they may want to.'

She was silent for a while.

'After each confrontation, I descended into a deep depression.' It was clear it was difficult for her to talk about. 'I felt immersed in the blood. I wanted to keep on killing. It took every bit of my restraint not to. I isolated myself in the caves or once even miles away, just to make sure that I didn't accidentally kill anyone from the village. Slowly, I managed to gain control and feel safe again.'

'Does this happen when you are the cat? Is it related?'

'No, I don't think it has much to do with the change. More with what I kill. As the cat, and sometimes as a human, I kill to eat, mostly animals in the forest, but then only what I need and to survive. It happens when I kill humans.'

'But it was to protect yourself,' Alex exclaimed.

'I know, that is how I explain it to myself as well. But sometimes it is not just self-preservation. With one of the attacks, I went much too far to keep it under the semblance of self-defence.'

Reliving the attack was an effort.

'There were six of them: five men and a woman. I think the leader was the General's brother or something like that. The resemblance was striking, and he was of about the same age, maybe two or three years younger. It was the first time they really wounded me extensively. I was shot four times. One bullet pierced my left lung. I managed to crawl into the jungle to heal but it took a long time, more than twenty-four hours. The damage was considerable. While I recuperated, I became more and more angry. They continued to hunt me in the jungle but couldn't find me. I turned the tables on them. The hunter became the hunted. I picked them off one by one and made sure they saw what happened to their comrades. It was frightening, unbelievably vicious. The last two to go were the General's brother and another man. I cornered them in a valley that ran into a dead end, a high cliff. There was no way they could escape. I wounded the General's brother and incapacitated him. Then I played with his friend. Like a cat plays with a mouse. Finally, when he died hours later, I turned my attention to the last one alive. What he had seen, and the fear he was under, drove him insane. He was foaming at the mouth and screaming. I killed him but felt cheated because his insanity robbed me of my pleasure.'

She looked Alex in the eye.

'I enjoyed the killing. It is not a feeling I get when I hunt animals, only when I hunt humans. This scares me, Alex. I don't know what you want me to do to help you but know what you ask. Please keep in mind the risks, and what may happen.'

'You shouldn't continue to batter yourself like this. Like my father and Marianna, I have faith in you and that you are able to distinguish between friend and foe. What you did with the people that attacked you was necessary. You had to kill them to be able to stay alive.'

'Yes Alex, I had to kill them. But I didn't have to enjoy it.'

Chapter Forty-Four

I found the first few days in the compound stressful. I wasn't used to having all these people around me: the noise, the smells, the nearness and lack of privacy.

At first, they tried to include me in the conversations. But it was forced and didn't feel right. After a few days most of the revolutionaries just left me alone. I was somewhat of an anomaly. The hermit who had lived in the jungle for so long. But who miraculously looked no older than thirty-five.

How was that possible?

Superstition was rife in the Latin countries and the revolutionaries were no exception. This strange woman who walked barefoot through the compound and had the ear of the council—of Jesus—was frightening for most of them. They had heard the rumours. That I somehow had a connection to the long white scars on Alex's arms.

That I was a killer.

I kept myself to myself and only occasionally spoke to others than Alex, Jesus and Dulce.

Having to be careful was so foreign to me that it cost all

my concentration. My senses were much more astute than those of the revolutionaries, that meant that I could hear visitors arrive before the sentries alerted the compound. Instead of alerting them to the coming visitors, I decided to ignore the signs and keep myself as low key as possible. Blending in was not really an option, so I just tried to attract as little attention as possible. But it was hard. Things that came naturally to me were totally scary for others.

I was so much stronger than even the largest man in the compound. If I helped them with anything it meant I had to keep myself in check all the time and constantly pretend not to be any stronger or more sensitive than any of the others.

Because I was so used to life alone, it took a lot of energy.

More than I wanted.

I yearned for the peace of the jungle.

But I had committed to this—at least to see what I could do.

So, I persevered. But it cost me.

I wasn't used to taking others into account. Life in such close quarters meant that everything was shared. There was no privacy. I suppose that was what irritated me most. That, and the fact that I couldn't change when I wanted to. After the breach of security when I strode into the compound, the guards were adamant I would not leave their sight. There was always at least one of them on my shadow. I commented this to Alex, who laughed and pointed out I only had myself to thank for that. I suppose he was right.

Alex stayed as close to me as humanly possible.

It was twenty-three years ago—all over again. His crush obviously survived the test of time.

At first, I was surprised he was still single. A man like

that should have been snatched up by someone years ago. He must be the most eligible bachelor in the compound. When I asked him about it, he laughed and said he was just too busy, and never got around to a regular life.

But I saw more than that in his eyes.

He had been waiting, waiting for the impossible.

Waiting for me.

It was cute really, flattering. But it was a complication, one I didn't need. I would have to do something about that sooner or later. Set the boundaries. Make it clear.

On the other hand, I enjoyed his company.

He always smiled, laughed a lot and was genuinely interested in me. He asked questions all the time about how I had lived, what my thoughts and plans were. He was also very open about his life, his goals. He wanted to help the people. Make sure everyone had at least a good chance at survival and a reasonable life. Alex was an idealist, but not naïve. He wanted to save the world but realised he would have to start small. His enthusiasm was contagious and soon enough I found myself caught up in his ideals and his plans.

Ever present was the memory of Julio.

'We never managed to get his killer,' Alex remarked one day when we were sitting with our backs to a rock in a small clearing, enjoying the warm rays of the autumn sun. 'We have a good idea who it was, or anyway which group of mercenaries. But they are hard to get near to. At least if you want to get back again.' He laughed half-heartedly.

'So, who was it?'

'We think the mercenaries that are in Ortiz's employ,' he continued. 'They lured part of our advance group into an ambush, killing most of the party, fatally wounding my father.'

I stayed silent.

'Thankfully it was quick. He was hit by a bullet near to his heart. We dragged him out of the battle, but he died soon after. Two of the others were less lucky. We heard their screams for more than twenty-four hours.' His head lowered in shame. 'There was nothing we could do about it to help them. We were so outnumbered and outgunned.'

I reached out and took his hand, he squeezed mine gratefully.

'It would have been suicide,' he continued with a sigh. 'We returned to the site late the next day, after the mercenaries left. They crucified our comrades and skinned the two wounded alive.' I felt the tremors that racked his body as he relived that day. 'There was one woman among the dead. I can't tell you what they did to her. It still haunts me. I'm just so glad she was dead first.' I could see the tears collecting in the corner of his eye.

His other hand moved over mine and he held on tight. He was probably not aware of the way he stroked the top of my fingers. Alex turned his head and looked me in the eye. He freed one hand and reached up to cup my chin.

'It's so good to see you again Tonal. I missed you so much. Somehow, I knew I would see you again.' His fingers traced the side of my face up to the outer edge of my eyes. 'Your beautiful eyes have been in my dreams for so long.'

We were silent.

What was there to say?

For a minute there I thought he was going to kiss me.

I don't really know what I would have done if he had. I was getting carried away by the emotions of Julio's death and the moment.

I probably wouldn't have stopped him.

But instead, he put his arm over my shoulder and pulled me close, turning back to the sun.

'I'm so glad you're here, I just wish it were for different reasons.' I rested my head on his shoulder. It felt good. We sat there like that for a while. His presence and close company comforted me. It felt so natural. Somehow, he made me feel good. I knew my feelings for him didn't measure up to how he felt about me. But for now, it felt good, and I was reluctant to let the moment pass. He seemed to know too and was content with the closeness and physical contact.

Soon we would have to talk about this—our relationship.

What it was and where it was going. I couldn't string him on like this. I had to bring it out in to the open, call it what it was.

But not now, not today.

Chapter Forty-Five

The first two attacks went off without a single problem.

The resistance devastated a bridge vital to the supply lines. It was wrecked beyond repair; the pieces fell into the wild river it spanned. To build a new rigid bridge would be a great challenge for the military, but they would have to, the fast-moving water prevented the use of floating bridges. It would prove to be a major setback for the enemy. The second target was a heavily used runway, the main artery for the transportation of cocaine out of the jungle. No planes would land there in the near future.

The attacks were part of the main offensive of the combined revolutionary groups and achieved the desired effect. By attacking multiple targets at the same time, they managed to keep the military racing around totally unstructured. Inevitably, retaliation by the government was centred on the civilians that supported the revolutionaries. Villages were targeted by the mercenaries employed by most of the big landowners and the government. Justly in fear for their lives, people fled into the jungle, where most of them joined the revolution. The density of the jungle protected them, at least for now.

After the initial assaults, the military stepped up its security on the main supply lines. It became almost impossible to launch an attack from close quarters and the revolutionaries lacked long distance weapons. They focused their attention on the first three human targets: Flores, his daughter and son in law.

The synchronisation of the assassinations was essential to their success.

Flores was less protected than the Reyes family, so the strongest team was sent to the husband-and-wife targets. Dulce was sent with a small group to bomb the Flores mansion now that his wife was out of the country. The second group, including Alex and Tonal focused on Domminga and Rolando Reyes. The assassinations were set for the middle of the night at around two a.m. The terminations had to be finished before the morning, preferably earlier.

Alex and Tonal finalised the details on the edge of the Reyes property. She would change and enter the grounds as the cat. It was her task to take care of the couple as they slept. The cat would be able to gain access where people couldn't.

Tonal jumped over the electrified fence and entered the grounds. A loud bark heralded the presence of dogs—quite big ones judging by the pitch of the sound. She moved stealthily through the scrub and trees and saw the house.

The large two-story building was very attractive. The Adobe style combined easily with the space that the two floors created. Hanging baskets on the balconies added to the friendly image, their smell quite heady in the midnight air.

The guards patrolled the outskirts of the mansion in a sequence of rounds. They passed her line of sight every ten minutes. They looked uninterested as they talked to each other while they walked. They didn't take notice of their surroundings or the dogs. Reyes would not be amused if he knew about this lack of dedication, mind you, after tonight —if all went well—he wouldn't care. No one would.

A car pulled up to the front of the house which caused the guards to stand to attention. An obviously drunk Domminga was supported by her husband as she staggered into the house. A few minutes later a light went on in one of the upstairs windows. It was consistent with the information Joaquin had amassed. This was their bedroom. It was also where Tonal was headed. After frenzied lovemaking, the couple turned off the lights and went to sleep.

The night was quiet while Tonal waited. She heard the soft sounds of nocturnal animals far away. Even the dogs decided to sleep.

Sure enough, the guards kept up their rounds, though they took slightly longer and were quieter—probably afraid that Reyes might hear them.

The air was nice and cool, welcome to her fur after the heat of the day. Humidity was reasonable, so the wait was pleasant.

Soon soft snoring came from the open balcony doors of the couple's room.

Cautiously she made her way to the house and kept to the shadows as much as possible. One great leap placed her on the balcony. However, The soft thud of her padded paws landing had been heard.

Rolando listened attentively. He had been sleeping, but something woke him. It wasn't really a conscious sound that he recognised, but all the same it was enough to put him on edge. He threw back the duvet and placed his feet on the thick carpet. His left hand searched for the pistol that he kept next to his pillow. Assassination attempts were frequent. Totally sure of his own prowess, he declined to wake his wife or call for the bodyguards. It was probably nothing and he didn't want to look stupid. Machismo was everything to him. He was the king of this domain—the most vicious one. He would take care of it, if there was anything there. He stood up and moved his impressive bulk towards the open balcony doors. Flexing his muscles as he went.

There were no more sounds, but still he wanted to be sure.

Tonal crouched in the deep shadows to the left of the balcony doors. The foot falls on the carpet were loud to her sensitive ears. She waited for Rolando to come to her. The soft snores of Domminga in the background were a clear signal she was still sleeping off her drunken stupor.

Chapter Forty-Six

Cautiously Rolando made his way out on to the balcony, his eyes trained on the area between the trees and the house. His arrogance prevented him from contemplating that someone may already be closer.

Tonal waited until he stood close to the balcony wall and then silently rose from her hiding place. His instinct must have hit in—he turned and raised the gun. Shock registered in his face, his eyes bulged, and his mouth opened to call out. No sound came, so big was his surprise and fear. He expected a man, not an enormous feline. Without hesitation she launched herself at him, closed her jaws on his throat and guaranteed his silence. He fell backwards and dropped the gun. His feeble attempts to dislodge her from his neck and chest failed miserably. She held on, bit down and broke the vertebra. His eyes turned in their sockets and he was still.

Tonal slowly left her kill and listened intently for sounds that anyone had heard the struggle. Nothing stirred.

She missed something. When she turned around to enter the bedroom, she realised what it was, the snores.

As soon as she set foot in the room Domminga attacked her. Brandishing a large machete-like knife, the woman screamed defiance and lunged at the cat, opening a large gash on its side. With renewed energy she pulled her arm back to lunge at the intruder again. Tonal saw her chance and swiped her outstretched claws over the woman's exposed throat and ripped it out. Domminga dropped the knife and grabbed helplessly at her neck, the fountain of blood splattering everything bright red.

It was over almost before it started, but the damage had been done.

Guards congregated at the bedroom in reaction to their mistresses' cries. The door flew open, and two guards rushed into the room. They stopped in mid-stride when they saw the unbelievable scene in front of them. There was blood everywhere: on the bed, the curtains, the walls. A daemon lion bigger than anything in their worst night-mares, stood over the blood drenched body of Domminga. A glance to the balcony confirmed their fears. Reyes body lay unmoving in its own steadily expanding pool of blood. One of the guards raised his gun, the monster roared, and any remnant of courage deserted them. They turned as one and ran out of the room screaming.

Tonal chose the balcony for her escape. There were guards outside—she could hear them—but it was the quickest and surest way out of the building.

Counting on surprise she bounded out of the room and on to the balcony. She roared as she launched herself off the balcony into the surprised group below. Panic and terror were visible on their faces, they crawled and stumbled to get away from the monster that had exited the room.

Tonal took advantage of the chaos, ran into the jungle and escaped almost without injury. One of the guards fired his machine gun wildly and a bullet had ricochet off a metal flower pole. It grazed her back leg—an irritation—not enough to slow her down. She cleared the high fence and made her way to where she had left the revolutionaries.

The sight of the bloodied cat was more than the men could take and the guns were levied on her. The colour in their faces vanished when she strode into the small clearing. Obviously, she had killed something, she was covered in blood. They saw her change before the assassination, but nothing prepared them for this nightmare vision. Her muzzle and paws were bright red, there were two cuts down her side, both of them already closing. Her intense gaze and Alex's somewhat tentative 'It's okay' barely convinced them to lower their weapons. They did so slowly—just in case.

She changed back into human form and wiped the blood from her mouth with her right arm. Grabbing one of the bottles of water she washed the grime off her face and hands, then gurgled the rest of the water to get rid of the coppery taste of Rolando's blood. She would never get used to human blood. The sickly sweet and metallic substance still assailed her senses.

Tonal turned to the revolutionaries and saw the shock and disbelief in their faces. It was one thing to talk about the assassination. It was totally something else to see the result so dramatically. She remained silent as she dressed in the clothes Alex held out for her.

'I take it that it is done?' Alex asked. She looked at him and nodded.

No more was said as they gathered their things and left the clearing, in the hope that Dulce's group had achieved the same level of success. The morning brought good news.

The other group also managed to kill both the target and his two sons. That combined with the success of the Reyes' assassinations effectively cut off the family's power. Already they heard terrifying rumours and tales of the monster that killed the Reyes. Superstition would aid the impact of the killings.

The revolutionaries who had accompanied Alex and Tonal on the raid remained silent about what had taken place. They all agreed it was for the best. Leave the actual details out and let the rumours and superstition do their work. The rest of the council was unaware of the exact extent of her talents. Tonal wanted to keep it that way. Even if it meant constant bickering with Dulce, who didn't appreciate being kept in the dark.

Her time would come.

Chapter Forty-Seven

We neared the climax, or what we thought of as the pinnacle of the struggle. It was time to take Ortiz out of the picture. The fact that he was probably responsible for Julio's death only strengthened our resolve.

But it would be no picnic. The man was seriously paranoid—and with reason.

His actions earned him the hatred of everyone who crossed his path. He killed without any semblance of empathy. Sparing only those beneficial to his cause. He left a legacy of bodies and blood behind him. Money and fear were the only things that kept him alive, and he had enough of both. Rich beyond measure, he was a ruthless psychopath. He kept his hold on the people and the rulers with vicious commitment and mercenaries who followed his every whim.

To go up against him was dangerous, but necessary. He had to be taken out of the picture. Even more important to the cause than El Presidente himself, taking Ortiz down was the pinnacle of our effort.

We thought up many different plans and dismissed most because of the extreme danger and only slight chance of success. One stood up to the measure. But it wasn't simple or safe. It was however the only option we had.

Dulce and I would infiltrate the tyrant's inner circle.

He was a known womaniser. Always looking for his next conquest. He favoured long legged exotic looking women. Mostly American or European. That was my cue. With my strange, ochre-coloured eyes, long auburn hair and—if I may say so myself—fantastic figure, I was sure to attract his attention. If, that was, I managed to get anywhere near him.

We thought up a plan. Something that was sure to interest him.

The initial story was put in place, complete with Internet and cloud manipulation to show my history and support the story we would spin. It was a scam—a big one. I was an international jet set figure on the search for potential business opportunities in Latin America. Bored with America and my home country in Europe, I craved challenges and was looking to new countries to satisfy my hunger. My history showed I was ruthless. I broke hearts and lives everywhere I went. I annihilated everything that got in my way. Because of a legal and personal hassle in Italy, I'd decided to move my headquarters to the southern Americas; to a town fifty miles from Ortiz's stronghold.

I specialised in exploiting the weak. That was bound to appeal to Ortiz. My company was built on the backs of the farmers around me. I bought their products for ridiculous prices, while I promised all kinds of extra benefits from housing to education for the children. When it came my turn to honour the contracts, I pointed out the small print and the farmers were backed into the corner.

It hurt to have to do this, but we recorded all the takings

and pledged to repay the farmers with interest after we'd managed to get rid of Ortiz. It was regrettable that we could not inform them, but we needed to keep up appearances. The scam required absolute secrecy and total authenticity to be successful. There were even rumours I'd ordered the brutal murder of one competitor and ruined many more.

It made for intriguing rumours.

Thankfully that was all they were.

Alex looked me up. He was anxious. The plan involved Dulce and me getting very close to Ortiz. This was an enormous worry for him: his sister and the love of his life.

Chapter Forty-Eight

Alex, Dulce and I travelled into the jungle. We stopped at a small cliff that was easily scalable for me, but quite a challenge for the others.

It was time to take out Ortiz. Besides the President, he was the only one left on the list of targets.

My undercover personage had finally gotten his attention. We'd taken our time because the story needed to be fool proof. The man was a monster, and any mistake on our part—however small—would be terminal. For the others, for me it would be unpleasant at the least.

Dulce and I cultivated a cover as a wealthy young businesswoman and her servant. My role was of an arrogant European woman, who terrorised her employees, or more appropriately—her slaves. The cover story was that she literally purchased them. Dulce was the personal assistant bought from her family long ago and brought up in the woman's mansion. I regularly pretended to abuse Dulce in public to consolidate the image. It wasn't real but looked authentic.

Ortiz was even better protected than the presidential couple. Quite understandable if you considered his reign of terror and the number of enemies he'd racked up in the past years. He was a very dangerous man without any semblance of a conscience who was led by his short-term lusts. In summary, he was a psychopath with limitless power. They don't get any scarier than that.

Ortiz fancied himself to be a Casanova. His taste was split into two kinds of women: the disposable ones—the prettiest of the peasants who died when he tired of them—and the trophy women. Tall, beautiful women with a status of their own. Preferably Caucasian and powerful. Though beauty was more important than power. His kind of soul-mate would be someone as scrupulous and vicious as the man himself. So that was my cover.

We determined how we would get into the fortress.

I would seduce him and take Dulce with me as hand-maiden. A woman of my stature traveling alone would arouse suspicion, so I needed a servant. Then, when we were finally alone, I would kill him, and we would escape.

That last part was thought out to the most miniscule detail. Today we travelled to this place to practice our escape.

Still unaware of the details of my special talents, Dulce had no idea how we would be able to exit the heavily guarded fortress after we'd fulfilled our task. She'd seen some of the results of my abilities that puzzled her but was still kept in the dark as to what had really happened. Today she would finally find out.

'This will do,' I said to Alex. 'This cliff resembles the high wall and moat at the fortress.' I dropped my pack and took off my jacket. The temperature was reasonable and thankfully it was dry. My two companions followed my lead and dropped their gear.

Dulce sat on a large rock. 'What's the use of practicing. There is no way we'll be able to get out. The wall is our least worry.'

She accepted that this would be her last mission, that she would sacrifice herself for the good cause. I had no such predisposition. We would get out and live to fight another day.

'The moat is filled with man-eating lions. If we don't kill ourselves in the building or on the wall, there's no way that we will be able to get past them,' she added. 'The moat extends for about three miles. We might be able to fool the lions for a minute, but after that we are like lambs to the slaughter.' Dulce looked at me, resignation in her eyes.

'I have no intention of dying,' I answered. 'Or of getting you killed. We leave through the moat, and I don't expect too many problems.'

She shrugged, not believing what I said. The whole situation amused Alex. He was no great fan of the idea of Dulce accompanying me into the fortress, but he knew there was no other way. I could not have a male servant. That would complicate things too much. And Dulce was petit and more important light, which was a necessity for our plan.

'Don't be so pessimistic, Sis.' Placing his hand on her shoulder he continued, 'besides, today you finally find out what is so special about Tonal. What her talents are. Cause you will need them to get out.' The mention of my special talents got her attention. Now that was the Dulce I knew. Her curiosity was killing her. It had been for a long time.

'Finally,' she exclaimed to Alex's laughter and my smiles. She proceeded to stand up, but Alex stopped her.

'You might want to stay seated, Sis. Get something solid under you.'

I walked a few feet away from them into the light and started to take off my clothes. The look on Dulce's face was priceless. She became more and more confused.

'Watch carefully,' Alex cautioned her. She turned to face me again. I was naked now and poised to change. Alex and I'd agreed I would take my time—not change too quickly—so she could appreciate what happened.

Slowly I started the process and watched her reaction all the time.

Her eyes opened to their limit, almost popped out of her head. Her mouth fell open.

Chapter Forty-Nine

While he kept his hand on Dulce's shoulders, Alex watched the change. He never tired of seeing the miracle every time she took feline form, enthralled by the beauty and raw power of the change. He felt the tension build in Dulce. Her body was poised, ready to run, but she was too fascinated and captivated to move.

What she saw was too warped and too fantastic to be true. Dulce sat open mouthed, hardly breathing. She took in every change and yet still couldn't register what happened. Her mind shut down; survival kicked in and convinced her this was some kind of visual trick. It wasn't possible. It couldn't be happening, defied everything, and yet... ... In some strange way, it fit. Fit with all the things that'd happened in the short time since this woman had been their companion. Fit with the unbelievable inexplicable things she some way—somehow—did.

The change was completed, and the massive cat sat on its haunches as it calmly regarded the two people.

The sun chose that precise moment to appear dramati-

cally from behind the clouds and shine a bright ray on her
—like a spotlight. It completed the moment.

No one spoke or moved for a while.

'Well, sis. What do you think?' Alex spoke softly, so as
not to startle Dulce's already frayed nerves.

Finding her voice again Dulce answered. 'That's some
talent.'

Alex doubled up laughing. It was so typically Dulce.
Slowly she regained her composure, calmed by the obvious
ease with which Alex dealt with this strange and fascinating
moment. Finally, Alex's laugh subsided to a chuckle.

'Come on Dulce, your curiosity must be killing you.
Let's go say hallo.' He walked in the direction of the cat.

Dulce hesitated and weighed the possibilities. She could
be killed and devoured by this animal, but then again, it was
her friend, or anyway it used to be. Or, nothing would
happen, and she could find out more about this unbelievable experience. As her brother so clearly noticed, the
suspense and her curiosity were overpowering. She
shrugged, decided to go for it and slowly walked towards the
two beings in the clearing.

The cat followed her progress with its eyes. Dulce swore
it was smiling, it laughed at her, like Alex. This spurred her
on. She stopped three feet from the feline and really
observed what was in front of her—a massive lion-like cat.
Big as a horse, at least five-foot tall at the shoulder. Tawny
brown with a hint of stripes on her shoulders and back. The
head was enormous, with slightly ruffled long hair along the
side. Not exactly a mane, more like the cheek fur on a
Siberian tiger. The cat's eyes were intense, ochre-yellow and
piercing. They looked into her soul. But she recognised the
strange colour Tonal had in human form.

Without a conscious intention, her hand moved as if to

stroke the cat's fur. Suddenly she realised what she was about to do, quickly pulled her arm back and hid it behind her back. She turned bright red—this was definitely not a house cat. It was completely something else.

'It's okay, Sis. She doesn't mind if you touch her, actually, she quite likes it.' Alex put actions to his words, placed his hands on either side of the cat's big head and moved his face towards her nose and muzzle. A strange rough sound came from the cat's throat.

Surprised and unbelieving Dulce exclaimed. 'Is she purring?'

'Yes,' Alex answered. 'She does that.' He turned his head to his sister, the cat followed suit. 'Give me your hand, come on.'

Slowly Dulce took another step forward, and another one and hesitantly extended her hand. Alex took her sweaty fingers in his and moved her closer to the cat. He placed Dulce's hand on the cat's shoulder. Held it there for a moment, then let go.

Dulce was fascinated. The feeling was unexplainable. The fur was soft and warm, the muscles beneath hard and massive. The power obvious. She couldn't believe this was really happening. It was all too much. Slowly tears left the corners of her eyes and ran down her cheeks. Disgusted with her excessive emotionality, she roughly rubbed them away with her left hand while she kept her right one on the soft animal, not able to take it away. The silence comforted her in a way. She took another step closer and took in the wild smell she'd smelled before.

The scene stayed that way for a few moments. It was finally broken when the big cat lowered itself to a more comfortable position. Alex and Dulce followed suit and sat down on the grass.

'I'm sorry you couldn't know, but there are people after Tonal,' Alex broke the silence.

'It's okay,' was all Dulce could bring herself to say, too preoccupied with the situation.

'This is probably the best kept secret in the world as we know it,' he joked. 'Papa wanted me to keep it that way. It has been difficult, especially since she has been helping us. People see the result of her talents, and they are hard to explain.' Slowly his words were getting through to Dulce.

'This is why Papa asked us to find her.' Understanding flooded her senses. 'How he got out of the lab in the first place. I knew she was strong, but this... this... is just too fantastic to believe.'

'Well, believe it, Sis, because this is what is going to get you out of Ortiz's fortress.'

'How?' She understood now why the lions would be less of a problem than she initially thought. But that was for Tonal, she couldn't replicate the bizarre metamorphosis.

Alex answered her questions for her, 'on her back.'

'What!' she exclaimed. This was ridiculous. How could she? You don't just get on a lion's back and ride out into the sunset.

'You heard me, on her back. You will ride her out of the fortress. Not like on a horse, but flat on her back so as not to hinder her progress. She will have to jump over the wall and needs excellent balance.'

He wasn't even smiling, so tentatively she started to accept what he implied. The idea was out of this world, but still maybe the only way that she would be able to fulfil the mission and live to tell the tale. Truth be told, she wasn't really ready to sacrifice herself. Life was too interesting to lose right now. Besides, she was still young and had so much to do and experience. So maybe—just maybe—this was an option.

'How would that work?' she asked softly. The cat turned its head towards her and rubbed its cheek against her hand. Obviously, she'd made the right choice. At least according to her friend.

'Good decision, Sis.' Alex was serious, all fun and games over now. This was a matter of life or death for his little sister. His whole life he'd taken care of her, looked out for her, and now here he was, planning a mission that was so dangerous and so downright suicidal he actually contemplated letting her ride a massive predator through a moat with man-eating lions.

He was either mad or desperate. Actually, his desperation, and that of the revolution was out of this world. The only way to get the final phase in the war going, was to get rid of Ortiz. And this was the only way to do it. Ortiz had survived more attempts on his life than he had eaten warm meals. At least once a week someone would try. Some even got so far as to wound him. Regrettably not severely and definitely nowhere near fatally. The repercussions were out of proportion. Whole villages were wiped out because one of their own was part of the conspiracy. Families were put to death in the most violent, most atrocious and brutal ways. Mothers watched while their children were fed to the lions. Some even jumped over the wall in a desperate attempt to shield their babies. All the time they were accompanied by the mad laughs and jeers of the lunatic Ortiz and his mercenaries.

And that was where he was sending his baby sister.

He was dying inside. The revolution was his responsibility. Not only his of course, they were all in this together, but they looked to him for leadership. He and Jesus made the final decisions on what to attack, where, when and by whom. He knew she was the best—no, the only person—for the job, together with Tonal.

They had tried to get to Ortiz for so long and finally there was a chance.

But Dulce? Did it have to be her? He wanted to stop her, veto the whole thing.

Tonal would be able to get out, she would be okay. But Dulce was mortal, and she was his family, his little sister. She was so petit, so young, so small, so fragile… … so stubborn, so strong, so competent. And she would not take "no" for an answer. Even from him, scratch that—especially not from him. He might as well resign himself to the situation. He would not win this fight. She was determined. He watched her as she in turn observed the turmoil boiling inside of him.

'I'll be okay,' she read his mind 'Tonal will take care of me.'

'I know,' he finally managed to say. 'She won't come back without you, and besides you are very capable of taking care of yourself. Still, we had better start to practice.' They stood up. Tonal stayed in her relaxed position.

'So how do I position myself?' Dulce was all attention. 'How am I supposed to sit?'

Alex motioned her to sit on the cat's back, a little over halfway down. She lifted her right leg and straddled the enormous cat. Carefully she lowered herself until she sat on its broad back. It felt so strange. She was very nervous. The cat noticed and once again began its rhythmic deep purring. She took this as a good sign and placed her hands on the massive shoulders.

'Like this?'

Alex nodded. 'We discussed the possibilities last night.

We think it would be best if you lay down on her back. Yes, like that. Then hold on with your hands behind her front legs and brace your feet before her back legs.'

Dulce followed his directions. She couldn't get a grip with her feet, so she took off her shoes and socks. Bare footed she was able to find a more comfortable way of positioning het feet. She didn't dare to hold on too tight, fearful she would hurt Tonal. But so far there was no other reaction than the constant purring. It soothed her. Her face was pressed to the warm fur near the cat's shoulder, the rumble of the purring continuing into her body.

'You comfortable, Sis?' Alex asked.

'Yep, feeling good, bring it on.' Dulce was a good equestrian, having ridden horses from an early age. How different could this be?

Tonal stood up in one easy and flowing motion and almost dislodged Dulce, who immediately tightened her grip both with her hands and her feet. Still no reaction from Tonal, so she decided to keep the tight grip. Slowly the cat moved, step by step. Dulce was so tense that she almost fell off twice.

'Relax, Sis,' Alex cautioned her.

'Yeah right,' she answered. 'Relax, like I do this every day.'

Laughing, her brother added, 'close your eyes, just listen to her heartbeat. Let her do everything. Just trust her.' She looked at him incredulously. 'No really, close your eyes.' Reluctantly she complied. The cat continued to move around. 'Concentrate on her heartbeat, on the purring, forget everything else.'

She concentrated on the soothing sound of the purring and the big cat's heartbeat. The sound was loud, almost overwhelming. It quickly blocked out all other noises. With her eyes closed tightly she found she could shut the world out of her senses. She concentrated harder and slowly— very slowly— she felt her muscles relax and started moving totally in sync with those of her unnatural steed.

Tonal felt the tension ease. She continued to keep up the same slow tempo. When she was certain Dulce felt comfortable enough, she quickened her pace. The tension returned slightly but was gone again quickly as Dulce adapted.

They continued to practice for another half hour, while Tonal changed her speed at intervals. She stopped and lowered herself down to the ground. Reluctantly Dulce sat upright. She was extremely relaxed and hesitant to break the soothing contact. The ride had been so intense, so much more than she expected.

'That was great,' Alex broke the silence. 'Great for the first try. Looked like you got into the rhythm quickly.'

He had mixed feelings. On the one hand he was happy that things were going so well, and that Dulce took to riding Tonal so easily. On the other hand, he was jealous. Jealous of the close contact Dulce experienced with Tonal. Jealous of the absolute look of awe that shone in his sister's eyes. His feelings for Tonal hadn't diminished over the years they had been apart and being in such close contact again only served to rekindle the fire of his youth.

'It was unbelievable,' Dulce exclaimed. The cat almost nodded.

'This is just the beginning though, Tonal will have to move much faster, scale the wall and jump down to the other side. More practice is in order.'

Taking control of his conflicting emotions Alex got down to business—the best way to mask his internal turmoil. 'But first, let's eat.' He produced some bread and a piece of cheese from his backpack, Dulce retrieved a bottle of water from hers. Tonal stood up and strode into the jungle to get her own lunch.

Alex and Dulce went over the plan for the assassination again. For Dulce it now took on a whole new dimension. She was no longer resigned to her death that previously seemed inevitable. Now the whole mission took on a new sense of adventure. She found that she trusted Tonal without restraint. She was certain they would both escape and live to continue their work for the resistance.

Tonal stayed away for about an hour and returned around two o'clock in the afternoon, which left at least another four hours of light in which to practice. The two humans had made use of her absence and set up the small tent they would use for their stay. They'd decided not to rush things and stay at least another day.

They practiced long into the afternoon and early evening. Dulce was at first apprehensive, sometimes even frightened at the antics the huge cat performed when she jumped up and down the small cliff. But slowly she got used to the motions and learned to relax. The situation was mutual. Tonal had to adjust her balance to take the movements and weight of her rider into consideration. Jumps that were usually so simple posed a problem at the start. Her balance was totally out of synch. She herself was too tense, and the unexpected shifts in Dulce's weight unbalanced her. She almost jumped into the cliff wall the first time they tried. But as time passed, both she and Dulce relaxed and started to move as one. Dulce surrendered to her and followed every movement. Tonal hardly noticed her presence anymore by the time the sun had set.

Alex started a fire and was cooking a stew of some dried meat and vegetables when Tonal walked over to the tent. She stood still and allowed Dulce to dismount. The solid earth under her feet felt strange to Dulce, as did the lack of motion. She sat down next to the fire and was dismayed to see the big cat move off into the jungle again. 'Will she change back again today?' she asked her brother.

He shook his head. 'I don't think so,' he answered. 'The change costs a lot of energy and seeing as we will practice again tomorrow there is no use. Besides I think she enjoys this form too much and wants to stay like this as long as possible.'

'Why has she gone off into the jungle?' Now this was the old Dulce again. All questions.

'To catch something to eat probably, like I said, it takes a lot of energy, and she needs to replenish it.' As if on cue, they heard a commotion in the jungle off to the left of the clearing, followed by a mighty roar.

'Sounds like she found something edible,' Alex concluded. 'I'm still not happy about you going into the fortress with her, but seeing you work together at least soothes the anxiety a bit. At the end you looked like one being. You moved totally in sync with her.'

'I followed your advice,' his sister answered. 'Relaxed and listened to her heartbeat. After a while it all seemed so natural, however strange that may sound.'

They ate in silence, Dulce listened to the jungle and hoped Tonal would come back. Now she finally understood the significance of the name that her father had given this strange woman. In old Mayan legends Tonal was a protector who could take animal form, more specifically that of a jaguar. This was no jaguar. She was much too big and powerful even for the majestic South American predator. But the analogy was obvious and fitting.

'What's her real name?' she asked Alex. He had been

his father's right hand and confidant. If anyone, he would have been privy to that information.

'I don't know,' he surprised her with his answer. 'Even papa didn't know, I don't think. She has always been Tonal to all of us. Now that you mention it—it is strange.'

'Will she come back to the camp tonight now that she has eaten?'

'Probably not, but she will be watching over us, so get some sleep, we'll get an early start tomorrow. I must be back in the compound before sunset.'

They retired to the tent. Dulce crept into her sleeping bag and listened to the sounds of the jungle. She almost pinched herself—it was all too hard to believe that this had happened today. She found she was exhausted and quickly drifted off into a sound sleep, confident in the protection of the biggest and most powerful being she had ever seen.

Alex lay next to her and heard her breathing slow down as she slept. The turmoil inside him subsided a bit, but he missed Tonal. He wished she were here in the tent with him instead of his sister. An hour later he too fell asleep. The rhythmic breathing and occasional snoring of its residents was the only sound that emanated from the tent.

Tonal softly padded over to the tent and lay down near the dying fire opposite the opening. She would watch over them, as she had heard Alex say. They were in her world—they were her responsibility.

They were also her friends.

Chapter Fifty

The sunlight woke Dulce. She'd dreamt a lot in the night and was unsure about what was a dream and what actually happened.

She lay awake in the sleeping bag until her curiosity got the better of her. She couldn't wait to see if the whole practice had been a figment of her imagination and was rewarded by the sight of the giant cat apparently sleeping on the other side of what had been the fire. When she stood up out of the small tent opening it became apparent that Tonal was not asleep. She raised her head and purred a soft welcome.

'Hi Tonal,' Dulce answered.

She felt strange calling this magnificent creature by her friend's name. She walked over to the cat, sat down next to her and leant against the soft warmth. The jungle cooled off at night this time of the year and Dulce was grateful for the heat emanating from her friend. The big cat purred again, so she took this as a sign she didn't mind the close contact.

'I thought it was all a dream,' she whispered. 'Glad it isn't though.' They sat like that for a while until it became apparent Alex was awake too. He stumbled around in the tent as he tried to dress in the small, confined space. He knocked the pole over and had to rummage around to put it back in place and lift the tent material off his head, much to the amusement of his sister who laughed out loud.

Finally, accompanied by swears and mumbles, Alex exited the tent. His head was bright red from the exertion added with a bit of shame. He'd pestered his sister so often, now it was his turn to be on the receiving end.

'Charming Alex,' she rubbed in the salt. 'Really charming, and so graceful.'

'Can it,' was all he could think of to reply. This naturally only spurred her on and she creased over with laughter. Even Tonal seemed to join in the merriment. Disgusted, Alex wandered off into the trees to relieve himself, leaving Dulce to her laughs.

When he returned, she'd regained her composure, even if she almost relapsed when she saw his face.

They rekindled the fire and positioned the tin of water to boil for coffee. The sun rose above the bushes and started to warm the clearing and its occupants. It was welcome, the night had been cold, and they'd travelled light, not adding any extra blankets to their packs. They warmed over breakfast. After clearing up, Tonal and Dulce continued their practice. Dulce was ecstatic that she could indulge in the close contact and adventure again.

Near noon, they perfected the jumps, turns and runs. They moved as one. Tonal hardly noticed the extra weight of the petit woman astride her back. Both of their confidence levels were at a premium. During the last half hour, Alex left them to their antics and started to fold up the tent and clear their camp. The remnants of the fire were scattered, and all signs of their stay were removed from sight.

When Tonal finally padded over to him he had finished tidying up and was ready to go. Tonal's clothes were lying on a pile, ready for her when she needed them. They had agreed that she would change back to her human form for the return trip. Positioning the backpack on the cat would be problematic, and as it was the heaviest of the three, it was no option to distribute the weight over the siblings. Dulce dismounted and walked over to her brother. She turned to Tonal and watched while the change was reversed, and the mighty cat once again became the familiar form of her friend. The change was quick, one fluid motion and Dulce understood that the first change was prolonged for her benefit.

Tonal dressed quickly and joined her friends. They shouldered their backpacks and turned to leave the clearing.

'Thank you Tonal,' Dulce finally managed to say. 'That was fantastic.'

Her friend smiled. 'You're welcome, besides we had to try out whether it would work.'

They walked single file over the small jungle track, back to the compound and real life.

Chapter Fifty-One

Dulce stayed even closer to me after that. Now she was party to my secret and having been so close to me, I fascinated her even more.

She bombarded me with questions.

How did I do that? What did it feel like? Did I ever want to stay like that?

And then the final question—could she do it?

Funny how everyone needs to know if it's contagious, how they could gain this fantastic talent. I knew though that with her, it didn't stem from jealousy, just curiosity. I answered as well as I could. I explained that I didn't know and that it wasn't something I could hand over to someone else. It had just happened to me, no specific reason. And no, it wasn't contagious.

I tried to explain that it also had its drawbacks.

She listened and nodded, but I could see she was too fascinated with what she perceived as the pro's, to even contemplate that there might be anything close to a con.

'Does your everlasting youth have anything to do with it all?' she asked me one day when we were walking patrol.

'I think so.'

She digested that.

'Seems like a great idea,' she said. 'On the surface.' I was curious what she would add. 'I mean, eternal youth, no crow's feet, keeping the figure. Must be a dream.' She was pensive. 'But if you're the only one, I would imagine it has a lot of drawbacks too.'

She was clever, this one. She'd thought it through after all.

'I mean, what about your family? You must have outlived them all by now.' She looked at me apprehensively, careful not to hurt my feelings. 'Do you have any family?'

I shook my head. No, not that I knew of. They were all long gone. Because I never had any children myself, I didn't really count time as others did. I didn't age and didn't have anyone to measure time by. Life as a hermit had its perks. But she was right. There were major drawbacks. Very perceptive of her.

'I don't think I could live with that. To see all my family and friends grow old and die and then be the only one left. I wouldn't want to make ties.'

She looked at me. I nodded. She'd hit the nail on the head. Long-term relationships had a different meaning for me than for other people. They would never be long enough. After I buried my husband so many years ago, I'd decided I wouldn't get involved with a man anymore. It simply hurt too much. The ageing, the loss, but also the jealousy that I lived on, and they didn't. They got aches and pains—I stayed the same.

'Is there anyone in your life now?' she asked carefully, anxious not to pry, but curious anyway.

I shook my head. 'No, no one.' We were silent for a while.

'You know Alex is madly in love with you, don't you?' she asked softly as she looked at me from the corner of her eye and gauged my reaction.

'Yes,' I replied after a while. It was out in the open—still it sounded strange.

'And you?' Now that was a question I didn't want to answer. Not to her, and not to me.

'I care deeply for him,' I answered cowardly.

'But you don't love him?'

'Not like that, no.'

She surprised me with her next question; 'why not?'

That stopped me in my tracks.

'Why not?' I was stunned.

It was not something I let myself think about.

The dismissed was so automatic. I didn't fall in love. I didn't get involved.

Well, I was involved here up to my neck.

So why didn't I let this happen. God knows, I yearned for the closeness Alex gave me. But the inevitable pain lay somewhere in the future—l would lose him as well. Like all the other people I'd known and loved.

Could I do that again? Go through the pain of the loss, the loneliness?

Could I sacrifice my peace of mind for love?

…Could I afford not to?

Dulce sensed my indecision and my struggle and left it at that.

But it gave me something to think about.

Later that night I went into the jungle. I changed and roamed the area in search of some contentment and peace of mind, but it eluded me. The questions that had been at the back of my mind were out in the open. What would I do with Alex? With his love? With my own feelings?

He definitely had an impact on me. The ease with which he sat next to me, held my hand, pulled me close, cuddled up without a thought. It felt so natural. Why was I resisting this? And what were my feelings?

I really cared for Alex. If truth be told, I think I actually loved him. In more than a brother-sisterly way. He was attractive, that was clear. He was my type of man. And to boot he was sensitive, loving, a good friend. Whatever I was, I was a woman, with physical and emotional needs. I wanted someone to love me, someone to love myself for.

But what about the longevity thing?

What about the loss I would ultimately experience?

What about the jealousy and the hate that was bound to slip into the relationship in time?

Was it worth it?

Was I being fair to Alex and myself to restrain the feelings, to avoid the love? To deprive myself of a real relationship.

Wasn't twenty-five years of love better than hundreds of years of loneliness?

I needed to think this through.

Chapter Fifty-Two

The progress was good.

Jesus was happy with how the missions were executed. Early on he noticed the difference Tonal made to the revolution. Not only with her "special talents", but also because she looked different from the rest. Her beauty and especially her strange, ochre-coloured eyes were a man-magnet. He employed this to the advantage of the cause.

She was not alone in this kind of mission. There were many more beautiful women in the resistance. They also led targets into ambushes. But when they needed the big guns, the more exotic type, Jesus called on her.

He had no scruples at all about the extent of the sacrifices he asked from her or the others. Though "asking" was putting it nicely. Everything was a means to an end. As long as the outcome was good; it was worth it. This kind of commitment was necessary to be able to carry out the missions the women were sent on. Men of power were easily seduced. That was clear. It would be an oversight not to make use of this advantage. However, it did have its dangers, not all the women came out of the struggle unscathed, either mentally or physically. Despite his practicality he was sensitive to these issues.

On the other hand, not fighting wasn't a guarantee you wouldn't be abused sexually or maybe even worse.

The mercenaries employed by many of the targets viewed the women of the nearby villages and towns as their own personal stock of sexual playthings. They kidnapped the women, abused them, and if the women were lucky, let them go. Too many of the victims ended up in a ditch somewhere or floating down the rivers. The inevitability of the abuse was what convinced many of the women to join the Resistance and to go to these extreme lengths to rid the country of the brutes that ravaged them.

Jesus needed Tonal's seductive powers for the assassination of Ortiz. She was exactly the type he would not be able to resist. The idea of making her a kindred spirit had also been Jesus'. Exceptional beauty alone would not keep Ortiz interested long enough to be able to force the advantage. Bait and assassin in one were an ideal combination. That he found in Tonal.

He regretted that Dulce had to accompany Tonal, but it was imperative. A male servant would not be acceptable, not for Ortiz. Insanely jealous as the man was reputed to be, it would be an immediate death sentence at best. Besides Ortiz wouldn't trust Tonal, not with a male companion. A gay male companion was even worse. Ortiz was extremely homophobic. That meant a woman was the only choice. The solution they chose for the escape bothered Jesus in that he could not be sure that Dulce would make it. Tonal would, but Dulce only maybe. But that was the nature of the revolution. You took risks for the greater good.

Initially Jesus didn't have a high opinion of Tonal. Sure,

her talents would come in handy. But she seemed unstable, especially after prolonged stays in the compound. The memory of the situation twenty-three years earlier was still fresh in his mind. She seemed better in control this time around, but appearances could be deceptive.

In all his years as the leader of the revolution Jesus had seen it all. He'd been hunted, wounded, started a family, and subsequently lost everyone dear to him. Violence was nothing new to him—his history was drenched in it. He didn't however dwell on the agony, and he left the mourning to others.

Except that one day each year.

The one day he allowed himself to remember.

She found him in the jungle that day. In retrospect she'd probably followed him.

'What are you doing here?' he was angry. This was his personal time. No one was allowed to disturb his peace and his sadness.

She just stood there.

He turned around and went back to what he was doing. The box of pictures was open next to him, the light of the fire just enough to be able to make out the features of the woman or the children on them.

'You're not leaving, are you?'

'No.'

'Then sit.'

She sat down next to Jesus, near enough to be able to see the photos if he handed them to her, but far enough not to encroach too far into his personal space.

She had never seen the big man look so fragile, so unlike the proud leader that inspired so many people to put their lives on the line for him and for the cause without hesitation. In the compound he was the stable foundation for everyone. If doubts arose, they were quashed by his total commitment to the cause and the charisma he effused. Everyone wanted to be like him and to please him. She also acknowledged he was a master manipulator. He had to be. The revolution was not a project with quick results. Something like this took stamina, perseverance and total commitment. Jesus had the ability and the charm to keep the revolutionaries together, to inspire people to keep following their goal, even when it was extremely difficult. To never give up, no matter what. And when necessary, he had the resolve and the guts to do the dirty work; to order and then implement the executions. He sentenced people to death and lived with the consequences. It took a very special man to make a lot of his decisions and still be able to look people in the eye.

He was a strong man.

He had to be.

Here, he was himself. For one night every year he let the image fall and wept for those he'd lost. For the people he'd killed. Those that died for him, those that suffered. And most of all, for his family and his personal loss.

He let his emotions overwhelm him. He needed this to stay sane the rest of the year.

As he looked down at the photos, he remembered.

The woman smiling back at him was immortalised in her prime. Not even thirty years old. A beauty in his mind with dark warm eyes and jet-black hair that flowed down over her back.

He handed the photo to Tonal. She took it in silence and looked at the picture.

'Mercedes.' Her name.

'A long time ago in a better life,' he said. 'She was my wife.' Silence.

'These were my children.' He handed her a new photo of two smiling faces. Round, dark features framed with the same jet-black hair Mercedes had.

'They were four and six when they died.' Tears streamed down his cheeks.

'How?'

'They were murdered. Before my eyes.' His voice faltered.

'The revolution had just started. I'd known Julio and his family for many years, they helped us as a family, gave me a job in the business. I was the manager of the ranch. I took care of the sales of the crops, managed the more than fifty staff and so on.' Reminiscing helped him to get through the night.

'Julio's parents were captured, along with many others who were on the premises at the time of the raid. I was in the city, for business. Mercedes and the children were in our apartment on the estate, they were taken with the others. The trials were a mockery. The executions of Julio's family public and televised. The rest including, the children, were killed the following night. They mowed them all down with a machine gun, after they raped the women in front of their own children. They shot Mercedes while she tried to protect the little ones. Her body fell on top of those she so vehemently tried to save.' He sobbed at the memory and handed more photos to her as he spoke.

'We watched from a distance, there was nothing we could do, nothing. I watched my family die.'

Silence.

'That was when I decided I would join the resistance.

And that I wouldn't rest until the country was liberated from the bastards who did this to their citizens.'

He reached the last photo; one of the whole family in happier days. In it he cradled his daughter in his big arms, his wife laughed at the small boy who squirmed in her grip. Posing for photos was not prominent in the little boy's idea of fun.

'That was when I decided I wouldn't allow myself to fall into self-pity. I would put away the grief and get to work. One day every year—today—on the anniversary of their death, I allow myself the grief and the sorrow. Then I cry, so that I can forget for the rest of the year.'

There was no need to say anything. It was a monologue. Jesus talked. Tonal nodded when appropriate and showed the intense empathy and sympathy in her eyes and her body language.

It was the first time he'd shared his pain with anyone.

It felt good.

He expected to feel her presence as an intrusion, but it felt warm and comforting. That she remained silent was probably debit to that. She was just there. And he was grateful for it, for her presence.

They stayed awake all night. Jesus talked, she listened. She spoke when an answer was required. They created a bond that night he hadn't deemed possible. She was so much more intelligent and emphatic than he imagined. So much more rooted in life. He knew she'd experienced a lot —Julio indicated as much. But she never pushed her experiences into the conversations. It was his night and her feelings spoke from the few remarks she made.

He was grateful for her company.

When he finally fell asleep totally exhausted, he felt better than in previous years.

In the first rays of sunlight, he woke and found he was alone again. She'd stayed and tended the fire until the early hours of the morning. Then she'd left him to get his act back together and return to the compound as the steadfast and unflappable leader.

Chapter Fifty-Three

Dulce and I played out the scenes and our story. She the servant—bordering on slave—me the jet-set bitch.

We moved into the enormous villa I'd rented for the scam. It was, as to be expected for the role, filled with every kind of comfort a spoiled rich person could wish for. The grounds were secured behind a high wall, patrolled and defended by a ragtag bunch of gangsters. Hired guns. As long as I paid them more than they thought they could steal —and scared their socks off—they would "protect" me. As a fall-back there were two partisans under cover in the villa, one as a servant, the other among the guards.

There was almost no contact with the compound. We expected Ortiz to investigate us as soon as we were in his line of sight. So that meant no trips back, and no regular news.

For me it also meant no changing. That turned out to be more of a challenge than I expected. The change was such an integral part of my life in the jungle—it happened at whim—that I really came to miss it. The hunt, the prowl

239

and just the enjoyment of the sounds and smells around me sustained me more than I knew. During the months in the compound, I'd managed to slip away every now and then. For the assassinations and other targets, I'd needed to be the feline. Now there was no opportunity. If I disappeared for a while, it would be suspicious. So, I stayed in my human form.

It cost me though. The tension started to build, and I became short tempered. Actually, that was quite good for the authenticity of the role, but nevertheless it was dangerous. I wished it would start. That we could finally move forward.

We were nearly there.

Ortiz started to show interest in me. He looked me up on the Internet, followed me on the cloud. The flags the revolutionaries set on the information showed he was taking notice. I had been to a few exhibitions Ortiz supported in his attempt at character improvement.

He desperately craved acceptance as one of the new rich, as a man of standing and culture. This was something he couldn't buy or achieve through terror. Not the real acceptance by the ancient upper class. In his grandeur he imagined himself to be a sophisticated man, not the murdering psycho degenerate he really was. Art and music were his favourite ways of showing his wealth and pretending importance, aside from of the mercenaries of course. He regularly hosted art exhibitions in his office buildings in the country's capitol. Heavily guarded naturally, and not always attended by Ortiz himself, but slowly his was "the place to be" if you were shallow jet-set people.

When I gate crashed the Salvador Dali exhibition, he wasn't anywhere nearby. News of my attendance however reached him, probably visually supported at that; the exhibition was televised. This was a risk, hopefully no one from my past would pick up the streams. But it was necessary to get his attention. The result was that I received an invitation for the next exhibition. He was still absent, but once again he was aware I had been there. Flowers were delivered to my door the next day, together with an invitation to have lunch in his penthouse.

I declined; played hard to get. He wasn't put off. Exactly the opposite. His people followed me everywhere and kept him informed about what I did. I upheld my image of a jet-set bitch, tyrannised my staff and was the ultimate diva wherever I went.

My own fame started to precede me. I was shown to the best places in restaurants. Maître-d's shuddered when I walked in. Cooks whimpered in the kitchen.

Invariably, I attracted a large crowd of admirers. Typical Latino men who thought the world revolved around them, that they were God's gift to women. My snide remarks and sometimes outright hostility soon brought them down a few notches. But there were always a few who were suckers for pain and didn't know when to stop.

My bodyguards usually made short work of them. I had no scruples about that, these were spoilt rich kids with no idea of the suffering around them, and if they did, they couldn't care less. I saw it as a piece of their much-needed education. Let them hurt for a change.

Ortiz watched at a distance. Probably laughing at the stupid men who sought my attention. He instantly recognised I was not interested in a nobody.

He invited me to dinner. This time I went.

For the occasion he booked the whole restaurant, a hot trendy French cuisine establishment. There were no other guests, just Ortiz and me. The place was however crawling with bodyguards and of course the restaurant staff, all of them scared stiff of their influential guests.

The meal was exceptional; the company wasn't.

As expected, he was arrogant, egotistical and narcissistic, and only remotely interested in who I was and what I did. Mind you, it turned out his research had the whole story so there wasn't much I could tell him he didn't already know.

'You don't seem to be bothered my dear, that I had you so thoroughly investigated,' he commented.

'Why should I be?' I said between sips of the extremely expensive champagne, 'It's no more than I would expect from a man of your standing. And besides I returned the favour.'

He laughed. 'You investigated me?'

'Naturally. I don't dine with everyone who sends an invitation, however nicely they ask.'

'And what did you think about what you found?'

'I'm here, aren't I?'

The rest of the evening was filled with nonsense, Ortiz attempted to show off his knowledge of art, his interest in travelling, and I nodded and occasionally added something from my side.

After the coffee and liqueur, he escorted me to the door.

'You will excuse me, my dear.' His tone was soft and friendly, belying his dangerous aura and the look in his eyes. 'There is some business I have to take care of tonight.' He kissed my hand. 'Until we meet again.'

I'd expected he would combine business with pleasure. He didn't come to town often. Probably too dangerous and much too great a hassle. I definitely didn't mind. I'd endured more than my quota of the obnoxious man for one evening.

His chauffeur drove me home.

In the week that followed, he invited me to a private screening of a film that was yet to premier, to the opening of yet another art exhibition and to lunch. Each time the conversation was almost exclusively about him. What he did, how he did it. What he wanted out of life.

Slowly his guard dropped an inch or two, and he started to confide more of the violent side of his persona with me. He would talk animatedly about hunts he had been on, the prey both animal and human, the end result was always the same. He explained how he gained his image as the reincarnation of Vlad Teppes, also known as Vlad the Impaler—the origin of the Dracula myths. He revelled in the fear he wrought on the villagers within his vast pseudo kingdom. The psycho was leaking at the seams of the art lover.

All through his narratives I smiled, laughed with him and generally encouraged him to continue his monologues. I wet my lips after each gory tale and showed a heightened interest in the bloody parts. I convinced him we were soulmates. Both extremely violent, both took pleasure from the suffering of the inconsequential victims. Occasionally, I would add a bloody tale of my own. I made sure that parts of the tale would be traceable. He would no doubt check them out.

'Soon, my dear,' he commented when he once again escorted me to the waiting car. 'You will come to my home, and I will introduce you to the ultimate killers. If you are lucky, you will be able to see them at work. My cats are sensational.'

'Don't make me wait too long,' I crooned. 'I look forward to it.'

Chapter Fifty-Four

Back at the villa, I took a long shower. It wouldn't be long now. I was getting under his skin. He was hooked. I could see it in his eyes. He viewed me as a new trophy, a new conquest. But more than that; he saw the psycho in me, a kindred spirit.

Dulce accompanied me to all the meetings with Ortiz, as was expected of a maidservant. During the visits she was with the other servants, near—but invisible. Just in case her mistress needed her. Back here at the villa, the role was slightly more relaxed. For the outside world we kept up appearances, with me screaming at her at regular intervals. But in the privacy of my rooms—which were swept daily for listening devices—we discussed the progress and next steps. Dulce provided valuable information she'd gleaned from the servants, which we used to help ready our battle plans.

Getting the news to the partisans was difficult. Sometimes the deliveries were made by one of the partisans, or a visitor would arrive under the guise of a business partnership. These were generally influential businessmen that clandestinely sided with the resistance. Their companies provided a good cover.

One such business associate; an elderly and influential lawyer, visited me in the villa. We discussed the legal sides of my business endeavours all afternoon, ate an elaborate meal prepared by my chef and laid down the strategy for the company for the next few weeks. His advanced age of seventy-nine sent him to his bed early and I decided to retire to mine as well. He would leave again tomorrow and relay important information to the partisans through his channels.

As I opened the door to my bedroom, I caught his scent.

He was standing behind the door, hiding in case it was someone else but me.

I closed the door quickly and turned to face him. 'What the hell are you doing here Alex? Are you nuts?' I whispered.

What was he thinking, coming here? He'd endangered the mission, not to mention himself. I smelt a faint gasoline odour on his clothes and deduced he was posing as the chauffeur.

'Great to see you too.' He smiled back and hugged me close. His eyes lit up with amusement at my anger. 'Come on Tonal, give me some credit. No one knows I'm here. Your cover is intact,' he added seriously. 'There's no way I would endanger you or Dulce any more than absolutely necessary.'

'So why are you here?' I was glad to see him, but there was no way I would tell him I'd missed him.

'I had to see you.' The tenderness and need in his voice soothed my anger.

We sat down on the sofa. He sat as close as possible, his arm around my shoulders, his other hand engulfing mine.

'Why? What's wrong?' Had something happened at the compound? Was there news? 'Should I get Dulce in here?'

'No,' he laughed softly. 'Nothing's wrong.' He stroked my hair. 'It's best if Dulce doesn't know I'm here. Having you bite my head off is more than enough.'

'So, once again, why are you here?' my voice was softer.

'For you.' He was deadly serious. 'I had to see you. Don't be mad with me. I couldn't sleep. Couldn't get anything done. No concentration at all.' His voice was so soft I almost had to strain to hear him, I gave up and rested my head on his shoulder. There was no stopping this man when he had an idea in that thick head, he was driven.

'You fill my every waking moment, and my dreams at night if I finally manage to sleep. I needed to see that you were ok.'

'Alex, nothing can happen to me, you know that. I'm invincible.'

'Ok, nothing physical,' he conceded. He had a point.

'But still, I needed to know how you are, and see for myself.' He was quiet for a few seconds. 'I needed to hold you, feel you near.' To add value to his words, he held me tighter. 'I need you.'

Alex cupped my chin in his hand and turned my face to him. 'I love you Tonal, you know that don't you?' The emotion in his eyes and in his voice was touching.

'Yes, Alex, I know,' I sighed.

'But?'

'But I don't feel the same as you do. I love you Alex, but not like that, not as you want me to, and it's not right.' Okay, so that was out. Now he would hate me.

'I know, Tonal.'

He surprised me. This was not what I'd envisioned.

'I know you don't feel as strongly as I do, and it's okay.' He smiled his deep and soothing smile. 'Of course, I would rather you shared my adoration. But I realise it's different for you. I have loved you from the moment I saw you. From that day in the clearing that you brought my father back to me.'

I wanted to speak but he softly placed his fingers on my lips.

'No let me finish. It's taken enough courage I don't usually have to broach the subject.'

I sighed and let him talk. His closeness was comforting. Warm, loving, comfortable. Maybe it wasn't so bad. Maybe I should just let myself enjoy the situation for the moment. In the past weeks the tension built and built. I need some release, some time for me. Maybe this was it.

'I love you Tonal, with all my heart and soul. If you love me less, that's okay—for now. In time you will learn to love me as I do you.' He silenced my arguments again before I'd spoken them out loud. 'Trust me, my love, I know. I have other talents than you, I can see into the future.'

'Yeah right,' I managed to get in.

He just laughed softly and moved his face closer. His lips came dangerously close to mine.

Oh, what the hell. I thought.

He kissed me, softly, cautiously and hesitantly. When I returned the kiss, he tightened his embrace, his passion clear.

My indulgence would haunt me later, but now it was all about physical and emotional gratification.

I was wound up like a loaded spring. Every fibre of my body cried out for release. If not in a change, then another way.

My fingers clawed at his shirt as I tried to pull it off over his head, but I wouldn't let go of his lips at the same time.

'Slow down, slow down,' he laughed. 'We have all night.'

I regained control over my passion and followed his lead. Slowly and tenderly, he undressed me. He took his time to discover every part of my body. I remembered he'd seen me naked before as a prelude to the change and wondered now how that had affected him.

Trying to be tender I pulled the shirt up over his head and let my hands roam over shoulders and upper back. I couldn't reach the rest yet. His hands moved up my sides and brushed against the side of my breasts, which sent tingles of electricity through my whole body.

Involuntarily I moaned, soliciting a subdued laugh and added fervour from him. His hands and lips roamed my whole upper body and left heated trails wherever they went. He drove me mad. My resolve for restraint was losing the battle over my physical need.

Alex was lost in his administrations and didn't notice my struggle. He moved back up my body and kissed my lips, in an attempt to push his tongue through to mine. I stubbornly locked my lips, scared he would feel the lowering canines I so desperately tried to hide, or taste the accompanying blood in my mouth. I felt the fur rippling up and down my spine. It sprouted up on my arms and receded immediately as I became aware.

'Please Alex,' I murmured through locked jaws. 'Now.'

He felt the trembles in me. Linked them to the impending change if the tension was not released. Hurriedly, no longer holding his own lust in check, he pulled my jeans and string down and off my legs. In one quick motion he removed his own clothes. We fell to the ground, and I could feel his erection pushing against my leg. I turned to accommodate him and pushed my pelvis up to meet his need.

He entered me with a strong thrust and pushed my pleasure over the brink.

I came with the first contact, and again, and again.

I felt the hairs burst through the skin and disappear again when he touched them. Now that would have been a mood killer. One minute he was making love to the woman of his dreams and the next to the killer of his nightmares. Slowly I regained total control of my body. I joined the lovemaking in a completely human manner and returned the passion and lust he emanated.

Alex thrust a final time. I felt him shudder as he let his own restraint loose. He moaned loudly, and I felt the bursts of semen in my body. I held my hand over his mouth in an attempt to stop most of the noise. It wouldn't do to alert any of the servants or guards to his presence in my room. Spent, he lowered himself down onto me, his head on my breast.

'Oh my God,' was all he could manage.

Chapter Fifty-Five

The depth of his comment, the absolute fatigue and bliss that was clear, made me laugh. He was like a child in a candy store. But I suppose he'd been dreaming about this for a long time.

We talked most of the night, well those parts that we weren't otherwise occupied.

I felt the tension that almost overflowed recede more and more.

It felt good.

I felt at peace.

Near daybreak, Alex finally fell asleep while I contemplated what had happened.

I'd let myself go.

Against all my resolutions, I'd let myself get caught up in a relationship. I didn't stop Alex, worse; I'd encouraged him. His love was whole, pure and I'd contaminated it. I selfishly took the release I needed and gave him some unfounded hope. His dream was realised and now I would have to break it apart again. He would be devastated. But I had to do it. I couldn't let this continue, let it bloom.

It was dangerous.

For him.

And for me.

I would have to tell him; 'No.'

He must have noticed something. His eyes opened, and he lifted his head to look at me. 'Okay, spill the beans,' he said, 'what's up.'

Where to start?

He beat me to the chase. 'Let me guess.' He was smiling. 'You've thought it through and now realise this wasn't such a good idea.' I nodded mutely. 'And you're sorry for leading me on. We should never have done this, blah de blah de blah.' The smile never left his eyes. 'That close?'

I had to laugh. 'About spot on,' I remarked.

He became serious again. 'Tonal, I knew yesterday, and I know today, that you do not have the same feelings for me I have for you. Nothing has changed. You haven't miraculously fallen head over heels in love with me. But I don't mind. This wasn't a mistake. It was great, fantastic.'

I couldn't argue with the last part.

'I won't get all love struck now; it was the fulfilment of my dream—well part of it. The rest will just have to wait until a better time.' His finger on my lips stopped my protests. 'This is not the time for a romantic relationship, we have too much on our plate as it is, and we can't use the distraction.' His fingers followed the line of my eye down to my chin. 'As much as I would like to continue this, I can't. And I won't. It's a bit selfish as well. I know you are not as committed to this as I am. And to be absolutely honest I don't want to know, not yet. So please let me have last night. No strings attached. Just the memories.'

'Just the memories?' I asked to be sure.

'For now.' The smile and twinkle in his eyes were back again.

Oh well. It would have to do for now. Coward as I am, I refrained from argument, just let it go. I stifled the small voice in the back of my mind that cried out I would live to regret the easy way out.

Alex kissed me one last time, got up out of the bed and groped for his clothes. They were strewn over the floor and mixed up with mine. 'Time for me to leave, before anyone notices anything.' He dressed quickly.

'Shall I tell Dulce you were here?' I asked.

'Better not, or we'll have to explain more than I'm comfortable with.' With a last smile he silently opened the door and disappeared to wherever he should have spent the night.

Lying back in the pillows, I tried to objectively rethink what had happened. It didn't help. I would just have to wait and see what happened.

But it had helped me. I felt better.

I slept like a baby and missed Alex and the lawyer's departure.

Chapter Fifty-Six

Seated in the back of the big black limo, Tonal and Dulce prepared themselves for their meeting with Ortiz. He'd sent for Tonal, and naturally Dulce came along. He had a treat for her, he said, something that she, as a cat lover, would no doubt appreciate. They had no idea what was about to happen. The limo was probably wired, so they didn't speak to each other, fully into their role. To fall out of character now would mean instant death for Dulce and the failure of the mission.

Ortiz sounded tense on the phone, there was a strange echo to his voice, as if you could hear his madness push through the carefully orchestrated façade. Certain that something had happened to enrage him, Tonal felt the heat and fury through the line. She cautioned Dulce to expect anything, and to make sure she didn't flinch or act any way out of character.

The driver steered the big black car through the town streets to the accompaniment of even darker looks from the passers-by. No one dared openly contest Ortiz, and because of the shaded windows, it wasn't visible who was in the car.

Soon they were out on the open road. There was only one road through the small town. South it led to the town of San Miguel. North offered only one destination—Ortiz's fortress.

They passed through the first of the roadblocks and checkpoints, still three miles from the buildings. Past the stakes and the remnants of the bodies that hung from them. The stench was overpowering and sickening. On either side of the road, one-hundred foot of jungle was cleared so that no one could ambush any convoys or cars that used the roads. There were high fences, so the chance that anyone would be able to attack from the jungle was small anyway. This was a seriously paranoid person, and with reason. You would need heavy vehicles to navigate the moat between the fence and the sides of the road. Heavy machinery was not something the resistance had. Also, their guerrilla warfare was not suited to open ground.

They passed the checkpoint without incident. After all, this was Ortiz's car and his driver.

The driver made good time and they passed the following two guard posts, each a mile apart. Soon enough, maybe even too soon for Dulce, they arrived at the drawbridge that straddled the deep moat. The bridge was a hundred-foot-long, the last twenty feet was the actual drawbridge, like in the ancient castles of the knights. The moat, however, was not filled with water. It was full of high grass and housed lions in its depths. It continued into the jungle on the opposite side of the fortress and ended in a high fence, two or three miles away. The guards at the checkpoints were in small high-fenced contained areas—small islands—well within the range of the lions that roamed the defence zone. Not the best place to be for anyone, safety was debatable at best. On the fortress's side, the moat ended up against a high sloping wall. There were spikes in the wall at about ten feet above the moat. The spikes were angled downwards, a deterrent for the lions to stop any attempt to gain entrance to the fortress. There was no need to have spikes facing up. No one in their right mind would choose to jump over the fortress wall into the moat. And if they did, it wouldn't matter for long.

This lapse in the defence was what Tonal was counting on. It was the way they would be able to leave the fortress when they'd accomplished their mission.

The car turned onto the gravel and stopped parallel to the steps leading up to the courtyard. There were several carts and nervous horses stationed in the same clearing. The car door opened on Tonal's side, and the driver offered his hand to help her out of the dark and cool interior. She placed her hand on his arm, extended her right leg out of the door and eased herself out of the car. Dulce opened the door on the other side and ran quickly to her mistress's side, where she bowed her head and stood diminutively behind the arrogant woman.

Tonal regarded the top of the stairs. Ortiz was there, his left arm bandaged and in a sling. That explained the anger. Something had definitely happened here. She strode up the stairs, brushing away the continued support of the driver. As she neared the top of the stairs Ortiz smiled at her.

'My dear, how nice of you to come.' He took her proffered hand and lightly pressed his lips to her fingers in a kiss. Ortiz was a man of tradition. He prized himself in his good manners and chivalry. Even if they were tainted by sadism and his vicious nature. It was a strange marriage.

'How could I not come,' she cooed. 'After you promised

me a good show.' She had cultivated her image carefully as the strong arrogant independent woman. Vicious in her own way, but never-the-less very feminine. She was beautiful; her makeup not overpowering, just enough to enhance her enticing deep ochre eyes that little bit more. Her dresses were designer creations. Made to measure, to hug and complement her fantastic figure. She moved with the grace of a feline, even on heels like today. This was what attracted Ortiz the most. That and her viciousness.

She purposely refrained from asking about his injured arm.

'This way, my dear.' He indicated she should accompany him to an area where a small pavilion stood to shade them from the sun.

To the right she saw a group of middle-aged and older men, elders from a nearby village. They were huddled together, in a feeble attempt to gain strength from numbers. The ferocious looking mercenaries interspersed across the whole area didn't help settle their nerves. And to make matters much worse, a man was tied to a frame set in the ground. He was wounded; badly battered. His gaze was locked on a stake near the edge of the terrace. Tonal followed his stare and saw a human head was speared on the pole. Tears slid down the man's face, every now and then he was unable to control his cries and this in turn resulted in a blow from the mercenary nearest to him.

Tonal walked over to the pavilion, careful not to stare or acknowledge the villagers and the prisoner in any way. She feigned curiosity and hoped Dulce was able to control her emotions. No doubt things would get worse, this was only the beginning.

Ortiz was all chivalry and manners to her. 'Here in the shade will suite you best, my dear.' He indicated an intricately carved chair with deep pillows. She sat down and looked around. The chair and pavilion were placed near the fortress wall and overlooked the moat. There was no movement apparent down there, but her eyes picked up the tell-tale signs that indicated the presence of predators. A combination of animal and human bones littered the floor of the moat. She also smelled the cats.

Ortiz walked over to the elders, who unconsciously retreated a few feet. They encountered the mercenaries behind them and—caught between the two—huddled together. The effect was pleasing to Ortiz, he traversed the remaining two feet to the prisoner and hit him across the face.

'This piece of shit is the father of the maggot that did this to me.' He indicated his bandaged arm. 'He attempted to kill me.'

The silence was total.

'As you see he failed.' He smiled as he turned to look at the young man's head on the stake. 'This family comes from your village.'

Once again, he approached the elders. 'You are responsible for what happens in your village. This, and what will happen as a result, is your fault. It is on your heads.' He chose his words carefully and articulated them slowly and clearly. Each one a blow to the huddled men.

'There are repercussions. You force me to make an example of this family. I will not accept this betrayal.'

When he lowered his voice, he became even more frightening. His piercing eyes locked on each man in turn. They paled under his gaze, even to the point of becoming physically ill.

'You are here to witness what I do with traitors and relay what you have seen to your people. Convince them revolution and betrayal will harm all, and not benefit any. You cannot kill me. I am protected by the devil. I have made a pact with him. He watches over me, and all my enemies will be delivered into my hands. I will deal with any adversity violently. This is my payment to the devil. He receives the souls of the traitors I slay. There is no rest for them, only pain and agony in this life and the next.'

The villagers were religious to a fault and endured the pain and horror of this world with tyrants like Ortiz because of the assurance of a better time in the hereafter. They were promised the heavens by the priests and teachers. Now even the afterlife was at the whim of Ortiz. He was a master of manipulation and played on the fears and anxieties of his enemies. Add pathological violence and sadism and it was a wonder anyone even remotely contemplated crossing him.

Ortis signalled to one of the mercenaries, turned his back on the elders and walked back to the pavilion. A servant offered him cool drinks. He took two and gave one to Tonal, who accepted the cool liquid with a smile and a nod.

'Now it gets interesting,' he whispered.

She turned her head to watch the scene unfold. In the corner of her eye she saw that Dulce still kept it together.

Chapter Fifty-Seven

Two mercenaries came into view dragging a screaming young girl with them. Instantly the prisoner called out to her, this was obviously his daughter. The mercenary behind him didn't bother to hit him—his grief-stricken cries now served a purpose.

She was a rather plain girl of about fourteen or fifteen years old, her face washed with tears. She screamed and called for her father as she struggled against the laughing soldiers. They stopped three feet in front of the prisoner, looked at Ortiz for the next sign as the girl strained against their arms. He nodded in their direction, and they started to rip the clothes off the poor girl, to additional desperate cries from her father.

'Please, please she is only fourteen, she knows nothing, she had nothing to do with Alejandro's attack, please, please.' His pleas had no effect. The mercenaries continued their task. Ortiz laughed at the scene—he clearly enjoyed it. The fear and apprehension of the elders, the pain of the father and the terror of the daughter.

Again, Ortiz nodded, and they positioned the girl on her knees opposite her father. The largest of the mercenaries pulled her head back and nonchalantly slit her exposed throat with an enormous hunting knife.

The horror of the unexpected violent murder caused Dulce to stifle a cry. Tonal heard her, but Ortiz thankfully missed the reaction, too enthralled by what he'd witnessed.

He glanced at Tonal, pleasure radiating from him. 'Now you get to see the surprise.' Offering her his arm he led her to the wall.

The mercenary that held the girl unceremoniously dragged her body to the wall. The second untied the prisoner and walked him to the same place. The old man fell to his knees and cradled his dead daughters' head. Another soldier pressed a button on a control panel on the wall and a siren went off. The sound was piercing, it continued for about twenty seconds and strained the ears of the spectators. The elders were herded to the edge of the wall that overlooked the moat. They were sentenced to watch the rest of the drama unfold.

Tonal saw movement in the bushes in the moat.

'There they are.' Ortiz was excited. He pointed to the massive black-maned lion that emerged into the clearing. Three tawny lionesses followed him. In the bushes she saw the heads of a few small cubs that peaked from the lower shrubs. The male lion looked her straight in the eye, confused by the mixed scents he picked up. The smell of another predator—one he could not recognise—made him anxious. But the prevailing scent of blood soon overpowered his concern, and he growled for his food.

The lions were majestic, though somewhat gaunt. Their growls of apprehension filled the air. They all smelled the death and blood. A fight broke out between two of the lionesses for the best spot underneath the watching people. The mercenaries grabbed the girl's arms and legs, tearing her from her father's grip, and threw her over the wall to the waiting lions. He jumped up and screamed his daughter's name. The sound was quickly drowned by the growls of the fighting cats.

'Let the old man follow his daughter,' Ortiz ordered. The soldiers grabbed the man and unceremoniously tipped him over the edge to new screams, this time for his own predicament. He slid down the wall past the spikes, trying in vain to grab one to stop his decent. The big male lion was preoccupied with the body of the girl, fighting two of the lionesses for the choicest pieces, ripping her apart. The remaining lioness focused her attention on the new prey, the man who struggled to scramble up the steep incline. She bounded up the bank and reached him within seconds. The cat bit into his foot and hooked her claws into his leg. Renewing his screams, the man fought the lioness, naturally to no avail. The massive feline pulled him down the moat wall and out into the clearing. Another lioness instantly bit the man in the neck and effectively silenced him. The elders averted their faces, not able to watch the vicious scene unfold.

Tonal didn't blame the lions, they did what came naturally. The blame lay with Ortiz and his fellows. The goal of the demonstration—besides feeding Ortiz's own bloody urges—had been achieved. The elders were sick to their stomach and would relay the scenes to the silly few who would dare to dream about opposing the tyrant.

'Remember what you saw,' he threatened them for good measure. 'You will be next, if anyone tries to oppose me again. I will throw your wives, sons and daughters to the lions while you watch. They will be torn apart before your eyes. You will see your loved ones go to hell. It is your responsibility—this rests on your heads.' He dismissed them with a wave of his hand and turned back to the feasting lions. The cubs joined their parents on the bloody bodies. There were three of them. Probably four months old.

Holding up one of their own, who no longer had the strength to stand on his legs, the elders hurried to their carriages, lest Ortiz change his mind and punish them further. The sights they had seen would haunt their nightmares for years to come. The man and his family were prominent members of the small community, the father had been a peaceful man who preached subservience. Even he had not been safe from Ortiz' wrath.

Tonal stole a glance at Dulce who was pale and shivering quietly. She managed to stop herself from reacting to the barbaric actions, but it cost her a lot of energy to stay standing where she was. Only the mission and the certainty they would succeed held her in her role.

Tonal in turn needed to delve into all her restraints to stop the change from happening here and now. She was so angry at the brutal and useless violence that had taken place. She was ready to take out Ortiz and all the mercenaries around him. Only the conviction that this would probably cost Dulce her life stopped her from doing just that.

The effort was enormous to stop the claws from breaking through her fingertips. Luckily Ortiz was preoccupied with the lions. Tonal felt she was being observed and turned her gaze to the right. There, the mercenary she knew as Croc looked straight into her eyes. He'd been watching her and sensed the inner turmoil. She had to be careful with this one. He was not convinced by her façade. She'd encountered resistance from him before and expected he'd been given the task of observing her throughout the "show". She smiled at him and raised her glass. Her hand was level, not a shiver to be seen. Tonal walked over to Ortiz and hooked her arm behind his as she joined him to view the carnage below. Happy with her reaction he lightly kissed her cheek.

'So, my lovely, what do you think of my cats?'

Radiating her smile, she answered, 'they are delightful.' She licked her lips to emphasise her words. 'So vicious, so wonderfully wild.'

They stayed there for a few minutes more until Ortiz tired of the scene.

He whispered in her ear; 'this show is over and I'm ready for the next one. Death always turns me on, I'm hard for you.'

He rubbed his groin up against her leg to demonstrate his libido.

'Let's go to my quarters.'

Chapter Fifty-Eight

Ortiz dismissed his servants—all but Croc—and steered her towards the villa.

She'd known this would probably have to happen to gain his trust. The plan was that she would seduce and kill him when they were alone. However, Croc followed them into the bedroom. In anticipation of her reaction, Ortiz cut off any discussion.

'He stays.'

Tonal feigned indifference. Shrugged and crept up closer to him.

'Move for me,' he whispered hoarsely.

She disentangled herself from his hold and moved backwards a few feet. Croc put on some seductive music. Tonal closed her eyes and started to sway to the tones. Slowly she moved her hands over her supple form, which excited Ortiz even more. She turned, bent and moved like a seasoned lap dancer and drove him mad. Opening her eyes, she regarded him while she slowly slipped the spaghetti shoulder bands of her dress down over her arms. She turned around and watched him over her shoulder. Tonal pulled the zipper down inch by inch, till it finally ended just above her bright red G-string. She bent over forward and slipped the dress off down her long legs, flexing the muscles of her buttocks and hamstrings. It was too much for Ortiz to bear and he grabbed her, turned her around and groped her breasts.

He was rough with no consideration for her feelings. She'd expected this and paid him back in kind. She grabbed his throbbing member and squeezed hard. He took as good as he gave, enjoying the tension.

She opened his pants to free his engorged penis. He pushed her head down and she took him in her mouth, biting down on the hard tissue. He called out, a combination of pain and unbearable excitement. Only able to take it for a minute he roughly pulled her up again by her hair and threw her on the bed where he ripped off her string. His pants down past his knees, he entered her brutally. She cried out in what seemed to be ecstasy. Ortiz banged away and viciously squeezed her breast as he came within seconds. Spent, he collapsed on top of her.

From the corner of her eye, she looked at Croc. He still observed her, dis-passionately so it seemed. The bulge in his pants belied this. She turned her head to look at him, openly eyed his erection and smiled, much to his discomfort. It had the intended reaction; anger coloured his face. She'd won the first round. But it was a dangerous game.

Ortiz rolled over off her and looked at her body. 'Take off the rest of your clothes,' he ordered and indicated her stockings and garter belt. She complied, and he pulled her back on to the bed. Softly, almost lovingly, he stroked her full breasts and flat stomach.

'You are beautiful,' he murmured. 'My soulmate.'

Chapter Fifty-Nine

It took all my restraint not to kill the bastard as he snored next to me.

I felt filthy, violated, soiled.

I desperately wanted to clean myself. Soak in a bath and scrub my skin until his stench left me. Until I could no longer smell his sickly hot breath. His sweat. His semen.

I let my mind roam. Back to Alex's visit and to the love-making I'd enjoyed. I tried to imagine his scent—his body here next to me. To no avail. I couldn't reconcile that night, that excitement with the revulsion I felt now. I would just have to grin and bear it. Worse than that. I would have to play along. Pretend my lust matched that of Ortiz and that my hunger for his body was real. Well, it was, but in a different way than he thought. That momentarily brought a smile to my lips.

I feigned sleep, rested and waited for the morning.

Chapter Sixty

Croc stayed the whole night. He witnessed the renewed libido of his boss and the further degradation of Tonal. She played her role well, even seemingly enjoyed the brutal sex and gave as good as she got.

She had no idea what had become of Dulce, and inquiring was out of the question. In her role she would not be the slightest bit interested in what happened to her servant. After all they were a dime-a-dozen. Privately, she was worried. Dulce could take care of herself in normal conditions. But what happened last night, and the large number of mercenaries in the complex was everything but normal. Tonal feared one or more of them might have tried to seduce or rape Dulce. She could do nothing more than wait until morning. She listened with her keen sense of hearing to pick up the slightest scream or cry from her friend.

She didn't sleep, though she feigned it. Croc stayed in his allotted place next to the door. He only moved to follow her into the bathroom when she needed to relieve herself and stood by the door during the process. There was no privacy, not yet, not until Ortiz trusted her. She expected that would not be anytime soon. This mission would take longer than expected. Ortiz was much more careful than we'd calculated. They would have to sit it out. The longer the mission took, the more dangerous it became, especially for Dulce. Tonal could get out any time, but not without Dulce.

The early morning light shone through the slatted windows. The pleasant chirping of the birds belied the tension she felt. Ortiz moved beside her and mumbled unintelligible words. Occasionally he thrashed out at some hidden enemy in his dreams. Was it possible that he suspected her? More than likely. He was paranoid to a fault. But it was functional, it kept him alive. She resisted the urge to accidentally hit him in his wounded arm. Instead, she stroked his manhood, slowly woke him to her administrations and mimicked lust. Ortiz opened his eyes and rolled over, so she could easily take him in her mouth. Tonal forced back the urge to vomit all over him, continued her acting and finally brought him to a climax. Her face became a mass of locked muscles, but still she smiled at him. He brushed her away and abruptly stood up, walked to the bathroom where he noisily relieved himself, much to the annoyance of Croc. This in turn amused Tonal.

Ortiz returned to the bedroom, dressed himself without bothering to shower, strapped on his gun and left for the door. At the last moment he remembered she was there. He turned and addressed her.

'The chauffeur will bring you back home, I have business to attend to. I will send for you.'

'Don't wait too long,' she crooned. That brought a smile to his face.

'I will need you soon.' Lust once again lit up his eyes, he crossed back to the bed, kissed her and viciously squeezed her breast, causing her to cry out. 'I will call for you before that bruise is gone,' he answered.

Tonal carefully forced the hairs on her back to recede and the claws to stay inside her fingers. It took an enormous effort. She would have to remember the bruise so she could reinstate it when he called. Her body would heal from such a small injury within a few seconds. She willed her body to ignore the bruise and not reabsorb the blood under the skin. Ortiz was gone, but Croc was still in the room.

Tonal stretched her athletic frame languidly as she stood up from the bed and strutted into the room. Croc constantly observed her. She bent over in his line of sight with her back to him and was delighted to see the unease and resulting anger in Croc's demeanour. She enjoyed baiting him, it was a dangerous game but consistent with the arrogant bitch she portrayed, and the only pleasure she could derive from this miserable business. When she turned around and put her hand seductively between her legs, it proved too much for the sullen mercenary and he left the room, the sound of her laughter ringing in his ears, his head a fine shade of red and an enormous bulge in his pants.

Tonal quickly bathed the grime and semen from her body, repulsed by the thought Ortiz's stench would stay with her one minute more that absolutely necessary. Her unease at Dulce's fate spurred her on as well. Dressed in the same garment as yesterday—minus the torn string—she left the room and headed to the veranda where the scene unfolded the day before.

To her relief Dulce already stood there, looking no worse for wear. Tonal indicated she remain silent, led the way to the waiting car and stepped into the dark and welcome interior. Dulce quickly followed, and the chauffeur started up the extravagant vehicle. They passed the main gateway and the moat. The lions were now out in the open, sated by their meal from the evening before. After they passed the checkpoints and emerged out on to the main road, Tonal allowed herself an internal sigh of relief. They had passed yet another test.

Returning to their hotel room, they remained in character. It was very possible, actually probable, that Ortiz had bugged the room. He didn't trust them out of his sight. By the end of the day, they packed up their belongings and, in sync with the cover story, were on their way to the city where Tonal had her business.

They finally arrived at the secure compound on the outskirts of the city that was their home away from home and were able to talk about the previous day and night.

Tonal quizzed Dulce and found out that she had found a small room belonging to one of Ortiz's servants and barricaded herself in the tiny compartment for the duration of the night. The servant told her the mercenaries had searched for her but abandoned the task for the easily available booze and two visiting whores from the village. The room had a view of the courtyard and Dulce emerged only after she saw Croc leave the room where Tonal was.

What had happened to Tonal stayed unspoken. It was obvious to Dulce how much her friend had sacrificed for this mission, and out of respect she avoided the questions that would humiliate her even more. Revulsion for the tyrant was written clearly across Tonal's face now they were in a relatively safe place. But no matter how repulsed they were by the brutality and arrogance of the psycho and his henchmen, they had no choice but to continue the mission and play by intuition, never knowing what would happen next.

Chapter Sixty-One

It took three days before Ortiz sent for her again.

The reunion was fierce and lustful—at least on his part. He almost dragged Tonal into his quarters the minute she arrived, ripped the costly dress she wore and forced himself upon her without the slightest thought for her feelings. In character, she went along with the show and even encouraged him all the way. The sooner he was spent, the sooner he would leave her alone again if only for a short while. As expected, Croc was present during the act.

Ortiz rearranged his clothes and threw a new dress on to the bed. 'Please wear this, my dear. I seem to have damaged the one you were wearing.'

Once again, he was all fake chivalry and manners, belying what just took place. 'I promised that we would be together again before the bruise faded, and I see I was right.' He indicated the soft yellowish bruise on her breast. It obviously pleased him that he had marked her this way.

'I have visitors that I would like you to meet, so please

clean up and meet me in the library.' He left the room, Croc hard on his heels.

That was new. He left her alone. Dulce entered the room and stood at the end of the bed, awaiting orders. After a shower, new makeup and perfume, Tonal slipped into the new dress. It was a tight fit and clung to her curves in a seductive and trashy way. She was the trophy, to be shown off to whoever was visiting.

Croc banged loudly on the door of Ortiz's bedroom twenty minutes after his master left her to escort her to the meeting.

"Whoever" turned out to be a group of Generals, all rough men, dressed up to look decent. As one, they stood when she entered the room escorted by Croc.

Ortiz beamed. The dress was superfluous, it accentuated more than hid any part of her body. That, and the expert make up administered by Dulce, made her even more seductive. The effect on the congregated men with their elevated testosterone levels was amusing. It was also exactly what that Ortiz had envisioned.

'Gentlemen, may I introduce the love of my life.' He put his arm around her, cupped her breast and squeezed lightly, pinching the nipple until it hardened, much to the jealous glares of the visitors. In turn, she seductively rubbed her body up against Ortiz and softly groaned at his adminis-trations.

'Here, my dear,' he managed to say in a throaty voice. 'Sit next to me.'

She lowered herself into the chair and leaned to his side as she observed the gathering. There were six men, four in their forties or fifties and two were younger—about mid-thirties. They sat and acted in a manner that showed that they were used to being waited on, their orders followed without questions. One of the younger men openly stared at her. He undressed her with his eyes. She returned the stare and then demonstratively hooked her arm in Ortiz's. This caused him to look up from his conversation and follow her eyes to the young General. His eyes hardened.

'Little brother, this one is off limits, even for you'. The younger man shrugged and lifted his glass as a toast.

'You always had impeccable taste, brother' He ceded to the one person in the room with total power. There was no love lost between the siblings.

The servants approached the gathering and stood in total silence until Ortiz deemed to acknowledge their presence.

'Dinner is served.' He stood up, offered his arm to Tonal. They crossed the room to the dinner table on the veranda. His hand left hers and rested on her behind where he slowly pulled up the flimsy material to expose her bare buttocks. The action was calculated. The Generals were all behind him and privy to his administrations. Ortiz pulled back her chair and indicated that she sit next to him.

Topics at dinner ranged from what the Americanos were doing to help the forces, the irritating partisans, fine wine and liquor, to which actors starred in which films. Talk was light, and the booze flowed easily.

After dinner, they retired to the library. Ortiz kissed her hand. 'I am sorry my dear, we must now talk business. I will send for you soon, before the entertainment.' He handed her over to one of the servants, took on a much more dominant demeanour and addressed the waiting Generals.

She was directed out of the room, back to the bedroom where Dulce waited. Croc was still with the Generals, obviously needed there. Tonal knew Ortiz wouldn't trust any of the gathered men, his brother probably the least of all.

Power was contagious, the more you came in contact with it, the greater the envy. One handy way to get your own power was to relieve someone else of his. As relatively decent as they had seemed at the dinner table, she knew they would all have to be almost as vicious and psychotic as Ortiz to be able to survive in his inner circle.

Once again, Tonal and Dulce played the waiting game.

Chapter Sixty-Two

The same servant came for her two and a half hours later. She was taken to the large reception room where the men convened. The discussions had obviously been fierce. There was a lot of tension, particularly visible in the face of one of the older Generals and Ortiz's brother. These traces of unrest in Ortiz's brother were immediately replaced by lust when she walked into the room. Her high heels clicked loudly on the tiles. The old General, not so easily swayed, attempted to continue the discussion but was abruptly silenced by Ortiz's stare.

'Ah my dear, there you are again, come sit with me.' He had a glass of what looked like whisky in his left hand and indicated she should sit on his lap. Tonal accepted his invitation and draped herself over him. He immediately placed his free hand high up on her thigh, the fingers under the hem of the dress where he stroked the soft flesh all the while observing the reaction this had on the others. She felt him harden again and she wondered what he took to keep up his unnaturally high libido. Whatever it was, he took a lot of it.

Ortiz nodded to Croc then addressed the waiting men. 'Gentlemen, enough discussion for one night. Now it's time for the entertainment.' His hand moved up higher under her dress and continued the soft stroking.

Croc opened the door and a group of eight women entered the room. They were without exception beautiful and very young. Music started, and they began to dance, moving in sync with each other to the cheers of the men.

Ties were discarded, uniforms unbuttoned further, and shoes kicked off. The women danced seductively closer to the waiting men, spurred on by their cries and catcalls. Slowly the dancers began to undress as they continued to move to the music. Clothing soon littered the floor.

Ortiz's brother stood up and grabbed one of the women roughly which caused her to cry out. She regained her composure and moved up against him, after all he was the boss's brother, a very influential man in his own right. She moved her hand down the front of his pants, opened the belt and unzipped his fly. He grabbed her by the hair and pulled her face to his.

'With your teeth,' he ordered. She dropped to her knees and to cheers and encouragement of all present, pressed on to comply with his wish. Obviously good at her job, she took the rim of his boxer in her teeth and proceeded to maneuverer it over the large erection, freeing it. With an exclamation of awe at its size—slightly overdone acting but still what the customer wanted—she opened her mouth and proceeded to expertly blow him.

Most of the men followed his example and grabbed the woman of their choice. The hierarchy between the Generals was obvious in the choices. By the time Ortiz's brother had turned his prize around and fucked her doggy style, all the men were engaged in some form of sex. Ortiz pushed Tonal off his lap on to the floor and her head on to his engorged member. He would observe the others while she administered to him. Her dress rode up around her hips, uncovering her naked form, much to the glee of the others.

The orgy lasted for some hours, fuelled by booze, drugs and Viagra. The women, except for Tonal, were swapped, sometimes used by more than one at the same time. One General enjoyed hitting and hurting his woman, to the encouragement of the others.

Finally, they were all spent, all except Ortiz. He'd held back, only climaxing once during the orgy, now he proceeded to show the gathering he was top dog. The one left standing. Her dress now also on the floor, Ortiz pushed Tonal over onto all fours and took her roughly from behind, pushing her face into the carpet. The rest watched and spurred him on.

At last, he finished.

'Enough Gentlemen,' Ortiz barked. 'The women will accompany you to your quarters. Please leave them whole, they are expensive.' Gathering some clothes, the women led the temporarily sated Generals out of the room to the quarters they had been allotted. Last to leave was Ortiz's brother.

'If you tire of her, send her to me,' he whispered to Ortiz, his libido still not sated, or maybe reinstated by the show. 'You always did give me your hand-me-downs.' He winked at her, threw one of the women over his shoulder, motioned a second to follow and left. Ortiz pushed her aside roughly. He no longer needed to keep up appearances.

'You did well, they all lusted for you. Men make mistakes when lust is foremost in their mind. I know now who to monitor.' Tonal sat with her back to the sofa and regarded him. He rearranged his clothes and sat behind the desk. Taking care of business. He ignored her. She knew enough to dress herself and leave the room.

'Don't leave the compound,' he called after her. 'I'm not finished with you yet.'

She went back to the bedroom, bathed and brushed his stink off her. Dulce was silent, intuitively she understood what happened was worse than last time.

Chapter Sixty-Three

In the small hours of the night she awoke to Ortiz's snores, he had at some moment joined her in the massive bed. His arm was draped over her.

Carefully she moved it to the side and slipped out of bed. Tonal sensed that Croc was nearby so she stayed in her role. She walked to the open balcony doors and gazed out over the now quiet compound. In the distance her acute hearing picked up the sound of someone crying, she thought the woman who had reluctantly followed the oldest and most vicious General. The one who could not follow through, never mind how much drugs or Viagra he used.

'What are you looking at?' Ortiz stood behind her, he had moved almost silently and now held her by the waist.

'Nothing,' she replied. 'Just looking out.'

Her answer didn't satisfy him. He pulled her away from the light.

'There is nothing to be seen out there.' He roughly pushed her in the direction of the bed then added, 'but here, we play a new game.'

The hairs on her neck stood up from the sheer menace clear in his voice.

'Stand here,' he ordered, stopping about two feet before the bed. 'Hold your arms up.'

She complied crooning, 'what are you going to do now, my love?'

He looked her deep in the eye. 'I am going to test your love, see how far you will go for me, make sure that you remember me while you are gone from here.'

He took her wrists and, with the help of Croc who materialised behind her, clasped them in broad leather handcuffs that hung from the ceiling. She had not seen these, so there must be some kind of mechanism that had silently lowered them while she was not observing. Croc left her and moved to the wall, where he pushed a button that was obviously linked to the cuffs. Slowly she was hoisted into the air until her toes barely touched the floor. Both men grabbed a foot, and pulled them to the side, where they fastened them to cuffs protruding from the floor. She was totally incapacitated, hanging from the ceiling with her legs spread wide. Dread crawled up over her back. This was the real Ortiz showing his true colours.

'What are you doing? she asked him. The expected tremor in her voice.

'Having fun,' was his answer. Croc beamed with pleasure. Finally, she would get what she deserved. Ortiz nodded, and Croc tore the short t-shirt off her body. He moved away from her and took up his position near the wall with a vicious grimace on his features.

Ortiz removed his boxers and walked to a closed cabinet. He opened the doors and flicked a switch that controlled two spotlights. One shone directly on her, the second illuminated the contents of the closet. It was filled with all manner of whips, clamps and other devices she attributed to bondage games. Ortiz picked up a leather head-cap before he moved back to her. His eyes bore into hers, even though she knew he could not kill her, she shivered at the pain and degradation she could expect.

'This isn't funny anymore, let me down,' she tried, fully into her role, but also meaning it deep down inside.

He smiled, held up the cap with one hand and slapped her viciously with the other. 'Now we do what I want,' he whispered. 'Now I have some fun. You are too independent my dear, too arrogant, you need to learn to adhere to my wishes, do exactly what I want.'

'But I did,' she answered angrily. 'Everything you wanted; I did. Even performed before those disgusting men. I did it all.'

He slapped her again. 'You were too arrogant, not quick enough to my needs and now you need to be punished.' It was clear that whatever she said would not help, he wanted to hurt her, and he used every excuse he wanted. Not that he needed any.

Croc held her struggling head, while Ortiz slid the leather cap over her face. There were holes for her eyes, but leather flaps were fastened over them that effectively shut out any light. She could breathe through a small pipe in the leather that Ortiz slammed into her mouth. The supple impenetrable leather covered her nose. Holding his hand over the opening of the pipe, he whispered in her ears, the only parts of her head that were uncovered. 'I determine whether you breathe, whether you live or die here, now.' He held his hand over the breathing hole for more than a minute to let his words land. She gasped for breath when he let her, then the game started again. Ortiz zipped the cap closed on the back of her head.

'Now you find out what obedience means,' he whispered.

The torture lasted for hours. Her eyes and nose were obstructed by the leather cap and all she could do was listen. Halfway through the ordeal she couldn't distinguish between Ortiz and Croc anymore. She was abused in every way possible. With nightsticks, dildo's, tasers and naturally a human dick, she was degraded and molested and left hanging when Ortiz was finally spent. Suspended from her wrists she was exhausted. He could not kill her, that was true, but he definitely hurt her. She healed—but she hurt. She concentrated on holding back her healing powers, and she tried to relax. Tonal lost all sense of time and slipped into a restless nap every now and then.

At some point in the early hours, she felt hands on her again. Softly, not pinching and hurting, stroking her— almost intimate. She raised her head and tried to get a sense of where Ortiz was. With only her sense of hearing and intuition to guide her she was confused. She heard and felt the man, he rubbed up against her with his hard penis sticking into her leg. But she also heard snoring. Was that Croc snoring or was he the one groping her. She could not get the scent through the sweaty leather cap. Straining against the restraints she tried to turn her head to the person behind her. A hand slid over the cap and closed the air pipe. He kept his hand there and cut off her breathing. She felt the panic rise. She relied so much on her senses, that the absence of them was frightening. He didn't speak, just held the pipe closed until she stopped resisting. Once again, she let herself hang in the chains.

The hand left the pipe and she gratefully inhaled more-or-less fresh air.

His hands moved over her body, pinching the nipples

erect. He moved behind her and positioned himself between her outstretched legs. He gripped her hips as he entered her. He felt different, his size, girth, not what she was used to, the rhythm slow and decided. It strengthened her belief he was not Ortiz.

Croc took an enormous chance, fucking her while Ortiz slept. But it was now or never. If Ortiz found out, he would feed Croc to the lions, bit by bit, dick first. She was his property, and his alone. But Croc was sick of the sadistic bastard. Oh, it wasn't the violence that irritated him, it was the arrogance, the way he treated Croc. No matter how he acted towards all the others, Croc was the leader of the Mercs, not some lowly servant or slave. He deserved more.

And then the bodyguard detail, waiting in the shadows while Ortiz rutted and defiled this beautiful but equally arrogant creature. He lusted for her—any man would. Hearing them at it only increased the tension. Now he had his chance. As long as he stayed quiet, and with a bit of sheer luck, he could pull this off. She would not tell, she could never be sure it was him, and his death sentence was automatically hers. If Ortiz thought she'd been defiled, he would ditch her no matter how beautiful she was. Croc climaxed as quietly as possible, then slowly pulled back from her. He softly stroked her hair and back.

She was furious, certain it was Croc. But she had no proof, and besides, why would Ortiz believe her?

The snores continued in the background—Ortiz was still sound asleep.

In the morning, heralded by the sounds of birds, she heard Ortiz wake up and move about the room. He ignored her, dressed and got ready for the day ahead. 'Get the handmaiden,' he ordered the ever-present Croc.

Dulce arrived. She had to use every shred of restraint

not to cry out when she saw her friend, soiled, bruised, bloody and hanging from the ceiling with a leather cap over her head. She had shallow wounds that looked like whip marks on her back and buttocks. They had not healed, so Tonal hadn't wanted them to.

'Get your mistress out of here,' Ortiz barked. 'Take her home and wait until I send for her again.' He left the room, Croc in his wake.

They left Dulce to find out how to free Tonal. She started with the leather cap, unzipped it and eased it off her head.

'Oh God, what happened...' she was silenced by the look in Tonal's eyes and remembered the room was probably wired, or maybe even filmed.

'Get me down,' Tonal hissed. 'The button on the wall.'

Dulce turned, searched the wall for the button and flicked it. The chains lengthened and slowly Tonal sank to the ground. Her cramped legs were unable to hold her weight—the muscles screaming for relief. Dulce ran over to her and unlocked the leather straps on her wrists and ankles. Tonal pushed her away, stood unsteadily and slowly walked over to the bathroom where she stayed under the shower for the better part of half an hour. When she reappeared, she was clean, though careful not to seem too resilient for anyone who may be watching.

'Get my clothes,' she barked at Dulce.

Ten minutes later they were in the familiar car headed back to the small town. Neither spoke. Tonal stared out of the window. She expected Ortiz to get violent, but not so soon, not like that. It took all her restraint not to kill him, no matter the consequences. There had been no way she could have escaped from the restraints and killed both men without a sound. This time she just had to bear the abuse.

Dulce was still in shock. The sight of her friend strung up and helpless, or at the least pretending to be, was so alien to her that the truth of the danger they were in finally sank in. On one level she saw the mission as a kind of adventure. Yes, they had a job to do, but she had not expected the price to be so high. She shivered at the thought of what was yet to come. Her own safety, her own sanity, was not so evident and secure anymore. She saw how the mercenaries and especially Croc looked at her, but dismissed the acute danger, sure in her conviction Tonal would not let that happen. That Ortiz would stop the threat to please his new love. What happened last night shattered her security, shattered her conviction. Everything was possible now.

Once back at the hotel, they packed in silence and continued their travel to the secure compound where they knew they were relatively shielded. They could not talk as freely as in the partisan's compound, but free enough that Dulce could finally voice her feelings.

'Are you all right?' she inquired softly. Tonal had not said a word more than absolutely necessary the whole trip. She now sat in the reclining chair with a stiff drink in her hand.

'No, I don't think so, but I'll heal.' She lifted her head to look at Dulce and saw the worry and compassion in her friends face and also the insecurity. She shrugged her shoulders, regained her composure—for Dulce's sake—and continued. 'I don't know, maybe the drugs, or the booze. He went over the edge sooner than I'd anticipated. Caught me by surprise.' She refrained from mentioning Croc and what she believed happened in the early hours of the morning.

They had to continue. There was no turning back now. So, she picked herself up and got down to business. Things would get a lot worse before they got better, that she knew for certain.

'Okay' she leaned over the table, shuffled through the maps and floor plans of Ortiz's fortress. When she found the floor plan, she queried Dulce. 'What did you find out?'

Reassured by the way Tonal took control again, Dulce told her about the rooms she had visited and the servants she'd spoken with. There was a feeling of dread amongst the people who worked in the villa. Frankly they were scared to death of both Ortiz and the mercenaries. The lions were their least worry. At least they had predictable behaviour.

Chapter Sixty-Four

It was too much.

I couldn't stand the feelings and emotions that bombarded me.

I felt so utterly soiled, humiliated.

I wanted to kill Ortiz, in an exceptionally painful and—for me—satisfying way.

In his absence I wanted to kill someone else.

Anyone would do. I was so out of it. I tried desperately to keep control of my mind. But slowly I felt reason and sanity slip away, a red haze sliding over my eyes and thoughts.

My dreams were violent. The sheets shredded every morning, witnesses to my troubled nightmares.

It was easy to play my role. I shouted and ranted at everyone, including Dulce. I frightened her. She knew what happened with Ortiz and correctly linked it to my obnoxious behaviour. But she didn't know about Croc, had no idea about the memories that resurfaced from the lab. She had no idea of the extent of my anger.

'Tonal,' her voice was soft, careful. 'Are you alright?' I had just thrown a tantrum and broken all the glassware and crockery at the dining table. The cook and maid fled the room trembling and crying. One of the guards stuck his head around the door to see what was happening, he was rewarded with the empty bottle of wine thrown at him that barely missed him full face. He slammed the door shut and retreated behind its relative safety.

I clenched my fists in an attempt to lower the level of tension and looked through the red at Dulce. She kept her distance, her attention on my hands. I followed her gaze and saw my hands were bleeding, the claws had pierced the skin. With sheer will power I forced my hands open, forced the claws to recede. The bleeding stopped instantly; the wounds closed. I must have looked frightening.

'I need to leave,' I managed to say. 'I need to change.' Not having to add the "or else." It was obvious. I would snap.

'I'll say you're sick. That you don't want to leave your room.'

She took control, I was so grateful I could have kissed her. But the abject fear in her eyes stopped me from moving any closer.

It was necessary. I would leave tonight. Go into the jungle and relieve all the anger that threatened to over-whelm me.

I had to get myself back on track.

Three hours later, in the early hours of the night, I changed and left the villa's grounds. The guards were focused on not letting anyone in—no one saw me leave.

The villa was in the countryside on the edge of the town, and I was under the cover of the jungle within minutes. The sounds and smells soothed me instantly. I ran and ran, feeling the soft undergrowth under the pads of my paws. The full moon shone on my fur and made me feel part of the night. My roar scared anything and anyone within a ten-mile radius.

This was the release I thought I craved. But still the red haze persisted, I needed to kill something. Feast on the forest as I had done so many times before. I stopped my head-on crashing through the jungle and switched to stealth mode. I padded through the trees, in search of the scent or tell-tale signs of prey, something that was big enough to satisfy my hunger, and if possible strong enough to offer a challenge.

In the undergrowth I found the scent of small mammals, peccaries and small deer. I was looking for something else.

The sand around a pool of water gave me what I wanted. This was the territory of a large caiman. A formidable adversary, but one without a hope in hell today.

I padded down to the water and waited. My presence would already have been noticed and the animal would be torn between hunting urges and uncertainty because of my unusual scent. Brashly entering the water, I decided to bring the fight to him. Sure enough, the gauntlet was picked up and a big black caiman glided through the water towards me. He understood this was a territory challenge and attacked.

The fight was short and sweet.

He didn't stand a chance. The massive reptile barely grazed me with his teeth, he never managed to get a hold. My teeth tore into his body as I manoeuvred myself up over his back. I closed my jaws around the top of his head, my immense canines crashed through his skull and killed him instantly as they entered his small brain.

I dragged the caiman to the shore.

He was big; at least four metres from head to the tip of his tail. I flipped him over and started to feast on the soft underbelly. The internal organs like the liver were my first treat, and I finished with the massive muscles of the tail. My hunger was sated.

But still something was missing.

I cleaned myself in the pool. I tried to wash off the dirty feeling I'd carried with me since my last visit to Ortiz. It wasn't enough. I would need to find another way to exorcise the images and the feelings of disgust.

I moved out of the water and walked back into the jungle. I left the carcass for the scavengers and travelled all-night and part of the morning. Without a conscious decision about the direction, I just kept going. I rested most of the afternoon and continued in the dusk and darkness. At just over midnight, I reached where I was unconsciously heading—the partisan's compound.

I softly circumvented the guards and padded over to Alex's quarters. This was my destination.

I had to see him. Feel him near, feel his love, let him cleanse me.

Pushing the downstairs window further open with my snout I softly jumped the short hurdle and landed in his bedroom. Only now hoping that he was alone. Otherwise, it would get embarrassing.

He heard the thud of my paws on the floor, sat up in bed and groped for his gun on the side table.

I changed.

'It's me,' I said in the husky voice that was always the result of the change.

'Tonal?' He made sure the safety was back on and put the gun down.

'Yes.' I stayed where I was, just inside the window. I

didn't know what to do. He got up and moved to me, his arms outstretched.

'Are you all right?' he asked worried. 'Dulce?'

'Dulce is okay, nothing's wrong,' I answered his unspoken fear.

He hugged me close and sensed my struggle. His arms felt good and slowly I thawed. My hands came up and I hugged him back. I felt the warm skin of his naked back. Let my hands slip lower to his buttocks. So, he slept in the nude, I thought, how convenient. I raised my head, sought his mouth and kissed him fiercely. He responded. No questions asked. Gave me what I wanted.

Alex picked me up and carried me to the bed where he lay me down on the clean sheets. I wouldn't let him go and he tumbled down on top of me. Kissing me as he fell.

We explored each other's bodies hungrily. Not staying long on any specific limb, too anxious and impatient to do anything else. He entered me and once again I felt the instant release.

This was how it should be, not the debasing act that Ortiz defiled me with, but the love Alex had. The all-consuming fire that raged from him, sought to please me and make me whole.

It worked.

We climaxed together and fell back spent.

It was rougher than the last time. But full of fire and passion. Full of emotion.

We lay in silence. He held me in his arms and softly kissed the top of my head. 'Are you alright?' he asked finally.

'I am now.'

'I'm glad to have you here. Tonal, but what happened?' I sighed. Had I thought I could avoid explaining my sudden appearance—my strange manner? I gave him the censored version. It was enough. I felt him tense as I circumvented the details. He filled them in himself.

'My poor love,' he whispered. He felt my hurt. Mirrored my anger at the bastard.

I felt tears well at the side of my eyes. Crying was something I hadn't done in decades. Now it was a release. As I lay in Alex's arms, I let myself go. I softly sobbed away, not only what happened with Ortiz, but everything that had bottled up all those years. He joined me in the cleansing. I felt the depth of his emotion, of his love for me. It was warm, comforting.

We stayed this way all night. As close as humanly possible. At one moment we slowly and softly made love again. The action natural and without active thought. It just felt good.

I knew I would be sorry later, but I just let myself ride the moment. Let myself enjoy the feeling of belonging.

'I have to leave,' I said as the first hesitant rays of the rising sun heralded the nearing dawn. He nodded but didn't release me from his arms. I was hesitant too. It was too comfortable. But I had to go before the compound woke up and I was discovered.

I also needed to get back to the villa. What if Ortiz tried to contact me? How would Dulce be able to handle that without making him suspicious? Reluctantly I disentangled myself from Alex's arms and left the bed. Good thing I didn't have to dress, I was in a hurry. Dawn comes quickly so close to the equator, and I needed to get back into the jungle.

He sat and watched me change.

'I love you,' he said as a parting gift.

I couldn't answer him in this form, maybe that was one of the reasons that I changed so quickly. Coward that I am.

He smiled anyway. I turned, leapt out of the window and softly landed on the dry sand outside. I hoped no one would notice the paw prints that went in and out of Alex's bedroom. Oh well, that was his problem now. Knowing Alex, he would probably enjoy that.

I loped back through the jungle and reached the villa in the deep of the next night. The caiman had been enough to sustain me until I returned back to human form in my room. Dulce lay on the sofa next to the bed and softly snored. She had waited for me to return. I felt terrible putting her through the anxiety of whether I would return or not, and in what state.

I picked her up, laid her on the bed and pulled the covers over her.

What I needed now was a shower. I closed the door to the bathroom behind me, stepped into the cubicle and stood under the rain shower for more than ten minutes, alternating between hot and cold water. It invigorated me.

The water and Alex expelled my dark mood, my blood-lust. The caiman and the jungle also helped. Once again, I was focused. The only nagging thought was that once again I'd played with Alex's feelings. That I had been so ultimately selfish and was once again leading him on. But that was something I would deal with after the mission. After all he hadn't needed much convincing. That brought a smile to my lips.

'Tonal, is that you?' The water had woken Dulce.

'Yes, it's me.'

'You ok?'

'Yeah, everything is back to normal.'

Chapter Sixty-Five

They enjoyed relative peace for almost two more weeks. Then the dreaded summons came; Ortiz wanted her to come. So, she complied.

He was happy to see her, even gave her flowers and a pretty little kitten. That was new.

The evening was pleasant and friendly, but late at night the real Ortiz surfaced again. He had a new toy that completely incapacitated her over a barrel-like contraption. She was fastened to it and had to stay in one position for the whole night, her muscles screaming out for relief. This time he didn't visibly hurt or damage her. 'I need you without blemish tomorrow,' was his only explanation.

Croc didn't try anything this time, she wasn't blind-folded or gagged, so the risk was much too great. Once again Dulce was summoned to free and help her mistress after Ortiz and his lackey left the room. Barking orders at the handmaiden, Tonal was fully into her role.

She spent the day relaxing at the side of the pool where she played with the kitten and occasionally took a dive into the cool water. Dulce remained at her beck and call, as was expected.

Around four in the afternoon she was joined by Ortiz, his soft hand-kiss in contrast to his administrations of the past night. He was obviously pleased at how she looked in the miniscule bikini.

'Very beautiful and effective, my dear,' he indicated the minute pieces of material.

'Thank you, I bought it especially for you,' she cooed. He expected her to enjoy everything he did to her, maybe not at that moment, but definitely in retrospect. So, she played along.

'This evening, we have important guests, my dear.' He sat in the deck chair next to her and accepted the offered cocktail from the white dressed servant. 'People who can be beneficial to me and my cause.'

He didn't elaborate, and she knew better than to ask. He made small talk, queried her about her business, how she spent the days they had been apart. He even seemed interested. In response to his friendly banter, she spun the yarn that she and Dulce cultivated so carefully. Her business was doing well, she had been shopping, her answers were enthusiastic, and he responded as any other boyfriend would.

Around them, servants bustled to hang up garlands of fresh flowers, clean every possible surface, set tables and stock bars. A platform was raised near the wall that separated the lions from the villa. Here music instruments were placed and tested. Whatever it was that was planned, it was big. Security was even tougher than normal. Croc was engaged in heated discussions with the many mercenaries that dotted the compound. There were more than usual. They'd even had a makeover and looked somewhat close to respectable—for a mercenary that is.

A stern looking man arrived with a contingent of muscle dressed in black. He summoned Croc to his side and proceeded to check the already high level of security. This was the vanguard for the VIP that would arrive this evening. It had to be someone very high up on the ladder to get everyone so riled up. Ortiz on the other hand was relaxed, at least on the outside.

'When does the party start?' Tonal enquired. 'I want to look my best for you, so I will need time.'

'You are so beautiful I cannot imagine you would need more than five minutes,' he answered. 'We start at seven, dinner is at nine. I have a present for you, something I know you will like.'

He stood up, took her hand and steered her in the direction of the villa. Holding his hand over her eyes for drama, they walked into the bedroom. On a dressmaker's dummy she saw the most stunning dress she'd ever seen. It was full length, with splits high up on one side and all the way up to the shoulder on the other, golden chains strategically holding the sides together. Soft cream with lace and shimmer, it was beautiful. Her intake of breath, and the sheer pleasure she managed to produce in her eyes was what Ortiz had wanted.

'It is beautiful, I have never seen anything like it,' she exclaimed, reaching to touch the soft material. 'It's made of air, so soft, so light.' She turned around and jumped into his arms. 'Thank you, my love, it is so special,' she cried convincingly.

His eyes sparkled. 'How special?' he asked.

She immediately understood what he implied, slowly sank down to the ground, opened his pants and freed his cock. She took him in her mouth, gave him the best blowjob he'd ever had and completely lived up to his expectations.

After he climaxed all over her hair and face, Ortiz thanked her—another first—and left her to bath and make herself beautiful. He indicated he would send for her, so she could make a grand entrance.

Dulce appeared and helped her get ready for the party. Tonal wanted to quiz her whether she knew who the mystery guest was but didn't dare ask outright. Her friend had tried to find out, but none of the servants were aware of who it was. They would just have to wait. Tonal mulled over who it could be. It had to be someone very important, not only to Ortiz. The amount of security that had flooded the compound indicated the mystery guest was at the least very rich. That much muscle costs a fortune. The most compelling reason that indicated the importance was how Croc was acting. He deferred to the chief security officer of the visitor without a flinch. Totally out of character.

Tonal relaxed as she soaked in the hot bath and decided to just wait and see. In any case it ruined any chance of finishing the mission this weekend. With so much security it would be impossible to leave the compound, even in the manner they had chosen. The risks were just too high. Not that there had been any real chances up till now. But she remained alert for any moment of relaxation on the side of Ortiz.

The dress was astonishing. It fit her like a glove. The clinging material followed every curve of her body and the colour contrasted fantastically with her bronze skin. The lace gave it the extra feminine detail. It was chic and sexy at the same time. Absolutely fantastic.

The makeup applied by Dulce was the finishing touch. It accentuated her unusual exotic ochre eyes. Her hair was fixed up in a simple but very effective way.

She admired the result in the mirror when Croc barged

in the room to announce that she was expected. He stopped his summons mid-sentence, too astounded to continue. She turned slowly and enjoyed the moment.

'You are summoned... uh...expected,' he stammered. 'Follow me.' He regained his composure, turned and walked to the door, holding it open for her. She glided out of the room, the hem of the dress lightly touched the floor and enhanced the image that she floated, her feet never touching the carpet.

Croc led her to the formal ballroom. It was decorated with thousands of flowers and the scents were overwhelming. Her entrance stopped all conversation as she moved through the large crowd that had already amassed. All the guests were dressed in formal evening ware. Men in tuxedo's, white and black, women in long dresses in a multitude of colours. These were not the whores of an earlier party, but the wives and trophies of the VIPS. Women of class.

The crowd parted for her amid whispers of admiration and jealousy. Many a man became the recipient of an elbow from his spouse in an attempt to stop his eyes from bulging out of their sockets. At the end of the tunnel of people stood Ortiz, beaming. When she was a few feet from him, he stepped down from the dais and walked the last steps to her. She held out her hand and he pressed his lips to her fingers.

'You look ravishing, my dear,' he whispered, just loud enough for the people near to hear. 'Clearly the belle of the ball. Thank you.'

'Thank you, my love,' she purred in return, 'As always your choice of a dress is impeccable.' She acknowledged he was the one responsible for her perfect attire. Tonal took his arm and allowed him to lead her to the dais. He stopped them in front of a couple flanked by the security chief and another muscle-bound brute in a tux. Ortiz turned to the man.

'Please allow me to introduce the love of my life; Tonal.' He addressed the man then turned to Tonal.

'My dear, allow me to introduce you to the Honourable Raimundo Esposito, El Presidente, and his beautiful consort, Señorita Salina.' Tonal did a small curtsy towards the president and bowed her head as was expected. So that was the mystery guest, well they didn't get very much higher up the ladder than this.

'Your beauty seems to have stopped conversation my dear,' he remarked. 'Quite an achievement in this gathering.' She saw the amusement in his eyes and smiled. When she glanced to the woman next to the president, she was surprised by the out-and-out hostility that emanated from the beautiful eyes.

'I am sure that it pales by the radiance of your beautiful lady,' she cooed. The hostility in the air lowered a degree. Tonal resolved to try and make the woman feel more at home. 'I cannot come close to your beauty and elegance.' She aimed her comment to Salina who acknowledged the compliment with one of her own.

'Your dress is as if it was made of air, beautiful.' More compliments followed, from both men and others in the inner circle. Tonal noticed that Salina only complimented her attire, never her person. It would take a lot longer and more than idle admiration to win this one over.

She observed the other woman: a petite dark beauty. The lines in her face attended to her Latin ancestry, but the mocha colour of her skin implied other race influences. She was beyond doubt extremely beautiful, with thick long jet-black hair that flowed beyond her hips almost down to the back of her knees. Her figure was impeccable. Tonal estimated her age at somewhere between fifteen and twenty. Despite her small stature and young age, she oozed strength. This was a very strong-willed young lady. Not one to dismiss easily.

Raimundo Esposito was a tall thin man of about sixty, his face was soft and friendly, his eyes though were hard and cold. He was comfortable in his stature, totally relaxed in these surroundings and his status. Fully content to leave his safety to the hired help, he was here to enjoy himself. Impeccably dressed in the latest fashion for formal ware, his tie and pocket handkerchief were in the exact same hue as Salina's dress.

Esposito continued his casual bantering as he downed his champagne.

A white clad servant appeared at Ortiz's side with a new tray of champagne, after Esposito had taken one glass, Ortiz took two, offering one to Tonal and one to Salina. He took a third for himself and dismissed the servant with a wave of his hand. The four of them were once again the only ones on the dais—the central focal point of the party.

Chapter Sixty-Six

Salina was a beautiful woman, but cold and distant. Her eyes weighed everyone and everything and found them wanting. This was not an easy woman to please.

The president held on to her arm in a way that was not exactly friendly. His fingers left red welts where they had obviously been holding her too tightly. Initially she seemed fragile, so small—petite really—but on closer look she was hard as granite. She had a will of her own, one that did not always find itself in line with Esposito's. During the evening, she never openly contradicted him, but her demeanour was enough. It was clear she was bored, and the luxury of the party did not make an impression. Later, the president gave up his attempt to steer her in the direction of his liking, and just let her do what she wanted.

Unlike him, she was sparse with alcohol—she stayed alert. She was also quite outspoken in her interest of the younger men in the official company. Ortiz's brother interested her for a few moments. But none could measure up to what she wanted and near the end of the evening she once again turned her charm and attention to El Presidente. He was used to her switching moods and not the slightest bit annoyed or surprised at her change.

She eyed me suspiciously for the first part of the evening but lightened up when it became clear that the president wasn't interested in me. Oh, sure, he acknowledged my beauty, admired the dress and what he could see of my body. But it never excited him like the other men around. Okay with me. I had my hands full with Ortiz.

His time would come later.

Chapter Sixty-Seven

The evening progressed easily with a lot of banter and casual conversation. Ortiz and Tonal stayed in the neighbourhood of the presidential couple all evening. They sat together at the immense dining table for the fantastic five-course gourmet dinner. And later retired to the second dais opposite the stage specifically built to offer the best place listen to tonight's concert featuring the best artists of the decennia.

Finally, in the early hours of the morning, the president retired to his suite of rooms. Slowly the other guests left, and the servants started to clean up. Ortiz took Tonal by the hand and led her to his quarters. He was friendly and even tender that night. It was also the first night Croc was not in the room the whole time. Esposito was also high on the list of the resistance and would have been a nice bonus. A shame she couldn't make use of the circumstances, but it was impossible.

In the morning, after a sumptuous buffet breakfast, the

president and Salina left, amid extensive thanks to Ortiz for his hospitality. Even Salina was all smiles and hugs.

Ortiz remained a gentleman for another hour while they had coffee at the side of the pool and chatted about the party. It was quite surreal.

'I will send for you again soon.' Ortiz stood up, kissed her briefly on the cheek and so dismissed her. He turned back and added an afterthought. 'You did well.'

Surprised at the change in Ortiz's demeanour, she called for Dulce and left the pool. They gathered her things, left the beautiful dress hanging on the dresser's dummy, packed and left the compound. Both were disappointed that they had still not been able to fulfil their mission and that they would have to keep up the façade and come back again.

It didn't take long for Ortiz to send for her. She was in the hotel for two days when Croc showed up at her door, demanding she leave with him. He was obviously disgruntled at being sent as a messenger and his temper was showing. Dulce raced to pack a small bag with the necessary items for a short stay. She wasn't quick enough to his liking and when she stumbled with the bag, he hit her across the face with his flat hand. Tonal felt the hairs on her back stand up, the claws ready to burst through, but feigned indifference. After all, Dulce was only her servant. Red faced and starting to swell near her left eye, Dulce doubled her speed and within five minutes they were seated in the car headed back to the compound.

Ortiz wasn't there when they arrived, she was ordered to wait at the pool edge. After more than two hours he arrived in a foul mood, covered in sweat and what looked like blood. Indicating she follow him—he strode to the immense bathroom in the main building. Tonal helped him undress and was rewarded with a back handed slap to the face. The result almost identical to that of Dulce. She knew enough not to comment or ask what the problem was. After a long and languid bath, where she was expected to wash his back and he almost drowned her pushing her head under water to administer to him, his mood was somewhat better.

She dried herself off and dressed back in the clothes she had come in. Finally, she asked what was on his mind.

Ortiz observed her closely as he recounted the mornings activities. The mayor of one of the villages in his domain had come forward to warn him about a possible attempt on his life. The mayor's only hope of diminishing the fall out shattered when Ortiz rode into the town with the mercenaries and proceeded to slaughter not only the alleged perpetrators but also all their families and neighbours. The mayor's son one of the innocent bystanders. Usually this would have improved Ortiz's mood, but the thought of an attempt so soon after the president's visit bothered him. The mayor said that the traitors initially wanted to kill the president and that was not a rumour Ortiz wanted spread around. The party was an enormous political success and he wanted it to remain so.

His rage sated; he calmed down. Outside Tonal could hear the mercenaries with one of the young girls they had taken from the village as bounty. The girl screamed; the men laughed. Tonal looked out of the window and saw they had her hanging upside down over the edge of the lions' enclosure. The lions bellowed, frustrated their prize was just out of reach. The bullies tired of the game and pulled the luckless girl back up and tore the clothes from her body. She and the other two girls that were taken were ravished by a large number of mercenaries.

Tonal joined Ortiz on his couch, seemingly oblivious to the violence outside the building.

After a long and boring meal, they watched the latest stream in the cinema room. Dulce and Croc as always near, then retired to the bedroom. Once again, the old Ortiz was back, as he hoisted her up by her arms and abused her. But the drive was gone, and he tired of the games quickly. He ordered Croc to untie her, let her clean the blood and gore from her body and join him in the vast bed. Totally unexpectedly, he sent Croc away. 'Go have some fun with the bitches,' Ortiz added.

'They are spent,' Croc answered. Earlier they'd heard the sound of at least one of the girls thrown over the edge and the lions fighting over her body.

'Maybe I'll take the maid.' It was not a real question, but he needed Ortiz's permission.

'Why not?' Ortiz laughed, looking at Tonal.

Her blood as cold as ice in her veins, she feigned indifference. 'Whatever.'

This was not part of the plan. It had always been possible, but she had pushed it from her mind, sure that she would be able to prevent it from happening. The smile on Croc's face broadened. He sensed she was unhappy with the situation, but there was nothing she could do. Finally, he had her over a barrel. If he couldn't have her again, then her petite servant was a nice pass-time. He would not kill her—Ortiz would not be pleased—but he could certainly hurt her a bit and have some fun.

Ortiz grabbed Tonal as Croc closed the door behind him. He pulled her close to him and started to pinch her breasts.

'The bruises are gone, my dear, I will give you new ones.' Her mind raging, she forced herself to play the game. She winced at the pain he inflicted. But she was distracted and forgot to stop the healing process, so the bruises disappeared almost as quickly as they came. This enraged Ortiz, and he intensified his administrations. She remembered—too late—and tried to halt the healing process. Ortiz was piping mad again. He rolled her over, straddled her and grabbed her by the throat. He folded his hands around her neck and squeezed hard enough to bring up bruises and almost stop her breathing.

She'd had enough.

Tonal grabbed his wrists and pulled his hands from her neck.

His eyes bulged, surprised at the enormous strength she had. Speechless, he strained to retain his grasp on her neck, to keep control of the situation.

The hairs were starting to grow through her skin on her back, and she let them come. Finally, she enjoyed the familiar tingling of the change. Tonal pulled his hands from her and broke his right wrist. She threw him off her and changed the tables. She sat on him and slowly let her muzzle form, her claws pushed through and pinned Ortiz to the bed. His stupor was replaced by mind-blowing terror.

'Now it's your turn,' the words were contorted by the change of her facial muscles and vocal cords but were clear none the less. Ortiz bladder emptied, he was so terrified by the sight of her muzzle, with the long canine teeth that slowly moved to his face and closed around his throat. With a last bout of terror-driven energy he tried to scream and throw this monstrosity off him, but it was too late. She had his neck in her jaws and bit down and almost severed the head. She held on for a few moments more, just to be sure before she finally let out all the pent-up anger at what this tyrant had done to others and to her. The violence, the degradation. At last, it was over, her anger bled out with Ortiz.

Tonal changed back and cleaned the gore off her body. It would not do to attract attention covered in blood. Then she pulled a shirt over her naked form and slipped through the door. No one would dare to disturb Ortiz' slumber until the morning, so she had time. Now she had to get to Dulce and stop Croc from hurting her or worse.

Chapter Sixty-Eight

She stayed in the shadows of the buildings and listened for the slightest indication of where he had taken her. Moving to the room that Dulce stayed in when she was here, she heard the sound of a hand striking flesh and the intake of breath when it hit. Her scent was strongest here. He had looked her up in the servant's quarters.

There was no one around at this time of the night. The servants didn't dare venture out of the relative safety of their rooms, and the mercenaries were sated with the girls from the village and the booze. Croc's laughter confirmed she was at the right place. She peered through the window and saw Dulce tied to the bed naked. She was bruised and bleed from shallow cuts. Croc stood over her, an enormous knife in his hand. He slid the blade down her form to the right nipple and mimicked slicing it off. Dulce begged and pleaded, but he continued his cruel game. He threw the knife to the side, pulled his shirt over his head and unbuckled his pants.

This was more fun than he had imagined. She was

tough and hadn't cried out until the last few minutes. Mind you, she would have to be strong to be with that bitch. Nice body too. Not the supple muscled form of her mistress, but certainly adequate for now. One of these days he would do away with Ortiz and take over. He made new friends at the party last week and the president's security chief indicated no one would mourn Ortiz's passing, should it occur. That was the backup he needed, so soon—very soon—he would feed Ortiz to his beloved lions. Piece by piece. And then he would be top dog. The bitch would be his. To do with as he fancied. Until he tired of her, and she ended up as cat food.

The thought alone was almost enough for him to climax in his pants. But that would be a shame. First this one. Croc pushed his pants down, stepped out of them and stood in his boxers.

A noise at the door spun him around.

Stunned, he just stood and stared. Tonal stood in the doorway, totally naked. Her seductive body reclined against the doorpost. The moon shone on her bronze skin and detailed muscle. She was sexier than ever. Not a blemish on that perfect form. Her hair accentuated the curve of her breast as it draped over her upper body.

'Are you really going to waste your time with the hired help?' Her voice the epiphany of seduction. She slowly moved into the room, closing the door behind her. He couldn't keep his eyes off her, this magnificent creature that filled his mind every waking and sleeping moment. The need was excruciating. He had to have her, he had to… …

Coming to his senses, he demanded; 'what are you doing here? Ortiz let me have her, you have no say in this.' Her fingernail moved from his shoulder over his pecs to the six-pack he was so proud of, almost but not exactly touching the bulge in his shorts.

'Is she what you really want?' she cooed, 'Or would you rather have all this.' Her hand seductively passed over her breasts and erect nipples, down her flat stomach to the fine triangle of hairs at her pubic mound. The fingers of one hand disappeared between her legs.

Croc shook his head in an attempt to clear his head and moved a step back. 'What about Ortiz?' Sanity was leaving in a hurry—lust was all that was left.

'He's asleep, and anyway, you're going to be the boss soon, aren't you?' Her eyes pierced his. Hypnotised him. She moved closer again. Her hand stroked his face and moved down to his neck. Before he could comprehend what was going on, she grabbed his neck in her talons and pressed them inwards as she forced him backwards to the wall.

'You pathetic piece of shit,' she whispered. His hands came up and tried to disgorge her grip. His survival training kicked in—but it was no use. She had him hard up against the wall, his feet no longer touched the ground. He kicked frantically to no avail. She closed her hand and ripped his throat from his neck. Desperately, he tried to press his hands to his bleeding neck. The blood sprayed around the room, colouring everything bright red as he stumbled and tried to get away. Croc fell to his knees, looked up at her form once more, tried to speak, and fell over flat on his face.

Tonal waited a few seconds. Just to be sure, she felt for a pulse and not finding any she moved to free Dulce from the bed. Dulce cried softly, stumbled off the bed, moved over to Croc's body and kicked him viciously, her anger centred on the body. Tonal let her vent for a few moments.

'Come on Dulce. It's done. Get dressed, we need to get out of here.'

Dulce wiped her face with her arm and aimed one last

kick at her tormentor. She turned around she became all business again. She found the clothes she'd picked for the escape, should it ever come; a tight-fitting stretch set that moved with every turn of her body. Her feet were bare, so she could hold on if needed. She packed her flat shoes in a small backpack, along with Croc's knife, the second gun he usually kept in a holster on the inside of his right calf and her cell phone. She slung the pack over her back and pulled the straps tight.

Tonal changed in the meantime and listened for any movement outside at the open doorway. She lowered herself to the ground and allowed Dulce to climb on her back as they had practiced so many times.

Chapter Sixty-Nine

They slunk out of the room and kept to the shadows.

One of the dogs started to bay when it caught her strange scent. It was silenced by a rough blow from a guard. The moon was half full, in and out of the clouds that moved over its surface and offered some light.

Tonal glided to the wall of the lion's compound, sprang up onto the top, looked back one last time and started the decent down to the moat's floor. She climbed and slid down, past the hooks and onto the sandy floor of the lion's den. Tonal wasn't expecting too many problems from the cats, they had been sated earlier that night, but anything was possible. She moved almost without sound as she skirted the area where the remains of one of the girls lay. Most of the lions lay asleep, their stomachs full. Most—but not all.

One of the lionesses was awake and nursing the cubs. She caught the strange scent and sprang up, growling in a low and menacing voice. There was no doubt this would awaken the others. The large male was between them and the way out. Instantly awake at the sound of his mate's growl, he rose to his full height and tried to pinpoint where the new threat came from. He was puzzled by the strange smell, and he curled his lips in an attempt to learn more.

Tonal moved to a large tree to her right and pushed up against its bark. Dulce understood, left her back and climbed up the branches as high as she could. Moving back to the wall, Tonal found a position with her back to the solid stone. The lion had found the intruders. The one in the tree he left to his lioness, the strange animal near the wall was another thing completely. He was confused. It looked like a lion, but was much, much bigger than anything he had ever seen. Even towering over him. The scent told him it was female, but that was impossible. Lionesses didn't get that big. One of the females growled and he decided that whatever it was, it was a threat to his family and had to be handled. Voicing his anger, he moved towards the intruder, flanked by two of his lionesses. The third was at the base of the tree and started to make her way up after Dulce.

Tonal had to get this over with as soon as possible, lions don't climb all that well, but they do climb. The lioness would get dangerously close to Dulce. She stood to her full feline height and roared a challenge to the lion. He charged; she met him halfway. The impact threw him off his feet. He stood quickly and attacked again, the lioness on her right attacked as well. Tonal swiped the lioness with her paw and sent it flying, turning just too late to stop the male's charge. His jaws clamped on her back leg, and he tried to shake his head, in an attempt to break the bones. She turned her back and raked her claws over his side. The lion let go and, leaving no room for chance, she pounced on him, closed her jaws around his head and ended his life in one jaw-crunching wrench. The lioness that remained turned and made her way to the cubs, determined to fight to the end to protect them. Tonal turned her attention to the one who had already climbed to the first branches of the tree where Dulce was perched. She reached up on her back paws, clamped her jaws around the lioness's right back leg and pulled her out of the tree. With a swipe of her right paw, she sent the cat tumbling to the body of her mate. There it regained its feet and joined the other female at the cub's side.

One last growl was enough to keep them at a distance. If possible Tonal didn't want to kill them all. It wasn't their fault they were man-eaters, and now they were just protecting their cubs.

Slowly Dulce climbed down out of the tree and took her place on Tonal's back. Keeping the lionesses in sight with a soft but clear growl, Tonal moved out of the clearing and into the trees. Once there she started to run while she listened whether the cats were following her. They weren't.

She reached the compound gates within a few uneventful minutes, slid past the lights and guards and continued on in the fenced enclosure. After another five minutes they reached the boundaries of the lion's compound. The fence was high and the current lethal. It was high enough for normal lions. Tonal was much larger and could jump much higher. But still it was close. She took a long run at the highest point in the landscape and only just cleared the fence, scorching the fur on her back legs. No matter, it would grow back. She continued at full tilt in easterly direction and ran for another half hour until they were sure they were relatively safe.

Dulce dismounted and retrieved her cell phone from the

backpack. She pressed speed dial on three and the dial button. She let the phone ring three times before she hung up. Exactly two minutes later she repeated the action.

She remounted and they continued in a more leisurely tempo in a south-easterly direction, where they arrived at the predefined destination an hour later. Alex and a few soldiers waited there for them. The bruises and cuts he saw on his sister's face and arms alarmed Alex.

'I'm okay,' she assured him. 'These are just superficial.'

Tonal had moved to the side and changed back to human form. One of the soldiers offered her clothes and she dressed quickly.

'It's done,' she told Alex. 'Ortiz is dead, and as a bonus we got Croc as well. They will probably not find out until the morning, so we should get away from here as quickly as possible.'

Hopefully, the fallout would not be extreme. With their leader and the moneyman dead the mercenaries would need to find new employment. The revolutionaries counted on them being disorganised and so egotistical that their own individual immediate survival would be the only drive. Regrettably, there would probably be some casualties among the servants of the compound. But Alex and Tonal hoped they would be the ones to find the two bodies and leave before the mercenaries woke up and plundered the place.

The assassination proved to be the major success they'd hoped. Alarmed by the manner of his death, Ortiz's supporters fled the country. The foreign support evaporated, and the president was left without anyone protecting his back. A vicious retaliation by the government's troops proved to be the catalyst that led to even greater support of the revolutionaries and so the presidential power waned. The revolution gained more and more ground and Alex became the face of the saviours. People flocked to their cause and foreign support in the form of money and arms swayed the balance in the favour of the revolution.

The march to the capitol was unstoppable.

Chapter Seventy

This was getting out of control.

What started out as the occasional tryst blossomed into a full-fledged relationship. We spent more nights together than not. By day we pretended nothing was going on. But who were we kidding? Beside ourselves that is.

I think everyone knew. At least everyone close.

Alex was ecstatic, he beamed.

That was what did it for me. The adoring way he looked at me. I could swear he was planning a lifetime of husband and wife, maybe with the chocolate box house and a Labrador. I enjoyed his company, thrilled in the sex and the release it gave me, but balked at the commitment and love he so desperately needed.

Don't get me wrong, I loved him. Just not as much as he loved me.

He tried to pretend our relationship wasn't his whole life, but it was obvious. He lit up when I was around. Paid no attention to anyone or anything else. He was the ultimate lovesick puppy.

And me?

I wanted to love him like that. But I couldn't. Part of me held back—all the time. In the lovemaking, the talks, the feelings.

Was my fear of loss so great I would forgo everything, so as not to have to experience it again?

What was I doing to him?

To myself?

I tried this before. I'd loved someone with all my heart. More than once. Only to lose them. Literally when they died, but mostly much earlier. When they started to resent me.

It always happened.

I suppose it's understandable. No one wants to get old, feeble maybe, and eventually die. Everyone wanted to stay young, beautiful—live forever.

Everyone except me.

What seems ideal from a distance is very different up close. For example—loss.

No one wants to lose their loved ones. For me it is a fact of life. Everyone I have ever loved, or ever will, is destined to die before me. It happens repeatedly. I outlive them all.

The pain doesn't get any more bearable with practice. So, it makes sense to avoid it. Not to love anymore—to isolate myself.

But that's easier said than done.

Alone in the jungle, it was a breeze. There was no one to love. No one to feel good with. Just me and my daemons.

Sometimes, lying in bed with Alex, him asleep in my arms, I cursed him silently for bringing me back and for shattering my peace. For making me part of a family again. Making me love.

I had been at least blissfully ignorant for a few years in

the jungle. Or maybe I just fooled myself all those years. But it worked.

Sort of.

And now the damage had been done.

I made someone fall in love with me. I strung Alex along.

What was I going to do about it?

It turned out to be a lot more acute than I thought.

Chapter Seventy-One

The mission had been blotched. We messed up big time.

Alex panicked.

But why? He knew I was virtually indestructible. There was no need for his rash involvement—for him blowing the assassination. I was okay. Would have been even if they caught me. And they wouldn't have. I can take care of myself. Alex's over-protectiveness screwed up the mission and sent the target into hiding.

So now we were here. Back in the compound.

Having our heads chewed off by Jesus.

And rightly so.

'What happened out there?' he demanded.

'I intervened.' Alex's stab at an answer.

Jesus focused on him. His very stance belied his calm voice. The man was piping mad. Very unlike the Jesus I knew. He was rattled. 'Why?' the question was curt, as if more would blow the lid of his restraint.

'I had to get her out of there.' Alex's pleas were getting more desperate.

No answer from Jesus.

'They would have captured her, maybe even killed her.' Jesus' silence intensified Alex's panic.

'And?' the big man finally said to Alex's shock. He looked to me for help, but none was to be found. 'I very much doubt that they could kill her,' the leader stated. 'Or even restrain her for that matter. Besides that, we do not abort an important mission because of one life, Alex you know that. Not even Tonal's.'

Adamant not to give up so easily, Alex tried; 'if we lose Tonal, we lose a lot more than one person. She is vital to us.'

'To us or to you?' Alex flinched at the harsh words.

I just sat there, let it happen.

The incident at the target's mansion brought home to me just how dangerous this relationship was. Thinking we could separate the "us" from our work was a fantasy at best. And now it put everyone in danger. Not to mention caused us to fail miserably on an important mission. We had to take him out. This had been the best opportunity. A new one would not present itself again in a hurry.

And it had been sacrificed because of Alex's perceived danger of losing me.

Jesus turned his back to us.

We felt like small children seated in the school bench, lectured by the irate headmaster.

'I have closed my eyes to your romantic involvement.' he chastised. 'I hoped that it would not influence your actions in the field.'

We felt terrible.

'That was an oversight.'

'What happened last night had nothing to do with our relationship,' Alex tried.

'Yes, it did.' I slid the nail in his coffin.

He looked at me, shocked to his core.

'Your fears are unfounded,' I continued. I winced internally at each word. I knew the pain I inflicted.

'They weren't. You were in danger.' His words were almost whispers—pleas that I would stop. That I would not say what was coming.

Chapter Seventy-Two

Jesus understood and left the room.

'Alex, this has to stop.' There was no sugar coating this. 'We can't go on. Our relationship endangers others, screws up everything we've worked for. We must focus on the job, and to do that it needs to stop.'

'I can't,' he said feebly. 'I love you.'

'You can, Alex, you have to. We have to.'

'No. Please.'

I let the silence talk for me.

Alex slumped down in the chair. His mind grabbed for threads. After a few minutes of silence, he seemed to pull himself together.

'Okay, we stop for now. Put it all on hold.' He'd found a way out. A desperate man, dying of thirst in a desert finds that one fata morgana.

'No Alex.'

The words cut him physically. 'We need to make a clean break.'

'No...' Tears welled in the corner of his eyes and started their slow journey down his cheeks.

It killed me inside to be so brutal, but it had to be done. I had to continue now I'd started.

'Please Tonal, don't do this. I will be better, I promise. I will put some distance between us for now, but please—not forever.'

He cradled my hand in his. Searched my eyes for any sign, any indication that I might change my mind. Come back on my decision.

'I need you Tonal. Please don't do this. You feel the same way, you love me, don't you?'

I remained silent, my eyes not touching his. I pushed the knife deep into his very being and shattered his heart.

It was for the best.

Then why did it always have to hurt so much?

His desperation made way for hurt, resentment and anger.

'So that was it, huh. You just switch off your feelings like that and expect me to do the same? Or did you even care for me at all? What was I? A plaything? Something to pass the time. A notch on your gun?'

I should have countered that. Told him how much he meant to me. That my feelings for him were exactly the reason why we had to stop this relationship. That I was terrified something would happen to him—more realistic than his fears for me. That I would be his nemesis.

But I stayed mute.

Coward that I am.

And that made it so much worse.

Chapter Seventy-Three

Alex avoided her after that terrible meeting. He made sure he was always physically as far from her as possible. After a week of leaving him alone she tried to talk to him. Tried to make him understand she wanted to be friends. Go back to how it had been before their friendship became sexual. But it was hopeless. He was hurt badly. His heart was broken, and his trust shattered,

She missed him. Badly. Maybe they should have just tuned the relationship down a bit. But it was too late now. He wouldn't talk to her, only reluctantly sat in the same room. The air between them was icy.

She let it rest.

Chapter Seventy-Four

Finally, three months later, the last major battle was fought.

To ensure success the revolutionaries once again turned to Tonal to take care of the president. She assassinated him one dark night in his own bedroom, circumventing the safety precautions, she leapt up from the garden onto the first-floor balcony. He was alone in the room, fully expecting any attack to come from the one locked and bolted door to the landing. When she crashed through the balcony doors, he felt his heart give out. Whether his death could be accounted to heart failure, or her claws and fangs was debatable, and totally insignificant.

As expected, his demise caused the main body of the remaining soldiers to flee the palace and that left just a small contingent of fanatics to protect the palace. The revolutionaries made short work of them and entered the palace grounds.

The smoke settled, and the noise receded as the group moved through the presidential palace rooms. They found a few additional soldiers and servants who offered no resistance. Leaving them to their comrades, the point group continued.

In the right wing of the palace, they encountered a heavily locked and barred door. They blew it up with Semtex and pushed into what turned out to be a row of dungeons and the entrance to the lower levels of the palace. The deeper they went underground the worse the cells became. Finally, on the third underground level, they found some survivors. Some of the men and women they recognised as missing resistance fighters or other opposition.

One cell held three women. An older woman—near to death—and two younger ones. Careful not to blind the three prisoners with their spotlights, the resistance group moved over to release the women from the chains that bound them to the bunks in the cell.

Tonal detected a familiar scent. She knew one of the young women. Where had they met? The figure was dirty and covered in rags and dried blood. Her long black hair matted and half over her face. Dulce offered her some water, which she took, raising her head to drink revealing her face.

Ah yes, that was where they had met—at Ortiz's party.

'Hallo, Salina,' Tonal said. The young woman stopped drinking and focused on the dust-covered revolutionary that stepped up out of the shadows.

'Well, well,' she said calmly. 'Look what the cat dragged in. The resistance, it figures.'

'You know each other?' Alex asked looking at Tonal.

'She was with the president at the party in Ortiz's compound.' Dulce answered for them. She also recognised who the prisoner was. 'She was his…consort.' She turned to Salina and added 'What are you doing here?'

'I angered him,' was the cold and emotionless answer.

The other young woman interrupted with a heartfelt plea. 'Please, help my mother, she is hurt.' The revolutionaries left the reunion for what it was, set to freeing the three women and transported them up out of the dungeons into the luxury of the palace. Alex called to one of the medics to take care of the older woman.

In the daylight Alex finally got his first good look at the young woman Dulce and Tonal identified as Salina. Of course, he had heard of her, but no pictures existed. She was the unofficial presidential consort. A beautiful prize that was the president's to do with as he wished. Obviously, he hadn't wanted her anymore. Why else would she be in the dungeons?

Salina felt his eyes on her. She turned her head to observe the man who was obviously in charge of the revolutionaries. He was not bad looking and strong, in body but also in mind. He was the natural leader, and so of interest to her. Latching on to power was a natural instinct to Salina. She let her eyes fill with tears and slowly made herself look vulnerable, wishing him to come to her aid. She was not disappointed; he moved to her side and took her in his arms and offered his shoulder to cry on.

Men were so predictable.

She held on tight and sobbed convincingly. Well almost. The woman she had seen with Ortiz stared at her. She saw through the farce. Salina would have to be careful with that one. Get her out of the picture as soon as possible.

'Please,' she whispered. 'Don't let them hurt me anymore. I'm so scared.' Alex stoked her hair and assured her she was safe.

Peace returned to the country, with the exception of a few isolated incidents. The revolutionaries installed their head-quarters in a large building near the presidential palace. The rebuilding of the country and its people started.

Alex remained the face of the revolution. He was charis-matic, and the people worshipped him. The council ruled the country in the meantime. Preparations were started for the transfer of power to a democratically chosen president and cabinet. There were several candidates for the presiden-tial position. Alex was one of them, spurred on by Salina and his popularity.

His romance with Salina was the talk of the country. The revolutionary and the vulnerable petite woman he saved. She played the media well; doted on Alex and referred to him as her saviour, her prince. Alex was smitten. She worked her magic. He wanted no more than to keep this beautiful and loving angel at his side. She understood him, to the very fibres of his being. She lived to make him happy. He had never experienced anything like this relation-ship before. Or so he thought.

For more years than he chose to remember he was in love with Tonal, but the short affair that once made him so happy ended badly. In his mind she didn't acknowledge his love—played with him. She broke his heart into a million pieces. And now Salina was here, healing him. She filled the hole in his being and more than that—she gave him a future.

She played him well and coached him into a career he never wanted, that had never been his ambition. She instilled a feeling of value in him, of self-importance and of privilege.

Tonal initially agreed with the relationship. Seeing how it made him happy. But deep down inside she mistrusted

Salina. This was a manipulative woman. One that was used to getting her way—a woman with her own agenda.

Slowly Tonal noticed the changes in Alex. He became more materialistic. Okay, in the jungle no one owned anything, which was out of necessity. That it wouldn't stay like that was to be expected. But Alex now leaned to the greedy side. She didn't begrudge him his pleasures, but the government picked up the tab. Alex's family fortune had long ago gone to help the resistance.

Maybe that was his reasoning why he was entitled.

Chapter Seventy-Five

I stalked into the room, my temper dangerously on the brink of explosion.

What was he thinking? He bought not one but two Ferrari's, not to mention the Bugatti Veyron that was delivered last month. I would give him a piece of my mind. This was a pure waste of money, and more than that, it was community money, tax money. Not his to spend. At least not like this.

His scent was absent. He wasn't there. But the cloying sweet smell of Salina's perfume filled the air.

She sat on the sofa with her legs folded under her and watched TV—some stupid soap. Seemed like her. Anything with more depth would probably bore her anyway.

'Where's Alex?' I asked brusquely.

'He's not here.'

'I can see that,' I answered. 'Where is he?'

'Why?'

I sighed, counted to ten under my breath. Seven, eight, nine, ten. Nope didn't really help. My temper was still up there near the clouds. 'Don't bother yourself with why, I need to talk to him.'

'About what?'

'None of your business,' I snapped. She was getting on my nerves. She did that a lot recently. She observed me with her sweet cloying smile.

'You don't like me do you, Tonal?'

'No,' I said on my way back to the door. Fuck tact. I was still fuming. I had no time for such a feather-brained manipulator. If she wanted to know how I felt about her, I would tell her.

'Well at least you're honest, this time,' She remarked. 'Anyway, it will not surprise you that it is absolutely mutual.' I stopped walking and turned to her. The past weeks she had really pissed me off. Maybe now was the time to unburden my feelings.

'You're no good for Alex. His actions the past weeks have been totally out of character. You have a bad influence on him. He should be busy rebuilding this country. Do you even love him?' I asked loudly, not caring who heard me now. 'You don't know what the word means. He adores you. God knows why. He should look through the veneer and see how rotten you are on the inside. How manipulative and totally narcissistic. The only person in the world who is important to you—is you. I wish his eyes would open. That he would finally see the damage you cause. The changes in his character, in him, all boil down to you. To your manipulations and greed. He might finally see you for what you really are—a money grabbing, emotionless sociopath.'

She only smiled.

'I should thank you really, you know.' She was enjoying this.

I stayed quiet. I should have stopped talking a while ago. I wouldn't give her any more reason to gloat.

'Thanks to you, he was extremely susceptible to me. You broke his heart, left it as ripe pickings for me. So really, the only one you have to blame for what is bothering you is yourself. Now doesn't that put a different perspective on things.'

'What do you really want with Alex?' I asked. 'Anything more than power? Money?'

'What's wrong with that? I've been abused all my life, since I was a small girl, men have wanted me, hurt me. Why shouldn't I get what I want out of it?' Her eyes blazed— finally some emotion.

'You have no idea how it's been for me. When I was five my mother pimped me out to a variety of men then sold me to the first rich paedophile she could find. You see, I was a beautiful child. With warm eyes, a small body and flexible limbs. I learned at an early age if I pleased these perverts, they would be nice to me, or at least not hurt me like my mother had done.' Unconsciously she pulled her legs up and hugged her knees. 'The pervert she sold me to, kept me as his so called "niece" for three years. By then I was too old for his tastes. He liked them young, and tight.'

Despite my hatred for the woman, I shuddered at her history.

'He sold me to a friend of his, a military man— someone with discipline and control issues. I was too recalcitrant, and he put me up for auction on the Internet. El Presidente bought me. I was nine at the time and shipped off to my new owner in a crate. Like an animal bundled in the hold of a plane.'

Was this real or just another attempt at manipulation?

'He chained me to his bed for the first nights while he

abused me constantly. He raped me any way he could think of and believe me that was one creative man. Not that I need to tell you. He and Ortiz exchanged ideas and stories. I heard about what Ortiz did to you. But that was peanuts compared with what I endured. Slowly I made him believe he had broken my spirit. I pretended to adore him. Led him on. In his own way I suppose he even started to love me. He kept me a lot longer than any of the others.'

'We found you in the dungeons,' I reminded her.

'Yes, I tired of him. Started to thwart him. He enjoyed it at first, it gave him a reason to beat me. But he was a simple man, with simple needs and I didn't fulfil them anymore. I refused to play along with his games, and he turned out to be harder to play than I thought. It worked for a while, but he tired of making compromises. Or maybe he just found my replacement. Anyway, I pushed him a little too far and he stuck me down there. He always said he would rather see me rot than allow anyone else to have me.'

'So, when we rescued you, you latched on to your next victim, your next meal ticket.'

'You have no right to condemn me, Tonal. I did what was necessary, and I will continue to until I have what I want.'

'And what do you want?'

'Everything.' Her smile was vicious.

'Alex is a man of the people, he never cared for material objects. His goals in life have always been to help his fellow people, to free this country from tyrants and money grabbers. You will not corrupt him. I will not let you.'

'You will not let me? What makes you think you have any influence left with him,' she whispered. 'He will do what I want. He wants to. He loves me. He will do anything to please me. I will get what is my due.'

'That you will,' I said 'but not maybe what you are hoping for. You're a manipulative bitch Salina. I'm sorry you had a bad start in life but get over it. You have the opportunity now to do something good with yourself. You could help Alex in his campaign to help the poor in this country. The oppressed and battered. People like those where you came from. Instead of only thinking about yourself, do some good.'

'I don't care about anyone else. I have absolutely no intention of tempering my goals just to help someone. Let them take care of themselves. That's what I did. No one helped me. Let them all rot.'

'Not at the expense of Alex's peace of mind, you won't,' I hissed.

She smiled her lopsided smile. Slowly she moved to me she and answered. 'I will do whatever I want. And aside of killing me, there is no way that you can stop me.'

Salina walked around me and whispered in my ear. It was infuriating. But there was no way I was going to react to her goading, no matter how difficult it was. What I wouldn't give to be able to change here and now, to rip her apart, limb from limb.

'You won't do anything, will you?' she laughed. 'Because he won't believe you. He will listen to me when I tell him you're jealous. That you begrudge him his happiness.'

She was right. That was the worst of it. I was afraid it was already too late to confront Alex with what she was doing. I questioned his decisions more often lately, especially where they concerned Salina. More often than not this resulted in heated discussions. Alex would not hear of any critique of his love. He was blinded to what she was doing, to the influence she had over him. His obsession for this creature surpassed even his love for Dulce or me.

'What are you going to do? Kill me? That would really push him over the edge. He would kill you. Now I would like that to happen, but not at my expense.' She was back in front of me. The top of her head was level with my chin. She was a small woman in stature, but her narcissism and arrogance made up for that.

Her breath was warm, her scent nauseously sweet. 'You could do us all a favour and leave now. That way I won't have to get rid of you myself. And I can, you know. You are not Alex's favourite anymore—you are way down on that ladder. He will get rid of you—I will make him. And you know I can.'

At that precise moment the door opened. I caught Alex's scent just as Salina cried out and staggered back, as if I'd struck her.

Alex stopped in his tracks. He caught my eye. His face first showed his confusion, then disbelief. Salina ran to him, sobbed and buried her face in his chest.

'What is it Salina, what happened?'

I lost the battle there and then when he closed his arms around this seemingly fragile creature. When he looked at me there was condemnation in his eyes.

I didn't have to hear her sobbing narrative to know it was my fault, that she convinced him I threatened her, terrified her. Alex knew what I was capable of, maybe that sealed the conviction for him. That—combined with his knowledge that I disapproved of Salina—was enough to convince him that I had done something.

'She scared me Alex,' she sobbed. 'I'm so terrified she will hurt me, and I don't know why. What have I done to alienate her so?'

Disgust shone in his eyes he scowled at me. 'Tonal, how could you?'

'How could I what?' He pissed me off. 'You know me better than that.'

He seemed to pull himself together after that. 'What did you want? What are you here for?' He still wasn't soothed.

Fuck it, I was in trouble anyway. Might as well say what I came for. 'The cars,' I said very distinctly and extremely judgmentally.

He blanched. 'What about the cars?' He strove to keep up an appearance of control.

'Oh, for God's sake Alex, Two Ferrari's? And you still have the Bugatti standing in the garage.'

Now it was his turn to be pissed off. 'A status car is part what is expected of me now. I'm an important figure, things are expected.' It must have sounded just as lame to him as it did to me.

'Expected by who? Salina? Yourself?'

His face coloured bright red. Was it anger or embarrassment? Could have been both. 'Back off Tonal. I can do what I want. If I want a car, I can buy one.'

'Not with the country's money you can't.'

'What's it to you anyway. It's none of your business.'

'You made it my business Alex, when you asked me to join the cause.'

'Well don't overstay your welcome.' He almost whispered that. But with my hearing he must have known I would pick it up. I looked at him incredulously. What was he saying? That he wanted me to leave? Was he so far gone?

Salina chose that moment to sob loudly, which caused Alex to shift his attention to her. His previous anger resurfaced. 'I know how terrifying you can be Tonal. If you can't restrain yourself around others, then maybe you should make your own conclusions.'

'Don't be ridiculous Alex.' I was close to real anger now.

'I wouldn't hurt or scare her, any more than anyone else close to you. You know that, give me some credit.'

'Then why is she crying?'

I looked at him, so possessive and protecting over this petite but brutally dangerous manipulator. The obsession for Salina was ever present in his stance, his very gaze.

'Why?' I answered. 'Because it works.'

It was useless to try to argue my side of the matter; to tell the truth. He was beyond listening to me—at least for now—while she sobbed in his embrace. She was a master at manipulation, and he fell for it hook, line and sinker.

I left the room to his soothing words. 'Salina, my love, it's okay, I won't let anything happen to you. You know that don't you?'

'She scared me,' was the sobbing reply. 'She is frightening when she's angry. What have I done to make her hate me like that? I just want to be friends. I know how much she means to you.'

I should go back and rip her throat out.

'Shh, my love,' Alex answered. 'You mean more to me than anything in the world.'

'More than her?' Softly.

Silence. 'Yes, much more.'

I had lost this battle.

Maybe the whole war.

Chapter Seventy-Six

Alex stood by the table and filled glasses with champagne when Tonal and Dulce entered the room. He smiled.

'Come in, come in.' He indicated they join him at the bar. He had a big grin on his face. Alex pressed a glass into their hands then motioned them to sit in the deep luxurious sofas.

'What's the celebration?' Dulce asked.

'I have great news.' Alex radiated happiness. The hairs on Tonal's back began to tingle. She had a sense of déjà vu and dread.

'She said yes!' Alex exclaimed. Dulce looked at Tonal, a puzzled blank look in her face.

'Who and why?'

Laughing, her brother continued 'Salina of course, silly. I proposed, and she said yes!'

Tonal placed her glass on the table next to the sofa, the champagne untouched. Her dread was now confirmed. Dulce took the other option and put the glass to her lips and drank deeply, anything not to have to react to the news.

Alex waited for the ecstatic reactions he'd expected to his fantastic news. He was elated that Salina consented to be his wife and he wanted no more than to share his joy with the two people closest to him. But their reaction to his announcement was not what he'd expected or desired. The silence was painful. Understanding crept in and pushed his elation back and out.

Slowly he lowered his glass, the smile faded from his face. Alex observed the two women who had always been the most important people in his life until Salina stepped into his world.

'You could at least congratulate me,' he said. His enthusiasm vanishing. 'It's a fantastic step. I'm getting married.' He desperately tried to keep hold of his feelings of joy, tried to lighten the black mood that descended on them following his declaration.

'Yeah, congratulations Bro,' Dulce said half-heartedly and totally unconvincingly. She didn't raise her head, to avoid looking in her brother's eyes.

Alex turned his face to Tonal. He almost pleaded with her to be as ecstatic about the news as he was. Or at least to pretend—for his sake.

'I can't,' Tonal answered his unspoken request. 'It's too soon, you can't be sure.'

Alex threw his glass on the floor and stood up. Anger replaced his initial joy.

'Why not?' he demanded 'How long we've known each other is irrelevant. She is my life. Salina is the one I want to spend the rest of my days with. I love her, more than anything else in the world, and she loves me.'

'Does she?' Tonal spoke the unspoken.

'What?' Alex turned on her. She remained quiet and calm in the sofa. 'Of course, she does.' Disbelief clouded his mind 'How can you doubt that? You see how she is. You see how she loves me. Can't you just be happy for me? I finally found the one and you both seem to resent that. Don't you want me to be happy?'

'Of course, we do,' Dulce answered.

'She's not what she seems,' Tonal said softly. 'She has an agenda, and you are just part of it—the next step on her ladder.'

She was painfully aware of how much she hurt Alex with her words but decided there was no way back now the subject was out in the open.

'I want you to be happy Alex. More than anything. But she's not the one. She's using you. Open your eyes, take a really good look at who she is and what she wants.'

Instead, Alex's eyes closed to slits, his face contorted in anger. 'I knew this would happen. For most of my life you were the centre of my world. The only love in my life. My reason to breathe. But you rebuked me, refused me. And now I finally have someone else—you're jealous.' He paused. 'Well, you've had your chance. Now it's too late.'

'I'm not jealous Alex. I care for you. I don't want to see you hurt.'

'That's a joke.' He was shouting now. 'You're the one who hurt me, now and for so long. You never allowed me to be happy. I was never good enough for you. Well, I don't need you anymore. If you resent the happiness I've found, then you are even more pathetic than I thought. You're not capable of love and resent others who are.'

His words cut her to the bone. Her healing powers were useless on the burning pain inflicted by her best friend.

'Alex, please,' Dulce tried.

But he turned on her.

'You... you could at least try to like her. But no, you

have to follow her example.' He pointed at Tonal, 'Think for yourself for once, instead of being her shadow. I took care of you all your life, sacrificed everything, now it's my turn. If you can't be happy for me then damn you, both of you.'

Tears blurred Dulce's vision. She had never seen her brother so angry.

'Alex,' Tonal tried. 'Salina has a bad influence on you, you're not yourself.'

'Bad influence?' he shouted. His face turned red. 'She gave me a direction in life. She shows me my destiny. Gave me the strength to take on the burden that has been placed on my shoulders. How can that be a bad influence?'

'You never wanted to be president,' Tonal continued softly. 'You were content to leave that to the revolutionary leaders—to Jesus. Your ambition was to help the people, never for your own gain. Now you're blinded by ambition and your ego. It has nothing to do with your ideals anymore, only personal gain—yours and Salina's.'

She stood up and moved to Alex. She placed a hand on his arm. He shrugged it off violently and moved away from her.

'You never wanted material things Alex, now you squander money like water. What the hell do you need three race cars for, or this stupid palace?' Her temper was showing.

'Why shouldn't I?' Alex ranted. 'I sacrificed forty years —the best years of my life—for the cause. I've earned it. I brought peace, I killed the tyrants, I freed the masses. Why shouldn't I reap the rewards? What's wrong with that?'

'That's not you talking, Alex. That's Salina. She's a creature of comfort and power. She's changed you. Made you forget yourself, your ideals. She's dangerous.'

Alex spun around and stared at Tonal. A vicious smile on his lips. 'Dangerous?' he whispered. 'That's a good one coming from you.' The contempt in his voice burned a hole in Tonal's heart. 'Dangerous… It looks like I have a fascination for dangerous women.' He walked over to her. His face close to hers. 'Is she more dangerous than you? No. I think not.'

Tonal didn't answer, but the truth screamed at her in the silence.

Alex sat down on the sofa. 'You should leave,' he ordered.

Dulce stood up, placed her glass on the table and walked to the door. 'We will speak later,' she tried.

'No,' he answered, his tone hard and cold. 'You misunderstand me. If you can't support me and Salina—my future wife—then there is no place for you in my life. Or here at the capitol for that matter.'

'You want us to go away?' Dulce was flabbergasted. This could not be true. She had been with Alex her whole life. They shared good and bad times. Surely this would not shatter all that.

'Only if you continue to oppose me,' he answered and pushed home the figurative but oh so painful sword that was dangerously near her heart. 'Join me and be happy or leave, the choice is yours.'

Dulce fled the room in tears.

'Do you even see what you are doing? What the result is of your obsession with this woman. She'll corrupt you, Alex. She's already started. You're pushing away everyone who really cares for you. Everyone who can advise you. Can help you lead this country to a good and prosperous future. If that is really what you want to do.'

'She said you would react like this.' Alex refilled his glass and drank it in one gulp, the bottle in his other hand. 'I hoped she was wrong, but she had you down to the smallest detail. Your jealousy, your so-called love and caring. You're in no position to talk about her that way. For years I followed your counsel and that of the others, and what has it brought me? A lot of pain and loss and nothing to my name. No wife and family, no possessions. Well now it's my turn. And if you can't live with that, then fuck you.'

She turned and walked to the door.

'You're becoming a liability anyway—what you are,' he added. 'Your use has come to an end. Go back to the jungle.'

Despite her resolution she felt the tears in the corner of her eyes. The last comment dismissed her entirely from his life. It shattered the last vestige of the intimate family connection she'd felt with Alex and his kin for so many years. Her best friend in the world had voiced his opinion. She was a freak and of nu use to him anymore.

Tonal closed the door behind her back and left the building.

From behind the drapes Salina emerged and walked over to Alex.

'My love,' she cooed as she took his face in her hands. 'I am so sorry for you.' Alex held her tight, his head on her shoulder. 'You did the right thing my presidente,' she continued 'It will hurt now, but they have done that. You had to get rid of them. Now we can be together and happy. It pains me to see you so hurt. I wish I could undo the anguish. But it is not of my doing.'

His head pressed close to her body, Alex failed to see the smile and barely contained bliss on her face. At last, she'd managed to get her staunchest opposition out of the way. She'd contemplated an assassination but disregarded the possibility because of the danger. It worked out so much better now the decision had come from Alex, or so he thought. Now she could work on her dreams. Make sure she got what she deserved. The revolutionary leaders couldn't oppose Alex's claim to the presidency. He was too popular with the people. Alex and his beautiful and loving wife—the perfect pair.

She could handle the leaders. They were men. The biggest danger had been the strange woman who had such a strong hold on Alex. She'd needed all her powers of persuasion and seduction to convince him Tonal had played him all this time. That she was pathologically jealous and incapable of love. There was no way back for him now. All she had to do was keep him convinced he was better off without his advisers. That he should listen to her.

Chapter Seventy-Seven

Two weeks later, they married in un-heard of extravaganza.

Salina materialised out of thin air in a radiant white dress of silk and diamonds. No expense was spared. Alex sold it to the people as the end of a dark era and the celebration of a new life for everyone.

Jesus and the other leaders reluctantly agreed to the spectacle, faced with the ultimatum of Alex's wrath, and were somewhat sympathetic to his argument that he had earned some recognition.

The absence of Dulce and Tonal was felt by all of them. Alex spun a tale that to himself seemed believable. But to Jesus, it sounded fabricated. He couldn't believe Tonal had threatened Salina's life out of jealousy. That Dulce helped her with an attempt. To start off with; if Tonal wanted to kill Salina, she would be dead. Party to her secret, Jesus was acutely aware of how dangerous Tonal could be. But to try to kill Salina out of jealousy. It didn't add up. Why should she try to do that? Salina was of no consequence—she had no power. She was just a small, beautiful woman without any guile, what was there not to like about her? What Tonal hated about Salina was hard to understand. For the first time in all the years Jesus had known Alex, the man was really happy. Well apart from the betrayal by his sister and Tonal. But somehow. Well, it just didn't add up.

So, they agreed to the party, and to so many things after that. One week after the wedding, Alex was inaugurated as president of the joint Latin countries. His courage and unrelenting passion for the cause and the people propelled his acceptance by everyone. He was the face of the revolution. He would lead them to a new and prosperous life. Finally, their suffering was over.

Chapter Seventy-Eight

Dulce and Tonal stayed together. They travelled deep into the jungle where they joined a village near where Tonal had stayed all those years ago.

The village elder recognised her and welcomed her back. She'd also heard of Dulce and accepted her into the fold without questions. This same woman Tonal saved from the mercenaries so many years ago wondered why the president's sister would prefer to live in the simple circumstances of the jungle than in the luxury of the palace with her brother. But that was not her concern. There would be reasons, she would know if they chose to share them.

Tonal and Dulce adapted easily to the slow and relaxed life in the village. The pain of the abrupt departure was replaced by a slow anger at the way that Alex had treated them. They didn't begrudge him his happiness. But this was not how he would ultimately achieve that. They hardly spoke about that afternoon. Somehow, they silently knew where they would go to and accepted that there was no other option.

Dulce settled quickly—much to her amazement. She'd thought she would miss the hectic life they'd lived with the revolutionaries. But she found that she was tired. Tired of all the fighting and the worry, tired of the endless strategy and living only for the cause. That part she could understand—that Alex wanted to do something else. But why he wanted to delve into politics—not his forte—she could not.

She helped with the children, taught in the small school, and soon felt at home in the slow pace of her new life.

Tonal alternated between the village and days—or sometimes weeks—that she roamed the jungle in feline form. Thoughts of Alex and his betrayal of their friendship receded to the back of her mind, aided by the tremendous joy she felt when she hunted in the close but endless space of the Amazon outreaches. The burden of the cause slipped down off her shoulders with the sound of the birds in the high canopy and the rain that fell daily, cleansing all the blood and stress from her fur.

Dulce even found time for romance. Against her will—or so she thought—she developed feelings for a quiet and friendly man from the village. Hector was attentive, but never overtly cloying. He was tenacious and dedicated to winning her over with flowers, poems, and all the romantic cliché's she would normally have waved off as superficial. He slowly won her heart. In her late thirties, she no longer yearned for children of her own, just the closeness of a companion who understood her every thought and just wanted to be with her. Hector was this man. He completed her.

Dulce and Hector were married in a small ceremony.

Chapter Seventy-Nine

Tonal abstained from romance. But she was a woman, or at least female and had her urges, like everyone else.

Sex only worked for her in human form. While feline, there was no male cat that dared come anywhere near her and she never actually came into season as a regular cat would. So, she cultivated an affair with a man from a town two days from the village where she lived. This offered her distance, and safety.

The villagers of her home were aware she was special. A creature unlike any they had encountered before. With Enrique she was just a woman. A very special one, but no more than that. She found relief in their encounters. Neither of them interested in questions or answers. Just the raw sex and pleasure their occasional trysts offered.

He was a well-built man, somewhere in his early thirties, independently employed and something of an idealist. They met three or four times a year when she suddenly turned up in his line of vision. For two or three days and nights

nothing else existed but them. Then they went their separate ways.

After two days of traveling Tonal was in the vicinity of
where he lived and changed to her human form in the small
clearing where she'd hid a case of clothes. She bathed in the
stream and washed her hair, using the soap-roots the forest
provided. Clean, invigorated and dressed in a pair of jeans
and an indiscriminate shirt she shouldered her backpack
and took to the road to walk the remaining two miles to
Enrique's ranch.

Chapter Eighty

The adobe building was situated on a large stretch of land and overlooked a river fed by the stream she'd just bathed in. It was a pretty one-story building with the characteristic thick walls that kept the sun out in the sweltering summer and the warmth in on the cold winter nights.

The last time she was here had been almost four months ago—somewhat longer than she usually preferred between visits. Enrique indicated last time he would need to go to Europe for a few weeks, so she waited a little longer to make sure he would be home. Even though the trip was always pleasurable, it was still a long way to go for nothing.

Tonal walked up the drive and saw him sitting in the hammock near the patio doors that led to the living room. He was working on his laptop. Silently she approached him, the more to surprise him. But as always, he felt her presence and looked up. His face brightened into a big smile. He placed his computer in the hammock, stood up and walked the last two yards to her, his arms open in a warm welcome.

His happiness was contagious, and she found herself smiling at this big but gentle man.

Their kiss was soft but held the promise of passion. Just as they were about to turn towards the patio doors, the peace was shattered by the two enormous mastiffs that had finally woken up and recognised her scent. Despite their two years, they were still massive puppies and fell over each other and Tonal to place wet and drooling kisses all over her face. Tonal had known the dogs since they had arrived as eight-week-old puppies and any unease they felt about her scent evaporated within ten minutes. Even now, after four months of absence they still treated her as their second most favourite person in the whole wide world.

Finally managing to calm the dogs, they retired to the living room where Enrique produced cool drinks. He had no idea where she came from but knew it was quite a long trip and refreshments would be in order.

'How was your trip?' she inquired.

'It was good. I spoke with the customers, and we have agreed on a larger monthly shipment of the goods to Europe. The farmers are very pleased and content to grow and harvest the crops without damaging the jungle, as long as they can sell them for a reasonable profit.'

Enrique was the middleman in the production of medicinal compounds harvested from the flora in the Amazon jungle. Use of the natural medicine was now more and more popular worldwide. It had the added ecological benefit that the farmers needed the Amazon as it was to be able to harvest some of the ingredients. Cultivating them in any way other than deep in the jungle had proven impossible. That meant keeping the Amazon intact became a financial goal as well as an ecological one. It proved to be a great way to increase the prosperity of the local people and retain the so important forest.

As a consummate naturalist Enrique was dedicated to the survival of the Amazon. He acted as middleman in the sale of the medicinal components, taking only a small percentage necessary to cover the overhead costs. His family earned their money a long time ago with oil and other natural raw materials. Unlike him, they ravaged the earth and Enrique saw it as his duty to at least try to rectify the legacy they left behind.

During the war, his small part of the jungle was spared because of its location. It was too far from anything remotely of value to the government, and not in the vicinity of the highways that transported the troops. Laying low, not attracting any attention—either from the government or the rebels—he continued to help the local people and build his small but effective business.

Enrique was not the party animal, he rarely attended festivities with the exception of the town carnival. There was no avoiding that and he enjoyed the dance, music and fun. It was there that they'd met. Tonal was visiting an old friend from the resistance who had settled in the small town. The coincidence with carnival had not been entirely by chance. She also enjoyed the fun. During the exuberant festivities she observed the big quiet man seated on the fringe of the crowd. She didn't have the impression he wasn't enjoying himself; he was just the quiet type. Her friend informed her he was one of the landowners involved in the conservation of the jungle—her home.

They were introduced and hit it off straight away. Two days later she left his farm to go back to the jungle. Though they never discussed their relationship, it was clearly how they both wanted it. No commitments, no obligations, just a lot of fun.

Observing this beautiful creature, he was struck by the revelation that he knew so little about her. She was obviously not local to this or any other Latin American country. Where she came from was anyone's guess, along with her age and occupation for that matter. She just materialised out of the forest, into his arms. The thought of taking the relationship to another level crossed his mind but was discarded because he was afraid she would lose her wildness, her mystery. She was an anomaly, mystical and secretive. That was part of the attraction. He was fully aware she would not stay with him, that she belonged somewhere else. Maybe even with someone else. So, he focused on the time they had together and enjoyed it to the max.

Later that night—their passion momentarily spent—they lay in the bed and talked. Enrique was one of her links to what happened in the world outside of the cocoon she and Dulce had chosen for themselves. The village was reasonably screened off from the world. News was not frequent and definitely not complete.

'There is unrest,' Enrique told her. 'The new laws are not popular. People compare them with the tyranny before the revolution. There are also disappearances.'

Her skin began to crawl with a sense of déjà vu. She had to know more. 'What kind of disappearances?'

'Not really organised, some of the opposition have left the country. Or that is what the stories say. But some of them cannot be contacted anymore. They seem to have disappeared off the face of the earth. It makes us uneasy.' He got up to pour a glass of wine for both of them, then continued. 'Jesus Valdez left the government, officially he retired, but there are rumours that he and the president no longer see eye to eye.'

Tonal accepted the wine and joined him at the window where she asked, 'where did he go to?'

'He has a holding on the coast.' Observing her face in the soft light of the moon, he detected worry. 'Do you know Jesus?'

She left the answer floating in the night sky. It had to do with the private part of her life he was not party to. He left it at that, even though he was becoming more and more curious about this mysterious woman he shared his bed with.

'The government and the president have more frequent run-ins,' he continued. 'Some of the bills Alex wants to pass are not popular with the ministers. He also replaced one of the ministers with an old military man. A man with a history. He fought on Esposito's side in the civil war. I know we should not judge a man only by his past, but I find it difficult to believe he has changed so much that he embraces the democracy.'

They spoke until deep in the night. Enrique was surprised by the knowledge she had of the revolution and that she recognised many of the names. Finally, they went back to bed and tried to sleep.

Listening to his deep breaths, Tonal reviewed the news. None of it was good.

As she expected, Salina had a massive influence on Alex. His trusted advisors—like Jesus, Dulce and herself—had left and the void was filled with people who were dubious to say the least. Enrique explained the new laws, the higher taxes and the effect they had on the country's people. The United Latin countries were slowly falling apart. Unrest was brewing, Alex was losing his hold on the government and the inhabitants. No longer able to rule on the basis of his heroic revolutionary history, he reverted to more stringent and less democratic measures. The military was called in to quell demonstrations. Large numbers of people were arrested and sentenced to a miserable incarceration in the overflowing prisons in mock trials. Opposition groups were tolerated, as long as they did not cross the line and openly call for Alex's abdication.

Chapter Eighty-One

Salina was having a ball by the sound of it. Regular trips abroad to luxurious resorts and immensely expensive shopping sprees filled her life. She was the queen-bee and loved it.

When she was in the country, she spent her time cajoling and manipulating Alex to pass new measures that would ensure her lasting wealth. In the times she was gone Alex was depressed and moody—not tolerating opposition or discussion. When she was there, he was distracted and ecstatic. All in all, he hardly ever attended to his country or his political and presidential responsibilities.

This was exactly as the new members of the government wanted it to be. They had full power and opportunity to manipulate the cabinet and push their objectives to the foreground. Slowly but surely, the democracy was hollowed out from within.

Tonal hated to be right in this case.

Secretly she'd hoped Alex would be able to handle Salina and stick to his own ideals and goals. But he was like a child, sick with longing every time she was gone. He lost interest in his tasks as president and preferred to spend as much time as possible with his wife. More and more, he accompanied her aboard and left the running of the country to his minions.

Salina fostered contradicting emotions about Alex accompanying her. On the one hand it proved her total power over the man, on the other it cramped her style. She was accustomed to enjoying the company of young and virile men during her trips. Alex's presence didn't stop her from these amorous trysts, it just made them more complicated.

Her love life was the subject of many scandals. Frequent streams and articles in tabloids screamed the woman's infidelity. Still Alex chose to ignore the news and rumours and desperately held on to his sanity and the pitiful remnants of self-respect remaining.

In the past months Salina tired of the game and openly flirted with anyone who took her fancy. She was still young, and Alex bored her. She needed new young men to satisfy her. She also relished the pain she inflicted on her husband and became more open in her extra-marital relationships. She even turned up at official banquets with the lover of the moment.

Chapter Eighty-Two

The situation was becoming intolerable. Alex slipped into a deep depression and had bursts of rage. The country was without its ruler and corruption blossomed. Slowly, it sank back into the dark and murky past they all fought so hard to get out of. They would have to see what the future brought.

In their village Dulce and Tonal were isolated from the rest of the country. Blissfully unaware of the extent of the struggle, except when the sporadic news reached the community. They held on to their peace and quiet persistently. But how long they would be able to keep that up was the question.

Finally sinking into a troubled sleep in the early hours of the morning, Tonal dreamt of Alex. She stayed with Enrique for another day, shorter than normal, but the tension she felt about Alex was building. She felt uneasy and Enrique naturally picked up on it.

A last lingering kiss and she was back on her way to the jungle.

Chapter Eighty-Three

They came in the night.

Seven mercenaries stormed into the village. They fired indiscriminately at anything they saw. The first shots and screams alerted the villagers, and they fled their beds to arm themselves where possible.

Three of the mercenaries targeted Dulce and Hector's house. They broke down the front door and stormed through the rooms in search of the inhabitants. Dulce's dogs attacked the intruders and bought precious time for their owners. Despite the relative quiet of the past years, her training kicked in immediately and Dulce reverted to fight mode. Hector grabbed one of the shotguns that stood against the bedroom wall and tried to barricade himself with her behind the door. The walls were thick so shooting through them was not an option for the mercenaries.

But they brought explosives and sent a grenade into the door opening. The resulting blast knocked out all the windows and part of the bedroom ceiling came down.

Dulce and Hector were able to duck and reach some form of cover before the explosion. Hector was wounded by shrapnel, but not critically. Both had been knocked over by the blast and were disoriented when the mercenaries came storming into the remnants of the room. Dulce managed to shoot one of them in the chest and grazed another on the arm but was soon overpowered. They were dragged out of the bedroom into the living space, where yet another mercenary waited. He was obviously the leader of the gang and smiled at the bounty.

'Well, look who we have here.' The cigar in the side of his mouth was so cliché Dulce almost laughed. He walked over to Hector and viciously kicked him in the ribs who doubled over. Screaming at him, Dulce attempted to free herself from the mercenary holding her.

'Still quite the feisty one, aren't you?' The leader turned his attention to her. 'Not bad either, considering your age.' He ripped the nightgown off her body. 'We should have some fun before we kill you. Salina only wants your head. What we do with the rest is our prerogative.'

The mercenary holding Dulce responded to the idea by cruelly pinching her breast. They all laughed at her resistance and Hector's angry calls.

Their fun was shattered by an enormous roar at the door to the house. The leader turned just in time to see the gigantic cat pounce with outstretched claws and open jaws sporting immense fangs. Tonal closed her teeth on his head and relished in the pleasing crunch when his skull split open. She instantly released him, spun around and went for the nearest mercenary. Dulce stomped the flabbergasted soldier who held her in the balls and freed herself. She grabbed his discarded gun, then shot him in the head.

Tonal made short work of the other man and stood over the body.

Dulce sped to Hector who was still on the ground. He bled from a number of what turned out to be shallow wounds. The only wound of real concern was in his left leg where a piece of shrapnel protruded from his thigh. It had missed the arteries and with a quick pull he dislodged it and threw it away. Dulce stelped the blood flow with the remnants of her nightgown pressed onto the wound.

'I am all right Dulce. You both should help the others.'

Sounds of fighting continued from outside. There were more soldiers than the dead bodies here. Tonal turned and bounded out into the fray. Dulce grabbed one of Hector's shirts, threw it on and followed her friend brandishing a submachine gun she'd retrieved from one of the fallen soldiers.

Within minutes the villagers and Tonal had dispatched the remaining three mercenaries.

Taking stock, the villagers had lost two of their own, a further twelve people were wounded in different manners and with varying severity. Both of Dulce's dogs had been killed. One of the homes was partially on fire, but the damage to it was not extensive. All in all, the result was not as bad as it seemed, although more than enough. The attack had been a complete surprise and only the presence of Tonal had been able to sway the odds. It was obvious that the mercenaries had not expected any real resistance and definitely nothing like her. They failed to take precautions and were overly confident that two women and a few peasants would not pose a threat to them.

The wounded villagers were taken care of by a doctor who arrived from a nearby village to stitch the wounds and help the more critically wounded. A group of men from the village—led by Dulce and Tonal—went out into the jungle to make sure there were no additional mercenaries waiting for the return of their comrades. In their arrogance the mercenaries hadn't left any sentries or additional forces to protect their vehicles. The whole party was in on the raid. The villagers found the two vehicles at the beginning of the road leading to the village. They were driven back and left near Dulce's house.

Tonal accompanied the group in her feline form. The villagers were party to her secret and felt safe in her presence. The enormous feline had been their protector for some years now. Most of them were brought up with the legends of the shape-changing guardian angel.

In the early hours of the dawn, the villagers finally retired back to their homes to rest and recuperate. Hector was in the spare bedroom because this was the only space that half survived the blast reasonably well.

Tonal stationed herself before her friend's house and stayed alert.

The next day Dulce, Hector, Tonal and the village elders discussed what happened. '

The leader said Salina wanted my head.' Dulce started the meeting. 'This was personal. It seems she wants to get rid of us, maybe views us as a potential risk—although I have no idea why. We haven't had any contact with Alex or Salina for about six or seven years. Not since we left.'

One of the elders remarked, 'there is widespread unrest about the government and especially about the Presidential pair. The rich are once again becoming richer, and the poor suffer and die.'

Dulce lowered her head while the elders spoke about Alex and the mismanagement of the country. She'd heard rumours of laws passed and of disappearances. Some even hinted at assassinations and murders. She'd dismissed the rumours as impossible and pushed the unsettling thoughts to the back of her mind. The attack on the village made it impossible to ignore anymore what stared her in the face. Still, she didn't believe Alex could have anything to do with the murder spree—she couldn't. That was just too much to grasp. She was still his sister, and family was everything to Alex. At least it had been. She couldn't imagine his morals would have deteriorated so much as to sanction this. Salina, now that was a different discussion all together. Dulce shared her friend's impression about the power-hungry bitch who had Alex dancing to her every whim.

Almost reading her mind, Tonal joined the discussion. 'This has to be something Salina initiated. I cannot believe Alex would condone the killing of his sister.'

'Alex is not the man you knew.' The elder continued 'He has changed. I knew him as a boy, and later as a man. He was a good man. Honest and compassionate. I voted for him to be our president. But now I hardly recognise him. Not in person and definitely not in his actions.'

Hector took centre stage. 'Alex has surrounded himself with the worst kind of people. His government is made up of many of the old powers. The same people he fought just seven years ago. Most of the old revolutionary figures have left—either voluntarily or by force. Some have disappeared. Even Jesus chose to go. Officially to retire, but we know he couldn't resign himself to the politics and what Alex was doing.'

Tonal had heard the news from Enrique. She was less surprised by the aggregation of bad news than Dulce, but still it hurt. She'd seen the influence Salina had on Alex, even tried to make him open his eyes. To no avail. The bitch worked her magic and corrupted him down to the bone.

'There are rumours that the old resistance has been reinstated.' The elder continued. 'That some of the old fighters have started to regroup and are going to take up arms again. Now against Alex. That is probably why Salina targeted you two. She must be afraid you would join the opposition and that would be a real threat. You are heroes of the resistance and think of the effect it would have on Alex if you were on the opposing team. I agree Alex probably had no knowledge of this murder attempt. But that doesn't exempt him from all the other things he has done and is still doing.'

Softly the elder added, 'he is becoming the tyrant he fought to overcome.'

The words cut to the bone.

But both Dulce and Tonal knew the elder was right. The rumours were too consistent, too clear, too frequent and detailed not to be true. Alex had sunk further than they liked to consider. The attack on the village consummated the terrible conclusion. The time had come for armed resistance, once again.

'If she wanted to stop us from intervening, she achieved exactly the opposite.' Dulce said softly.

'We have to go. She brought the conflict to us.' Tonal nodded. It was inevitable. They would have to react now. Salina would wait for the return of the mercenaries, when that didn't happen, she would definitely try again in the knowledge her adversaries had been warned.

The village needed to be protected while Dulce and Tonal were gone because it was in the direct line of fire, unless Salina was sure her targets were no longer there.

That meant going out in the open. Plans were made to fortify the village and to work with other settlements close by to protect the people and homes.

Hector—as expected—insisted on joining the two women. He would not leave Dulce. Reluctantly she agreed, and they started to make plans for their departure.

They would take one of the mercenaries' vehicles, the one without a locator, and leave it in an open place far from here. A friend took the other mercenaries' car and ditched it in a different location because it would probably have a SAT NAV locator too. This was a clear message to Salina that the mercenaries didn't need them anymore. They packed what they deemed necessary in Hector's truck, then said their goodbyes, secure in the knowledge the villagers would be able to protect themselves with the measures they had initiated.

The drive to the vicinity of where they expected the new revolutionaries to be took all day and part of the next morning. The new compound was in a different location all together because Alex was party to all the locations used in the past. Tonal had heard about the general vicinity from Enrique and visiting old comrades on the way confirmed they were on the right track. They met up with their old friend Juan Torres from the council and made their way to the small group of fighters.

Once they were close, they ditched the truck and resume the trip on foot. This posed a challenge for Hector with the fresh stitches in his leg. Eight hours later—soaking wet from the rain—they arrived at a small camp deep in the jungle, invisible until they were almost on top of it. There they were greeted by Jesus. He had aged alarmingly, his hair was bright white, and his stance bent and uncomfortable. He walked with a cane.

'It is so good to see you both, even though I wish it was under different circumstances.' He embraced both women in turn.

'I wish I could say that you look good, Jesus,' Tonal said —direct as always.

Chapter Eighty-Four

'The past few years have taken their toll on my health, I'm afraid. The situation is very troubling, and I am no longer a young man. Camping in a tent doesn't agree with me as much as before,' Jesus answered. 'Come in. Get out of the rain, dry a bit.'

The meeting was a heated one. Some of the revolutionaries were new to the cause—or at least new to the group—and had not known Alex personally. They viewed him as any other enemy. Others had known and fought with him and felt betrayed. They wanted revenge. Jesus, Dulce and Tonal were reluctant to act without at least trying to reason with Alex. For old-time's sake.

Ultimately, they all wanted a solution. One they could all live with. It was Jesus who had the swaying vote. They would attempt to speak with Alex. Give him one last chance. Tonal would do the honours. That she was extremely difficult to kill was one of the reasons. The other was the consensus that Tonal would probably make the most impact on Alex. Dulce was too emotionally involved, and Jesus too valuable, old and feeble to chance an armed encounter, even if he didn't agree to all the reasons.

During the next week they gathered information about Alex's whereabouts. Being the political figure that he was, his official itinerary was easily found on the web. This offered no options, as he was heavily guarded and never accessible. One of the revolutionaries turned out to be a master hacker and they managed to gain access to Alex's more personal agenda. They found out he would be at his estate in the La Pedrera region as of the following weekend. A small affair, no guests, just the presidential pair. They would leave for the estate Friday afternoon and be back in the capitol by Monday eleven o'clock. It was a six-hour flight by helicopter for Alex, and that would leave him Saturday and Sunday for relaxation.

The resistance decided on Sunday. Nowadays, Alex was a heavy drinker and after two late night booze sessions he would probably be less on his guard. Hopefully the same would apply for the guards.

Additional hacking produced out-dated architectural plans of the estate and the enormous grounds. A small team of three was sent in advance for recon work. They would try to determine the best way to gain access to the grounds and meet up with the main group later on.

Chapter Eighty-Five

The main group left for the estate on Wednesday.

They travelled on foot for the first leg of the journey. Nineteen miles from the compound they borrowed horses from a farmer sympathetic to the cause. They travelled until Friday afternoon. The horses were left at an abandoned farm, and they continued on foot for another hour which brought them three miles from the edge of Alex's estate. It was a gigantic mansion in more than four hundred acres of land, eighty percent of which was jungle. The rest was cultivated land and gardens.

They set up camouflage tents on the edge of a stream— just inside the tree-line— and settled down to wait for the advance group. Their meal was dried meat and army biscuits—no fire would be started. They were too near the estate for that.

The night brought the familiar sounds of the nocturnal animals. Hunters like the jaguar and the ocelot, prey like the tapir and capybara. Insects made the stay unpleasant. After dark Tonal moved into the jungle and changed. She would do her own recon, go where the others couldn't.

Some of the revolutionaries had been informed of some of her strange talents. It was necessary to explain why she was the ideal person to talk to Alex. She would be in the most dangerous position and her healing powers may come in handy. The change shocked most of the inner council. They had only seen the end result. The other revolutionaries had not, they were left in the dark about that part.

She returned to the tents early the next morning with a full stomach and information about the estate. She'd changed back and dressed before she joined the others. The advance party was expected in the course of the morning, so they waited. At half-past-eleven one of the sentries brought two of the three recon men to their waiting companions. They spoke for almost an hour.

The grounds of the estate were extensive and therefore impossible to close off entirely. The jungle animals had trails that they used to enter the grounds when they wanted to forage, most of which were known to the groundskeeper, and subsequently monitored with cameras. But the recon party managed to find two relatively new and unknown trails. Slipping through the perimeter they found an enormous tree that offered a reasonably comfortable perch from which to observe the mansion and its inhabitants. Camouflage nets completed the hide and made them invisible to the house's occupants.

An hour before the helicopter arrived, they'd noticed an increased activity in the grounds and the house. Some of the bodyguards arrived early and proceeded to secure the area. They had not been happy with the preparations so far and with a lot of shouting and posturing spurred the home security employees to a higher security level.

Alex and Salina arrived in a helicopter late Friday evening, somewhat later than expected. This resulted in foul moods for both of them. A contingent of nine bodyguards accompanied them and fanned out over the area near the mansion.

The recon group saw Alex rise early Saturday morning with an obvious hangover. Nursing his first drink of the day, he sat in the gardens of the mansion until he felt better. After breakfast he saddled a horse and rode in the ménage for an hour. Salina woke up and took a swim in the pool. She was naked which caused the first row when Alex returned to the plush seats rimming the blue water. The bodyguards were used to the bickering and didn't react, either to the argument or to her exhibitionism.

The recon party chose this time to leave the scene. One stayed behind at a safe distance, the other two had made their way to the rendezvous site.

Chapter Eighty-Six

In the course of the afternoon the group decided on a plan. They would move into the grounds of the estate in the late hours of the night when the guards were at their most vulnerable. There, they would wait for an opportunity either in the house or on the grounds. Preferably on the grounds far away from the house. They did not want to endanger any of the servants or other innocents.

The group slept in shifts and rested until the time came to leave. They packed the few belongings they had and scattered any signs of their presence before they left for the estate.

The trails were dark, the ground wet and sticky. Around them they heard the sounds of the jungle: strange howls, rustling leaves, the screams of the prey animals.

Tonal walked point, her senses attuned to the smells and sounds. Her vision changed the gloom into almost daylight. They crossed small streams, pushed their way through dense vegetation and reached the perimeter of the estate around three in the morning. One of the original recon group went to the lookout where they left their comrade the day before. The others proceeded to a part of the grounds where the forest was exceptionally dense. There were no manmade trails in this part of the grounds. Chances were slim that they would be found here.

Settling down to wait, they posted sentries anyway.

In total there were nine of them. Dulce wanted to come along but was stopped by Jesus' veto. Not that he didn't trust her to stay quiet, but he wasn't taking any chances. Hector also stayed in the revolutionary's compound, officially to support Dulce and because of his bad leg, but mainly to make sure that she stayed put.

Tonal was glad they had not accompanied her. She didn't need the distraction. Her mind was already in turmoil. She was excited to see Alex again, but apprehensive about how he would react. Against her better judgment, she hoped he would be receptive to their arguments and would change his ways. That the Alex that she had known would surface again and make amends. Deep down inside she knew it was wishful thinking. But still she hoped.

Around eleven in the morning, one of the recon-group rushed into the hiding place and informed them the jeeps were being readied at the house, probably for a hunt. Alex and Salina were both dressed in camouflage gear and sported rifles. There were three jeeps for the presidential couple and the six bodyguards. The remaining five soldiers would stay at the mansion.

With one last check of their own weapons, the revolutionaries moved back to one of the trails in the grounds that led from the mansion into the jungle. They chose a spot where there were no motion detectors or cameras. The track was just large enough for a jeep to drive though— deep tyre tracks were evidence it had been used before. It led to one of the watering holes where animals congregated. The revolutionary's expectations were proven right when the last recon man joined them with news that the hunting party was headed their way.

They fanned out into the foliage on both sides of the road for maximum coverage and made themselves invisible.

The rain from the previous day turned the ground to mud, made any real speed impossible—even with a four-wheel drive—and caused the jeeps to almost crawl down the tack.

Chapter Eighty-Seven

The open Jeep stopped in the middle of the dirt road. The driver was uncertain what to do.

About fifty metres in front of the car stood a seemingly unarmed bare-footed woman framed by the jungle on either side of the path.

'Why are you stopping?' Alex demanded, looking around. 'Have we arrived at the site?'

The driver pointed ahead.

'Oh my God.' It was Salina who spoke, she instantly recognised Tonal.

The bodyguards stormed out of the following jeeps and moved to the front of the vehicles.

Slowly they became aware of bright red luminescent spots that dotted their faces and bodies. The laser sights were familiar, and they froze—referring to the bodyguard seated in Alex's jeep next to driver for guidance. He in turn looked to Alex.

'Lower your weapons,' Alex ordered 'I know this woman.'

The hairs on the back of his neck stood upright. He'd never dared contemplate that she would appear so suddenly. Part of him hoped she would turn up at his door and just look him up, that things would be as they once were. But deep down in his heart he understood that was impossible. There was no way she would agree with his current policies and strategies. That, and the way they parted ways, bode no good. Her appearance in the jungle, coupled with the red laser dots was the certainty he needed to know she was not here for a courtesy call. She was also not alone. That meant that some form of resistance had gathered again. Probably more of the old clan. Only now to oppose the new president—him.

The subdued light of the sun through the treetops shone on her face. She looked good. Her deep tan showed she'd been out a lot. The familiar ochre-coloured eyes mesmerised him once again. Like they always did.

Tonal walked closer to the congregated soldiers and jeeps. She stopped about fifteen meters from them and nodded to Alex.

'You've noticed I am not alone.' She stopped for effect. 'Sit and listen, Alex.'

'Are you going to let her talk to you like that?' Salina screamed hysterically 'You are the president, kill her.' One glance from Alex silenced her.

'Tonal, it's been a long time. I see you are well, though I wouldn't expect anything else. Not with you. Is Dulce here as well? How is she?' He looked past Tonal anxiously to see if his sister was there too. Truth be told, he missed them both a lot.

'She is well, all things considered,' she answered. 'No thanks to Salina.'

Alex glanced at his wife, who shrugged as though unaware of what she meant.

He asked the unspoken question. 'What do you mean?' His stomach sank. 'What has Salina got to do with Dulce?'

'She sent a group of mercenaries to kill us, specifically to take back Dulce's head.'

'That's ridiculous. That isn't possible. I wouldn't allow it.' Regarding his wife, his conviction evaporated.

'They're a big threat to you and to your position. I told you years ago they should have been taken care of. You wouldn't do it, so I did.' The flatness of her tone was unbelievable and so typically Salina.

'How could you? She's my sister!' He was fuming. Salina was not impressed and sulked.

'That's not the only thing I am here for, Alex,' Tonal continued. He turned back to look at her.

'You've screwed up big time. There is nothing left of what you were, of the ideals we all fought for. You are becoming the tyrant you deposed. Worse even, you should know better.'

'I was entitled,' he retaliated 'It was my turn to have some of the benefits, some kind of reward.'

'What part of the entitled reward are you on now Alex?' Her voice was calm and soft, which only intensified the impact. 'How much more than this do you need? How much of this do you really need?'

She paused. 'You have received more than enough for your effort. The wealth that you amassed has been over the backs of the people you once fought for. You used to be the people's saviour, what happened to you?'

Her words cut deep. Somewhere deep-down Alex knew that he was on thin ice at the least, had known for a long time. He'd noticed he was having trouble making the decisions his advisers and Salina coached him to make. But somehow, he couldn't turn back on the path he'd chosen. He'd gone too far. There was too much to lose. He stayed silent.

'Do you even remember why we fought Alex?' Her eyes pierced his soul. 'How can you sanctify what you have done? How can you reconcile yourself with the pain and suffering you cause? You used to fight the tyranny. It was your life, your goal. You were one of the people. Julio would turn in his grave if he saw what you had become.'

'Leave my father out of this,' Alex retaliated halfheartedly.

'How can I? He was the driving force behind the revolution, behind what we did. Go back to what you were, to the ideals you used to have. Become the man you should be, the man you were. Make amends and start helping the people. Do your job. Be the president.'

'It's not that simple,' he spat back. 'You have no idea what politics are, the pressure that I'm under. It all looks so simple from where you are.'

'So, retire. Let the people chose a new president. One who is able to withstand the intrigue and stress. Get out or do something about it. Stop whining.'

'I can't, there are people relying on me.'

Softly. 'Yes, Alex there are... .... the people of this country. Your old friends and comrades.'

He was silent. There was no answer to that.

'I don't feel sorry for you Alex. You made this bed, so lie in it. You wanted to be president. So be one. Be a good one. Take responsibility for your people. For the country. Do some good for someone else, instead of only for yourself and the rich. The people are no better off now than they were before the revolution.'

Her words cut so deep.

'I'm here to warn you Alex. Change your ways. Go back to your old ideals, your old goals. This is your first and only warning.' The silence was palatable.

'Don't make me kill you, Alex.'

Chapter Eighty-Eight

Alex finally raised his head and looked at her. He had no doubt she would make good on her threat. He knew her, knew what she was capable of.

Tonal turned around, walked back to where she'd appeared and moved into the jungle. The red dots disappeared from the soldiers and the presidential couple.

Salina instantly screamed. 'Get them, go on, kill the scum.' Alex waved the soldier still.

'No, leave it. There is no way we will be able to get them anyway.'

The main bodyguard countered, 'we should at least try. Kill as many as possible.'

'Kill her!' Salina screamed.

'I said NO! We go back to the house.' Alex was adamant. Reluctantly the bodyguards took their places in the cars and reversed until they reached a clearing where they could turn around.

Alex was visibly rattled by the encounter.

He had felt safe and secure in the grounds of his

mansion—certain no one would be able to get through the security measures. This illusion had been shattered. Not only Tonal got through, but enough others to hold them all under shot until she was finished.

He turned to the bodyguard in the front passenger seat. 'This is an unacceptable breach of security. You'd better get some answers quickly about how they managed to get in the grounds and who screwed up, or I'll have your head. This is intolerable. They could have killed us both. I want your report before five this afternoon. With the solutions to the breach in security.'

As an afterthought he added, 'and get the helicopter ready, we leave within the hour. I'm not staying here any longer than necessary.'

Alex left the jeep and stalked back into the mansion.

Just before the opened door, he turned to Salina. 'Get in the house. I want to talk to you.'

He was so angry that even Salina decided to comply. Alex strode into the house, straight to the bar where he poured himself a very large, very mature whisky. He didn't ask what she wanted.

He was seething and turned to face her. 'What the hell did you think you were doing? She's my sister, for fuck's sake.'

She just stood there, not answering.

'Did you think you could just get this past me, that I wouldn't find out?'

'It would already have been done,' she answered serenely as she walked to the bar and poured herself a glass of the same whisky. She held the bottle up. 'A refill?' she asked sweetly.

He was flabbergasted. She put her glass and the bottle down.

'Oh, come on Alex. She might be your sister, but she and that bitch Tonal are also your—no our—biggest enemies. They begrudge you your happiness. How much do you have to do for them, for this country, before it is enough? How much more do we need to sacrifice before you can finally have what you want and need from life? What you deserve. They didn't love you, not really. Otherwise, they would have been happy that you had found your soulmate, that you were finally happy. But what did they do? They left. They couldn't win and stalked off like the two spoiled brats they are. They abandoned you. You hear me, ABANDONED you.'

It sounded so ridiculous, but at the same time, some of the things she said rang true. They had abandoned him. They had left at his finest moment when he wanted to celebrate his newfound happiness with those closest to him. They deserted him. Hated him. But still... ...

'Well maybe they were right.' He screamed at her. 'Look at what you do to me now. You make a laughingstock out of me. You screw around with anything with a dick. Tonal warned me about you. Said you were only out for status and money.'

He refilled his glass and turned his back to her.

He felt her move closer. Her arms slowly, softly encircled his waist. She pressed her tight body against his back. He felt himself melt. His anger seeped out of his pores and was replaced with lust and what was it? Yes, still love. He hated himself for this. How could he still love her after she tried to kill Dulce. How easily she manipulated him. But she was his lifeline. His reason for living. He couldn't live without her. And they had left.

'My love,' she said softly and seductively. 'You know you're my reason for living. That I breathe only to please you. I will behave, I'm sorry. It's my history, I can't help it sometimes. But if you help me, then we can start again.'

He felt his resolve fade even further, his anger dissipated. He couldn't stay angry at Salina.

But this was just too much. She tried to kill his only sibling. The only one left of his history. And Tonal. Even though that would never have happened. Nothing could kill Tonal, But Salina didn't know that.

Determined to stay angry, he disentangled himself from her arms. Turning, he threw the last drops of his whisky down his throat and pushed Salina out of the way. 'What you do is up to you, I couldn't care less,' he said and stalked out of the room.

Chapter Eighty-Nine

All Tonal said was true. He'd abandoned all his ideals. And what for? For a wife who didn't love him, a position that was a straight-jacket—forever tightening—his country a spoilt and unthankful child. He sank down in the bedroom sofa and took his head in both hands. How was he ever going to get out of this?

How was he going to stop her from killing him?

Chapter Ninety

Alone in the back of the helicopter Alex pondered his options. He had no illusions about the revolutionaries, having been one himself. Their resolve was one hundred percent. He knew how tenacious people like Jesus and Dulce could be. Not to mention Tonal. It was pure survival for him now. There were basically two options. Fold or fight.

As expected, Salina had decided to stay at the mansion, secure in the knowledge the revolutionaries had come for Alex—not for her—and that they'd left. Three of the security detail stayed there as well. With a sharp pain in his heart Alex recalled how she chose the three most handsome and robust bodyguards to keep her company, and no doubt entertained. Her infidelity was already legendary.

Angry about the assassination attempt on Dulce and Tonal and her involvement, Alex hadn't spoken to Salina at all since the morning.

But still it hurt.

Telling her he was about to change his strategies and

revert finances back to the population would probably not help their relationship either.

He had decided to fold.

His conscience had been plaguing him for the past years and it was time to do something about his mismanagement. His decision to revert back to his initial goals and ideals offered him some peace. It would not be easy, that was for sure. There were all kinds of interests involved here, and all kinds of people.

People he should have stood up to a long time ago.

Dangerous people.

Chapter Ninety-One

Back at his office in the capitol, Alex prepared to implement his new resolves. He called the finance and education ministers to a meeting. The two men arrived somewhat curious about why they had been summoned. Generally, they decided on the strategies and Alex only ratified them.

They were astonished and furious that Alex ordered full disclosure on all financial and educational budgets. What was the money being spent on and particularly, what were they doing about aiding the poor? The tension was palpable. As he paced the room, Enrique Salazar, the minister of finance, was barely able to restrain his anger.

'What is this shit? Since when, do I need to justify every cent in my budget?'

Alex was not impressed and calmly took in the spectacle.

'Don't you trust me anymore, or us?' The minister gestured to his equally aggravated colleague Antonio Esposito.

'Don't fool yourself,' was Alex's calm reply. 'I've never

trusted you. And I don't doubt that the feeling is mutual. Only now I've decided I want to be more involved with what is happening in my name, and with this country's money.'

It felt good to finally stand up to these creeps. 'As of now I will personally approve every budget payment above two-hundred thousand.'

The effect of his words on the minister's face was priceless. Flabbergasted, Salazar sat down in one of the chairs in front of the desk. His incredulous gaze first centred on Alex, only to pass to his fellow minister in a desperate search for support.

'You can't do that,' Esposito blustered 'It's undemocratic... ... It's against the laws... ... it's it's...'

'It's what?' Alex demanded. He was tired of the two men. 'That's a laugh coming from you Salazar—undemocratic. Since when are you interested in anything democratic? Well now's a good time to start. I expect detailed plans from both of you by Wednesday. In the plans you will specify a new strategy to aid the poor, offer free education and explain where the money will be rerouted from.'

'You are dismissed.' The final insult.

Fuming, both men left the office.

Alex sat back and mulled over what he had just done. His power was based on the allegiance of these men. No longer the people's hero, he'd sold his soul to the upper-class and the politicians. Accustomed to the luxury and wealth he and Salina had amassed in the past years, he wondered how he would convince his greatest supporter this was the right choice; to go back to the support of the people. That meant alienating the upper-class and basically walking a tightrope for the immediate future. This was not something that Salina would enjoy.

Despite his anger at her actions regarding Dulce—and her infidelity—she was still the love of his life. Maybe misguided, but he was certain they would climb out of the pit together and once again be happy and content with less. Like they were in the beginning. At the time they were with the revolutionaries. They lived on meagre rations and their love. It was enough then. It would be enough once again. Well maybe not the meagre rations, that was pushing it. But they could definitely do with less.

Who knows—in time—maybe Dulce and Tonal would even forgive them a bit and maybe they could even meet again under less stressful circumstances.

He decided to discuss this with Salina the moment she came back. Thinking about her like this, he realised he missed her already. He phoned her mobile, got the voice mail and forced himself not to dwell on why she didn't answer at this time of the day. He waited for the beep.

'Salina, it's me. I'm sorry I was so brusque yesterday. I was just so surprised and angry about Dulce. And quite thrown that they were able to penetrate our defences. Anyway, I miss you, and I wish you were here with me. Please come back as soon as possible, we have a lot to discuss about how to tackle this together.'

She hadn't been in the middle of a heated love bout as he suspected. She was on the phone with the Prime Minister.

Salina was filled with rage at what had happened What did Alex think he was doing? This was all the result of the meeting with that bitch Tonal. Alex's conscience was playing up, or he was frightened, probably both. He was such a wimp. So easily manipulated, so fickle. In all, that had been advantageous for her and made it easy for her to shape him into what she wanted. The status, wealth and power she now had were her only motives for the marriage. He was a means to an end.

One day she would get rid of him, and the allegiance of the ministers would shift to her only. Frankly this was already the case, but they needed the front man—the old hero. Even that shine was fading. And if he continued on the path he had obviously chosen; his use would evaporate even faster. But it was too soon—she was not ready yet. She wanted to be a second Eva Peron. Only better.

She resolved to get back to the capitol a.s.a.p. after she listened to the voicemail. Salina turned back to the bed and addressed the bodyguard.

'Get the helicopter back here and prepare to leave.'

He shot up out of the covers.

'Not yet, you fool,' she added seductively as she moved back to the cushions and the handsome naked man. 'Afterwards.'

Chapter Ninety-Two

Salina returned to the capitol late in the evening.

She completely surprised Alex who was unaware that she had left the mansion. He was ecstatic when she flung herself tearfully into his arms and proclaimed her undying love and adoration. The night was passionate. No mention was made of Alex's new plans or the attempt on Dulce's life.

She made sure he was sated and glowing from the attention she bestowed on him before Salina finally broached the subject of Alex's plans. It would do no good to directly oppose his ideas. That would only strengthen his resolve. She softly stroked his chest and pretended enthusiasm. Lulling him into disclosing what he wanted to do, only offering small unimportant comments on details, she planted the seed for what she would cultivate in the following days, or if necessary, weeks.

When the ministers came to present their plans of finance and educational support for the poor, Salina stood behind Alex. As agreed, the ministers were calm and complacent. The plans didn't have as far-reaching goals as

Alex wanted, but he let Salina dampen his disappointment by viewing this as the first step. He barely registered the lack of opposition from the ministers and chalked it up to his persuasive talents. They had come around to his way of thinking. Okay, Rome wasn't built in one day. He would be patient. At least they all agreed.

The overt glances the men and Salina shared belied his conclusions, but he missed them. They were once again playing him. Salina had managed to convince them the way to achieve their goal was through deception. They would string Alex along—as they had done for so long. Let him think he was making a difference. In the meantime, all results would be minimal—highly marketed and publicised for his sake—but minimal. In the end, they were sure this "for the people" phase would fade. It had before, and otherwise they would look for a more permanent solution.

The main thing was that they were once again in control.

Chapter Ninety-Three

Initially the propaganda worked. It soothed Dulce and Tonal's misgivings. Billboards were hung up that indicated new educational plans for small villages and town schools. Government officials visited some of the poor families and promised help. New initiatives were started. Small food banks were instated where the needy could go to get the bare essentials. The propaganda machine ran full steam, Alex's face was once again prominent, with—naturally—his ever-loving wife at his side.

Relieved, Dulce was quick to believe Alex really was changing. After all, the evidence was there. Tonal and Jesus were less gullible and anticipated this was all too good to be true. Salina would not give up her privileges without a fight. They toned down the revolutionary activities and waited.

The farce continued for three months before the resistance concluded it had all been easy promises and propaganda. Nothing worthwhile changed. Sure, there was some food available, but that flow dried up fast. The rest were empty promises. None of the schools received any additional funds. Corruption was ever present, and no real improvements were made.

The outside still looked good, but it was skin deep. In the end no progress was made. The initial optimism faded. Any opposition was quickly quelled—secretly, so that no word reached Alex. In the middle of the night people were lifted from their beds and taken away, never to be heard of again. Rumours of midnight executions were substantiated when the revolutionaries found a mass grave.

Chapter Ninety-Four

Standing at the edge of the pit my heart sank.

So, this was the extent of Alex's conversion back to his old values and his commitment to helping his country's people. The smell of blood and gore was overwhelming and caused most of the revolutionaries to gag and divert their faces.

Beneath the steep dirt walls of the pit, the level floor was littered with decaying bodies. Rats and other scavengers scuttled over the corpses; angry their feeding had been interrupted.

I counted what I thought were at least thirty-seven bodies. Men were predominant, but I also saw women and even two small children. Many of the bodies carried gunshot and machete wounds, some missed extremities. Heads were bashed in—the children's as well. The earth was haphazardly thrown back over some of the bodies, insufficient to conceal what was there, but enough to show how little respect there had been. Littered around the pit were empty liquor bottles, used condoms and a burnt-out campfire. All evidence of a wild violent party that had taken place here. A party culminating in the death of all these people.

I heard one of our group cry out and run to the edge of the jungle where he lost his last meal.

'The fire.' he gagged.

I moved over to the embers and saw what had spooked him. There at the bottom of the smouldering logs were the remains of a child. Not much older than a baby. The corpse was still recognisable as having been human.

What kind of monster burns a baby—maybe alive?

I hoped against hope the child had been dead before they tossed it into the fire. Images filled my mind: of the child, its screams, the mother desperate to save her infant, maybe the father trying to attack the killers.

Ortiz had been a monster, but this matched whatever he had done.

My blood started to boil, the familiar tension flared, and a red mist clouded my sight. I willed it to subside and fought for control. The hairs on my back and arms pushed through the skin. Hector's restraining hand on my arm helped. It made me focus. The only living people here were friends, I couldn't lose control and possibly hurt them. It was deathly quiet—all eyes on me. They were all pale and held assorted pieces of material to their noses to try to dampen the smell of decay.

'Document everything.' Hector took change of the scene. 'We need streams of the bodies and the fire.' His words produced the intended result and the revolutionaries bustled into action.

I pointed to the jungle and told Hector I would explore the treeline for evidence or anything that could point us in the direction of who was responsible for the massacre.

As I slowly patrolled the undergrowth, I tried to shut out the smell of the decomposing bodies from the pit and concentrate on other foreign scents. My heightened senses gave me an edge over the rest. The findings however were meagre: a few cigarette butts, human excrement and some tyre tracks. The deep tracks suggested the people were brought here by truck. A lingering smell of diesel substantiated that. I counted three individual sets of tracks. Three trucks. Judging by the profiles they were military trucks. Human footmarks led from the place where the tracks were deepest and had probably parked. The ones in the centre were mostly from bare feet, the ones on the outside bore the heavy markings of a soldier's boots. Another confirmation the perpetrators had been military.

Back at the terrible scene, I shared my suspicions with Hector. They were consistent with other evidence we found. The conclusion was obvious.

'I'm so glad we left Dulce back at the compound,' Hector said. 'She didn't need to see this. The ramifications will break her heart.'

Dulce was desperately hoping against hope her brother had changed, that he really was the old Alex and things would go back to something resembling how they used to be. Hector and I tried to temper her enthusiasm when she saw the billboards and other signs, which she immediately translated to what she needed. She was adamant—Alex had listened, and it was just a matter of time before things would improve.

The realisation that the terror had upped a notch would devastate her. It would mean she really would have to fight her only sibling—her beloved brother.

Being the pessimist I am, I was never convinced Alex had indeed listened and taken the appropriate action. I hoped, of course. He was my friend too. To see him as the enemy was so foreign—so sickening. We fought the old regime together. He gave his all. We all had. And now it had come to this.

The bodies were laid out on the ground near to the rim of the jungle. These were all someone's loved ones. They had to be brought home and buried properly. In all, we counted thirty-two corpses. Less than I initially thought, but way too many. Some bodies were so decomposed or scavenged they were barely recognisable. Identifying them would not be easy. Some had an identity card on them, but most would need the heart-wrenching personal identification of their next of kin.

A sound to the left of me announced the arrival of some horse-drawn carts the revolutionaries had borrowed from a nearby farm. We wrapped the dead in blankets and sheets, loaded them onto the wagons and left the depressing scene.

Our first stop was the neighbouring village. The id-card of one of the bodies showed he came from here. Wails and tears welcomed us into the village square. I smelled the remnants of a fire and spilled blood. The villagers confirmed there were eleven people missing. Most men, but one family with three small children.

The identification was, as expected, heart-wrenching. It boiled my blood to see the devastation wrought on this small community. Tears flowed freely on all sides. The bodies were identified and claimed by their next of kin. The villagers informed us that more people were missing from other villages nearby.

We pressed on, our feelings and senses blunted by all the pain and suffering.

At the end of the next day, we'd managed to identify

almost all the bodies. One remained, but the last village offered to bury him too.

Dirty and tired—our emotions hardly bearable anymore—we returned to the compound.

Word of our findings preceded us, and we were met by Jesus and Dulce, along with most of the compound inhabitants. The welcome was quiet. The pain obvious in our faces. Silently we were accompanied to our tents. I chose to go to the stream instead to try to wash away some of the grime and stink of the past days.

The outside cleaned okay.

The inside was a totally different matter.

Chapter Ninety-Five

I felt soiled. Deep down inside I always hoped it would not come to this. That we would be able to solve the situation without a new war. Killing still impacted me in an extremely unpleasant way. Somehow it even seemed like an addiction, as strange as that may sound. The more I'd killed in the previous wars, the more I'd wanted to. Coming back from that had been traumatic.

Control was essential for me. After all these years I was still petrified by the possibility that I would lose it and kill indiscriminately.

The cat's power was phenomenal. It made me feel so alive—so fantastic.

But it had a dark side. It wanted more. The massacre scene at the pit and reliving it every time we arrived at a village, took a lot out of me. Each screaming relative added to the enormous load of emotions already fighting for control of my mind and body. At one moment I left the group and headed off into the jungle. I changed and ran and ran and ran until even I was tired. My howl in the night had probably frightened every living creature within a few miles. It didn't help my mind, but at least it relieved some of the physical tension.

The water of the stream calmed me a bit.

I knew what was coming. We would have to formulate a war plan. This massacre and no doubt others that had taken place, was the last drop.

It forced a reaction.

Once again, we were at war.

Chapter Ninety-Six

The next day saw the first of many meetings where the revolutionaries discussed and debated the options available. Dulce joined the meeting with a pallid face and red eyes. With no remaining viable options, she realised there was no other way. But it hurt.

Once again, the group planned military strategies aimed at weakening the infrastructure of the army. Secondary to the fighting, the revolutionaries would build up their own propaganda campaign.

The support of the people was tantamount to success. Without it they would not be able to continue.

One of the main objectives was to get the news about the massacres out into the world. To show the government's promises were empty propaganda and worse. The inhabitants of the country wanted to believe better times were coming—a new war would not be popular. But the truth had to get out, it was unavoidable.

The revolutionaries made use of all media options they could, and the story was told.

The government's reaction was immediate and vicious. The military landed hard on all known or perceived opposition. People were picked up and disappeared. The night curfews were reinstated, and all illusions of democracy vanished.

The dictatorship was back with a vengeance.

Chapter Ninety-Seven

Alex was alone in his office in the capitol. The room was dark and intensified his depressed mood even more.

This was not how it was supposed to go.

He'd tried to change the government's strategy to a more democratic and fairer one and it was working. And how had they reacted? With vicious accusations and all out attacks on his person. The revolutionaries slandered him and the government. They concocted horrendous tales of massacres and slaughter.

He'd sent observers to the so-called stricken villages. They returned with news that contradicted the revolutionary's accusations. Nothing had happened in the regions, and no one was hurt. The observers assured him that they were welcomed as honoured guests and that the villagers once again proclaimed their undying support for Alex and his government.

Still the propaganda continued.

Now with streams and photos. Why did they continue to spread these terrible accusations? The General even opted that if they existed at all, the murders may have been carried out by the resistance themselves—to fuel the campaign against him. Could they be so vicious? Why were Dulce and Tonal mixed up in all this? He had shown his good intentions. What more did they want?

They were forcing him to react in kind—with violence. All his good intentions were made redundant by the revolutionaries. Supported in his disappointment by his advisors and Salina, he saw no other option. If it was war they wanted, it was war that they would get.

Alex reconvened his generals and gave his support to the planned actions meant to annihilate the revolutionaries once and for all. Some of the plans seemed out of proportion and excessive, but the generals assured him they were necessary to make this a short and successful campaign. Stop the resistance as quickly as possible and restrict the damage to the country and its people. He signed the declarations and the new laws. Reluctantly, but spurred on by his advisors and his intense disappointment.

The military came down hard on all suspected revolutionaries, and some non-suspects—just for fun. The resistance retaliated with their own attacks. The violence escalated and—as always—the civilians were caught in the middle. Many made their way deeper into the jungle where they often joined the revolutionaries.

The revolution that put Alex in power had been only seven years ago. Most of the people fought alongside the revolutionaries then. They delved deep into their experiences and were quickly back in war mode.

The attacks on the military convoys and the more remote outposts were intensified and finally brought the intended results. Slowly the rebels gained control over more and more of the country's provinces. Most of the larger towns and the capitol were the domain of the military. There they held the inhabitants as hostages and so deterred large attacks there by the resistance.

Alex tried to gather support from the neighbouring countries, but they themselves were either caught up in the more global struggle or sympathised with the revolutionaries.

In the previous war a very large portion of the Americas was liberated from dictatorship. The area spanned many old countries like Puerto Rico, Guatemala, Honduras, Puerto Rico and Panama. Alex was president in Columbia, other countries had new presidents that stayed loyal to their democratic ideals. The encroaching tyranny posed a risk for their safety as well as that of Alex's constituents. They sympathised more with the revolutionaries than with the official powers. Some of them were even old friends of Jesus from the old struggle. With their support, the resistance gained even more terrain quickly. Aided by the unrest in the government and the desertion of many soldiers, their influence boomed.

In the government, the rats fled the sinking ship.

Many of the rich had gathered their possessions and moved to quieter grounds where money still bought safety. Salina once again shed any veil of compliance or good judgment. She reverted back to her main objective in life— herself. She submerged herself in egotistical exploits, aimed solely at her own satisfaction and was totally oblivious to the struggle in the outside world.

Chapter Ninety-Eight

This was the moment they'd dreaded most.

Gathered in the meeting room, the council was subdued and jittery.

All eyes went to Jesus, Dulce and Tonal who sat on one side of the table. Photos and printouts of documents littered the surface. Most were long-distance shots of the capitol, the palace or maps of the vicinity. On top was a close-up of Alex.

He looked old in the picture; old and worn. Tonal couldn't take her eyes off the image. For the past few weeks all the efforts had geared up to this moment.

Decision time.

What do we do with Alex?

Behind Dulce, Hector placed his hand on her shoulder. He knew how difficult this was. Dulce acknowledged him and was grateful for the support. She placed her hand over his and kept it there.

'It is time for the next step.'

Victor was always direct, and now was no exception.

Not having known Alex in the previous struggle, he had less scruples about broaching the subject. 'The capitol is our target, and naturally the president.'

Dulce winced and squeezed Hector's hand even harder.

Jesus took control of the meeting. 'Let's start with the strategy to take the capitol.'

They discussed options for the better part of the afternoon. Frontal attacks. How to lure the soldiers out of the city. Cutting off the supply lines and long waits for something to break.

Some were discarded straight away because they posed more of a risk to the city dwellers than to the government. Others because of the sheer magnitude needed. The rebellion had grown enormously and was well armed thanks to support from the countries around them. But an all-out attack would cost many lives, especially on the side of the civilians.

Alex's supporters had barricaded themselves inside the city where they rallied around their leader. The military, supplemented with mercenaries, crowded the grounds of the palace. Alex never left the security of the palace. He conducted his business from one of the offices in the vast property. Many of the remaining ministers also moved their families to the vicinity of the complex in the hope this would increase their security.

Alex finally achieved some diplomatic success and awaited the arrival of supplies and a military force from the Americas. His lobbying paid off, that and his promises of the country's natural resources. He'd sold his soul to the Americans, but then, there was little soul left to sell. The devil owned most of it already.

It was imperative for the revolutionaries to capture the

palace before the promised support arrived. More than that, the resistance needed to break the power centred around Alex. He was the central support of the current initiatives the government was taking. All power reverted to him. Finally, he had taken control. He was the spill of the government's efforts. Taking him out would collapse the last government resistance, stop the foreign engagement and scatter the mercenaries. The revolutionaries would be able to take control.

That was the main reason for this meeting.

They needed to name the unmentionable.

Ask the unaskable.

It was Jesus who finally uttered the dreaded words. 'Alex has to be terminated.'

The sharp intake of breath from Dulce, and the hint of a sob were the only sounds in the room.

It was final. It was said.

'Is there no alternative?' Hector held on to his wife who was openly sobbing now. 'Couldn't we talk to him one more time? Give him a deadline.'

'We already did that.' Victor again.

'But maybe once more, let Dulce talk to him. She's his sister.'

'Yeah, the one he tried to kill.' Another of the newer members of the council said.

'He didn't.' Dulce screamed. 'He wouldn't.'

'No,' Jesus answered softly, silencing everyone. 'Salina did. But he stayed with her all the same. He didn't prosecute her for the attempt. Didn't take any action.'

Renewed sobs from Dulce indicated that the message was clear.

'I will not endanger your life Dulce, Not let the bitch try again. And I don't trust Alex anymore. He should have acted on the attempt. Should have done something. Family means nothing to him anymore.'

The finality of the statement pushed Dulce over the brink. She broke down in Hector's arms. He held her tight. Softly, he picked her up and left the meeting.

It was quiet. No one spoke for more than ten minutes.

'Now the question is how?' Victor spoke what everyone was thinking. Well, all but one. 'How can we get close? His protection is even better than what Ortiz had.'

Slowly faces began to turn towards Tonal. They wanted to know what she would say.

'I'll do it,' She stated and stood up.

She turned her head towards Jesus. The anguish was apparent. Her face was a mask, but her eyes showed her pain—she was dying inside.

She left the tent.

It had to be done.

Chapter Ninety-Nine

How would I ever be able to do this?

Yes, he was a tyrant.

Yes, he was unredeemable.

Yes, it had to be done.

But could I do it?

Could I forget everything that Alex had ever been.

Before.

A long time ago.

When he still loved me.

When I loved him.

Could I do it?

How could it be anyone else but me?

Chapter One Hundred

Alex opened the door and entered his suite of rooms. He left the light off, the dark suited his mood.

The bitch was gone again, with all the drama that was standard in their relationship. She flaunted her infidelity in front of him and anyone who wanted to know. This evening it had been the dinner with his generals. Salina stood up and declared she was leaving; she was bored. Taking the bait, he ordered her to stay. That of course was like throwing petrol on a fire—Salina didn't take orders.

Their relationship had sunk to an all-time low. Salina blamed Alex for everything. The revolution, the danger to her lifestyle and wealth, her unhappiness.

She had a string of lovers, picking them up wherever she found one that took her fancy. Usually young and handsome, with the exception of the American general she seduced in front of him two months ago. Just to spite him.

Rallying her guards, Salina would take the car into the town streets and look for new meat.

Her favourite places were where there were manual

labourers: loggers, steel workers, anyone with muscle and youth.

'They amuse me.' She would say adding, 'and at least they can keep it up long enough to pleasure me.'

He was left to take care of the loose ends when she tired of them. The general proved to be a challenge. But for everyone there was a fitting "accident".

This evening, she really pushed the spite level to a new high. She humiliated him in front of the convened generals and their consorts of the hour.

After she left, conversation dropped, in volume and in level, he could hear the quiet sneers and giggles. He sent them away. Now all he wanted was peace. Something he would not get. In his mind Alex saw Salina writhing in the arms of yet another lover. He should divorce her, or in track with his current manner of solving things—make her disappear.

Tomorrow, he would confront her, tell her to get her act together, explain the importance of her acting as the president's wife she was supposed to be. He would give her a deadline. Either she complied, and became the loving wife again or else…

Or else what?

Who was he kidding? Tomorrow he would crawl back to her. Beg her to stop this madness and love him again. He would forgive her for everything as he always did. She played him. Could make him do whatever she wanted—and she did—just for her amusement. If she could not goad him into the preferred actions, she would seduce him, throwing her beautiful supple body into the fight. He would crumble, and she would win again. Always.

The balcony doors were open, and he walked out onto the ledge. It was dark, and quiet. Mercifully, even the dogs were silent for a change. Their constant baying irritated him. But that was what they were for—guard dogs. "Vicious monsters" was the more appropriate label. He'd watched them rip into a goat the mercenaries put in the pen to liven things up.

Mercenaries, it had come to that.

The peacock called in the background, another of Salina's short time obsessions. She had "needed" one, so he made sure she got it.

Alex turned back and walked into the dark room.

Something nagged at the edge of his consciousness. Something was not quite right. He tried to figure it out, but Salina invaded his thoughts again.

He walked over to the cabinet and poured himself a generous amount of vintage whisky. Then he turned back to the window and forced himself to focus on his nervousness. What was out of place? What gave him the sense of déjà vu?

Slowly it dawned on him. The balcony, the doors were open, the light was off.

Alex placed the glass on the table, walked back to the ledge and flicked the light switch. Nothing happened. The hairs on the back of his neck stood upright, he felt the dread start in his lower back and creep up past his shoulders to the base of his skull where it stayed, throbbed and pushed him to flee this place.

Slowly he comprehended the situation.

Chapter One Hundred One

She was here.

She'd come for him.

His initial fear was replaced with a temporary resignation. If she was really after him, there was no escape. And he was sure she was in the room somewhere. The fact he didn't know where just added to his conviction. He picked up his glass as he passed the table and sat down on the sofa facing the balcony.

'Hello Tonal,' he said softly, sipping the whisky. There was no reply. Still, he knew she was there.

'Quite the déjà Vu.' Alex continued. Talking felt good. 'That was what alerted me. This is almost the same as when you took care of the previous president.'

'It isn't the same.' The voice—her voice—came from his right near the drapes.

'He wasn't my friend. I never loved him.'

Alex folded his hands around the glass. 'Ah yes, there is that.'

The silence was heavy. She didn't move.

'Please Tonal,' Alex pleaded. 'Please show yourself, I want to see you.' He turned his head towards the drapes in the hope she would comply with his request.

Slowly she moved into his line of vision.

Naturally, she was naked. That was to be expected. The moonlight shone on the skin of her shoulder, her arm and her torso. Alex's heart fluttered. She still had that effect on him, after all these years, after everything that had happened. He felt twelve years old again. Totally fascinated by this beautiful creature.

Chapter One Hundred Two

'Is this it?' he asked. 'The end of the line for me?'

I let the question hang in the air. It hurt me to think about it. It was so definite. So irrevocable.

In the discussions with the war council, it seemed so clear, this was the only choice left for us. That it had to be me was obvious. No one else would be able to get anywhere near Alex, not without losing their own lives.

I was ready for it, at least that was what I thought.

It had to be done and I convinced myself I could put the small residue of feeling I had left for this man aside and just do the job.

After all that's what it was—a job.

I'd stopped counting the number of assassinations I performed while with the partisans. It was what they'd recruited me for, what I was ultimately and totally suited to do. Long ago I buried my internal ethical deliberations about killing human beings, smothered them with "The Cause". It was for the best, and it needed to be done.

To be truthful, killing the bad guys also relieved my

bloodlust; the continuous struggle I had with my inner beast.

My feelings of guilt and debasement were irrelevant. An occupational hazard.

And that brought me here. To this monumental place and time.

Naturally, it wasn't that easy.

He might be a tyrant, but he was also Alex.

My Alex.

The only person I really opened up to in the past three decades.

Someone who gave me at least a semblance of normality.

And now I would kill him.

What did that make me? Besides a murderer.

I'd shut off my feelings for so long I'd convinced myself they were absent.

Feelings of disgust at myself, at what I had become.

Feelings of isolation, because I was this mythical creature that no one really dared to approach.

Feelings of self-loathing and confusion. For my urges, for the gratification that I got from killing humans.

People.

People with families.

People with lives and ambitions. People who didn't want to die.

And Alex didn't.

'I would say it's good to see you, but that isn't the case, is it?' He broke the silence.

'Can we talk about this Tonal?' he tried. 'For old time's sake.'

I remained silent. My ultimate weapon, and one that got me into this fix in the first place.

'We used to be friends, lovers.'

Why did he have to remind me? The memories cut through my heart and my resolve as it was.

I shook my head, to clear my thoughts and pull myself together, and as an answer to Alex.

'Please Tonal, I'm begging you. Don't let it end like this.'

Tears appeared and slowly ran down his face. I wanted to scream; stop it, don't you know how this is killing me already.

'I'll change, you'll see. I will Tonal, I promise.'

'You've tried before. That option has passed,' my voice was hard in an attempt to quell my internal turmoil.

'I mean it. I will divorce Salina, abdicate, organise democratic elections.'

He was ranting, trying against reason to hang on to his pathetic life. He must have known it was a lost cause. I mean—I was there. There was only one reason for that, and he was it. He knew I would not change my mind, could not. But still he tried. Pushed the red-hot poker deeper into my heart.

'No.'

'Please Tonal, I beg you, I don't want to die.'

'It's too late for that. You brought this upon yourself.'

His posture deflated.

There was no hope. The grim reaper had come, and I was it.

Crying uncontrollably, he put his head in his hands.

I let him. I tried to isolate myself from the emotions that spoke from his sobs. For the finality of it all.

Against all logic I waited for more than five minutes, until he had himself under some semblance of control again. Why? I suppose for old time's sake. And to postpone the inevitable.

Even these circumstances were better than no time at all with Alex. I realised how much I'd missed him. How important he still was to me.

I chastised myself for not trying harder to get through to him, for leaving him to Salina's administrations and manipulations. He had been like a puppy, under the influence of a vicious and cunning owner. I should have saved him from that.

Saved him from what was to come now.

I should have...

I shouldn't have broken his heart.

That was the catalyst to all of this.

If I hadn't broken off with him so brutally, he wouldn't have been susceptible to that bitch.

If... If... If...

Yeah, right. That was about as much use as his begging for his life. It wouldn't change anything. Things being as they were, there was no going back.

What was done was done.

The present was what was important.

And that present sucked.

Big Time.

Chapter One Hundred Three

The initial resignation resurfaced. Alex knew it was inevitable. And maybe, just maybe, even the best solution.

But he had to get it off his chest. All that he had done. He had to tell her, make her understand and maybe hate him a little less.

'I'm sorry Tonal,' the confessions came easily. 'Sorry for what I have done, what I've become. We set out to stop the tyranny, to make a better life for everyone, you, Dulce, Jesus, me.'

He didn't want to stop, his need to unburden himself was so great.

'I screwed up, big time. I became the very thing we fought, like you said. No, worse, because I should have known. I betrayed everything that was dear to us. Alienated everyone who really cared. I wish we could turn back time, go back to the time that we fought together. Before Salina. She ruined everything she… …'

He shook his head.

'No, it was me, I take full responsibility.'

425

'How can you?' Finally, she moved into the room. 'How can you take responsibility? Do you even recognise what you have done? Why Alex, Why?'

Her voice was soft, but it cut Alex deeply. Tears once again began to leak from the edge of his eyes.

He felt tiny, insignificant, ashamed. His father would turn in his grave, had probably done so for a long time. After all, he had indeed betrayed all Julio had stood for.

'I have no excuse.' There was defeat in his voice. 'I cannot change what I have done. And now this is the ultimate betrayal; I force you to kill me... I wanted to do it myself, I knew that I must die to make amends for anything. I even tried. I sat here for hours with the gun in my hand, getting up the guts to finish it all. But I lack the courage even for that. I'm a total failure. And once again, you must clean up the mess I made.'

His tears came with a vengeance now.

'I wish I could stop, save you from doing this, from killing again. But when she comes back tomorrow morning I'll cave in again and it will all continue. You can't let me live. Please help me Tonal.'

He begged for release now. 'I have ruined so many lives. Killed so many people. Even the actions of the General and Esposito fade in the light of what I've done. I can't live with myself. But I'm too much of a coward to finish it. The guards won't let me out of their sight outside of this room, so I can't put myself in the way of a bullet. I need you to do it.'

Alex talked for another ten minutes. Finally, he unburdened his conscience, in the knowledge he would not find redemption. His actions wrecked all hope of that long ago. But he found that talking and voicing his remorse at least lifted the dread for what was to come.

She watched him, listened. Slowly the old Alex returned. The man she had known so many years ago. Silent tears slid down her cheeks, she had loved this man. Still did. This one, not the monster he became. And yet in all his power abuse, in all his tyranny, he'd kept her secret. Not even Salina knew who and what she was. What her talents were. Even then, he stayed true to the promise he'd made so many years ago. She walked around the sofa and put her hand on his shoulder. Touching him brought back memories—good ones.

Alex stopped crying, finally at peace and resigned. His hand touched hers, felt her emotion, her hand trembled.

'It's okay.' He said.

Alex bent his head back against the sofa and closed his eyes. She wrapped her arms around him and cupped his chin softly in her hand.

'Thank you,' he murmured.

With one quick wrench she broke his neck.

Alex died instantly, without pain, the vague smile still on his lips.

Sliding to the floor behind the sofa she wept in earnest.

Chapter One Hundred Four

I lingered in the room for more than an hour, willing someone to come in. Preferably a mercenary, someone I could vent my anger and sorrow on. But no one came.

With an extreme effort I finally pulled myself together, stood up and walked to the balcony. I turned one last time to look at my long-time friend. He looked peaceful, finally at rest. So at odds with how I felt.

I left the way I came. I clung to the face of the building with the tiny handholds that only I could find, changed as soon as I felt the grass under my feet and ran past the side of the building.

The dogs were silent, they would bay no more, I'd taken care of them on the way in. Past the pens and the outbuildings, I approached the high fence. With a mighty bound of my powerful back legs, I easily cleared the high voltage fence and disappeared into the jungle beyond—bound for the rendezvous point.

I ran as fast as I could for the first few miles. I looked for the release I so desperately needed in physical exhaustion.

But it didn't work. The emotions overwhelmed me, and I stopped. Raising my head to the sky I howled out my pain. The roar carried deep into the jungle. Even the familiar sounds and smells of the forest could not comfort me now.

I'd killed my best friend.

One of the people who made my life worth living, made eternity bearable.

Slowly I continued my route to where I'd arranged to meet Dulce.

Every step was a torture.

He was her only sibling.

I'd killed her big brother.

Her anchor in life.

Chapter One Hundred Five

Dulce was a nervous wreck as she paced back and forth in the small clearing. Torn between fear for the safety of her friend and the knowledge that her return would mean the death of her brother.

They'd all agreed that it was the only way. Alex had to die. It was a unanimous decision by the war council. But that didn't mean that it was an easy one. Many of the council members were long-term revolutionaries who'd fought by Alex's side. His betrayal lay heavy on their minds and was the validation for the decision. It almost pushed away the memories of those other times.

Of the other Alex.

Almost, but not quite.

In the silence and privacy of their own quarters they all shed a tear for their old friend and for their own souls now they'd condemned him to die.

There was only one choice for the assassin. Only one person who could and would do it. The consensus didn't need to be spoken out loud. It was evident.

They had left for the palace that morning. In the clearing Tonal left her clothes with Dulce, changed and disappeared into the jungle. Leaving her here to pace back and forth, biting her nails.

Five minutes ago, she heard the enormous roar. She was certain it had been Tonal, in no doubt of what it meant. The tell-tale sound of frightened birds heralded the arrival of the majestic cat. It slowly passed through the bushes at the edge of the clearing and approached Dulce.

Tonal stopped a foot away.

'So, it's done?' The tears began to escape her eyes, regardless of her resolve. She wanted to be strong for her friend.

The big cat dipped its head and stared at the dusty ground. Dulce took the last step forward, threw her arms around the big neck and buried her face in the warm fur. Sobs racked her body.

Finally, she loosened her grip and sank to the ground. Tonal sat down next to her. They stayed this way for a long time as the darkness of the night faded into the vague glow of the new day.

'You're not changing back.' It was more a statement than a question. Dulce felt Tonal was done with human form and everything it entailed. The big head rubbed up against her shoulder, confirming her assumption.

'I have to contact Jesus,' she said. She stood up and walked over to her small backpack to retrieve her phone. She punched the speed dial for one, let the phone ring five times—the agreed signal that Alex was dead. Phoning was not an option—all calls would probably be monitored. Besides this saved her from saying the words out loud. Tears flowed again. and she returned to the comforting warmth of the big cat where she curled up against its great flank and wept uncontrollably.

Finally, her tears dried up. She shouldered her backpack and kicked off her sandals, then crawled on to the cat's back. Taking her old familiar place, she lay her head on the massive shoulder and closed her eyes.

Tonal slowly stood and walked out of the clearing into the forest. The close contact comforted her as much as it did Dulce. They would travel back to the rebel's compound this way and take comfort from each other.

Chapter One Hundred Six

Early the next day—after a long trip—they arrived back at the compound. Their entrance caused a stir. Though there had always been rumours, the actual extent of Tonal's talents were not widely known among the rebels. Dulce remained mounted with her hands on either side of Tonal's shoulders. Children's frightened screams alerted the camp and armed soldiers appeared.

Dulce refrained from comment, her stare enough to make sure the guns were lowered. Screams and cries were silenced. Jesus appeared with his lieutenants and viewed the scene. He nodded to Dulce and beckoned them to follow him. To the crowd he said, 'go back to your work.' His deep voice pushed the people into action. Reluctantly they left to continue with their tasks.

Dulce dismounted and entered the large, camouflaged war tent after Jesus, followed by Tonal who settled down in the corner, her massive head resting on her paws.

'Why does she come here like this?' he asked softly.

'She won't change back. I think she's done with humanity,' Dulce answered. 'I can't blame her after what we asked her to do.'

'No one asked her to do it, she volunteered,' Victor sputtered, once again the first to voice his opinion. He was silenced by the coldness in Jesus' eyes.

'Oh, we asked her, even if no one said it out loud. She has taken care of our dirty work for too long. If it were me, I wouldn't have done it. Alex was her friend. They go back a long way.'

Jesus walked over to the big cat and addressed her 'Thank you Tonal. I am sorry you had to be the one.'

The cat lifted her head and looked intently at the large man, himself close to tears. Alex had been his friend too, his protégé. Tonal acknowledged him and his pain and lowered her head once more where she continued to observe the surrounding revolutionaries. All those present had been privy to her secret but were unprepared to face the fact so suddenly and so clearly. Knowing from a distance was very different from being in the same tent as the massive predator.

'Now we prepare for the deciding battles.' The warlord was back in control.

The tyrant was dead. The backbone of the power broken—but by no means defeated.

There were long battles, assassinations, infiltrations and a lot of death. On the political side the resistance gained more and more support. Now Alex was dead, the power struggle in the government and military erupted. Assassination became the preferred way to deal with the competition. This suited the revolutionaries just fine. Their enemies were doing their work for them.

Briefly Salina came out on top, backed by the vicious

mercenaries. But when they departed for greener pastures, she was left in a void.

Help came from an unexpected quarter. A military man from the northern states looked her up and promised his help and a way out of the situation she was in. He would take her back with him and they would regroup from the north. In turn she would help him with another matter. Looking into his piercing blue eyes she recognised a kindred spirit.

Chapter One Hundred Seven

Tonal fought alongside the resistance.

In feline form, she wreaked havoc among the military and became the nightmare of every government soldier. Whenever there was close combat, she would appear and annihilate her enemies indiscriminately and viciously. Her fame preceded her. Soldiers deserted as soon as they had any indication she would be involved in the fighting. Nobody knew the full story—that she could change—only that a massive feline murdering machine was somehow on the side of the resistance, and that nobody could kill it.

It was the devil incarnate.

Slowly but surely the resistance got the upper hand. They gained ground and support with every battle and every death. Key figures were assassinated, many of them killed by Tonal, their throats ripped out which strengthened the nightmare. Her recklessness fuelled the belief that she was immortal.

Supporters flocked to the revolutionaries, adding to the power and might of the resistance.

Victory was on the horizon.

Chapter One Hundred Eight

This was what we had been fighting for all the time. The final battles. Now that Alex was dead, we had to push our advantage quickly, make sure we obtained—and kept—the momentum.

But it was difficult. Alex's death touched us more than we would confess to.

Dulce was a wreck. Hector kept her out of the fighting for the first few weeks.

Jesus seemed to take out his guilt in endless strategy meetings where he pushed the partisans even harder and blocked out everything but the final struggle.

Me, I just killed and killed. A useless attempt to drench my sorrow and guilt in blood.

The enemies blood preferably, but in their absence, any animal in the jungle.

I killed for the killing.

The act itself a statement.

The violence was abominable and out of any context. Totally without restraint. I ripped the victims to shreds. On the battlefield I played with some of the enemy. Hamstringed them and then slowly, excruciatingly painfully, incapacitated them further to finally finished the job and move on to the next one.

But it didn't help.

I could still feel Alex near; could still hear his sobs and begs for his life.

The loud sound when his neck broke rang in my ears and overpowered everything else, even the cries of the dying. Every time I closed my eyes, I relived the scene in the Presidential Suite. I tried frantically to imagine other outcomes—naturally to no avail. Besides it wouldn't have helped, probably even made things worse if I dreamt up an alternative, now, after I killed him.

He filled my waking and the few sparse sleeping moments.

I let myself go. No restraints on the battlefield. I let the beast out. All self-control I'd spent years learning went out the window.

Blood and gore were my rewards. The killing went on and on and on.

But it didn't seem to make a difference.

The peace I fought so hard to achieve eluded me. What seemed helpful earlier to reduce the tension—killing the enemy—now only increased the red haze and bloodlust. I wanted more.

What was happening to me?

It was ever more difficult to control myself.

Differentiating between friend and enemy became vague and a chore. Besides Dulce, I avoided everyone. I growled when they came too close, scaring them off. The distance was as much for their safety and for my sanity. Dulce, I shadowed. She was my friend and the only link to

Alex. I convinced myself I was protecting and comforting her, but it was a two-way street. Her closeness was necessary to keep that last little thread of my sanity.

But even that eluded me of late.

Recently there were voices in my head. My conscience probably. And the primal urge. All vying for my attention and support.

'How could I do this?'

'Easily, it's in my nature.'

'I have to stop.'

'Why?'

'Killing is unethical and runs against everything I believe in, every fibre in my body.'

'Then why am I so good at it?'

I hardly ever slept. Afraid my conscience wouldn't wake up with me in the morning. That I would be delivered into the hands of the beast only. That I would lose every semblance of humanity inside me.

That I would lose me.

But who was I anyway? For that matter—what was I?

How could I hang on to something I might not even have?

And the ever present and unanswered question.

Why me?

Chapter One Hundred Nine

Tired and weary, Dulce pushed open the door to the room she was allotted in the new camp.

Hector was fighting on the southern front. They'd just won a decisive battle and she'd spoken to him on the phone. He would now come to the capital to help the attack on this front.

Today they decided to mount the final offensive to gain control over the capitol. The troops were ready, and Jesus had just spoken to them, motivating them for the final battle. But she was tired. Continuous fighting for more than two years had drained all her energy. It had been eight months since Alex had died, the pressure was unrelenting, not allowing her any time to grieve.

She missed her brother.

He'd been gone in person for many years, but still deep down, she knew the real Alex was there somewhere and hoped maybe he would return as the same big brother she had known and grown up with. Now that was impossible. He was dead.

Since his death, Tonal was almost her shadow. Wherever Dulce was, Tonal was one step behind. Though she appreciated the protection, Dulce missed her human friend. Missed being able to talk to her and receive an answer back.

Last week Tonal finally let her be on her own in the compounds, surrounded by the resistance's soldiers, and created some distance.

Dulce turned on the light and walked into the room. Immediately she saw her friend sitting in the chair—in human form. The fact she was in the room was not as surprising as her current physique. She'd changed for the first time since Alex's death.

Goose pimples ran up and down Dulce's arms, dread mounting.

'You're leaving, aren't you?' Understanding flooded her mind.

Tonal nodded. 'I couldn't just go, I wanted to tell you why.' Her voice was almost too soft to hear. 'And say goodbye,' she added.

'You can't leave now,' Dulce blurted out. 'Not when we're so close to victory. We need you.'

'No, you don't, not anymore.' Dulce had to concentrate to hear the soft words. 'The killing must stop. This has to be the last battle. Or you won't be any better than the rest.'

She avoided looking at Dulce and directed her words to the floor. 'You must start rebuilding, stop the blood. My special brand of violence is a liability to the movement now. You must distance yourself from me and all I stand for. My work is done here. I can only harm you now.'

Dulce sank into the chair opposite her friend and looked at her. In the harsh light on her naked body, she looked tired, dirty and soiled. Her skin was blank, her hair flaccid.

She looked like hell.

'I have to leave,' she continued, as she held up her hands, the skin brownish and coarse 'I'm covered in blood. Even my soul is drenched. If I don't stop now, I never will. I won't be able to stop the violence—I enjoy killing too much. It's taking over.'

'It's the cat,' Dulce tried, 'If you stay like this, it will be better.'

Sighing Tonal resumed 'No. It isn't the cat. That's the only thing that's kept me sane. It's the blood, the killing, and it's Alex.'

The silence said it all.

'I have to heal.' Tonal lifted her head and pleaded with Dulce. 'This is no way to spend eternity, I'm dying inside.'

Dulce's heart went out to her friend. She was close to tears. She'd known for a long time that Tonal was stressed, that things were not right. But her own needs had blocked out her friend's. Understanding filled her, but still she had to try.

'I need you,' She whispered.

'I'm sorry Dulce.'

Then silence.

'No, you're right, I'm sorry. I'm being selfish. But I don't want you to leave. You're my family, my friend.' There was remorse in her voice.

Both studied the floor, as if it was interesting what the carpet looked like.

'Will I ever see you again?' Dulce asked. Before Tonal could answer she added. 'Scratch that. Don't answer. I couldn't bear to hear you say no.'

'Where will you go to?'

'I don't know, far away. Somewhere I can't do any damage.'

'You're leaving tonight, now?' More a statement than a question.

Tonal nodded and slowly stood up from the chair. Dulce stood and moved towards her, they embraced, both barely able to hide the tears.

'Thank you.' The words were halting. 'Thank you for everything. I'm still going to keep hoping we will somehow, someday, see each other again. Let me know every now and then how you're doing, please.'

'I will Dulce. Live well and keep safe.'

Tonal turned towards the door, changed again and ran out into the night.

She left Dulce alone in the dark with her sorrow. It was bound to happen; she knew that she'd felt the distance Tonal purposely created the past week. Blocking it out had seemed like the best thing to do at that moment. But it was inevitable.

She pulled herself together, wiped her tears with the back of her sleeve and left the building to talk to Jesus.

I was back where I belonged.

Next in the Primal Series

vinci-books.com/natureofthebeast

Immortal. Powerful. Bloodthirsty.

She doesn't age. She doesn't die. She can transform at will into a
deadly beast. But her immortality comes at a high price: she must
kill to maintain her sanity, or else risk flying into a bloodthirsty
rage.

Turn the page for a free preview…

Nature of the Beast: Prologue

I never really thought about what constituted being human until it no longer applied to me.

Have you ever thought about it?

What is the definition of a human?

What does it mean to be a human being?

Some of the least appreciated characteristics are that you wither and die. Humans are born, go through predefined stages in life—childhood, adolescence and adulthood, into old age and finally, you die. You are susceptible to all kinds of diseases, pain and misery. You interact, live by certain values and ethics—or the lack thereof. Your life is predetermined for the most part. Generally, your existence, your health, strength and other aspects fall between pre-set borders.

To be quite blunt, your life is mostly short, preordained and boring.

This doesn't apply to me.

I don't age, don't die, don't get sick and am significantly stronger than any of your kind. I don't fit the mould and therefore I must be something dangerous. The jury is still out on what I actually am though.

I was human for so long it never occurred to me that might change. Why should it? It didn't for anyone else.

Strange things happened to me, but the big picture eluded me for a long time.

They say that knowing what "isn't" helps with figuring out what "is." Well, that's overrated. Understanding that I'm not human hasn't helped me find out what I am. I've been trying to find the answers for the past two hundred years. There are many hypotheses, but the right one is anyone's guess. There have been revelations that seem right, or maybe that's just wishful thinking on my part. But I'm running ahead of the story. You will find out about them later on.

This story begins where the last one ended, give or take a decade or two.

I was no closer to answers than when I was the focus of experiments in the lab. Every day I encountered new aspects of my "differentness", new reasons for why I don't fit anymore.

Funny that humans need to fit everything and anyone into a predetermined box. Anything that doesn't conform is a threat. Because it's different, it's strange and you can't get your head around it.

One thing you humans definitely are not, is flexible.

Nature of the Beast: Chapter One

The fighting didn't stop when America lost the war.

Outside of the borders maybe, but within the former "American Territories", the violence escalated. The Free World Coalition won. But how do you police the loser when they make up more than fifteen million square kilometres of hostile territory? And that was just one of the challenges that faced them.

America may have lost, the government and military surrendered, but it was by no means a unanimous decision or, for that matter, supported by the majority of the three-hundred seventy-eight million inhabitants.

With the fall of the government came the disintegration of law and order. The army was disbanded. The police and fire workers—no longer pulling an income and the target of mass aggression—gave up on their job and fled.

The Coalition stepped in and with the help of the newly instated government, a semblance of order was returned to the Northern States. However, the farther south you went in the American territories, the less influence the Coalition had and the greater the chaos. There, lawlessness reigned supreme.

The NUS, or New United States as the reforming country called itself, slowly expanded its influence, thanks to the Coalition. New order was enforced with extreme prejudice. That, in turn, caused the criminals to move further south, which made the situation much worse there.

The north was liveable, the south was anarchy. That suited me just fine. I kept to the south and initially stayed in the territories America annexed in the southern continent.

After my self-inflicted expulsion from society decades ago, I lived in the dark recesses of the Amazon jungle hoping against hope I would find some semblance of peace, that I would be free of the bloodlust that accompanied my "talents" like the bad side of a penny. I was sick of the killing, sick of the rage, of the blood and the guilt. Sick of what I had become.

I moved as far away from humans as possible. I didn't want to mingle, didn't want to care about anyone anymore. Didn't want to feel. Just be me, whatever that was.

The first months were okay. I finally managed to unwind and find some form of relief. I was the master of the jungle in my feline form. I hunted when hungry, relished the sun, even enjoyed the tropical rains. I didn't need people. Didn't need anything more in my immortality than this.

I was so wrong.

After almost nine months, I started to see red again. Killing to eat was no longer enough to feed the primal urges inside me. Reluctantly, I changed back into human form, hoping to relieve the tension.

It didn't help.

The familiar pressure returned in my head, the red haze over my eyes, and the unbearable anger that terrified me.

Was I going mad?

Again?

I changed uncontrollably from human form to feline and back again, sometimes even a mix of the two, but nothing helped. Nothing relieved the tension that drove me insane. In these moments, I massacred all the animals around me, anything that was stupid or unlucky enough to wander within five-hundred metres. Even that didn't help. My vision coloured red and got brighter by the minute.

In my insanity, I drifted from my self-imposed isolation to lightly inhabited regions of the jungle. It wasn't a conscious thing. I was totally out of it by then. With no idea where I was or what I did.

I woke up one day next to the body of a man. I'd killed him. Tore out his throat, almost dismembered the body. His blood was all over me.

I was horrified.

In my primal rage, I'd killed another human. Someone I didn't know. Just a person. I had no recollection who he was or even why I'd killed him. I just knew I had. And I was devastated.

Once again, I fled deeper into the jungle. I was all right for a while. My thoughts stayed coherent. I was repulsed by what I had done, but I was thinking straight for the first time in months.

Slowly, after a few weeks, the tension returned.

I lay on a ridge in feline form and tried not to think of the inevitable—that I was going insane again. My sensitive ears picked up the sounds of a scuffle. Uninterested, I tried to zone it out.

My head snapped up; these were not the regular hunter and prey sounds of the jungle. I heard voices. Human voices. Raised in anger. Then one in terror. I rose from my perch and softly made my way in the direction of the sounds. The intensity increased with every step. I heard a scream, sped up, and within seconds overlooked a small clearing where a uniformed man with a machete hacked away at the body of another man.

With a bloodcurdling roar, I sprang from my cover and landed on top of the soldier. His terror paralysed him. I lunged, took his head in my jaws and crunched down, killing him instantly.

Once again, I'd killed a man. And once again, the tension was released.

Understanding washed over me, and with that, revulsion and horror. To relieve the blood rage, I needed to kill. But not just kill prey, I had to kill people! Killing animal prey never brought the same result. Sanity only came with killing humans.

How could I reconcile my newfound clarity with my morals and ethics? I needed to kill people to stay sane. My body yearned for the release I experienced when I killed a human. But how could I stay sane if every fibre of that same sanity screamed this was unacceptable. It was the classic catch twenty-two. Damned if I did, damned if I didn't. And, it meant dead humans, whichever choice I made.

The revelation spiralled me into a deep depression.

I even tried to kill myself. In human form, I threw myself off a high cliff on to jagged rocks hoping to impale myself and end my suffering. The beast inside had other ideas. Against my conscious will, my body changed mid-fall and I landed on all fours. Injured, bleeding and in great pain, I slunk off into the jungle where my body worked its magic and I healed.

My own death wasn't an option.

I needed to find a way to come to terms with the inevitable—I had to kill. Whether by choice or not, the beast inside would not be denied its blood.

My options were limited. To ignore the need would mean the rage would win. I would be overcome by the bloodlust and kill everyone I found. Fleeing into the jungle wouldn't help; that was clear from my first kill. The urge would send me to the populated areas and God knows what I would do in a village or town. I was immortal. Nothing anyone could do would stop me. It would be an all-out slaughter.

I had to come up with another option. How could I feed the need and keep myself from another kind of insanity? The kind that refers to me, to my beliefs. What would make me less of a psycho? Make me something I could live with.

Killing was a given. Who I killed, however, was up to me.

That was where I had a choice. What if I killed those who didn't deserve to live? The dregs of society. People the world wouldn't miss and would actually be better off without. That way I could counter the blood insanity and possibly even make a difference in my own twisted way.

At least then I could live with myself — maybe.

How to determine who was entitled to live posed another dilemma. Who was I to decide whether someone has the right to live or to die? I would be playing God. Me. A killer — frankly a murderer myself. Quite the contradiction.

As I mulled over the alternatives, I finally felt some form of peace. At least I was working on a solution. That made me feel marginally better than the past months. But thinking about it and finding a way to reconcile myself to the ideas forming in my head were two totally different things. I would actively hunt humans again.

I moved back down to the clearing and dragged the two bodies into the jungle. I buried the peasant and left the soldier to the scavengers.

I didn't trust my new resolve yet or feel comfortable with the idea, so I stayed in the caves for another two weeks to get my mind around these strange and frightening developments. That I wasn't a man-eater was a small comfort but still didn't sooth my conscience about the killing. The more I debated the issues, the more the final option seemed to gain merit. Not specifically because of its strong points, but because it was the lesser of the evils. At least I had a solution for the time being—until better options presented themselves.

The main issue now was how to put my newfound strategy into place. How would I determine who would merit termination—the word sounded so much better than murder—and what would the criteria be? Where would I find the next candidate and how long would I be able to fend off the bloodlust until the opportune moment? At the back of my mind, I screamed my sorrow and frustration at the road I was forced to choose. But now it was plain and simple survival, both physically and mentally.

I was sentenced to eternity. I had to get through it as best I could.

I changed back to human form and started to pack my few belongings. Human form would make travel easier and allow for interaction with people. That was a necessity — after all, they were my new prey. I set out for the nearest large town and started to work out the details. An identity was needed or at least a name and a history that would appear more or less believable. It didn't have to be fool proof. I wouldn't be around long enough to have to pass detailed scrutiny.

Leaving the country was also one of my first priorities. I didn't want to start my new life here. Not while there were people who would recognise my 'modus operandi'. I hadn't exactly been inconspicuous in the last civil war. I needed the anonymity of a new environment.

During the next decades, I went steadily north through the Latin countries, New Mexico, Texas, and finally into what was originally Louisiana.

On the way, I slowly fell into a kind of rhythm. Initially, the killings needed to be frequent—once every two to three weeks. In time, I managed to extend the period to a comfortable four weeks. More than that clouded my judgement, which was not a good thing in my new line of work. If you extrapolate the number to the decades I roamed, the total is astounding.

I don't keep count.

The further I got from my original habitat, the less careful and more brazen I became. Basically, I'm indestructible, so I became complacent. That all came to a halt when some of the General's old henchmen found and tried to kill me. They didn't succeed, obviously, but man, it hurt. After I got rid of them, I decided to be more careful. The long reach of the General's clan had shaken me. Frankly I forgot about them, and the reminder was bloody and painful.

How to find the potential targets? I wasn't in one place

long enough to get to know the area and determine who was eligible for termination. While I kept to the shadows again, I rethought how to continue. Some kind of research on an intended target would lower the exposure and danger for me. But how could I determine who the target should be?

That was when it hit me. Enlist others to find targets. It sounds easier than it is. Hiring myself out as a hit woman to the highest bidder would clash with my morals, plus it necessitated that I left some kind of a trail, so the right people could find me.

I needed to continue to kill those who didn't deserve to live. I resolved only to take the contracts that met my criteria and God help the client if he or she didn't.

So now almost all my targets are supplied by clients. New clients need to be referred by former employers. I work solely by referrals. It's almost impossible to find me without them. That's a necessity. I make a lot of enemies in my line of work.

Hiring me is a dangerous undertaking anyway. In the initial contact, the client needs to convince me of two things: why the intended target should die and why the potential employer shouldn't.

If the client turns out to be on the wrong end of my criteria, he or she ends up dead along with the target. I am very clear in my contracts. The target needs to deserve to die, the client must deserve to live. Anyone who double-crosses me lives just long enough to regret it. I made an example once and it wasn't pretty. More often than not, I turn down the payment after the actual deed. I have to live, but my needs are few. I find food in the forests and only need weapons as an optical deterrent, as I carry my own built-in arsenal. My real payment lies in the relief I experience.

But killing still doesn't comes naturally, even after all this time.

It's not easy to kill someone, not even for me—not even if my sanity depends on it. For me, each kill has to be validated; needs to be a choice for good, an "ethical" choice. Each contract necessitates ample research into the target and the client. I must be sure. I have to quell the constant doubt within me. Am I doing the right thing? Is the kill a justified one? Will I be able to live with myself again? Or am I just kidding myself to bypass the remnants of morals and ethics I have left?

I like to think it's justified.

The last contract brought me to The Big Easy, the city built on the ashes of New Orleans. When the hurricane hit in the early twenty-second century and wiped out the whole city, the survivors built a new home some ninety kilometres inland, away from the gulf coast. They named it after the mother city, using one of its nicknames, "Easy."

For most of the inhabitants, it was anything but.

Nature of the Beast: Chapter Two

All eyes turned my way when I walked into the dimly lit bar. Even though a dark cloak covered my body and hair, I still managed to attract everyone's attention, as expected.

It was a motley bunch of people. As I looked more closely at the clientele, I noticed I was possibly the only female in the building who wasn't joined at the hip to one of the macho punks or flogging her wares and favours to whomever was interested and could afford them.

I moved between the tables towards the back of the room, pulled an elevated chair away from an empty corner table and sat down with my back to the wall.

The murmurs and pointing continued for a while. An enormous, heavily tattooed woman of about forty in a much too-skimpy skirt loomed over me.

'What'll it be?' she demanded. 'Drinks are mandatory.'

'Beer,' I answered without looking up. She turned and repeated the question to the people at the neighbouring table with the same charm and outgoing personality. A few minutes later, she returned and placed a bottle of beer in front of me. I paid without a word and took a sip of the brew. In my long years, I've tasted better, but at least it was cool and wet.

I had been on the road too long without "work" before getting this contract. The tension was building up inside me again. Travelling didn't diminish my anger or any other emotion. As I moved around in populated areas, I couldn't change properly for a while. It hadn't been opportune. All in all, I was spoiling for a fight. This seemed as good a place as any to be in that mood. I was dangerous to others and myself. Well, mainly to others.

I also needed to eat and drink, so I came to this dark hole in the wall. Finding a place to stay was next on my list. The weather was atrocious and a stay outside in this town was not really a good option anyway. Besides, even I need at least a minimum amount of comfort. Other than that, my direct future wasn't clear. I had no plans on how to work this contract. I was basically winging it.

Sure enough, after about six or seven minutes of relative peace, three rough looking characters approached my table. The leader sported tattoos over most of his face, an intricate pattern of tribals; black and red, angry and threatening.

There's no accounting for taste.

'Well now, what do we have here?' His question was directed at his comrades. He sat uninvited in the chair next to mine. Close—too close for me.

'What brings you to our fine establishment?' he crooned.

I raised the bottle and answered without words.

'Ah, our local brew, the nectar of the Gods.' Laughing he added, 'there are other pleasures in this room.' He reached into his pocket and pulled out a collection of plastic bags containing multi-coloured pills and spread them out over the table.

'No thanks, I'll stick to the beer.'

He stuffed them back as his tattooed visage contorted into a sneer. 'Maybe you're looking for other thrills.' He moved his chair closer, gripped the edge of my cloak and pulled it back off my head to expose my face and hair to the lustful gazes of his companions. '

The three of us would definitely be able to rock your boat, lady.' He appraised what he could see of me with unbridled lust in his eyes. If he got any hornier, he would start drooling.

I shook his hand off as I replied, 'not interested.'

Okay, not the answer he expected or wanted. His face contorted and he pulled back a bit. 'What are you, some kind of dyke?'

How original.

His voice had an edge you could cut yourself on. One of the other two moved to my left side. 'We can cure that,' he said in what I suppose was meant to be a seductive voice. 'Can't we, guys? One night with us, and you will be saved. Or maybe we would need two nights if you're lucky.'

He was definitely drooling.

Tattoo-face took over again. 'Let's leave and retire to a more comfortable…'

He stopped mid-sentence.

While he was laughing, I'd moved my right hand under the table and held his balls in my extended claws through the material of his jeans. The colour slowly drained from his face.

'Like I said,' I repeated. 'I'm not interested.'

'Who cares, bitch. We are and you're the minority.' The

thug next to me was not going to be put off so quickly, mind you, his balls were not in a vice. A very, very sharp vice.

I looked at Tattoo-face and raised my eyebrow.

'Back off, guys,' he managed to stammer.

'What? Why? No way, we're just getting started.'

I tightened my grip, and the claws drew blood. The skin around the threatening tribal tattoos on his face went decidedly pale. 'I said, back off!' he shouted.

Lust was gone, replaced by cold anger and obvious pain. His dirty look convinced his comrades, and they backed off. With one last twist, I let him go and retracted my claws. I took another sip of the beer.

Tattoo-face pushed his chair back and reluctantly—but very painfully—got to his feet. He looked sick. Red blood spots showed on his pants. As he staggered away, he added 'this isn't over yet,' and retreated to the other side of the room where the bar lady waited with an ice pack.

About ten minutes later a fresh bottle of beer appeared on the table in front of me. I looked up but saw no one.

'Down here, beautiful.'

The voice came from the other side of the table. A little person, with a big smile and his own bottle of beer stood next to the chair Tattoo-face recently vacated.

'Okay if I sit?' he asked. When I didn't answer, he pulled back the chair and struggled onto it, his short legs dangling. 'I'll take that as a yes. They call me Toad.'

He stretched out his hand over the table to shake mine, I left it there. 'For obvious reasons,' he added, unfazed by my silence and unfriendliness. He pulled back his hand and sipped his own beer. 'Welcome to our beautiful city. Are you visiting, passing through or planning to stay?'

Despite my reservations, he intrigued me. 'What makes you think I'm new to this town?'

'Well, the way you manage to make friends so easily for one.'

He shrugged his head in the direction of where Tattoo-face was still seething. 'The guy you alienated back there, old picture-face, he's one of the head honcho's main men around here. His boss owns the city and controls it with a hard hand. He kills anyone who gets in his way, slowly. Doesn't discriminate between men, women and children either. Picture-face over there is his number one enforcer. Well, next to his psycho son. That one's a real character.'

He lowered his voice. 'Not the kind of person you want as an enemy, beautiful.'

'Neither am I.'

'No, I guess you aren't. Not the way you had him by the balls. You have some nails, lady.'

I guess his height had put him in an optimal position to observe what took place under the table. Dark as it was, he'd seen enough to be impressed, and careful. He scrutinised me for a while.

'I believe you can be very dangerous when you put your mind to it.' I refrained from answering and took another sip instead, I was getting used to the beer.

'So, what brought you here, beautiful?' he asked again, and when I didn't answer he started fishing. 'You piss someone off? Sleep with your best friend's guy?'

He was actually amusing, and I warmed to him a bit. While he rambled on, I observed him in more detail. He was quite a character. His face was rugged, his eyes soft, handsome. If it weren't for his size, he would be a real woman magnet. Mind you, he may be anyway with his charm and if the rumours are true. I thought I recognised a slight Australian accent but could be mistaken. Anyway, his enthusiasm and friendliness were contagious.

'Nope,' I answered. 'None of the above.'

'Ok, let me think.' He looked at me, his eyes softened even more, and became serious. 'It was a man, wasn't it? It always is.' Once again, he took my silence as a yes. 'Broke your heart, betrayed you, did he?' He sat back to observe my reaction, or lack of it. 'You're young and beautiful, but your eyes are older. You've seen too much. He really hurt you. So, what did you do to him?'

I took another sip and only answered him after I placed it back on the table. 'I killed him.'

'Yeah, figures.' That shut him up—for all of thirty seconds.

'Anyway, you need a new friend and a guide to this hellhole, so how about me?' he continued. 'Why our fair town?'

'I'm here on business,' I tried.

'Well, then this meeting was preordained. If you want to know anything about this hellhole, I'm the person to talk to.' He placed his hand dramatically on his chest to emphasise the fact. 'What kind of business?'

Damn, I would have to think of something quickly. This was no fool. He would see through any half-witted stories. I decided to keep up the silent treatment for the moment.

'Okay,' he continued. 'We'll get to that later.' There was no fazing this guy. 'Anyway, I expect you will need somewhere to sleep and probably something to eat. I wouldn't advise you eat here very often if you value your health, actually not at all would probably be even better. I know some places that are reasonably kosher.'

Food, now that was an idea. I'd been on the road for the past two weeks with sporadic access to food. Three nights ago, I half changed and hunted out of desperation more than anything else. The small boar I killed barely managed to scratch the surface of my hunger. That was always the dilemma. I needed to change to hunt for food, but the change cost me dearly in energy and necessitated even more food. The ultimate vicious circle. I had no idea how long it would take before I could do it again. The tension inside was already almost at boiling point, the change relieved it just enough to make it bearable.

But back to food.

Should I trust this guy? My gut feeling said "yes", and I trust my instincts. He was momentarily scared stiff of me, even if it wasn't apparent on the outside. I could smell the fear on him. He camouflaged it well. Even more reason to find out why he sought contact to start off with. I smiled. I like a challenge. Besides, how difficult would it be to over-whelm him if it became necessary? Even the shotgun slung nonchalantly over his back would only temporarily slow me down if that.

'So, where do you eat?' I asked him.

'Why don't I show you?' He smiled that winning smile.

He struggled down off the chair and led the way out of the establishment, carefully avoiding the corner where Tattoo-face and his comrades quietly smouldered. From a distance, I smiled sweetly at the pained leader and angered him even more. One of these days I would regret winding people up so much. But it was fun. And besides, I'm invinci-ble. So, what do I need to worry about? A bit of pain? I'm used to that.

Grab your copy...
vinci-books.com/natureofthebeast

About the Author

USA Today bestselling author Monique Singleton writes compelling stories that mix fantasy and science fiction with realistic psychological suspense and unique insights into the minds of the main characters.

As the daughter of a British soldier and his Dutch wife, Monique was born in an English military hospital in Germany. The family toured the world where she was exposed to different cultures in many countries. Finally settling down in the Netherlands, she pursued a career in art and later in consultancy.

In 2017 Monique started to put the scenes she had running around in her head, down to paper. Scenes led to a story, the story to a book, and the first book to a series. The rest is, as we say, history. She has now penned many books in multiple series.

From her Dominion series, The Devil You Know was runner-up in the Page Turner Awards 2024 and won a Readers' Favourite 5-Star award. It also won two PenCraft awards in 2024: one for literary excellence and the Fall Seasonal Book Award.

In addition to her writing, Monique still holds down a full-time job as a business consultant. She lives in a beautiful old farmhouse in the south of Holland with her two sloppy monster dogs, a horse, and two cats.

The cats are in charge.